THE FRUIT *of* ATROCITY

D.L. WATERHOUSE

THE
FRUIT *of*
ATROCITY

TATE PUBLISHING
AND ENTERPRISES, LLC

The Fruit of Atrocity
Copyright © 2015 by D.L. Waterhouse. All rights reserved.

No part of this publication may be reproduced, stored in a retrieval system or transmitted in any way by any means, electronic, mechanical, photocopy, recording or otherwise without the prior permission of the author except as provided by USA copyright law.

Scripture quotations marked (KJV) are taken from the *Holy Bible, King James Version,* Cambridge, 1769. Used by permission. All rights reserved.

This novel is a work of fiction. Names, descriptions, entities, and incidents included in the story are products of the author's imagination. Any resemblance to actual persons, events, and entities is entirely coincidental.

The opinions expressed by the author are not necessarily those of Tate Publishing, LLC.

Published by Tate Publishing & Enterprises, LLC
127 E. Trade Center Terrace | Mustang, Oklahoma 73064 USA
1.888.361.9473 | www.tatepublishing.com

Tate Publishing is committed to excellence in the publishing industry. The company reflects the philosophy established by the founders, based on Psalm 68:11,
"The Lord gave the word and great was the company of those who published it."

Book design copyright © 2015 by Tate Publishing, LLC. All rights reserved.
Cover design by Rtor Maghuyop
Interior design by Angelo Moralde

Published in the United States of America

ISBN: 978-1-68028-404-1
Fiction / War & Military
15.02.02

If God Is Not Up There

If God is not up there
or
God is not down here,
Then how did we appear
And where would we know to go
To find a heart of love,
To catch our falling tear
If God is not down here

If God is not up there,
Then how would passion burn
And babies be
Or how would we all see
The leaves of autumn turn
Or nations finally learn
That if God is not here
And if God is not there,
The future's crystal clear,
There is no hope,
And we are doomed
To repeat the errors
Of those in tombs
And die again through every year.
We do not know that God is here
If God is not up there.

Acknowledgments

When I wrote the side plot of the Russian smuggler into my first book, *The Sequel to Alfred Creek*, I had no intention of writing an entire book about it. Later, after *The Sequel to Alfred Creek* had gone live, I began to formulate the initial ideas for this book, *The Fruit of Atrocity*.

The difficulties arose out of the back story that had already been written in the first book. Such as: The time period, the age of the children, the Chinese girl and how to make the connection with Arthur Bold and the pilot of the Antonov AN-2.

After several *chapter ones*, had been tossed into the waste basket, I finally settled on the *chapter one* you are about to read. By the time my protagonist had made it through the second chapter, I was totally out of ideas. I realized I had no plot, no plan, and no more story. Then, it occurred to me. Make the story a *metaphor*. So that is what I did.

I hope you enjoy it as much as I enjoyed writing it. It was exciting to watch the story unfold in my mind, as if it had been locked in a vault awaiting the right moment to reveal itself.

The spiritual connotations are the whole purpose of this fiction adventure; like a horse that carries its rider, it carries the fundamental truth of the gospel of Jesus Christ; conveying a glimpse of the gospel of grace, by which men are saved; through faith. During which time, I hope, the reader is so enraptured with this adventure and the romance of the time period that he, or, she, will remember with fondness their time spent reading. If that is you, thank-you.

Finally, I would like to thank my dearest wife, Florence, from the bottom of my heart, for providing me every opportunity, support, provision and encouragement during the three years this work was in process. I love you forever. Only you could ever understand how important writing is to me.

Often times I am asked how I come up with the names of certain characters in the story. Frequently, they are the names of certain people I know. One name in particular, Major Yuan, has been borrowed from my very esteemed cardiologist, who was born and raised in China. Dr. Yuan has shown a considerable amount of interest in my research of the war in China. Therefore, in tribute to him, I have borrowed his name for one of the characters in this book. I certainly hope Dr. Yuan doesn't mind that the character was somewhat unscrupulous.

There are others that I wish to acknowledge, due to the fact that I appreciate so much their willingness to help this struggling author. Many thanks are deserved and offered to Sue, who labored through an unfinished and unedited manuscript yet provided much appreciated confirmation. Also there is Sheri, who despite letting her father, Dennis, my friend and flying buddy, rope her into editing a huge manuscript written by someone she neither knew nor had ever met while raising three teenage daughters and working a full-time job, nonetheless consented to help. Thank you, both.

Finally, I would like to mention my friend Phil Stiffler for sharing with me the knowledge and experience he gained from many years of flying the DC-3 in Alaska. I appriciate so much the time you spent with me involving the performance and flight characteristics of the DC-3. Many thanks to you all, hope you enjoy the book.

Introduction

This is a fiction novel. For purposes of analogy and story telling, I have taken many literary liberties. All portions of this story are fictional with the exception of the spiritual connotations and reference to the Authorized King James Version of the Christian Bible along with the actual historical events that took place during the time line of the story, such as the atrocity of the Rape of Nanking China in 1937. Other historical facts, recognizable by the astute reader, also have been incorporated into the story.

Research into the war in China during World War II and the invasion of China by the Japanese was conducted from several sources: the Internet, various documentaries, war movies, and books. One of which I would like to give special credit to is *The Flying Tiger* by Jack Samson. It is the opinion of this author that it is the most complete, detailed, and authentic biography of General Claire Chennault ever written.

However, regardless of how reliable the information from the these sources claim to be, this author assumes no responsibility into the accuracy of details acquired from any source. For instance:

- The actual number of people slain during the Japanese occupation of Nanking China from December 4, 1937, until that occupation ended.

- The actual number of women raped and murdered during the massacre of Nanking seems to vary, depending upon which source the information comes from.

The same is true for other estimated information, like the population of Nanking and Chungking during that time in history.

There is one more resource for information on this terrible atrocity that I would like to recommend: *John Rabe*, a film, "based on the international best-seller *The Good Man of Nanking*. "Based on actual events, John Rabe tells the story of a German business man who rescued more than 200,000 Chinese during the 'Nanking Massacre' in China by courageously negotiating a safety zone to protect innocent civilians from the Japanese Army" (excerpts from the DVD jacket, promotional copy).

Three more well-respected, real-life characters of that time and place in history found their way into this fictional work—such as, Brigadier General Claire Chennault, Genneralisimo Chaing-Kai shek, and the Madam Chaing-Kai shek. These renowned heroes of World War II are certainly worthy of recognition for their role in the freeing of China from the invasion of the Japanese imperialists. The intention of this author in giving them a place in this fictional work is for the purpose of bringing attention to an atrocity of war that in actuality did, in fact, take place as well as give credit to these very special war heroes for the part they played in putting an end to the despotic empire that commited the horrible atrocities. Certainly, no disrespect has been intended or implied by their part in this fictional story.

The story of Charlie and his band of "Little Devils," this author believes is more folklore than it is factual. However, it seems that in 1945, a movie was made called *China's Little Devils* starring Harry Carey and Ducky Louie. The picture was made by Monogram Pictures Corporation and produced by Grant Withers. It is noteworthy that at the beginning of the film the narration begins by making the claim that the story is base on *"absolute fact."* And there seems to be just enough plausibility to it that the reader might be safe either way—believing or not believing.

THE FRUIT OF ATROCITY

For me as an author, the main purpose for writing Christian fiction is that the reader catch a glimps of the purposes of God in not only war and it's atrocity but in every life and circumstance of every believer. And as believers in God our Father and Jesus Christ His Son, we may have the assurance, at all times, in all places, and under all circumstances, that God is *there*, that God is in control, and that God is *love*.

Prologue

Genneta Williams sat at her desk in the flight school office of the William Shearer Center for Learning. Suspiciously, she studied the pictures and other documents handed to her by Mr. Lou Worley only moments before. Sealed in a glass jar and stored in a teakwood chest with close to three gallons of uncut diamonds, it had survived more than fifty years at the bottom of a lake in northwestern Alaska.

Lou Worley had made his fortune in the gold mining industry. Ten years before handing Genneta the teakwood treasure chest, he had paid the expenses for both her and her husband Jeffery to move from their home in Sikeston, Missouri, to Alaska. Soon Jeffery began working as a pilot for Worley's Mining Corporation. When Worley began building the learning centers, Worley assigned the job of designing and building the flight school, as well as superintendent of Fight School Operations to Genneta.

Twelve years had passed since Genneta's father, Arthur Bold, had retired and sold his property to Mr. Worley. After which he moved back to his original home, the home where he had been born and raised and where he would, ultimately, spend the remaining years of his life, living with his estranged daughter.

Before Arthur passed away, he had entrusted his daughter with a large manila envelope containing an assortment of newspaper articles and maps. Included in it was a letter he had written requesting that she forward the package to Mr. Lou Worley in Wassila, Alaska.

In 1953, according to the newspaper reports, an old Russian airplane, and its pilot—presumed to be a diamond smuggler—had entered the Alaska Territory from Siberia only to disappear. The Russian pilot was presumed to have gone down somewhere in northwestern Alaska. Arthur Bold believed he knew precisely where and that Lou Worley was just the man who could find him. Genneta did as her father requested and forwarded the package to Mr. Worley.

Over the next ten years, Genneta had forgotten about the manila envelope, and its contents, until one spring day while sitting at her desk in the learning center's Flight Operations Center in Bettles, Alaska; into her office walked Mr. Lou Worley, the billionaire who had financed the construction of the learning centers.

"Genneta," he said. "I have something I believe belongs to you, more than it does to me."

Puzzled, she glanced at the teakwood chest as he placed it on her desk.

"That doesn't look like anything that belongs to me, nor have I ever seen it before, but it certainly is beautiful."

"Remember that manila envelope you sent me from your father?"

"Yes, something about a Russian airplane that went down somewhere, supposedly a diamond smuggler."

"That's right. Well, I found the airplane, and this chest was hidden in a secret compartment in the floor that I would have never located if it had not been completely rotted out. I think you should have a look inside. There are some documents, and pictures, you might be interested in."

Genneta opened the lid and inhaled so deeply he thought she would explode. "Oh, my god! Are those real diamonds?"

"Yes, ma'am, they surely are, and I've come to the conclusion that they are yours."

"I want you to be right, but why are they mine?"

The Fruit of Atrocity

"Have a look at the pictures and documents in that glass jar, and see what you can learn about those people. It's possible they may be members of your extended family. Oh, and don't make this public. It wouldn't be in anyone's best interest for the news media to know anything about it. Just take them home, and if you want to sell any of them, let me know. I'll buy some, or all of them, from you for fair market value. On the other hand, if you want, just keep them."

Genneta studied the pictures. The shorter individual in the first picture was wearing a pair of mechanics coveralls and was evidently the owner of the 1947 Antonov AN-2, Bi-wing.

Another tall, handsome young man in his early thirties, wearing a sealskin full body–length flight suit stood next to the shorter man. It was evident that the two, posing next to an Antonov AN-2 Seaplane with their arms over each others shoulders, were good friends. A notation on the back of the picture read: "Jay and Elmo Manchuria—1949."

Another picture featured the same tall, handsome one, alone standing next to a shiny, polished aluminum DC-3 Red Cross hospital plane parked on her father's grass airstrip in Wasilla, Alaska. A note on the back of that picture read: "Brother Jay Bold—1949."

Tears welled up in Genneta's eyes as she considered the possibility that the young man in the picture could have been her father's younger brother, an uncle, she never knew existed.

Other possibilities also occurred to her. Was her father involved in a diamond smuggling operation along with his younger brother, Jay? If so, was this uncle—she had never seen, nor heard of—the pilot of the Russian AN-2? And was Glacial Lake, Alaska, the place where they both had ultimately lost their lives?

Genneta slid the teakwood treasure chest closer to her where she could examine its contents more closely. Reaching inside, she grasped a handful of the diamonds, slowly letting them drift through her fingers, fascinated by their mysterious beauty.

Only a few months before handing the box of diamonds to Genneta, Lou Worley had met with a very unfortunate accident. While searching for the lost aircraft, he inadvertently crashed and sank his beloved

Cessna 180 to the bottom of Glacial Lake where it had, fortuitously, come to rest next to the old Russian ANT, the same aircraft that had gone missing long ago in 1953, thirteen years before Genneta was born. In his efforts to recover the teak chest full of diamonds that had lain buried under that lake for nearly fifty years, Mr. Worley had nearly lost his life in addition to losing his airplane.

Genneta recalled again the words Mr. Worley had spoken to her, "I believe..." he said, "that these belong to you."

Now, upon reflection, Genneta was not entirely sure she wanted them. Questions swirled around in her mind: Where did the diamonds come from? What did this, man—who apparently was her uncle— have to do with any of it? How many other people were involved? And more importantly, at what cost and by whose blood were the diamonds acquired?

A year later, Genneta received another call from Mr. Lou Worley.

"Did you get a chance to look through those pictures yet?"

Genneta paused for a moment as if she were about to start up a long, steep hill and needed to shift gears first. "Yes...I have studied them quite a bit since that day, and I have a lot of questions. The problem is: I have no idea who has the answers..."

"What kind of questions?"

"Well, for instance, why didn't my father tell me I had an uncle? Was it none of my business? Or was he ashamed because his brother was a diamond smuggler? Furthermore, if he knew his own brother was smuggling diamonds and had crashed somewhere, why did he not try to find him instead of waiting all those years and leaving it to you? It makes me wonder if my dad was involved in the whole operation. Maybe that's why my mother left him and took me back to Missouri. Maybe she wanted to avoid any potential ramifications that might come from it. Now I'm not sure I want that box of diamonds."

Worley wasn't sure if Genneta should be bitter over the whole deal or happy for the opportunity to learn something involving her family history. Feeling obliged to tell her what else he had learned, he said, "It may not be what you think, Genneta."

"Well, that is the problem, isn't it? I have no idea what to think."

Worley sensed Genneta's frustration and anger, even betrayal. He was glad however that she felt comfortable enough with him to let it out. He was about to speak again when she broke in with more questions, throwing them out on the table like pieces of a puzzle that not only didn't fit but had no business being in the box.

"And who is this Chinese nurse, and all those kids?"

Without realizing it, Genneta had asked the question in two opposing tenses, as if the girl in the picture, who was much older, was somehow a relevant part of her dilemma, but the children never were.

"Genneta, do you remember when my wife and I took Beltray to meet his mother for the first time?"

"Yes," she answered, almost in a whisper.

"His mother, Loraine, is a member of a church in West Juneau, the one that Beltray Gibbons is now the pastor of—he lives in the duplex next to the parsonage."

Her voice became stronger. "Yes, I am aware of that."

Lou Worley continued, "The congregation's pastor passed away only six months before Beltray met his mother, and the pastor's wife had passed away only six months prior to that."

"Yes, I am very glad for Beltray, but what does this have to do with me?"

Lou Worley paused a moment, not sure if he even knew that answer. He decided to let her arrive at her own conclusion the same way he had.

"Genneta, she was Chinese, and many of the church members were of mixed Chinese/Japanese descent." He paused again.

"Mr. Worley, I still don't get it."

"When Kati and I were there, we saw a wedding picture hanging on Loraine's [Beltray's mother] wall of a young Caucasian man and his Chinese bride. They were both about thirty years old. It was your uncle and the same girl in the picture that you have."

Lou could hear Genneta quietly crying. She didn't say anything for several minutes. Finally, she spoke. "Mr. Worley, thank you...I'm really very grateful, but there are still so many unanswered questions." She paused again, regaining her composure.

"Are you saying he was the pastor of that church at one time?"

"Yes, not only the pastor but the one who started the church in the first place."

"What do you think happened? Who were all those children? How did they...?" Again, she wept.

"Genneta, I can find the answers for you if you truly want them, but there's no telling what else may come to the surface. Maybe wonderful discoveries about your family history, and maybe some not so wonderful, you will have to let me know. I can also tell you what I think if you like, and you can either let my speculations be your truth or give me the go-ahead, and I will begin an investigation that will reveal the whole unadulterated facts of the story, from the very beginning."

Again, Genneta waited a long moment before replying, "I would appreciate both, Mr. Worley."

"Good, well then, according to the information I have so far— which is purely heresay—your uncle's name was Jayson Baldwin. I am not sure if he had a different father than Arthur or if he just changed his name from Jayson Bold for some reason. My source also suggested that he may have been a missionary in China, which may have been where that photo was taken and where the two of them met."

"A missionary? I find that hard to believe."

"Why?" he asked, surprised.

"I don't know. I guess because I never heard of anyone in our family who was Christian."

"Well, either way, he was in China for some reason. Maybe he was in the army or something. Maybe that's why he changed his name and Arthur never spoke of him. Maybe your father was trying to protect him from his past. Maybe—"

"Maybe what, Mr. Worley?"

"Maybe he was in the army when he met the girl and deserted to run off with her. I told you, you might not want to know. What may be theory at this point could be real life at another."

THE FRUIT OF ATROCITY

"That's why I would like to have both. Where do the children fit into all of this?"

"I'm not sure, but it is possible that she was a teacher as well as a nurse, and the children were her students or maybe she worked in an orphanage or something. Anyway, I get the impression that your uncle was trying to get them all out of China and, for some reason, maybe resorted to smuggling diamonds to fund the operation. This could have placed the time frame around about the fall of Shanghai to the Japanese and the 1937 invasion and Rape of Nanking where, it was reported, that over three hundred thousand Chinese were massacred in less than a month. I did some research and discovered that during that same month, over eighty thousand women and young girls were raped—most of which were murdered. You cannot help but notice that all of the children in that photograph are apparently the same age. I would venture to say their birthdays are all within three weeks of one another, which would explain why they appear to be mixed race, Chinese/Japanese. Furthermore, I believe that whatever your uncle was originally involved with in China, he evidently abandoned it to concentrate on saving that girl and those children. And during that time, at some point, I believe the two of them fell in love.

"It is possible the mechanic was involved in it all as well. Maybe he was the one who owned the AN-2. Who knows? At any rate, that's about the only feasible scenario I've been able to come up with. There is one more thing that seems clear though. When your uncle finally did get them all to Alaska, he hid them all in Juneau, started a church, and apparently changed his name. If I were you, I would let it go at that. In my opinion the guy was a hero..." (Revised excerpts from *The Sequel to Alfred Creek* by D. L. Waterhouse)

Chapter 1

Twelve Chinese freedom fighters, armed with assorted rifles and automatic weapons, stood atop an outcrop of jagged rocks overlooking a treacherous narrow canyon, deep in the heart of the Himalayan Mountains. It was midmorning, and the rising sun warmed the young men as they rested from their arduous climb up from the dense jungle below.

Most of the young patriots were dressed in US army green fatigues with ammunition belts that crisscrossed their chest and backs. Australian-made Akubra jungle hats, attached by a leather thong, hung loosely from around their necks, while long black silk bandannas, tied about their foreheads, trailed over their shoulders, fluttering in the morning breeze.

These fighting men were not part of the regular National Army led by Generalissimo Chiang Kai-shek but rather civilian militia, self-appointed assassins of the hated Japanese aggressors that had invaded, and occupied, their beloved China for nearly a decade. These ferocious and fearless young men answered to but one man, who, revered for his bravery and leadership, stood dauntlessly above them at the highest point on the rocky ridge.

Charlie Nee motioned for his men to be still as he cupped his hand against his ear, straining, to hear some faraway sound that only he had detected. He was not imagining it; it was there, and it was coming closer, a distant hum that soon would dispel their morning respite. Momentarily, the others would hear it too, the unmistakable drone of an airplane approaching through the long, narrow canyon that lay like an enormous crocodile for twenty-miles to the west of their position. The intimidating rumble of the huge radial engines grew louder as the aircraft came closer.

The young Chinese jungle fighters were well acquainted with the various unique sounds of the warplanes in the Asian theater. In fact, they knew very well the identity of each one, friend or foe, merely by the sound. There was no question that this airplane was American, most likely one of the C-47s making its daily run across the Himalayas to Kunming, China, from one of the several American bases in India supporting the war effort against the Japanese. There would be nothing to fear from this aircraft—this was China's only ally.

The young squad leader pondered, *Why is the American pilot so far south of the Burma route? And so dangerously low in the canyon?*

The roar of the twin, 1,200 horsepower Pratt and Whitney engines, grew louder, and the young squad leader said to his men, "Mericonn airplane, maybe trouble, maybe crash—"

In that instant, the huge freighter emerged from around the bend in a frighteningly steep bank, narrowly negotiating the tight turn. Now, less than a mile from where they stood, the raiders could see the army pilot working feverishly to slow the heavy freighter as it rapidly descended toward them.

Closer and closer it came. The young men grew wide-eyed and looked about for a place to run, but there was no time. Impressed, they watched their leader, Charlie Nee, fearlessly standing his ground as the C-47 roared past a mere thirty feet above their heads. So close in fact, the young raiders could plainly see the terror in the eyes of the pilot as the huge aircraft briefly blotted out the sun.

Fascinated, they watched and listened as the cargo plane continued its descent into the bottom of the dead-end canyon, soon disappearing from sight. For a brief moment, all was still while the jungle turned strangely silent. Then, the thunderous, sickening sound of the aircraft's fuselage impacting the earth reverberated throughout the canyon.

Charlie Nee stared wonderingly in the direction where the plane had crashed. A huge cloud of dust began to rise, billowing above the meadow where they had spent the previous night. Slowly, he shouldered his weapon. Turning to his men, he said to them, "We go back, see…maybe, mericonn pilot no dead."

High in the Himalayan Mountains of western China near the border with Burma, and somewhere southeast of the Burma Road, a twenty-four-year-old American pilot lay on an army stretcher: bewildered, injured, and staring at the moss-covered ceiling of a dark, damp rocky cave.

The airman's befuddled memory struggled to recall the sketchy events leading up to the moment he awakened from the only true sleep he had had in over a week.

Lying on his back, his body wracked in pain; his brain struggled to recover from a concussion. Fragments of memory occasionally flashed through his mind like pieces of a puzzle floating about in zero gravity.

A few things had already become clear to the injured pilot; his name was First Lieutenant Jayson Bold, and he was one of a squadron of cargo pilots assigned to the Seventeenth Military Air Transport Division of the United States Army Air Corp based in Ledo, India. He knew also that he had just spent the last eleven months as pilot in command of a C-47 Transport, flying one, sometimes two, round-trips a day the seven hundred miles across the treacherous Himalayan hump to the Flying Tigers based in Kunming, China, day after day hauling freight desperately needed in support of China's war effort against the Japanese.

It was the spring of 1943, and three hundred round-trip missions across that treacherous range of mountains was supposedly enough to qualify any pilot that lived that long to a thirty-day leave of absence—stateside. However, with but three missions to go, something terrible had happened, and the lieutenant had yet to recall exactly what it was.

The cave was wider than it was long, about forty by one hundred feet. The only light came from a small fire some thirty feet from where the injured airman lay and where nearly a dozen young Chinese men ranging in age from fifteen to nineteen years sat in a circle around a fire. They talked in low tones among themselves and, with their fingers, ate rice from oversized leaves that served as plates. Occasionally, in the half light and void of any expression, one or two would glance ominously in the lieutenant's direction.

The fighting men, some of whom were dressed in American GI uniforms, did not appear to be soldiers of either the US or the regular Chinese army. For weapons, they carried an assortment of Japanese 6.5 millimeter bolt action rifles and US M1 thirty-caliber carbines. One of the weapons the lieutenant recognized was a US army issue 7.62 caliber BAR (Browning Automatic Rifle) proudly owned and operated by the oldest, and obviously the leader, in charge of the twelve-man squad.

Other weapons included a mixture of ancient and relatively new Japanese-, German-, and Russian-manufactured small arms. The lieutenant calculated they were weapons confiscated from dead Japanese soldiers, soldiers that this small band of raiders had more than likely killed plenty of.

The leader of the jungle fighters glanced at Jayson and noticed he was finally awake. Speaking in his native dialect, he ordered the youngest member of his team to take the injured pilot some food and water.

Jayson's memory, for the most part, only included the events of the last three days since the crash. Even then, he had frequently slipped in and out of reality, sometimes for extended periods.

During intermittent times of cognizance, Jayson occasionally tried to communicate with his captors, or rescuers, he wasn't sure which. And because Jayson did not speak Chinese, and apparently none of them spoke English, his attempts at communicating had not gone well.

By now, the lieutenant's backside was getting numb, and as he tried to roll over on his left side, a searing pain in his rib cage reminded him that he was seriously injured. Once again, another fragment of memory returned.

Vaguely, at first, Lieutenant Bold recalled lying on the cold, damp earth, somewhere in the jungle. Above him, he remembered, bamboo trees swaying gently in the breeze and sheer rock cliffs towering perilously overhead. The sky was white with high cirrus clouds where patches of sunlight occasionally pierced through, bringing with it a searing pain to his bruised and sensitive brain. Vaguely, the lieutenant recalled the hands that had lifted him onto the stretcher, the same hands that had also searched through his pockets.

For the moment, that was all he could recollect. He was tired again, and it made his head hurt to think. But the question that plagued him was how he managed to get his self all busted up, flat on his back, and on the ground in the first place.

The young Chinese man approached the injured airman and placed the food and water beside him. Jayson took hold of his arm and spoke to him, "Do you know what has happened to me? Can you tell me where I am? I must go Kunming, you"—Jayson motioned in the direction of the other men—"you, take me Kunming, Flying Tiger, airbase?"

Without realizing it, Jayson had tried to mimic the broken English he supposed his escorts would most likely understand.

"Kunming? You know Kunming?" Jayson looked into the eyes of his benefactor for any trace of understanding, or acknowledgment. But the eyes that stared back, projected only a blank stare.

As the young man returned to his place beside the fire, the leader of the band of men set aside the leaf from which he had been eating and shuffled his way to where the lieutenant lay.

Jayson immediately noticed the army issue Colt .45 strapped to his waist, which heightened his sense of vulnerability even more.

Squatting beside the injured pilot, the Chinese rebel leader reached his hand across Jayson's body and gently touched his rib cage on the right side. He then proceeded to speak the only English the lieutenant had heard from any of them.

"Okay?" He patted Jayson's side again and repeated the words, "Rib okay?" Jayson nodded though he was not sure just how *okay* his ribs actually were. Suddenly it occurred to him.

"English! You speak English?"

"Speak Engleh…little bit, you bet."

The lieutenant felt a huge sense of relief at the prospect of finally being able to communicate with someone.

Jayson had a hundred things he wanted to know but was not sure how much of the English language a "little bit" actually amounted to.

"What is your name?" he asked.

"Charlie," the young man responded, pointing his thumb at himself.

Eagerly Jayson answered, "My name is Jayson Bold, First Lieutenant, United States Army Air Corp."

Charlie considered the name a moment and slowly repeated his Chinese version of Jayson's first name, using two distinct syllables. "Jae-sonn? Okay? Jae-sonn?" He repeated it again as though inquiring if his attempt at pronunciation was adequate.

Jayson nodded. Charlie, patting his own chest and arching his arm in the direction of his men, said to him, "Lito Devos."

Jayson noticed that Charlie's face lit up with an expression of pride as he spoke the name given to his band of boy soldiers by the AVG (American Volunteer Group) in 1939.

Lieutenant Bold—as well as every other pilot in the Seventeenth Military Air Transport—had heard many stories of the *little devils* and especially of their leader—Charlie Nee. The stories of their underground war, consisting of acts of terror-

THE FRUIT OF ATROCITY

ism and sabotage against the Japanese ground troops, extended as far back as 1937 and had literally become folklore among not only the Flying Tigers but the Chinese Regular Army and the American Army Air Corp as well.

They were all much younger then. Charlie would have been barely twelve years old. They had lived in an orphanage run by a Christian missionary named Alfred Blair, whom the orphans affectionately called Baba-Wanjuxiong—or Papa Bear.

Then one day, the Japanese bombed the orphanage, taking the life of their beloved father figure and the only parent Charlie, and most of the other orphans, had ever known. It was a sad day, and it was *that* day that Charlie Nee declared his own personal war upon the armies of Japan. For the next two years, Charlie and his adolescent raiders wreaked havoc on Japanese supply depots, barracks, and radio transmission stations from Nanking to Chungking. Their successful feats of sabotage quickly brought them notoriety among the AVG flyers. Even Claire Chennault, the commander of the AVG, recognized their contribution to the war effort by providing the Little Devils sanctuary and support.

Unfortunately, the stepped up Japanese advancement deeper into northwestern China in 1939 eventually overwhelmed the Chinese Regular Army along with its Air Force. With their airbases virtually destroyed, and the Chinese Air Force effectually decimated, Chennault and the AVG disbanded, leaving inland China completely indefensible from the air.

"I thought you and your friends were all killed in the bombing of Kunming in 1939?" Jayson asked, remembering the historical account of the heroic *China's Little Devils*.

"Flyem Tiger, tell everyone Charlie dead, Devos dead. Very good story for Charlie. No Japan soldier look for Devos no more." The leader of the band of raiders poked his thumb against his chest as he proudly verified, "Charlie no dead, Devos no dead, still kill many Japan soldier."

"Are there more of you or just these men you have with you?"

27

"Many more, many, many more Devos. We go now, you see."

Immediately, Jayson felt a deepening concern for his future. "We go where?" The lieutenant thought a moment, deciding it would be a good time to ask the question that had bothered him most. "Am I your prisoner?"

"No, no, prisoner, you Mericonn, Mericonn no prisoner. Devos help Mericonn pilot. Charlie take you safe, okay?" The head devil pointed off to some distant place in a direction Jayson was not sure existed.

"Then why have you taken my weapon?"

"You eat now, get much rest, then we go more…long way." Charlie rose to return to his leaf/plate of rice.

Jayson called after him, "That Colt .45 is US government property, and I want it back." Charlie was all through talking and, without replying, returned to his campfire.

Lieutenant Jayson Bold resumed eating the rice and drank the water the young man had brought him. He was of course relieved to know that he was not in enemy hands, but nonetheless, the lieutenant had many questions as to Charlie's intentions. He thought, *If they could carry me through the jungle to the southeast, why couldn't they carry me northwest toward Kunming? Then again, maybe the mountains are impassable in that direction, or maybe they are taking me to some place where there is an airfield and a hospital. I'll just have to wait and see.*

Jayson slid the empty leaf/plate away and once again fell asleep. When he awoke, his memory had fully returned.

Before the Japanese attack on Pearl, the US involvement in the Chinese war with Japan had been an unofficial one, involving only a small squadron of American Volunteers—the AVG. Later in the war, the very same airman would gain unprecedented notoriety as the infamous Flying Tigers, based in Kunming, China.

THE FRUIT OF ATROCITY

From that airbase and several other smaller bases between Kunming and (since the fall of Nanking) the Capital City of Chungking and during the six months prior to Pearl Harbor, the AVG and their small squadron of P-40 fighter aircraft had effectively destroyed hundreds of Japanese Zeroes at an unprecedented kill ratio of twenty-five to one.

The Japanese bomber sorties, raiding among others the new Capital City of Chungking, numbered three hundred a day. The continual assault practically decimated the city of over twenty-nine million civilians. The Flying Tigers had made both the bombers and Japanese Zeroes pay dearly for their sorties until the bombers were forced to resort to only flying at night where their losses from adverse weather and inadvertent encounters with the terrain were, nonetheless, extremely high.

Since the objective to retake the Burma road had been accelerated, Lieutenant Jayson Bold began to see more and more of the Japanese Zeroes. So far, he had either been lucky or especially protected by a higher power, for each spotting of the enemy had failed to result in any serious repercussions. Until one day, in the spring of 1943, a mere week before Lieutenant Jayson Bold awoke in the cave, neither scenario proved to be the case.

The Japanese pilot that spotted the lieutenant as he emerged from a cloud dove his fighter toward the American cargo plane at full speed; his 20 mm wing mounted canons blazing even before he was within range.

Jayson immediately initiated an aggressive diving turn to an easterly course that would place the Jap fighter directly into the morning sun.

Recently added to the fleet of Transports—that until the spring of 1943 mostly consisted of C-47s, more affectionately referred to as the *Goony Bird*—was a new freight hauler with the military designation, C-46, that soon became known as the Commando.

The more powerful C-46s could not only carry a much larger payload but were also capable of climbing to higher altitudes,

altitudes that kept its pilots and crew high above and far away from the limited range of the Mitsubishi Zeroes based in Hanoi.

Lieutenant Bold's C-47 was a military modified version of the McDonald Douglas DC-3 that had become the workhorse of the war effort both in Europe and, since Pearl Harbor, the Pacific and Asian theaters.

Lieutenant Bold's freighter was loaded with fifteen fifty-five-gallon drums of aviation fuel for both the American fighters and transport planes based in the Yunnan and Taungyyi province's of western China. At maximum gross weight—plus 605 lb.—and due to the inclement weather at the higher altitudes, Jayson stayed closer to the lower elevations of fifteen thousand feet and below while crossing the Himalayas. Unfortunately, this scenario invariably placed him exactly where the dreaded Zeroes were most likely to be.

On that fateful day, as Lieutenant Bold's C-47 cargo plane emerged from the clouds, he instantly saw the Japanese fighter at the same moment the Japanese fighter pilot saw him. As Jayson executed his evasive maneuver that took him deeper into a canyon, he hoped and prayed the camouflage-painted exterior of the '47 would somehow make the vulnerable cargo plane invisible.

The C-47 had no armament like the B-17 bombers that were winning the war in the European theater nor were there gunners incased in swivel turrets at strategic locations throughout the airplane that could shoot in all directions. Lone pilots and pilots with crew on board were frequently lost in treacherous weather and wicked downdrafts en route through the Himalayans, and in their efforts to avoid the hazardous conditions, at times, would fly through the lower elevations, often meeting their demise at the hands of the Japanese Zeroes. Losses were staggering, and the fleet of '47s was necessarily reduced to a one-man crew— the pilot.

Only six days prior to waking up in Charlie's cave, surrounded by dense jungle, First Lieutenant Jayson Bold, as usual, was the only soul aboard his aircraft, and if he were to survive, it would be from a display of exceptional maneuvering through the treacherous southeastern extension of the Himalayan range—as well as a miracle from Almighty God.

Before the war, Jayson and his older brother Arthur owned a crop dusting business in Sikeston, Missouri. Together, they waged a war of a different kind against the boll weevil, saving the cotton crops for growers up and down the Mississippi Delta from Cape Girardeau to New Orleans.

Arthur Bold was three years older than his brother Jayson. Together, they had sold part of the farm left to them after both their parents perished in a tragic automobile accident shortly following Jayson's fifteenth birthday.

In 1934, the Huff Deland Duster Corporation left behind the business of crop dusting on their way to becoming Delta Airlines. Arthur, barely eighteen years old, and his younger brother Jayson traveled to New Orleans, where they purchased two of the remaining fourteen crop dusters from the Duster Corporation at a price of $800 each.

The Huff Deland Duster—often referred to as the Puffer—was a cantilever biplane, powered by a 200 hp Wright Whirlwind J-4 engine. The Puffer was the only airplane Jayson had ever flown until his enlistment into the Army Air Corp, other than an old surplus WWI Jenny in which he had first soloed.

Both Jayson and Arthur held flight instructor certificates and, as such, would supplement their income during the winter months when there were no boll weevils left to bomb.

Expecting a terrorizing spray of machine gun bullets to come ripping through the fuselage at any moment, disintegrating him and his cargo plane into a massive ball of flame, Lieutenant Bold dove the freight hauler, loaded with 825 gallons of gasoline, deeper and deeper into the long canyon. Flying only a few feet above the canopy of the bamboo forest and not sure where the long, narrow valley would take him, he frantically prayed while searching for any way out.

The canyon was much too narrow to execute a 180-degree turn and too short to climb back up to the altitude needed to cross the high terrain that lay just ahead and on either side. All of which was assuming he had effectively given the Jap fighter the slip. It had become increasingly apparent to the lieutenant that he had inadvertently trapped himself in a dead-end canyon.

Jayson had not seen the Zero since he began his accelerated dive and was not sure if he had ditched the Jap fighter or not. The one thing he *was* sure of: the canyon was making a hard left turn to the northeast, and Jayson had no idea what was around the corner. He prayed, "Lord God, I've gotten myself in over my head here. It appears that this is the end of my life on this earth. Oh merciful God, please don't let me die, I pray."

Banking the overloaded C-47 into a sixty-degree steep left turn, Jayson rounded the corner. Suddenly, the lieutenant drew in a deep breath and held it for a long moment. There, through the front windshield, where the pilot is supposed to see blue sky, Jayson could see nothing but the towering gray mass of solid granite, a vertical cliff wall extending ten thousand feet above the floor of the canyon in which he was flying, and toward which he was accelerating at over two hundred miles per hour. Frantically he checked the distance between the canyon walls, but there was no space to turn around. He was much too low and far too heavy to attempt to execute a Channdelle. Again, he prayed to God.

As the breath he was holding slowly escaped his inflated lungs, he heard a faraway cry for divine help, hardly realizing it was his own. He looked around, not sure that the cry had actually come from his own lips. But there was no one else there. He was all alone, strapped to a flying bomb that was hurtling itself toward a granite wall. Then, he heard it again, like someone screaming at the top of their lungs, "Oh God…oh my God!"

Without consciously thinking about it, the lieutenant's experience and emergency procedure training took over. Quickly, he simultaneously reduced the power to twenty-three inches of manifold pressure. As the airspeed deteriorated, Jayson gradually raised the nose of the ship while simultaneously applying flaps to maximum extension, slowing the aircraft. With airspeed dangerously close to seventy knots, only slightly above a stall, and the ground speed as slow as it was ever going to get without stalling, Jayson let the freighter descend under power lower and lower into the dead-end canyon.

While manipulating the throttles to control the aircraft's vertical decent rate, he frantically searched for some survivable place to land.

Passing slightly above and narrowly missing a smaller ridge lying perpendicular to the lay of the canyon, he noticed movement on the ridgeline. For a brief moment as he passed over their heads, he could see men with small arms and realized they must be soldiers of some type. Suddenly, the most beautiful meadow Jayson had ever seen appeared in the windscreen of the C-47, less than two miles directly before him. A long clearing is all it was, but it was the one and only option left, and the lieutenant knew that regardless of the outcome, it was the place where his mission, that day, would abruptly end.

Without extending the landing gear of the aircraft, the lieutenant effectively belly-landed the overloaded flying bomb onto the undulating field at over eighty miles per hour.

It was as if time had switched to slow motion. At only a few feet above the tall grass, Jayson cut the fuel to the Pratt and Whitney engines, both of which abruptly stopped. Instantly, the aircraft ceased flying and, like a porpoising projectile, slammed repeatedly against the uneven terrain.

As the aircraft hit the ground for the last time, the rough ground violently hammered and tore at the belly of the ship, a ship that had abruptly become a giant cross-country ski. The aircraft pitched up and down, its momentum launching it from side to side in first one direction, then another, rolling with the undulations of the uneven land. Violently, Jayson felt himself yanked, first to the right and again to the left. As the aircraft transferred from higher ground on the one side to lower on the other, one wing would dip low, crabbing the airplane in a yaw to one side while still speeding straight ahead. Tall grass mixed with brush and chunks of dirt and sod shot across the tops of the wings. Finally, the left wing settled onto the surface of the long meadow, realigning the nose of the airplane straight ahead as the aircraft finally slammed into the upward slope of a small rise and abruptly stopped.

The impact burst the binders that secured the fifty-five-gallon drums of gasoline. Two extra drums of fuel doubled stacked in the forward cargo area, which had contributed to the overload, broke loose from their bindings; the tremendous momentum launched them skidding on their sides, across the narrow aluminum surfaced catwalk of the flight deck, and into the cockpit. The first drum of fuel to arrive smashed into the pilot's right side rib cage, knocking the lieutenant unconscious and nearly crushing him against the instrument panel.

Finally, a terrible stillness replaced the incredible violence of the crash landing. Lieutenant Jayson Bold, still fastened into his pilot seat, sat pinned against the pilot's side window, badly injured and unconscious yet miraculously alive.

It was the middle of June, and especially in the Himalayans, the monsoon rains had been the heaviest in years. On the morning Lieutenant Jayson Bold departed Ledo, India, with his cargo of

THE FRUIT OF ATROCITY

aviation fuel, the adverse weather southeast of the Burma Road project had briefly turned to broken clouds and partly sunny skies.

Jayson knew not to expect any organized search for his downed aircraft. The war effort could not spare the pilots, aircraft, or fuel required for searching or risk the potential of encountering other Japanese Zeroes, chancing the additional loss of more men and equipment, especially the precious cargo which was more often than not fuel for Chennault's P-40s. Besides, it would be like looking for a needle in a haystack a million times multiplied.

There was, however, a search and rescue group known as Blackie's Gang recently organized by a Captain John Porter based in Chabua, India. The Seventeenth MATS Squadron often called upon Blackie's gang to search for downed pilots in the event they had a reasonable idea of the location where the transport presumably went down. There had actually been a few Airman rescued by the unit who were then returned to flying status. Jayson knew it would be unlikely any of them would find him, and he was confident that his recent acquaintances were not taking him in a direction that would increase his chances of rescue. Furthermore, his diversionary flying had taken him far south of the designated route over the hump, and the chances of someone inadvertently finding the crash site was, as the crash site itself, extremely remote.

Jayson now recollected the individuals he had seen on the ridge just before his off-airport landing. For the first time, he realized his rescuers were one and the same.

Jayson had no idea where he was. The three or four days of following invisible trails with secret markings through the dense jungle foliage, while dealing with a concussion that kept him disoriented most of the time, had the lieutenant totally confused geographically. Disorientation, which in addition to everything else, contributed even more to his feelings of vulnerability.

Nonetheless, Jayson admired the moxie of the young raiders and felt some degree of assurance that they were at least capable,

35

if not willing, of getting him back to his unit, whether in fact that was their intention remained to be seen.

Lieutenant Bold was a handsome young aviator. He was lean and strong from years of hard work on the farm. Standing well over six feet and two hundred pounds, he posed a striking picture of young American manhood. His thick black hair, dark-brown eyes, and square jaw garnished his rugged features and chiseled physique.

Jayson wore the same heavy, flyboy clothing issued to every other transport pilot for the cold temperatures of high altitude flights. His quilted military flight suit, Army issue wool lined leather flight jacket, and combat boots—only provided to the hump pilots—was not only warm but considered to be more valuable than diamonds, especially to the enemy. Now that he was on foot—or at least on a stretcher—Jayson was faced with a new problem: his flight suit unmistakingly distinguished him as an American pilot and certainly would guarantee his torture and probable death in the event of capture by the Japanese—making it imperative they avoid discovery.

The lieutenant had also thought of the possibility that the Japanese fighter pilot who had chased him into the canyon might have seen where he went down and reported Jayson's location to his superiors. Silently he prayed that they would not find him.

Morning inevitably happened again, and Charlie and his band of raiders prepared to leave the cave.

Charlie approached the lieutenant and said to him, "Jai-sonn walk now, okay?" Jayson felt like it was time for him to regain some control of his situation.

"I walk now if you give me back my sidearm," Jayson said sternly. Charlie was silent for a moment and slowly unbuckled the army issue Colt .45 semiautomatic from around his waist.

THE FRUIT OF ATROCITY

"Okay, you take now." Jayson was somewhat surprised that Charlie had no objection.

"You better have your men bring that litter along. I'm not sure how far I can go, or how long I will last."

"You drink this." Charlie offered Jayson a cup of some kind of liquid.

"What is it?"

"You drink, no hurt."

"What is it?"

"You drink, now." Charlie pushed the cup toward the lieutenant's lips.

Jayson peered suspiciously at Charlie wondering if the potion was some kind of drug that he would end up addicted to. Yet on the other hand, he knew the pain would likely be more than he could take if he didn't, so reluctantly, Jayson took the cup from Charlie's hand and tasted its contents. *Tastes a little like baking powder*, he thought. Due to the fact it was not entirely disgusting, he drank it all down.

A few moments later, Jayson began to feel a euphoria he never imagined could be experienced so far from heaven. Slowly he stood up and began to move about for the first time since the crash. The unstableness caused from the concussion had dissipated, and the lieutenant made his way toward the group of raiders, who were not only intrigued by him but for some reason found him quite humorous.

Charlie barked an order, and the band of raiders gathered their belongings and set about eliminating any trace or evidence of their overnight bivouac. That completed, together they emerged from the cave entrance and quickly disappeared single file into the jungle. Jayson picked up the rear followed only by the last, and youngest, of the raiders in line.

The lieutenant finally had his sidearm back, but how effective he would be with it in an encounter with the Japanese, remained to be seen. Slowly and quietly, the small group of men moved through the jungle, sensitive to the injured pilot's limitations to keep pace.

Jayson was feeling no pain nor did he any longer have any feelings of vulnerability. Often he would pause to examine a strange flower or exotic bird screeching at them from its perch on a limb, apparently irritated by the strange procession. At which time, Jayson would feel a gentle nudge from behind reminding him to keep moving.

Soon Jayson's thoughts drifted nostalgically back to his childhood and fond recollections of his parents and the wonderful times they had together. Suddenly, he seemed acutely aware of the aroma of his mother's cooking in the kitchen, carried by the morning breezes through the open window above the sink as it saturated the country air far out even to the fields where his father worked. Jayson could vividly see his father sitting on the old Farmall tractor as he worked the row crops, preparing the fields for planting. Tears of nostalgia stained Jayson's face without his being aware of it.

As a young man back in Sikeston, Missouri, Jayson occasionally accompanied his mother when she attended a small church on the outskirts of the town where they lived; although, he had never actually become a member. Jayson had come to realize early on that his theological views were somewhat eccentric compared with mainstream Christianity and the diversity of their teachings. However, the young man was not ignorant of the true gospel and knew precisely what he believed. At an early age, he had accepted the biblical teaching of the Son of God, Jesus Christ of Nazereth, who had come as a man to die on a Roman cross in sacrifice for the sins of humanity. Jayson's faith proved strong, and he never deviated from it regardless of the pressure to do so by his peers.

Suddenly, from behind, Jayson heard the sharp report of a rifle, and the limp body of his rearguard fell against him on its way to the ground.

The Fruit of Atrocity

Snapping out of his nostalgia, Jayson did an about-face desperately trying to fight off the fog that befuddled his brain, interfering with his connection to reality. Slowly it dawned on him that he was now all alone in the trail and watching eight men dressed as Japanese soldiers running toward him, yelling at the top of their lungs, "Ameri-conn, hands-up, Ameri-conn, hands-up."

Slowly the lieutenant raised his arms, realizing that his rescuers had vanished, and he was about to become a prisoner of the dreaded enemy. As if in slow motion, the Japanese patrol advanced closer to the American pilot. The leader approached Jayson with his sword drawn, brandishing it next to the pilot's throat. From a mere twelve inches away, Jayson looked into the insane, demonic eyes of his aggressor as the man screamed at him,

"Ameri-conn pilot, you die, you d—" A shot rang out. Then another. Suddenly Jayson heard an explosion of automatic gunfire coming from the thick jungle foliage on either side of the path where they stood. A volley of bullets sprayed the Japanese soldiers; small, bright red pieces of flesh, bone, and splattered blood torn from the soldier's bodies flew through the air in scores of directions. Beginning with the Samurai warrior, all nine of the Japanese soldiers slumped to the ground lifeless. Not a one of them had fired another shot.

In seconds, it was over. The lieutenant stood alone in the trail surrounded by a pile of dead men, his befuddled mind desperately attempting to figure it all out. He had not even drawn his pistol.

As the raiders slowly reappeared from the jungle, Charlie approached the confused airman with his hand outstretched.

"Charlie take pistol, now." With no further argument from the pilot, Charlie unbuckled the Colt .45 from Jayson's waist and strapped it to his own.

Quickly the band of raiders stripped the dead bodies of everything that could be useful for themselves: clothing, boots, weapons, ammo, even the food they carried in their packs. From their mouths, they extracted gold fillings, from their persons, rings, and jewelry. In a short time, the Japanese soldiers had completely disappeared from the face of the earth, buried in unmarked graves.

Charlie's raiders so totally camouflaged the area they completely eliminated any evidence of the skirmish. Yet sadly, there was one evidence that remained with Jayson forever—his rear guard, the young raider who had brought his food to him was dead. Although he had not known him personally, it saddened him deeply, for he had given his life to protect Jayson's. As for Charlie and his band of jungle fighters, apparently, without remorse and without saying a single word among themselves, they buried their comrade in yet another shallow grave, picked up their packs, and continued on their way.

Over the next two weeks of marching through the jungle, Charlie weaned the American flyer away from the somewhat hallucinogenic herbal concoction. Though it would take several more months for his ribs to fully mend, for the present, the pain had diminished to a tolerable level. Although Jayson regained his senses, he often remembered with fondness the euphoria that came with that awesome painkiller. Fortunately, he survived the befuddling side effects that accompanied it. Without reservation or comment, Charlie returned the Colt .45 to its rightful owner who was once again capable of understanding when and how to use it.

The jungle trail paralleled a treacherous crashing river that abruptly descended into a narrow canyon, evolving further into a deep gorge, finally terminating at the confluence of two additional drainage systems.

The three rivers, swollen from the deluge of monsoon rains, converged together to crash over a gigantic cliff towering seven hundred feet above a bowl-shaped basin completely encircled with a cylindrical shaped sheer rock wall. The enormous waterfall made a deafening roar, and Jayson wondered where all the water ultimately flowed to, for there did not appear to be any outlet, and the cylinder would certainly fill with water unless there were somewhere for it to go.

Jayson followed Charlie and his remaining raiders as they made their way carefully down the treacherous path. The trail eventually led to the bottom of the cliffs and soon emerged out of the jungle to the base of the thundering waterfall.

The thick mist reduced Jayson's visibility dramatically as he followed the raider in front of him. The narrow trail hugged the perimeter of a large whirlpool of water at least three hundred yards in diameter that violently flushed itself into a huge cavern in the earth. The rocky trail, wet from the constant curtain of mist, soon turned to slippery shale rock as it led them along a narrow ledge behind the falling apron of water to what appeared to be a dead end.

As the lieutenant approached, he saw the procession had stopped. The spray, from the water cascading off the cliff looming high above, swirled in the air, creating a fog that diminished visibility even more. Jayson wondered why everyone had stopped in a place where it was raining harder than the monsoons they all had endured for the last three weeks.

The thunderous roar of the water was deafening. Jayson noticed that Charlie was talking to someone he couldn't recognize. Suddenly he became aware that the head count of the group had increased by at least four or five heads, heads that were wearing bamboo grass hats instead of the camouflaged green jungle hats the raiders wore. Jayson inched his way closer to see the additional people that had joined their party, curious as to where they had come from.

It appeared the trail had ended at the far side of the waterfall, but suddenly, the additional people along with the raiders, one by one were mysteriously disappearing into the rock wall. The raider who had been staying pace with Jayson on the jungle trail turned to him and said, "Jai-sonn, you follow, stay close." Jayson could barely hear above the roar of the water and was surprised to hear him speak his name. Until that moment, Charlie was the only one of the raiders that had communicated to him, and he didn't think the others spoke or understood any English.

Jayson followed close behind as one by one those in the lead melted into the granite wall. Behind the waterfall, at the far end of the rock shelf where they had gathered, the path continued on to make a sharp left gooseneck turn behind a giant rock slab leading to the opening of a small cave. The farther they continued into the cave, the darker it became. Jayson could only faintly see the outline of the raider in front of him who was now the only one left in the procession and the only one who had stayed behind to help him find his way.

Water seeped from the cracks in the rocks dripping onto the floor of the cave. The two men stayed close to the right side of the rock wall as they passed through. The light had been completely extinguished by darkness. Jayson began to stumble. For a moment, he could feel the onset of vertigo disrupting his spatial orientation. As he made his way along, he leaned against the wall of the cave for support and guidance.

The lieutenant was becoming weary. The march had taken its toll on his endurance. Sharp pains shot through his side with every stumble, or misstep.

His senses told him the cave was making a wide counterclockwise turn. Suddenly, Jayson bumped into his guide who had unexpectedly stopped in front of him.

The young raider, whom Charlie had called Chi (pronounced *Chee*) said to him, "We rest here."

Jayson sank to the damp floor of the cave, thankful for the opportunity to rest a moment. The lieutenant was curious as to just how much English Chi could understand.

"Where does this cave lead to?" He asked.

"Path down steep, Jai-sonn, be vera careful."

They had only been resting about ten minutes. Jayson wished it had been an hour, but Chi stood and remarked, "We go now."

The raider was correct. The cave began to descend turning back to the right, and Jayson could no longer see his guide who was less than an arm's length away. The shale floor of the cave was wet and slimy from the perpetual stream of water, and algae that grew on the surface of the smooth layered rock. For the next two hundred yards, the pilot held to Chi's shoulder with one hand and to the wall of the cave with the other. Any misstep, or slip, would risk further injury to his still fragile ribs.

Finally, they reached the bottom where the floor of the cave leveled out and made a ninety-degree hard turn to the right. The two men began to see a trace of light illuminating the side walls of the cavern. Within minutes, they emerged from an opening in the side of the mountain looking out over a huge symmetrically round basin beneath a cauldron of sheer granite rock rising a thousand feet above the floor of the basin. It was a most beautiful setting, and Jayson held his breath a moment as he took in the incredible view. He had heard of a place in Dutch New Guinea, in the Belem Valley, called *Shangri-la*. He wondered if it was as beautiful as the valley spread out before him, this valley he had been brought to, somewhere—he knew not where—in the Himalayan Mountains.

The basin appeared to be eight or nine miles in diameter with a slight downstream slope covered in a thick forest of vegetation with a deep and meandering river worming its way for miles through the forest to the far side of the basin. It was obvious to Jayson that it was the same water that originated at the upper end of the cave. Both men stood together, quietly taking in the incredible view.

Chi said to Jayson, "Here we live, home now, Jai-sonn, you come." Chi turned to follow the path nature had cut out of the wall of the cauldron, leading from the cave entrance down the approximately 8 percent grade.

The path got wider the farther down it went. They hugged the towering cliff wall. Nearing the bottom, Jayson could hear voices, and Chi's pace increased at a rate Jayson could no longer match. At the bottom of the path, Charlie waited with his raiders who were affectionately greeting a group of people, all of whom appeared to be friends or family.

Jayson felt a little awkward, like he was an uninvited guest. He wondered why Charlie would bring him to a place that was obviously his own personal home, a place that would require absolute secrecy for reasons of life and death. Was he someone that Charlie believed could be trusted? Or on the other hand, was he someone that once invited in, could never be allowed to leave, someone they would, if needed, kill before risking the disclosure of their secret world?

On the other hand, the downed pilot had no reason to distrust the band of devils. They had risked life and limb as well as losing one of their own men to save him from certain death, death that most certainly would have come at either the hands of the Japanese or exposure to the elements following his rough landing.

During his trek through the jungle, Jayson had not had much time to reflect on the events of the day he went down. In one shattering moment, his world had gone from C-47 pilot, First Lieutenant United States Army Air Corp, to a busted up tagalong straggler marching through a jungle of bugs, beasts, and bushes to who knows where, completely dependent on a bunch of teenagers for his survival.

Only three weeks before, he had methodically repeated the same daily routine of flying his cargo plane to and from Ledo, India, to Kunming in the Yunnan province of China, awaiting the day he would receive the set of orders that would send him home. Since then he had been everything from a prisoner to a patient. At times, he felt like he may never again find his way back to his unit. Surely, God's divine hand must be behind the circumstances that had dramatically changed the course of his life.

On the other hand, things were actually looking up. A dozen, or so, friendly faces approached the pilot with huge betel nut smiles full of betel nut–stained teeth and knurly betel nut–stained hands loaded with more food than he had seen in nearly a month. Suddenly, the Seventeenth Military Air Transport Division had become a distant and faded memory.

Chapter 2

First Lieutenant Jayson Bold, awoke to the sound of children playing and the murmur of voices outside his grass thatched bamboo bungalow.

Stiff and sore from three weeks of trekking through mountains, gorges, streams, and thick jungle while sporting several broken ribs and a concussion, Jayson evaluated his circumstances and decided things could be worse—like waking up in a Japanese prison camp.

He thought about his army buddies back at his home base in Ledo, India, and wondered what they must be thinking. Jayson and his best friend, First Lieutenant Carl Prichard, had met while in line at the recruiting office in St. Lewis Missouri and had stayed together all through their officer cadet school and flight training.

Carl was five years older than Jayson, whose advanced maturity intrigued Carl and helped to embolden their friendship. Together with two other rookie, second lieutenants, they had shared a cabin on the ocean liner that brought their unit of eighty-five new recruits across the big water from San Francisco Harbor to Rangoon. All of the recruits started out as second lieutenants until they reached first pilot status, which usually occurred after thirty round-trips across the hump to China.

Jayson felt bad for Carl; he knew that his friend would find it hard to accept the fact that he was missing in action and would go out of his way to look for him, enlisting as many other pilots as he could to join in. Predictably, the big brass would turn a blind eye for a month or so, then would issue a bulletin, stating, in effect, to cease flying irregular routes and get back to flying direct to the destinations assigned. In other words, *Forget about Lieutenant Jayson Bold. We have bigger fish to fry.*

The lieutenant needed a bath and yet had no idea where to go to accomplish that, or any other personal hygiene. He groaned as he rose from his bamboo grass mat. Glancing around for his weapon, he realized it was gone.

As he emerged from his guest room to go in search of it, he immediately encountered Cheng, one of the raiders with whom he had just spent the last three weeks in the jungle. It alarmed Jayson to realize that Charlie had posted a guard at his door. Jayson looked at the young man suspiciously, noticing that he was still armed with a rifle.

"Where can I get a grunt and a bath?" Jayson inquired bluntly.

"You come…we go…you see." Cheng stood and motioning for the lieutenant to follow headed in the direction of the river.

The lieutenant pondered, *That's what I thought, another one that speaks English—a 'little bit.'*

Jayson followed, looking around as he memorized where his guest room was located in relation to the other surroundings.

Speckled among the forest of bamboo trees in the little valley were the grass huts and dwellings of a small village of Chinese peasants. The dark, rich soil of the village completely cleared of brush provided protection from snakes for the many children playing happily together. They all paused and stared at the army pilot as he walked by, still in uniform, except for his government issue Colt .45 and cap.

It appeared to Jayson that the population of the village was somewhere between four and five hundred—not counting the fighting men that numbered at least a hundred. He based this on the rather large group of people who had come out the day before to greet their men returning home and the expanse of village huts extending all the way to the river three miles away. Most of the people were women, children, and elderly.

The majority of the men did not carry their weapons around the village, but the lieutenant counted at least twenty-five heavily armed men stationed throughout the village and at the entrance of the cave, visible from just about every location in the valley. Some men stood watch in bamboo towers separated by approximately three hundred yards around the entire circumference of the camp. Jayson assumed it must be their alarm system in the event of an attack.

The lieutenant followed his posted guard through the camp of men, woman, children and grandparents, to the place where the river valley emerged out of the canopy of trees under the open sky. It was at the downstream end of the river where it disappeared into the cliff as abruptly as it had inexplicably emerged at the upper end but at the opposite side of the basin.

Just below the line paralleling the forest of bamboo trees, approximately five hundred yards above the river's edge, the lieutenant's escort stopped and pointed to a row of parallel trenches, one foot wide and a foot deep, that had been dug into the earth. Along one side, paralleling the trenches, the dirt formed a neatly piled Burm several hundred yards long.

Jayson immediately realized he was looking at the community latrine. A couple dozen people, including women, children, and men were already involved in the very thing Jayson needed to do. There did not appear to be any additional toiletries such as newspaper or leaves.

Beyond the latrine area that measured a hundred yards wide and three hundred yards long was another area the same size that obviously served as a garden or rice patty. It did not take much more than a third grade education to figure out what was making all those vegetables grow so large.

Beyond where Jayson stood lay a dozen fields, duplicates of the one in which he was standing. It occurred to him that the people had a rather sophisticated and organized system for cultivating human waste into rich topsoil; their gardens, located farther up stream, certainly testified to its effectiveness.

The lieutenant completed his contribution to soil enrichment, and his guide directed him to that portion of the river where all bathing took place. At the lower extremity of the river just above the place where it disappeared into the cauldron wall was an area where the water spilled onto a lower portion of the bank forming a broad, knee-deep pond approximately the size of a football field. Overgrown with marsh grass, it was the place where the villagers bathed themselves and washed their clothing. The tall grass, growing two to four feet high, provided some degree of privacy; although after experiencing the public latrine, Jayson surmised that they were not overly concerned with modesty.

Cheng said to him, "We go now...talk Charlie." Jayson was actually more interested in food and lots of it. He could tell he had lost a few pounds since his ordeal began back at the miracle meadow.

The people had fed Jayson some dried fish and a bowl of rice when he first arrived, but the lieutenant's stomach had shrunk during the last three weeks of living on rationed food, dolled out by the *devils*, who were obviously reluctant to consume more than what was absolutely necessary during the trip. By the time he had finished the small bowl of rice, he already felt full, but that was twelve hours ago, and Jayson was ready to resume the process of unshrinking his stomach.

About two miles from the river, the lieutenant followed his guide through another more populated section of the village community that took them to a large open circular clearing measuring several hundred yards in diameter.

Many of the bamboo thatched roof huts, constructed on stilts with a single pole ladder as their only access from the ground, were the personal dwellings of the villagers. Dozens of bungalows lined the circumference of the clearing where in the center, yet another large oval shaped building stood separate, overshad-

49

owing the rest of the camp. Jayson noticed it had no windows and only one door but deduced from its size and shape that it must be the village City Hall. The lieutenant scrutinized the structure and determined its size to be about two hundred feet long and, at its widest point, which was where the main door was located, approximately one hundred feet wide.

Again, the villagers stopped what they were doing to watch the American Army Air Corp transport pilot and his escort as they passed by. Cheng barked a command to one of the younger boys that appeared to be around ten years old. The boy immediately broke into a run and disappeared into the City Hall.

A few minutes later, Charlie appeared, along with at least twenty men of varying ages from fifteen to fifty including six of the elders in the village, who—judging from their weathered appearance and bent posture—must have been in their seventies or eighties. Charlie approached the army pilot and said to him, "Jai-sonn…you come…meeting with council…eat later."

Jayson wanted to ask Charlie a few questions, like, when are you going to help me get back to the Seventeenth Transport Squadron? Or why do I still feel like I'm a prisoner? Regardless of how cordial my captors have been. And one more thing, how did you find this beautiful paradise?

The lieutenant politely followed Charlie and his attaché to the thatched roof, bamboo structure where they entered through the fifteen-foot-wide side door.

Inside was a twenty-five feet by fifty feet platform directly in the center of the large auditorium. The platform was elevated a few feet above the ground on which sat a bamboo table ten feet by twenty feet in size situated directly in the center. Crudely constructed bamboo chairs—more than Jayson bothered to count—were neatly position all around. Other than that, there was no other furniture in the building.

A crowd of onlookers gathered by the entrance while Charlie, Cheng, Chi, and several others from the squad of jungle fighters, along with several of the elders, ascended the steps to the platform. Jayson followed, as each took a seat at the far end of the table. Charlie motioned for the lieutenant to sit, facing the entrance, and the growing crowd of spectators migrating closer to the platform.

Jayson was feeling a bit vulnerable and was wishing he had sought Charlie out sooner in respect to the whereabouts of his .45 auto, but the head *Devo* had made himself scarce, which left Jayson thinking he might be avoiding the subject.

As the lieutenant took his seat at the far end of the table, the rest of the committee followed suit, except for Charlie, who came around to the end of the table and stood next to the army pilot to face the board of trustees—and the spectators. Jayson had the feeling he was sitting before an inquisition which was about to decide his destiny.

Charlie began speaking, and of course, it was not in English. The lieutenant watched the expressions of the jury members for any clue as to what this town hall meeting was all about. All the members of the panel, except for two of the elders, eagerly expressed their opinions and views with a significant amount of fervor, not to mention all at once.

It seemed to Jayson that Charlie was trying to sell them on some idea he had cooked up during their long hike, and the rest of the members, apparently, were of the opinion that he had been smoking his breakfast. Oh, how he wished he had a secret interpreter whispering in his ear.

Jayson was sure that he was the subject of their controversy and only hoped that at some point he would get included in the discussion. However, for the present time, he had the disconcerting feeling that his future was about to take another unexpected turn. Silently in his heart, Jayson prayed that somehow God would get him back to his army unit.

Suddenly, into the pavilion came a young woman. The gathering of people immediately grew quiet. The onlookers stepped aside to make a path for her as she made her way toward the platform.

She was stunningly beautiful. Her long black hair glistened in the filtered light as it cascaded down her back past the sleek curves of her buttocks to the backs of her knees. She wore a white silk short-sleeved top that laced together down the front and sleek matching slacks, not too tight, yet splendidly tailored. Her smooth skin was the texture of fresh whipped cream and glistened in the soft light. Her face glowed as if she had just descended from the Mount of Transfiguration with Jesus and the disciples.

It took a minute for the lieutenant to realize he had stopped breathing. His eyes were riveted to her every movement, and hope sprang up within him that she might have come on his behalf.

With confidence and poise, she walked directly to the platform where she climbed the steps to the podium, bowed first to the panel, then to the assembly, and took a seat at the table across from Charlie and within inches of where Jayson sat at the very end—completely mesmerized.

The lieutenant's heart leapt within his chest, and he was sure she could hear it pounding. As she turned to look at him, he was embarrassed to realize that he was still staring at her. He tried to divert his gaze but could not. For a brief moment he thought he detected a slight smile form across her voluptuous lips.

Jayson had lost all awareness of the table full of inquisitionists. It seemed to him that the gorgeous creature who had sat down beside him held some special influence with the panel of government representatives, and now he thought, maybe, he might also, because she had smiled at him. Then, she stood to speak.

His heart sank a little as he realized, she too was speaking a language he did not understand. It made him feel vulnerable all over again. She must have realized what the army pilot was feeling and occasionally turned to him with a look of assurance that renewed his sense of security. If only he knew what they were saying.

Jayson's thoughts began to wander. Try as he may, he could not keep from thinking of her—her form, her walk, her lips, her eyes, her form…repeatedly, he imagined her in his mind. "Stop," he whispered to himself.

Jayson had never been with a woman before. The moral standard he had long ago committed himself to, compelled him to keep his body, and his mind, pure for the bride the Lord would someday give him as a gift.

She appeared to be somewhere around five feet and four inches tall, or so, and a petite 110 lb. Making her perfect in every conceivable way.

Completely oblivious to all that was going on around him, Jayson softly spoke to her, "What is your name?"

The voices stopped again, and this time, all eyes were riveted on him. At that moment, a pin falling to the floor would have sounded like thunder. She looked at him and answered, "Ah-lam." The lieutenant could not speak. She smiled again, and the whole panel of board members glanced at each other smiling and chuckling among themselves, except for Charlie, who did not seem at all amused.

English! Jayson exclaimed to himself. *She understands English!* Ah-lam finished what she had to say to the panel and sat down. When it occurred to him that she might be rising to leave, his heart felt a stab of panic. *Where will she go? Where does she live? How will I find her? What if…I never see her again?*

She bowed again to the City Council, and they disbanded to make their way down the steps from the podium. Charlie, Ah-lam, and Jayson remained seated at the table.

"You will come with me to the dispensary," she said to him, in near perfect English, heavily flavored with a French accent. She reached out and touched Jayson's damaged ribs and said to him, "I will examine your injuries."

"Ah-lam, doctor," Charlie interjected. "Ah-lam, Charlie sister."

Such a difference a *little bit* of English can make. Suddenly Jayson felt like part of the family. Once again, she was smiling at him, and her gaze so paralyzed him, he could not look away.

For a moment, the lieutenant hoped he might be fortunate enough to get some time alone with Ah-lam, where they could communicate and he could ask her a few questions. He wanted to know who this remarkable creature was and how she happened to cross paths with a US army pilot, who three weeks before had crash-landed a C-47 in the jungle in front of her brother who just happened to be standing on a ridge watching the whole thing. There was so much unexplained logistics to the events of the last three weeks, almost as if it had been preordained, even down to the moment he saw her, and his heart did a flip-flop within his chest.

Was there some divine schematic in play that was manipulating the events and circumstances? Had God designed for it all to happen just the way it did? If so, then why? Was it God's plan that Jayson have these feelings that were already stirring within him, feelings that had begun the moment he first saw Ah-lam? What was to happen, now that he was completely infatuated with this beautiful creature? Suddenly, Jayson was not sure if he really wanted to get back to his unit after all. Charlie interrupted his thoughts. "Charlie...go to."

Thanks a lot.

Charlie led the way, and Jayson followed. Ah-lam intentionally matched pace with Jayson so she could walk beside him. The lieutenant's heart was in his throat, and his throat had long ago gone dry. For the first time in his life, he could think of nothing to say. He stole glances at her as they walked along toward the dispensary. Jayson wanted to tell her what was going on inside of him in hopes that she would help him understand what it meant and if the same thing had happened within her. However, his brain was confused, so he remained silent.

"My brother tells me that your name is Jayson, is that correct?" Her voice was like the soft music of a harp.

"Yes, First Lieutenant Jayson Bold, and your name is Ah-lam. Did I say that right?"

"Yes, Ah-lam Nee, that is correct."

"Your English is extremely good. Where were you educated?" For a long moment, she did not answer. Jayson feared that he had touched on a subject that she might rather avoid. He was about to apologize when she replied, her voice distant.

"Nanking..." Her voice trailed as she looked up at him, and she asked, "You are a pilot?"

"Yes, I am."

"Charlie says you crashed, and he rescued you and then saved you from the Japanese."

"Yes, that is also true."

"I am glad. It is safe here. You can live with us."

Her statement shocked the lieutenant back into reality. He said to her, "As soon as I'm able, I need to return to my unit, the Seventeenth Transport Division in the Assam valley."

Ah-lam was quiet. Charlie stopped. Pointing at a large hut nearby, he turned to Jayson and said to him, "You go to there, sister fix you up good. Tomorrow, we have big feast. Everybody come, Ah-lam and Jai-sonn come, Charlie come too, eat much food." Charlie turned to leave, and suddenly, it was just the two of them.

Jayson felt a sense of elation that they were finally alone with each other. Then just as abruptly a concern washed over him, the realization of an inherent carnal liability that came with his humanity; maybe he should not be alone with this woman whose stunning beauty had left him trembling and weak in the knees from the first moment he laid eyes on her. Ah-lam pulled back the curtain that hung in the doorway and invited him into her dispensary.

Lieutenant Jayson Bold sat on the edge of a bamboo table covered with several grass mats. Dr. Ah-lam Nee helped him remove his coat and shirt so she could examine his injuries.

"There is much severe bruising. You should have never hiked so far coming here. They should have carried you all the way." The doctor's tone exuded irritation with her brother for letting such a thing happen. Jayson grinned as he imagined her scolding the leader of, *China's Little Devils*, whom in his own right was a hatred driven cold-blooded killer, but that was out there, in the jungle, on the other side of the cauldron where a war was going on and people were being slaughtered by a demonic regime that long ago had become so full of themselves they had lost all control and reason. Jayson felt that Charlie would have been a much different person were it not for war.

"I will bind a protective padding around your ribs to cushion them to help keep the body heat in. You will come to the dispensary twice a day for hot and cold application of hydrotherapy, which will stimulate the circulation in the injured area. You must be very careful not to do anything that will pull the fractures apart. It will take a couple of months before you will be well enough to travel again."

Travel? Jayson cringed at the thought, and a feeling of dread shot through his heart at the notion of ever leaving the exotic creature standing next to him. Where would he be traveling to? He took her hand and pressed it against his heart.

"I don't want to travel anywhere that would take me away from you."

Ah-lam looked shocked; her voluptuous lips parted, and her eyes glistened with moisture. She reached upward pressing the palms of her hands to each side of Jayson's face.

"I know," she said and lightly stroked his cheeks.

The lieutenant did not understand what she meant by "Ready to travel," nor did he know what she meant when she said, "I know." His experience with women and with love had only just begun.

"Do you know something I don't?" he asked the doctor. "Am I scheduled to travel someplace I am not aware of?"

She took a step backward and said, "You told me you wanted to go back to your unit when you are well enough."

"Then I don't ever want to get well enough," Jayson remarked, looking squarely into her eyes. Suddenly he realized what had just come from his lips. For a moment, he felt paralyzed by the implication of his words. *Not returning to my unit is not an option. I can't walk away from the army because I met a girl. What on earth am I thinking? Have I lost my mind?*

Jayson shook his head to clear his brain of the trance that had come over him. Not at all sure it accomplished anything, he looked back at Ah-lam. She smiled and handed him his shirt.

"Would you like to walk with me tomorrow?"

"Yes, and I would like to walk with you now as well."

"Then I will go with you to your quarters, and we will walk again tomorrow also. But first let me prepare for you something to eat. When is the last time you had food?"

The lieutenant was famished, and his heart was pounding in his chest in anticipation of spending more time with Ah-lam. He still had had nothing to eat since the night before when he arrived. It began to dawn on him why there were no overweight people in the village. He wondered if he would ever get three meals in one day again. He answered, "Shortly after I arrived yesterday."

They walked together, back to the City Hall, where a group of villagers were preparing food for their families. Ah-lam spoke briefly to one of the women, and she invited Jayson and Ah-lam to join them for a meal of bread and fish.

He said to Ah-lam, "Why are they having a feast tomorrow?"

"It is to welcome you into our village and our home."

"Me? That's a bit of a surprise. What all did they talk about at that meeting this morning? I didn't understand a word, but it sounded like some of them wanted to string me up, and now you say they're making a feast for me."

"Our village government is a very democratic one. We escaped to this place to get away from not only the Japanese but also the communists that are winning the civil war in China against the Nationalist. When they have succeeded in taking over the government, there will be no more free choice. We know that our community will some day be discovered and our democratic home will be taken from us, but until then, it is important that we do all that can be done to keep it a secret. Charlie brought you here without first consulting with the committee, and they were not happy. However, it is okay now. They want to make this feast in your honor and welcome you as a citizen of the *Ziyou-di*."

"Is that the name of this place, Ziyou-di?

"Yes."

"How do you say that in English?"

"Freeland. We have lived here five years now. Charlie found it and, with the help of his jungle fighters, brought us all here a few at a time to escape the Japanese and other oppressions. There are over five hundred of us and more that still need to be brought here, if they are yet alive."

Jayson and Ah-lam talked and walked late into the evening. Ah-lam introduced Jayson to many of her friends and villagers. Finally, it grew late in the evening, and she walked him home.

"What time tomorrow do you want me to come to the dispensary?"

"Come early, and I will prepare a morning meal for the two of us."

The lieutenant said to her, "I have things I want to say to you, but I am not sure I should."

Ah-lam pressed the palm of her hand against Jayson's heart and said, "Then, wait until you are sure." Again, she smiled at him, and this time he could not shake it off.

Jayson retired for the night, but sleep came in bits and pieces as his mind kept seeing her slender figure, her eyes, her smile, her skin, and especially the sound of her voice. Ultimately, it was the music of her voice that finally put him to sleep.

The feast went well. Ah-lam and Jayson sat together, staring into the each other's eyes as the rest of the village took humor in their rapid plunge into love. Jayson had no idea they were being so obvious about their mutual infatuation.

The lieutenant looked for Charlie and his *little devos*, but none of them had made it to the feast. Of course, he never knew them to be that big on eating anyway. Jayson glanced up at the black hole where he had emerged into his Shangri-la world a mere two days before. Two guards, armed with machine guns, stood at the entrance. Jayson wondered if their job was to keep people out, or keep them in.

For the next six weeks, Jayson revisited the dispensary twice a day for treatments. The circulation around the broken ribs gradually improved and the bruising was rapidly dissipating.

Every day Jayson's feelings for Ah-lam deepened until he could no longer hide them from even the most naïve. Frequently they walked together through the village holding hands or embracing as they strolled.

Ah-lam and Jayson spent more and more time together relishing every moment as if they were unsure how long the moments would last. It was wartime, and lifetimes were brief. Who knew, if there would even be a tomorrow.

The lieutenant wanted to learn as much as possible about the doctor but was waiting until the right moment to ask the kind of questions he expected would be difficult for her to answer. Then one day while walking by the river, Ah-lam said to him, "You said there were things you would like to say to me but you were not sure if you should. Have you decided yet if you should say them?

He thought a moment, a bit shocked by her frankness, yet wanting desperately to share with her the feelings within him that begged for expression.

"Actually, I'm afraid if I don't I will wish I had for the rest of my life. Yet I feel so awkward because we have only just met."

"I wish that you would tell me because I have something I would like to say to you as well." She stopped and turned him toward her to look into his dark eyes.

Jayson knew that to take this unexpected relationship to the next level would change his world forever. It meant he could never go back to his unit, never go back to his army life; though to them, he was dead already. No one in his unit expected to ever see First Lieutenant Jayson Bold alive again. As far as the army was concerned, Lieutenant Bold was a casualty of war, and both he and his unit had already turned the page. By now, he had been replaced by another flyer who was so concerned about the weather and Jap fighters; he didn't have time to wonder whatever happened to Lieutenant Jayson Bold.

In the interim, Jayson had fallen head over tea cup in love yet was tentative about telling Ah-lam how he felt, realizing what a vulnerable position it would place them both in. He knew that in moments like this, hearts either become *one* for life or are broken beyond repair. He wondered which it would be; then he gambled. How could he do otherwise?

Her eyes were black as jade, her skin soft as fresh cream. He studied her loveliness as he looked into those beautiful eyes. Finally, unable to contain himself another moment, he said to her, "I have fallen in love with you, Ah-lam. I love you with all my heart and every fiber of my being and have since the first moment I laid eyes on you. You are the most beautiful creature God ever made, and I am so incredibly smitten with you, I have lost all other reason. In the short amount of time since we've met, the rest of my world has disappeared. I could never imagine ever leaving you, or being without you. I know we barely know each other, but it doesn't matter. I want to marry you and make you my wife forever. I want to be your husband. I want our hearts to beat in symbiotic rhythm until the day we have lived out our years together." He knelt on one knee, his face only slightly below hers. "Will you marry me? I promise I will get you a ring someday, and I will take you far away from this war where we can live in peace."

Ah-lam looked stunned, and for a moment, Jayson thought she would faint. Quietly she broke into tears. He gently picked her up in his arms, hardly aware of the stabbing pain in his side; with her head tucked into the base of his neck, her arms firmly clasped around him, he could feel the warm moisture of her tears on his skin. Her head moved as though she were nodding.

"Yes! Yes!" she said. Tears rushed from his eyes; he shuddered from the flood of emotion within him. In the distance, they could faintly hear people clapping and cheering. It came from the many villagers working in the gardens who had stopped to witness their moment.

Jayson carried her to the dispensary where she lived along with a few helpers that would come and go from time to time. He gently placed her on the table where day after day she had treated his broken ribs. There they held each other without speaking.

Their hearts were overwhelmed with love, but even more with grief. For Jayson, buried within him was the unresolved loss of his parents taken from him so soon and so violently and for whom he had never taken time to grieve. Finally, he felt relief as he gave his heart to the one God had given him that would fill that lonely void.

For Ah-lam, it was more, much more.

"Jayson..." He held her without answering. "I must tell you of my past. I was seventeen years of age when they came." She unconsciously turned her face toward the bamboo wall, staring distantly into her past.

"It was December 1937. I was in school at the University of Nanking. It was China's capital city then.

They came by the thousands and thousands and thousands." Her voice broke, and her lips quivered. Jayson gently stroked her hair.

"They killed for mere pleasure, over three hundred thousand citizens murdered in less than a month in the city of Nanking alone. Eighty thousand women, both mothers and young girls, were raped repeatedly, most were killed. Many were put to work as *comfort women* for the Japanese soldiers."

Jayson spoke softly, "Ah-lam…you don't have to…"

"But I must, my love."

"Very well then, how did you escape?" Jayson asked.

"I prayed to God, and I hid and kept moving from one hiding place to another."

Jayson lifted her head and turned her face to look at him, then asked, "How did you know about God? Isn't everyone in China Buddhist?"

"Charlie and I lived in an orphanage since before I can remember. The communist factions had killed both our parents. The only real parent, I remember, was a French Christian missionary we called Papa Bear. He ran the orphanage and taught us of the One true God in heaven and His only begotten Son whom He sent into the world as Substitute and Surety and Savior to all men. That was all I remember him ever teaching us: "… Jesus Christ, and him crucified" [1 Corinthians 2:2, AKJV].

"Tell me more about how the Lord spared you through that time."

Ah-lam looked into Jayson's face, her eyes welling with tears.

"You are Christian too?"

"Yes…I am!"

"I knew God is the one who sent you to me, and when I saw you, I loved you instantly and then wondered how that could be."

"Why do you think God sent me?"

"Because I prayed for someone who could save my children." Jayson stiffened.

"Children? You have children?"

"It is a long story. They are kept in an orphanage far from here, and I call them my children. I need to get them away and bring them here."

Jayson's heart felt as if it had been ripped from his chest.

"So you have pretended this love for me so I will help you save some orphans?"

"No, no, Jayson, it is not like that." She threw herself at him and clung to him with her arms clasped tightly around his waist. "I prayed to God, but I didn't know that the one He would send would capture my heart as well."

Jayson held her head in his hands and kissed her brow.

"Well, apparently he has."

"I want to tell you the rest of the story so you will understand."

Jayson sat next to her and whispered, "I'm listening."

"There was a man named Rabe."

"Who was Rabe?" Jayson asked.

"He was the German chancellor that had lived in Nanking with his wife for twenty years or more. He saw to the financial business interest and investments of the German industrialists and Nazis yet remained unsympathetic toward the Nazi's fanatical leanings. He and his wife loved the Chinese people, and if it were not for him, there would have been many more thousands killed."

"What did he do?"

"The Nazis and the Japanese had been allies until the invasion of China when the Germans became displeased with the loss of their financial interests due to the destruction of the industries and the economy. Friction erupted between them, yet in the midst of it all, Mr. Rabe managed to get the Japanese commandant to agree to a secure *Safety Zone* around the hospital and university dormitories. Amazingly, they agreed on the condition that no Chinese soldiers would be allowed sanctuary within the

Safety Zone perimeters, or, the Japanese would come and kill us all.

"Where were you while all this was going on?'

"The women all cut their hair short to look like boys, and I stole a Japanese uniform so I could sneak out at night to find girls that needed help getting to the Safety Zone. By the end of December, the city was completely destroyed, and the Japanese slowly began to leave. Thousands upon thousands of Chinese had been beheaded, and the human heads decorated the flower pots in the windows of every apartment and adorned the lampposts lining the streets. Dead bodies of Chinese soldiers piled in heaps on the street corners were left to rot. I, along with many others, fled to Chungking, where in spite of the bombings, I continued my medical education and training at the university. I only returned to Freeland during the summers. I attend the university during the school year. But I really am not a doctor yet, only an intern."

"What about the children you were telling me about. Where did they come from?" Jayson had no more than asked the question, and the look on Ah-lam's face told him all he needed to know. Even before she explained, he understood why she had given him the details of the Rape of Nanking.

"They are *the fruit of the atrocities* that took place in Nanking."

"You mean, children, of the rape victims?'

Ah-lam nodded her head.

"Yes, at least, what is left of them, hundreds were slaughtered. They are of mixed race, half Japanese and half Chinese. They are now five years old, will be six this coming December, and their birthdays are all within three weeks of each other. They have no homeland and are foreigners in the country where they were born. China does not want them because they are a reminder of the terrible atrocities. When the war is ended and the communist government takes over the country, they will never consider them for citizenship but instead will surely kill them. Japan will never want them. If they were to be discovered by the Japanese, they would all be murdered because after the war, they would serve as evidence of their war crimes." Ah-lam stopped to take a breath and placed her hand over Jayson's heart. "There is only one who wants them. It is *God*, and it is *He* who has sent you to us to take them away where they will be safe and can live free."

The lieutenant held Ah-lam, her head still pressed against his chest. "How many?" he asked.

For a moment, she was quiet. Jayson asked again, "How many children am I smuggling out of China?"

Ah-lam lifted her head, and looking into his eyes, she sofly whispered, "Sixteen."

"Sixteen! Jayson exclaimed. "Where are these children now?"

"They are in an orphanage in Chungking north of here, about three hundred miles."

"How am I supposed to smuggle sixteen children plus you and I out of China, and where am I suppose to take them?"

"There is one more thing you must know," Ah-lam added.

"What's that?"

"Charlie did not rescue you so that you may save the children. He is fighting a private war against the Japanese, and because he saved your life, he now considers you his personal property. He plans to use you as his pilot in his own covert operations against the enemy."

"How do you know this?" Jayson asked.

"It is what he explained to the committee the day after you arrived."

"I have news for Charlie, the only one who owns me is God. Besides, where is Charlie going to get an airplane?"

"He has gone away to make arrangements to have your airplane fixed so he can use it and you in his war against the Japanese."

"I can tell you this, that's not going to happen. As soon as I'm able, I am going back to my unit and taking you with me. I can speak with my commander and try to make arrangements for getting those children to someplace safe, but other than that, I have no intention of working for Charlie, or anyone else. Besides, I love you, and right now I don't want to think about anything else except being with you." Jayson pulled Ah-lam closer to him and held her firmly against his chest burying his face into her soft, silky black hair.

Ah-lam said to him, "I want to be with you too, but first we must be married." Jayson pushed her away to look into her eyes.

"Don't you believe our vows of love and the Spirit of God will constitute our marriage?"

"Yes, I believe that as well, but we must have a Chinese wedding ceremony and make our vows before the entire village."

Jayson thought for a moment, smiled, and said, "Actually, that sounds like a lot of fun, count me in."

Lieutenant Jayson Bold stared at the thatched roof of his guest hut as he lay on the bamboo bed. His mind swirled with scenarios and questions. Every idea he entertained involving some method of whisking sixteen children out of China collided with the lack of feasibility of it all and especially the complication of his enlistment in the armed forces of the United States. For that matter, where could he take them where they wouldn't need papers? Maybe, he would need to work for Charlie after all so that he, in turn, could use Charlie. But how?

Jayson had sworn to serve his country. That undoubtedly meant that if captured by the enemy, he would never cease making every attempt to escape and/or frustrate the enemy's purposes. Jayson was sure it also meant, if he was lost in the jungle, he would be expected to make every attempt to find his way back to his unit: the Seventeenth Military Air Transport Division based at Ledo, India.

Ah-lam was right about everything she said. The children would most certainly be killed, and sooner rather than later. Somehow, Jayson had to figure out a way to get them from

Chungking to some neutral place, maybe even the *Ziyou-di*—Freeland. Then, maybe, he could come back from the dead and return to his unit.

Like any other daunting task, this one would have to be broken down into doable objectives: First, his ribs needed to completely heal; then he would need an airplane. Thirdly, he would need an airport and, above all, a steady stream of miracles from the hand of God. He thought to himself, *Was Ah-lam right about that as well? Was she right about God, calculating and calling into play the events that brought me to this time and place? Had God designed it all for his own purposes, purposes that God alone understood? If so, then God was the one who was using Charlie, not the other way around.*

At first, Jayson had felt contempt for the Japanese fighter pilot that was responsible for his dilemma. Now, he thought of Ah-lam whom he had fallen so head over heels in love with, how his heart beat for her, and her alone. Suddenly he realized, Ah-lam *was* right. Of course it was God who engineered the events and circumstances that had brought them both together. Jayson could now see that the Japanese pilot was the greatest blessing he had ever had. His off airport landing was not a catastrophe but a calling of God to a special purpose.

Ever since Jayson had joined the Army Air Corp in service to his country, he had felt that God had a greater work for him to do. His experience flying crop dusters had qualified him for a seat in a P-40 fighter, but Jayson declined the offer and chose the Military Air Transport Squadron instead due to his definitive spiritual convictions regarding the taking of human life. It was clear now that God had called and chosen Jayson, and at that moment, he realized, somehow, he would get those children to a place the Lord had prepared for their safety, and for the rest of his life, Jayson would remain dead to the army.

Jayson's restless night finally turned to morning, and he dressed to go to the dispensary. As he approached the large hut where Ah-lam resided, his pace slowed as he noticed a group of villagers huddled around her door talking to Ah-lam who was standing in the doorway.

Two of the women in the group, who were a bit more advanced in age than the others, saw Jayson approaching and, turning toward him, waved him off, chattering something he did not understand. He looked toward Ah-lam who, still standing in the doorway, waved to him and smiled.

Taking him by the arms, the two women turned him toward the river and, with one on each arm, escorted him to the marsh where they removed his clothing and proceeded to bathe him.

Jayson had been going to the river every other day or so for a bath over the last three weeks since his arrival in Freeland. He did try to avoid going whenever women or children were present, and if they inadvertently showed up, he would conceal himself as far as possible. He knew their customs were a bit more liberal than his and tried to adapt as far as he could without sacrificing his own modesty.

The woman giggled at his shyness and persisted in their objective. From their bag of toiletries they had brought along, they produced sweet smelling perfumes and powders, which they generously applied all over Jayson's body. It almost felt like they were preparing him for burial. Jayson was ignorant to many of the customs and rituals of the people that he was living with, but he wasn't completely stupid. It may have been slowly, but he eventually realized, they were preparing him...for marriage.

The wedding planners wrapped him in a red Chengsam (male) swirl with a snug-fitting button-down black silk coat and motioned for a young boy who was among the curious onlookers witnessing Jayson's bath to gather up his flight jacket and uniform, which he did, disappearing into the jungle in the direction of the village.

They were a people of integrity and pride but were completely uninhibited when it came to personal interaction and biological function. Family and fidelity were of utmost importance to them, and the marriage of two people in love, they celebrated as a holiday for the entire village, a village that to them represented city, country, nation, and even their very society.

Jayson saw it as a custom that was far more forthright than the customs in his own country. In America, it was just the opposite. Be modest in public, and behind closed doors practice every conceivable kind of promiscuity. The decline in moral integrity over the last twenty years had dramatically diminished public modesty, and American morality had become more and more outrageous, which Jayson saw as an evil that would in some future generation bring about the demise of its society, and ultimately, he was sure, the end of America as he presently knew it.

The women led him away toward the City Hall. The group of villagers, who had observed his public bathing, had grown in size, and some of the young girls had formed a circle around Jayson and were showering him with petals from the white orchids that grew everywhere in the valley. Many of them sang and danced, some chanted, and others stared at him as if he were some sort of an aberration, which actually, was not far from the truth.

Eventually, they arrived at the clearing, stopping short of the City Hall a hundred yards away. A small temporary igloo-shaped hut had been constructed and adorned with flowers of every description as well as large green leaves that covered the bamboo roof. On the path leading to the door, Jayson saw a strange display of rocks, sticks, and ditches that not only led to the hut but encircled it as well. The gate to the path was about fifty feet from the door of the hut, and Jayson had been positioned ten feet off to one side of the gated pathway.

Suddenly he heard more noise and celebration coming from the opposite direction and could see another procession of people coming toward him. Then he saw her; laced throughout her long glistening black hair were petals of white orchids, and she too was wrapped in a red Chengasm (female) swirl, laced with white, red, and silver embroidery that wrapped tightly around her slender form, finally terminating at the top of her throat. Closer and closer, she advanced, stopping directly opposite of the groom.

Jayson and Ah-lam now faced each other, positioned a mere twenty feet apart. She was truly the most gorgeous creature he had ever seen. Her black eyes sparkled in the light as she smiled at him. The filtered sun danced sparkles of gold and silver light from her jet-black hair.

Jayson no longer harbored reservations concerning his military service. He was no longer an officer in the United States Army Air Corp. As a citizen of Ziyou-di, he had crossed the line of people and culture to their own secret Shangri-la, far from, but not unlike, the Belem Valley.

Ah-lam stood before him like an oriental ornament; so beautiful, she took his breath away. Time reverted to slow motion as he memorize every second of the ceremony. Every detail of her hair, her costume, her look, her movement, and, especially, her intoxicating smile, recorded in a wedding book in the recesses of his mind where it would remain forever. This was their wedding day. Silently, he prayed, *Oh, Lord my God, in heaven. We have no Christian minister, no little white church, and no organ music. However, we know the Holy Spirit of God is upon Ah-lam and me to unite us in holy matrimony. Thank you, in the name of our Lord and Savior Jesus Christ, amen.*

From what seemed like a mile away, Jayson could hear the sounds of musical instruments that three weeks prior would have sounded like fingernails scratching on a blackboard, yet on this day, it was the most beautiful orchestra he had ever heard. Jayson and Ah-lam simultaneously walked in unrehearsed but coordinated step toward each other. She was holding a bouquet of white orchids in her hands, clasped together against her stomach forming a bed of flowers below her bosom.

Finally, within arm's reach, they clasp hands and side by side began a slow stroll down the path to the door of the marriage hut. Together, they stepped across each obstacle that lay in their

THE FRUIT OF ATROCITY

path. First, the stones, then the sticks, and, finally, the miniature ditches, each representing the trials and sacrifices they would endure throughout their life together.

At the door of the marriage hut, they turned and bowed to the multitude, then together entered the hut, pulling the curtain closed behind them.

Candles lined the circumference of the circular blanketed floor casting a soft, sensuous light upon their marriage bed. They sat cross-legged facing each other. Jayson was quivering with anticipation, shaking from the uncertainty of what was to happen next. Her hands caressed his face, and he looked into her eyes; then their lips met for the first time. And their bodies melted closer and closer together until finally, they that, until this moment, had been two became one.

Chapter 3

Summer turned into winter, and the people of Ziyou-di ushered in a new season of planting by celebrating the Lunar New Year. Four months later, Jayson and Ah-lam also celebrated the birth of their first child. They named her Ching-Lan. It is interpreted as "beautiful orchid." Like her mother, Ah-lam, whose name interpreted "like an orchid," she too was stunningly beautiful and perfect in every way.

Jayson's ribs had finally healed, and he had built an addition onto the dispensary to accommodate his growing family.

Charlie, who was still unaware of his sister's marriage to Jayson, and his band of raiders did not return to Shangri-la until early summer of the following year, one month after the birth of their daughter.

At first, he was aghast at the news, as if something catastrophic had happened. Ah-lam talked to him for many hours trying to help him understand. It was a new era for China, and love and survival were the only traditions left they could afford to defend. Ah-lam was unsuccessful in her attempt to persuade her brother, but he no longer argued with her. Eventually, Charlie began to accept Jayson, if not as his brother-in-law, at least as an opportunity. With time, he became somewhat friendlier.

One day, a month after his return, Charlie came to visit, calling to him from the entrance of their bungalow.

"Jai-sonn…you come. Charlie talk."

"Come on in, Charlie, what's on your mind?"

"Charlie talk sister long time, too much talk. Sister want Jai-sonn bring orphans to Freeland from Chungking."

THE FRUIT OF ATROCITY

"Yes, I know. She mentioned that to me but still hasn't told me where I am supposed to get an airplane."

"Charlie say, okay, but Jai-sonn work for Charlie, or no can do."

"What kind of work?"

"Jai-sonn, fly Charlie airplane."

"You have an airplane?"

"Charlie have airplane…you bet. Charlie make many men fix Jai-sonn airplane. No more Jai-sonn airplane, Charlie airplane now. You fly airplane to here, then we go Chungking, bring home orphans. Then you fly for me, help Charlie kill many Japan Soldier."

"What do you mean *fix*? That freighter will never fly again. In the first place, that meadow is too uneven, not to mention *short*, and besides, when that plane hit the ground, those props were probably damaged beyond repair, meaning the crankshafts were likely fractured. There's no way in the world I would ever try flying that plane out of that meadow. Even if both engines were rebuilt, at that elevation, the crate would never get airborne. Attempting a takeoff over all that uneven ground and under full power, the whole ship would come apart on me."

"No sweat, Jai-sonn, we fix no sweat. Charlie have mechanic fix engines. Many more men fix runway, almost all done. We go… you see, then come back Ziyou-di. But first—"

"You rebuilt the engines!" Jayson interrupted.

"Charlie have many friends, no sweat."

"I can hardly believe that. Well, even if we did make it out of there, where are we supposed to land when we get back to Freeland?"

"Village men make runway. Jai-Sonn mark place for landing runway down by river. Charlie get many men, make very good for landing airplane."

Jayson glanced at his wife sitting next to him. Ah-lam was holding the baby, her eyes closed. Tears streamed down her face. Jayson knew she was praying. He placed his arm around her.

"Okay, Charlie, if you say so, but you still didn't answer my question." Charlie started to leave. "Wait a minute. When you said I would be flying for you, where exactly will I be going?" Charlie was through talking and did not look back as he disappeared through the door.

Only a month had passed since beginning construction on the airstrip, and the work was progressing smoothly. Over two hundred of the villagers, many of which were women and children and many of the men who guarded the place, worked from daylight to dark seven days a week. In another week, or so, the four-thousand-foot-long airstrip would be adequate for landing and taking off. Charlie had left within a week after their meeting, and Jayson had not seen or heard from him since.

When Jayson was not helping and supervising the building of the runway, he was at home with his wife and newborn child. He did not want to miss a minute of time with his family knowing that he soon must leave to embark on a mission fraught with danger and uncertainty.

Ah-lam did not seem nearly as enthusiastic about Jayson saving the orphans as she was at first. Her emotions were conflicted now that the only pilot who could make it happen was both her husband and the father of her child. Their beautiful life in Shangri-la had only just begun, and the enormous risk associated with the endeavor scratched at her faith. Throughout each day, she repeatedly knelt beside her bed to place her trepidations before the throne of grace.

Since his father and mother had perished in the automobile accident, Jayson's feelings for the most part had become numb to both life and death. He did not want to die nor did he hate living; he just no longer had a *zest* for life or *fear* of death. At least that is what he thought. But on the day he turned the corner in the canyon and saw that enormous rock wall closing in on him at two hundred miles per hour, for the first time in years, *living* suddenly became an absolute priority, and now, more than ever, his reasons for living a long and healthy life had tripled.

When Jayson awoke to the realization he had survived the crash and been rescued, it hit him for the first time that God must have a purpose for his life. However, what apparently was being expected of him by Charlie was certainly a purpose he never expected, or even imagined.

Jayson had managed an assignment to the Military Air Transport Division for the purpose of avoiding a fighter group. However, as far as he was concerned, flying a cargo plane over the hump was every bit as dangerous as being in a dogfight with a Japanese Zero. The towering cumulus nimbus (thunderstorms) that built up over the Himalayas during the afternoons that matured into gigantic monsters capable of ripping the wings off even the largest of airplanes were far more terrifying to the pilots than a Japanese Zero. Unfortunately, not all pilots understood the real dangers that lurked within those monster storms.

It wasn't entirely the pilot's fault, of course. The ever increasing need for supplies in China exacerbated the pressure on the pilots to deliver the freight at any risk, and even cost. The airman of the Seventeenth had no choice. Day or night, regardless of weather, the cargo had to go through. Many Japanese ground troops, who—inadvertently—discovered the downed cargo planes, often resupplied their provisions from the scattered freight lost in the battle between a cargo plane and a thunderstorm.

Jayson, side by side with the love of his life and the mother of his child, prayed that God would strengthen them for the work He had selected them to do. Then one evening in an especially Spirit-filled atmosphere, the Lord spoke to them, not in an audible way but in a calm assurance that said to them: "The work I have given you is not the work of man. It is the work of the great, *I Am*. Do not forget who has sent you. For *I Am* your strength, *I Am* your guide and guardian. *I Am* your defense and protector.

Your work is to simply *have faith*, to be at rest, and watch the arm of God move in your behalf. *I am God, and there is none like me"* [Isaiah 46:9, AKJV].

Ah-lam sat silent, head still bowed in prayer. Jayson jumped to his feet, his body stiffened, his arms outstretched as if nailed to a cross as the power of God suddenly flashed through his humanity, lighting the prayer room with a brilliant white light. Ah-lam stood, her body encased in her husband's arms. The light from within him glowed through her as well. There they remained until the power of God released them. Exhausted, they fell again to their knees praising God the Father and His Son Jesus Christ.

When they arose, Jayson began to prophesy. "Ah-lam," he said, "the Lord has shown me that He will save us all, including the children in Chungking, not one of us will be lost."

In amazement, Ah-lam said to him, "Jayson, you are speaking perfect Chinese!"

The village, with the exception of the City Hall, was well concealed under the canopy of Bamboo trees, and, for the most part, was not visible from the air. However, the gardens by the river lay spread out in the open. As Jayson studied the environment, he fully expected that a plane flying low enough over the basin might see their landing strip.

Jayson had only a vague idea where the Ziyou-di was located in relation to the Himalayan Mountain Range, but he felt sure it was in the southern region possibly as far south and only a few hundred miles from Rangoon. Evidently, it was not an area where American or Japanese planes crossed frequently, for neither Jayson nor anyone in the village had ever seen an airplane flying over the Freeland.

However, in the event that one did—and eventually it was bound to happen—the new runway, still under construction, would certainly be an eye-catcher. Jayson calculated that it would

THE FRUIT OF ATROCITY

just be a matter of time, and before that happened, he needed to come up with an idea to camouflage the airstrip during the day.

Hearing the sound of someone approaching, Jayson turned to see Charlie coming toward him. He was especially surprised to see another man, an American, accompanying him. The stranger was somewhat heavy-set and shorter than Jayson by maybe three or four inches, wearing quilted coveralls of the type mechanics usually wear.

"Jai-sonn…you come now. We go to airplane."

Jayson, excited to see another American, extended his right hand for a good old-fashioned American handshake, which he had not had in over a year.

"How do you do?" he said, refraining from giving his name and wondering why Charlie had brought a stranger into the Freeland.

"Elmo Barker," the man replied as he vigorously shook hands with Jayson. "Glad to meet you. You must be Lieutenant Bold?"

Jayson felt a twinge of uncertainty at the realization that this stranger knew his name. He wondered, *How many others know of my survival?*

"I'm not a lieutenant any longer. I guess you could say I've been reassigned." Jayson looked at Charlie and continued, "I'm surprised Charlie let you in on that little secret. I would appreciate it if you didn't refer to me as a lieutenant ever again."

"I understand, but your secret is safe with me. I just spent the last half of last year and the first part of this one fixing that beat up C-47 you parked up there in that box canyon. Let me congratulate you on your flying skill. I don't know many pilots who could have pulled that one off and walked away."

"Neither do I, nor *did* I. Charlie's men carried me on a stretcher for a week before I was able to walk on my own."

"Well, anyway, I'm glad you made it. And for your information, I'm your mechanic, so from now on, you'll be seeing a lot of me. You won't need to worry about what all I know about you. I'm just here to help."

"Jai-sonn…we go airplane now," Charlie said again, impatiently.

"I can't go anywhere right now, Charlie. This runway we're building may be detectable from the air, and we need to come up with some way to camouflage it."

Elmo said to him, "I don't think you need to worry much about that, Lieutenant. Once you see this place from the air, you'll see what I mean. Any pilot flying low enough to see this place will be more concerned about the terrain in front of him than what is below him. Normally they fly at altitudes high enough to cross the bigger terrain that looms less than fifteen miles directly ahead. And unless they don't plan to cross the mountains in the first place, it's unlikely they would notice this place. Besides, most of the Japanese bombers flying in this neck of the woods are either heading directly from Hanoi to their targets or from their targets back home. Of course, the fighters go with the bombers to protect them. Plus, they all have one thing in common, every one of them will be low on fuel. So not much to worry about right here."

"Do you have any idea what the elevation is here?" Jayson asked. Mr. Barker studied the ground as he stroked his chin.

"Somewhere around five thousand feet if I'm not mistaken. How long did you make your airstrip?"

"Approximately four thousand," Jayson answered.

"Fully loaded on a hot day, that could be a little close, I'd have them extend it a little more."

Charlie was getting more impatient.

"We go now, hurry, must go now."

Jayson was wearing his military issue flight suit and bomber jacket that no longer sported the silver bars identifying him as an officer in the Army Air Corp. With a packsack of dried fish, bread, and rice and with a heavy heart, he said good-bye to Ah-lam and Ching-Lan. Ah-lam was quiet and somber, hiding her feelings

THE FRUIT OF ATROCITY

well. She knew the possibility existed that she may never see her husband alive again. That part she left with God.

Charlie, Elmo, and Jayson worked their way up the trail that took them up the face of the escarpment to the mouth of the cave. A dozen of Charlie's raiders accompanied them, well armed as usual. Before disappearing into the cavern, Jayson turned to look at the beautiful aerial view of Ziyou-di. The last time he had stood there, he had felt like an uninvited guest. But no longer was he a foreigner in a foreign land. This time, he was a part of what lay below on the floor of that basin; it was now *his* home and *his* family he was leaving, the home and family he would be thinking about and praying for, every minute he was away.

Charlie had long ago given Jayson back his Colt .45. And before they left to salvage the C-47, Charlie had insisted he take it with him. One by one, the men entered the cavern and made their way up the steep incline through to the other side, emerging out of the cave under the waterfall. Jayson had not returned to the spot since he had first arrived at Freeland the year before.

Back then, injured and intoxicated from Charlie's formula, it had taken three weeks to make the trek from the crash site to the Freeland. The first week, the raiders had carried him on a litter. The remaining two weeks, they had patiently waited for him as he slowly made his way through the jungle under his own power. He remembered how painful and laborious it was and was suddenly anxious to do the same hike under different circumstances.

Charlie offered Jayson a rifle to carry, but he declined, expecting that the sidearm was all he would need to defend against snakes or wild boar, and he wanted to travel light.

They made good time, covering ground at least three or four times as fast as the last time he had made the journey. In addition, he was making more sense of the terrain and recognizing landmarks he had seen during his first trip through the jungle.

In less than a week, they were at the cave where Jayson discovered for the first time that Charlie spoke, a *little bit* of English, also where they could spend a night and for the first time make a fire with the least risk of detection. Charlie and the raiders were on the alert every minute, carefully checking each clearing and water source before approaching it, a required skill that kept them alive. Once again, Jayson breathed a prayer of thanksgiving to the Lord, who had provided the *miracle* meadow and the men who had rescued him. He shivered at the thought of what might have been had it not been for God's grace and provision—*a pile of bleached bones in another pile of twisted metal.*

Jayson had questions as to what repairs Elmo was able to make to the C-47. The aircraft had two 1,200 hp Pratt and Whitney radial Wasp engines that turned three individual prop blades on each engine. Jayson knew that though he had shut the engines down and feathered the props before putting the aircraft on the ground; at least two of those blades would surely need replacing. He wondered how Elmo would get major parts such as propellers that surely must have suffered some degree of damage in the hard landing. However, before he got into all of that, Jayson wanted to know a little more about his new mechanic.

After a meal of root spuds, dried fish, and rice, Jayson turned to Elmo and began a casual conversation.

"Where're you from, Mr. Barker?"

Elmo looked at Jayson for a long moment, as if he was not sure he wanted the—just recently retired army pilot—to know too much about him.

"Alaska."

"Alaska!" Jayson was intrigued, "That's interesting, what part?"

"Palmer. It's across a channel called the Nick Arm, northeast of Anchorage. Which reminds me, I know a fellow up there with the same last name that you got. When I met you, I wondered if you two might be kin or something, but when you said you were from southeastern Missouri, I figured it was unlikely. However, the guy I know does have an accent like yours, and you even favor him some."

THE FRUIT OF ATROCITY

"No, I don't have any relatives in Alaska that I know of. What's his first name?"

"Let's see…I think it was…Art."

Jayson's face turned ashen. "Art! As in, Arthur?"

"Could be. He just told me his name was Art Bold."

"Did he say where he come from?"

"No, but he had just moved to Alaska from back in the Midwest somewhere."

Jayson moved closer to sit next to Elmo by the fire, his interest in Art Bold of Alaska intensified. *Could my brother, Arthur, have sold the farm and moved to Alaska without my knowledge? Surely, this was not the same Art.*

"Elmo, does this man have any other identifying features that would distinguish him from the average guy? For instance, is there any evidence of an injury he may have had at some time?" Jayson held his breath for the answer that he somehow feared he already knew.

"Yes, as a matter of fact, now that you mention it, he does have a bit of a limp, looks like maybe he got his right hip hurt some time or another."

Jayson stared into the fire and for a long moment did not speak.

"Do you think he might be your brother?" Elmo asked.

"Yeah, that's him. He crashed one time and broke his hip, walked with a limp ever since. He must have sold the farm after I left. Oh, well, I guess I can understand it. He must not have been able to make it work by himself. I don't blame him, for that matter, we barely got by with the two of us working it together, fifteen hours a day seven days a week. I remember, he was kind of mad at me because I ran off and joined the Army Air Corp. I guess I left him holding the bag, probably figured I wasn't coming back anyway."

Jayson moved away from the smoke that had drifted into his face. Muttering to himself, he said, "So he moved to Alaska! How about that? So where did you say the two of you met?"

"He bought a piece of land not far from a place called the Wasilla Road House and started building a hangar and log cabin. He hired me to run a dozer for him for a month or so, plus do some work on his airplane. While I did that, he worked on the hangar."

"His airplane? Did he take the Puffers up there too?" What was he planning to do up there anyway?"

"Puffers? What's a Puffer?"

"It's a crop duster. We had a crop dusting business back home before I left."

"Well, I didn't see any Puffer, but I know he has a 1931 Stinson SM2AA, five-seater monoplane, and has plans to fly for hire. I expect he'll do well up there too, especially if he was a crop duster. That experience could keep him alive a little longer than his competition. Most of the good pilots joined up to fly fighter planes. I'm actually surprised they didn't put you into one of them coffins, what with your experience."

"They tried. I didn't want to shoot people."

"I'll let you in on a little secret, Lieutenant…oh, sorry, I mean Jayson. Them Japs, they aren't people anymore. They quit being people and started being monsters a long time ago, and if the rest of the world is going to live free, every one of them needs to be killed and the whole country sunk into the ocean."

Jayson didn't respond to Elmo's expressions of hatred. He knew that the Japanese people responsible for the atrocities against the rest of humanity thought they were doing what was necessary for the survival of their own race and country; apart from God, and apart from any knowledge of His Son Jesus Christ, in their minds, the war they started was justifiable homicide.

"Elmo, you said you repaired the Goony Bird. What all did you have to do to it, and how bad were the propellers?"

"Actually, I don't know how you did it, but the props were perfectly fine. All we had to do was lift the airplane and lower the gear. Then, once we had it standing up, we ran it, turned it around, and about fifty men are up there right now leveling out a runway for you. They got started on that last year, but it was too big a job to do by hand in only a few months, so they took the winter off. But they're back on it and will have it completed soon enough. Hell, it might even be ready by the time we get there."

"How long is the runway?"

"The length of that meadow, whatever that is. There's a downhill slope to it. You landed uphill, which helped you get stopped and was also the reason why there was not that much damage to the aircraft. You can look at what you got to work with, and if you want, we can lighten some of the load."

Jayson thought a moment. "I think we should unload it all. We'll stand a lot better chance of getting in the air at empty weight."

"We already unloaded the aircraft. We had to do that to raise it. But if I know Charlie, he's going to want to take every bit of that fuel back to Freeland before we go on to Chungking. We'll need it there eventually anyway. We can reload with whatever you think you can carry, after all you're the captain."

"I'm not so sure about that anymore," Jayson said. "But we should at least get it down to half a load. I can always make another trip if I need to, providing the runway is adequate enough and we live through the test flight. Did you say there are fifty men up there? Where did you get fifty men?"

Elmo chuckled. "Well, you had no way of knowing it, but on the northeast side of that rock wall you almost ran into, within about ten miles or so, is a little village. Charlie uses it as his headquarters, and it's where most of his men live. He has a virtual army over there, and the Japanese don't know anything about it."

Jayson shook his head. "Why doesn't that surprise me? So is Charlie part of the regular Chinese army?"

"No, but he's real tight with Generalissimo Chiang Kia-shek and, the general's wife, Madam Chiang.

"Really!"

"Oh, yeah, and General Claire Chennault. Charlie works for the gimo directly, and Chennault gives him any support he needs. They go way back to 1937, at the time when Chennault started the AVG."

"Yes, I remember hearing about that. Well, I'll be doggoned, what exactly is Charlie's job description?"

"From what I understand, he's what you might call the head of China's National Intelligence."

"National Intelligence? I suppose that means he's planning on engaging me in his intelligence gathering. I wonder what that's going to look like."

"I can tell you this much," Elmo replied. "When it comes to Charlie's country and his private war with the Japanese, everyone is expendable, and that includes you and me. So I wouldn't let him suck you in too far."

"I'm not so sure about that, Elmo. He needs that C-47, and he needs his pilot and his pilot needs his mechanic. I think he'll think twice before he exposes any one of those commodities to too much risk."

"Well, at least you understand one thing."

"What's that?"

"That with Charlie, you are no more than a commodity."

"Yes, I do have that figured out."

Jayson thought hard about the risks associated with working for Charlie especially in the light of what he had just learned from Elmo. But he also believed God had chosen him for this special mission of saving Ah-lam's orphans, or he would never have deserted his commission in the United States Army Air Corp in the first place. He now committed himself to believing that God would provide for every difficulty that may arise in the process. Because it was Gods will, Jayson resigned himself in the confidence that God would keep him, his mechanic, and, of course, the airplane, safe from any and all harm. As far as the ramifications of his leaving the army, Jayson expected that he already had been classified as MIA (missing in action) and the success of this mission would depend, in large part, upon his remaining that way—one more issue that must necessarily be left in the hands of God.

Jayson's recent conversation with Elmo and his learning of his brother that moved to Alaska had given him an idea. Alaska, as yet, was still a territory, and might make a perfect place to start a new life with Ah-lam, Cheng-Lan, and the sixteen orphans. The only problem, of course, was the distance. Alaska is the other side of the world from Freeland, an impossible journey from the perspective of a lone pilot without an airplane or resources for fuel and other provisions that would be required. Nonetheless, it was worth considering and, of course, remembering that nothing is impossible with God.

Upon their arrival at the cave, Charlie had stationed two guards at the entrance. Three hours later, he ordered two of the men who had finished eating to relieve the other two guards who had not eaten as yet. One of which was Cheng. The guards rotated three-hour shifts with two men on duty at all times during the night. The two raiders picked up their gear and stepped toward the cave entrance.

Suddenly, gunfire erupted from the darkness outside. The young raider closest to the opening died instantly falling backward into the cave directly in front of Jayson. The lieutenant jumped up, immediately drawing his Colt .45. Charlie hollered to his brother-in-law and pointed at the dead raider.

"Jai-sonn, you take rifle." Jayson did not argue. He quickly grabbed the dead man's weapon and headed to the door of the cave. Charlie immediately grabbed him and shoved him against the granite wall to the right of the entrance.

"Jai-sonn, stay...cover Charlie." Elmo took cover behind Jayson while Charlie and the remaining raiders disappeared into the blackness of the night.

Jayson holstered his weapon and examined the American army issue M-1 carbine he had taken from his dead comrade. It was locked and loaded and ready to fire. Jayson took all the ammunition the young man carried along with his bag of trail food and crouching low stayed as close to the rock wall as he possibly could. He said to Elmo, "You stay put. Don't leave this cave." Then Jayson too disappeared out the door.

Sticking close to the stone cliff, he moved approximately fifty feet off to the right of the entrance, tucking himself into a place of concealment that provided a level of cover while he guarded the entrance to the cave.

The shooting had stopped temporarily, but Jayson knew it would start again at some point. For the next several hours, he waited, listening for the sound of any one who might be approaching the cave entrance.

Elmo was the only one left in the cave and the only one of their group that had absolutely no training in hand-to-hand combat. Jayson had not had much more but at least his basic training had included rifle training with an M-1, with which he had scored high. However, this was not a gun range, and Jayson was not in boot camp. This was war, real war—the kind of war he had hoped and prayed to God he would never have to experience. Jayson had never pointed a loaded gun at another human being before, much less actually shot at someone, and had prayed the day would never come when it would be required of him. Now, he wondered, *Had it come anyway?*

Jayson had no idea where Charlie and the other raiders had gone. He expected, they were doing what they do best, seeking out the enemy and eliminating them one by one. He felt some small comfort in knowing that Charlie was not only capable but more than willing to squeeze a trigger and take the life of another human being—maybe he even liked it.

Somehow it did not seem right. In fact, it seemed downright hypocritical that he should hope Charlie and his men would do his killing for him. Jayson struggled with the morality of it all.

"Oh, God," he whispered. "Why am I here, why am I in this war?"

You joined up, remember?

Jayson remained where he sat, listening, thinking, praying.

Hour after hour passed. Time after time he fought back the desire to fall asleep. Soon, it turned colder, and the fog began rolling in. Jayson expected it would shortly become daylight. Erie gray outlines of the surrounding jungle suggested that the confrontation would soon resume.

It was not yet light enough to identify any particular individual, or what uniform he wore. But there was enough light for Jayson to make out the outline of several men just below the entrance, only a hundred feet away. At first, he could not tell if they were Charlie's raiders or Japanese soldiers until he noticed that their hats were different. The raiders wore Akubra jungle hats. The hats these three men wore reminded him of the confederate soldiers' hats in the war between the states back in the 1860s.

Jayson drew a deep breath as he watched the silhouettes of three Japanese soldiers crouched low and moving through a hedge of tall grass, cautiously approaching the entrance to the cave. He wondered, why had he not heard any response coming from the raiders. Where had they all gone? Now, a mere fifty feet from where Jayson was hiding, they stepped into plain view to peer into the cave entrance. Jayson slowly shouldered the M-1 carbine and flipped the safety to the off position. "Please, God, where is Charlie? I don't want to do this."

Jayson leveled the open sites at the head of the nearest soldier as his finger moved into place against the trigger. Then, it happened. The voice of conscience in Jayson's mind spoke loud and clear: "Thou, shalt not kill!" He paused to make sense of it.

Theologically, Jayson believed the teachings of Paul the apostle to the Gentiles. And that as a Gentile believer, he lived: "By grace, through faith..." in the completed work of the Lord Jesus Christ on the cross of Calvary not under the law of the Hebrew Old Testament, that law of Moses handed down to the ancient Jews at Mount Sinai applied only to the Nation of Isreal, the natural descendants of Abraham who still operate under its dictates. However, as a Gentile Christian living in the new dispensation of grace, the old law of the covenant had been completely fulfilled by the life of Jesus Christ. That was the *good news* of salvation. That was the message the Apostle Paul had clearly preached to the Gentiles. Yet somehow, Jayson knew it was the voice of God that had spoken those words to him... "Thou shalt not kill" (Exodus 20:13, AKJV). That of course was the whole idea of the gospel of grace; that instead of the "law" dictating a man's behavior, the Holy Spirit of God would fulfill the righteousness of God within them "who walk not after the flesh, but after the Spirit" (Romans 8:4, AKJV). Calling every believer to rise above the miasma of this world and put all his faith in the arm of God to move in his defense and in the defense of his calling.

Yet surely, the Lord did not expect him to let those vicious killers stroll into that cave, kill Elmo, and walk back out again, leaving behind nothing but the murdered remains of his mechanic. Jayson was running out of time. He had to make a decision—soon. More words of Scripture appeared in his mind.

"*I Am*," your defense. "*I Am, I Am.*" He breathed a sigh of relief and began to pray, "Yea, though I walk—" Suddenly, a burst of 7.62 Browning Automatic Rifle fire erupted from just below the cave entrance, and in less than a moment, all three of the Japanese soldiers lay in a heap at the entrance of the cave. Jayson lowered the carbine from against his cheek. Sweat ran into the corner of his eye. He continued, "Through the valley of

the shadow of death, I will fear no evil: for thou *art* with me…"
(Psalms 23:4, akjv).

Like a ghost, Charlie suddenly appeared from out of the fog.
He approached the entrance to the cave and looked down at the
dead soldiers. Jayson stood and made his way toward his brother-
in-law who looked first at him, then at the bodies, then back
at Jayson. Reaching out his hand, he said, "Charlie, take carbine
from Jai-sonn, give to Barker." Once again, Jayson surrendered to
the wishes of the leader of China's National Security.

"We go now. Jai-sonn and Barker, stay close to Charlie."

Jayson asked, "Where are the other raiders? Are they—?"

"Devos bury Japan pigs." For the first time since joining the
Air Corp, Jayson fully comprehended the finality of war.

Jayson could not get the picture of those three Japanese soldiers out of his mind. He had seen dead men several times but
never as much as he had since arriving in Charlie's world. He
felt he could never get used to it. But what bothered him most
was the realization that had not Charlie intervened, Jayson would
have, in one more second, pulled the trigger, and those three soldiers would have been dead by his hand instead of Charlie's. *What
if Charlie had not come in time? What if the soldiers had arrived a
minute sooner?* The thought made him shudder. It also made him
realize: he was no different than Charlie or any other soldier of
war who fought, killed, and died for the preservation and way of
life of their civilization and society. Had God chosen Charlie as
a killing machine so Jayson could go through the war without
ever getting blood on his hands? It didn't seem fair to Charlie,
but then again, maybe Charlie didn't mind, maybe he liked killing. Jayson lifted his hands to his face and stared at them—they
were shaking.

With the bodies buried and the spoils of war distributed
among the raiders, Charlie led the way down the path on the last
leg of their journey to Jayson's miracle meadow.

By noon of the second day since leaving the cave, Jayson and his friends stood on the same ridge he had flown over moments before his last flight had ended in the meadow below. Tomorrow he would fly that airplane again for the first time since that terrifying moment thirteen months before.

From the top of the ridge, Jayson could practically see all the way to the meadow nearly two miles away. He strained to see around the bend to the place he had set the aircraft down, but the forest of trees concealed it well.

The group of men made their way down from the open ridge and began slashing their way through the last two miles of jungle, finally emerging at the far southwest end of the meadow. Charlie stopped for a moment, listening. Then, staying close to the tree line, he led the men the long way around, skirting the area in a clockwise circle.

Carefully and quietly, they followed in single file until they were positioned directly across from the spot where the C-47 had skidded to a stop, only two hundred yards away.

A rustic bamboo structure built on the northeast end of the meadow appeared to be an improvised hangar, and Jayson assumed the freighter must be inside. Also, between their present position and the building was yet another lean-to type of structure under which were stacked, fifteen fifty-five-gallon drums of fuel covered with tarps.

Charlie studied the open area for the better part of an hour until he was satisfied there were no Japanese soldiers present. Motioning for everyone to stay put, Charlie made his way toward the hangar. Moments later, he emerged from the thatched-roof-covered-bamboo structure and signaled that it was safe to come out.

Bamboo poles covered with foliage leaned unfastened against the front opening of the makeshift hangar. Jayson went inside, and there, sitting on all three wheels as though nothing had ever happened, was his C-47. Nostalgia flooded over him. He thought he would never be back to the meadow again and certainly never expected to see that cargo plane back in flying condition. He climbed up the ladder and through the man door into the forward cabin of the Goony Bird. There he saw the damage caused by the barrels of fuel that had broken loose from their bindings and slammed into the cockpit.

For a brief moment, Jayson recalled the terror that had come over him as he turned the last corner of the canyon, only to see the massive granite face of a mountain looming directly in front of him. Silently, he breathed another prayer of thanksgiving to God for creating that lovely meadow at the last minute before he slammed head on into the sheer rock face of the mountain.

He turned to Elmo standing directly behind him.

"Barker, are you sure this plane is airworthy?"

"Sure enough that I have no reservations about going with you."

Jayson climbed into the pilot's chair and grasp hold of the control yoke. He manipulated it from left to right, pushing the controls all the way forward and all the way back, checking for unrestricted range of motion and free play.

"The controls feel good. Did you check all of the cables and pulleys?"

"Sure did, went through everything. Charlie wanted me to do a good job 'cause he says this is his airplane now, kind of like, 'finders keepers, losers weepers' if you know what I mean."

"Unfortunately, I do. When are we going to load it up?" Jayson asked.

"Charlie is out checking the strip to see how the leveling project is coming along. Do you want to go see it? It will be up to you to decide if there's enough runway to get in the air?"

"Yes, I would. But do you think my opinion would make any difference to Charlie, even if I did say it's too short?"

"Well, if it doesn't, he can fly the dang thing out of here by himself."

Jayson looked across at Elmo. Until he had joined the army, he had not been around that many people who swore. Arthur was the only one in his family that did and only on occasion if he was really mad and only after their parents had passed away.

"So would you back me up if I refused to fly this wounded duck?"

"Lieutenant, if you say it won't get off the ground, you can bet I won't get into it either."

"Well, before we get too paranoid, let's go have a look at the runway.

Together, Jayson and Elmo began walking down the crudely modified meadow. What had at one time been an undulating tabletop of uneven earth and jungle was now a cleared and level field of dirt. Only one problem: it was just slightly wider than the landing gear and not even a thousand feet long.

Jayson stammered, "I…can hardly believe it's the same meadow."

"Yeah, they certainly have done a lot of work on it."

The workers were all the way down at the far end of the strip, and as far as Jayson could see, they all had done an excellent job. He pressed his foot into the soft, freshly disturbed soil.

"We'll need to get everyone together to trample this dirt down. It's way too soft, cost us too much takeoff roll."

"We can mention that to Charlie when we get to the other end."

As they continued down the runway, Jayson asked his mechanic, "How did you get involved with Charlie in the first place?"

Elmo didn't answer immediately, and Jayson glanced at him out of curiosity. The look on Elmo's face puzzled Jayson, and he asked again, "Just what all is Charlie involved in? And I take it that whatever it is, you're involved too, am I right?"

"You're nobody's fool, Lieutenant. I can see that and so can Charlie, but I can't go into it right now. After we get in the air tomorrow, I'll fill you in. And by the way, don't think for a minute you're not involved too."

Jayson thought a minute and nodded. "I've already figured as much. That's why I'd like to know more about it."

THE FRUIT OF ATROCITY

Jayson suspected that Charlie had more going on than met the eye. Although he wasn't sure what it was, he had resigned himself to the fact that God had brought the two of them together to accomplish His purposes in the lives of not only those sixteen orphans but a great many other people as well.

He knew also that at times it might seem like God was leading them into a trap or maybe a circumstance so drastic it would require more of a sacrifice then he could endure. He thought about Ah-lam and his brand-new, beautiful child Ching-Lan and prayed to God for their protection, that he would live to see them again soon. He also prayed for Charlie and his band of devils that God was using as warring angels. And he prayed for Elmo. "Father in heaven, you have provided these men and others I have as yet not met as instruments for the carrying out of your purpose. Let them see the hand of God in all that you do for us as we carry out this endeavor and let them understand that it is your hand that guides us and provides for us. Amen."

Elmo and Jayson reached the far southwest end of the airstrip where some forty men worked on finishing the remainder of the landing strip while Charlie and his raiders stood guard. The working men also carried their weapons, and Jayson assumed that they too were part of Charlie's underground army.

Jayson was impressed with how well trained they all were. He also noticed that most of them were older than the raiders that had saved his life the year before in this same place. He wondered how Charlie, who had only been twenty years old for a couple of months, managed to keep his spot at the top of the pecking order.

Jayson asked Elmo, "What do you think the elevation is in this part of the world?"

"About five thousand feet, I'd say."

"That's what you said about the Freeland. Isn't this place considerably higher?"

"I don't know. It's hard to say."

"Well, in that case, I am going to need a point of reference at the halfway point. Do we have a flag, or something that will be easy to see?"

"I'll go look. I'm sure I can find something. What will that do for you?"

Jayson looked at Elmo and asked, "Are you a pilot?"

"Yeah, but I'm a float plane pilot."

"Well, you've probably heard of it. It's called, the 50/70 rule. If you're not sure of the elevation and temperature and cannot determine the density altitude, you can use the 50/70 rule to keep from dying."

Elmo looked at him quizzically.

"You'll have to explain."

"Just go to full power until you get to midfield or 50 percent of the length of the runway. If by then the aircraft has not achieved 70 percent of its rotation speed and doesn't feel like it is darn close to lifting into ground effect, it would be prudent to cut the power, turn around, and unload some of the freight. If you don't, that ridge out there could ruin the whole rest of your day." Elmo immediately turned on his heels and headed back to the hangar to find a flag.

Charlie saw the two men talking and came over to speak to Jayson.

"Jai-sonn, how you like airport, okay? Jai-sonn like?"

"They have all done a great job, Charlie. Only two problems: the runway is too short and the first half is too soft. The whole thing will need to be lengthened at least another thousand feet and packed down until its hard pan."

"No can do, Jai-sonn, no can make longer."

"Why?"

"Ground too steep down. No can fix. Runway must do. Jai-sonn good pilot. Jai-sonn make airplane fly...zoom." Charlie made a gesture with his hands, imitating a takeoff into the air.

Jayson stared at him dumbfounded.

"Charlie, are you serious? Do you realize I might not get that tub into the air? Do you want everyone to die?"

"Jai-sonn can do, no sweat."

"I'll tell you what I'll do, Charlie. If I can manage to get the thing airborne, I'll take Elmo and fly it back to Freeland by myself, empty. You and your men can hike back and meet us there."

"No can do. Charlie go too. Take three men and all the fuel. Jai-sonn need fuel for later, must take all now. No can come back no more."

"Charlie, you don't understand. There won't be any later. Don't you get it? We're dealing with several factors here: number 1, the high altitude, a runway that's too short, even at empty weight, not to mention the retarded takeoff role due to the soft surface. Why wouldn't you want to play it safe?" Charlie pointed up at the sky.

"Jai-sonn talk Father God, we go, no sweat."

Jayson felt like he had just received a lesson in the art of having faith in God. How could this killer, and whatever else he was, teach him anything about having faith? Nonetheless, he just did, and Jayson could still feel the sting.

There was of course the necessity of being practical, and for a pilot that was a given. But practicality played no part in the Israelites crossing the Red Sea, and the same God that had provided for them, had not only called him to do this thing but also had provided a meadow, which was the only reason he was alive to have this conversation.

Jayson headed back to the airplane to get it ready for departure. On the way, he met Elmo, returning from the hangar, carrying a stake with a red rag attached to it.

"Will this do for a flag?" Elmo asked, holding up the shredded remnants of a red shirt he had fastened to a bamboo stick.

Jayson answered, "That's okay. We won't need it."

Elmo started to speak, "But what about the 50/70—"He stopped in midsentence and turned to look at the ridge sitting just off the end of the runway. Suddenly, it seemed to loom twice as high as it had just twenty minutes before.

The workers finished tramping the runway and loaded the C-47 cargo plane with all fifteen of the fifty-five-gallon drums of airplane fuel. Jayson remembered that when he had left Ledo, India, he was 605 pounds overweight.

Leaving Ledo, India, overloaded was not that unusual for the fleet of 47s. However, at Ledo, the elevation was only five hundred feet, and there was a ten thousand feet concrete runway to work with. And some days, it would be as much as 112 degrees in the Assam Valley. During takeoff, Jayson would easily use up four or five thousand feet of the runway getting the overloaded cargo plane off the ground, staggering into the hot air at just above stall speed. Often, depending on the temperature, he would have to circle the valley for an hour, or more, to gain sufficient altitude to safely cross the Himalayas.

Jayson realized, on this day, they were far short of enough runway at gross weight. Though it was a *miracle meadow*, it was nonetheless at a much higher altitude than Ledo, which, of course, meant the air was thinner and, more than ever, he would need another miracle. He thought of the story of Daniel in the lion's den. Would God have saved him a year ago only to let him die now, right here in the same meadow? At this point, it made no logical sense to do anything else, but believe.

It was seven hundred miles to Kunming from Ledo, India, and the flight time en route, including climb out to altitude, took about four hours. Jayson had been in the air two and a half hours when he landed the freighter in the meadow, which meant he had burned off approximately eighteen hundred pounds of fuel. However, he was still sitting within a half a ton of gross weight, which for the 47 was 26,200 pounds. Furthermore, he had now had five additional passengers. He reasoned, *I should exercise my pilot-in-command authority and make Charlie leave all that fuel behind.* However,

Jayson knew, as Charlie did, that when he got to Freeland, he would need to refuel if they were to go on to Chungking.

Charlie said to him, "We load barrels now, fly Freeland today."

"Absolutely not!" Jayson vehemently objected. "We'll wait until morning when the air is cooler."

"No can do, too dangerous. No can stay no more. Japan soldier come any time now." Jayson looked at Charlie and clenched his jaw.

"Well, it's too dangerous to take off in the afternoon. The air is too hot. We'll go in the morning. One more night isn't going to make any difference. If your people need something to do, they can keep trampling that dirt all night. That's final."

Charlie did not approve but gave in to the decision of his pilot.

The men spent the night in the hangar. Ten men per four-hour shifts guarded the perimeter of the airfield. As morning arrived, the fog moved in encasing the airport vicinity in a gray coffin of visible vapor.

It wasn't very deep, maybe only a thousand feet, but it was deep enough to close an airport at any government controlled facility. Although Jayson was chief pilot, Charlie was in control, and this time his orders were nonnegotiable. He ordered the makeshift hangar door removed.

When Elmo originally parked the aircraft, they had built the enclosure around it right where it sat. Jayson approached Charlie.

"How are we going to pull this plane out of the hangar?" Charlie looked at him like he was joking.

"Jai-sonn start engine, drive airplane away."

"Charlie, this structure is not very well built, and I'm concerned that the prop blast will disintegrate it when I power up, which could damage the tail of the airplane before we get all the way out from under it. I suggest we dismantle the building while we let that fog burn off."

"No time, must go now."

"Okay, I'll give it a try, but if it starts to break up, you better holler so I can shut down before the plane gets damaged.

Jayson hollered to Elmo that it was time to go. Charlie yelled at his men to stand out of the way.

Jayson climbed aboard the aircraft and belted himself into the pilot seat; a quick check to make sure no one was standing near the props, and he fired the starboard engine, four, five, six times the huge propeller turned over. Finally, the 1,200 hp Pratt and Whitney choked, coughed, and sputtered to life. Jayson waited for the oil pressure to come up and checked the voltmeter; everything was in the green. Two times, three times, the port side engine turned over, then started. Both engines were running smoothly at 1,000 rpm. He studied the flight controls for any sign of vibration indicating possible damage to the props or internal parts of the engines.

Jayson looked out over the port side wing where he could see chucks of roof thatch flying away in the hurricane of air, generated by the prop blast. He knew it would take at least twenty-three inches of manifold pressure to get the loaded cargo plane moving and dreaded to imagine what might happen when the rest of the structure blew apart.

Then Jayson saw Elmo and Charlie hurrying toward the aircraft. Elmo entered the cabin and secured his self into the copilot's seat. Charlie, standing in the cockpit doorway, leaned close to Jayson and yelled, "Charlie ready, go now."

Gradually, Jayson simultaneously increased the power on both engines until the Gooney Bird slowly began to move. Immediately, he went to full power, and instantly the additional power launched the cargo plane out of the hangar.

Jayson wanted to look back to see what was left of the structure or even to inspect for any damage on the aircraft's tail section, but from where he sat, he could not see behind the aircraft. Furthermore, the ship was moving faster and faster, and he could not afford to divert his attention, possibly sacrificing the aircraft's momentum over the soft surface.

The loaded cargo plane rumbled along over the spongy surface as it struggled to build airspeed. Jayson saw the red flag Elmo had stuck into the ground as they passed the midpoint of the field, and he thought about the 50/70 rule. By then, the tail wheel should have already been off the ground and the aircraft skipping over the tops of the dirt clods. By the three-quarter point, the freighter should have already lifted free of the earth into ground effect where it could build the necessary airspeed to lift them above the ridge, looming directly before them. However, none of those three prerequisites had as yet happened. Jayson was glad for the fog that obscured their impending doom. Disaster is much easier to take when you can't see it coming. He breathed one final prayer to God.

"Lord, you promised there would always be a lamb in the thicket for us. Now would be a good time to provide it." Suddenly, something incredible happened. Long after the option to abort had passed and only a moment before they ran out of flat ground, an unexpected headwind blasted the nose of the aircraft. The force of the wind was so strong, it slowed the takeoff role of the airplane over the surface of the ground, as if someone had slammed on the brakes. Amazingly, the overloaded freighter lifted into the air only to disappear into the cloud of fog. Jayson had now lost all outside visual reference. Now, completely reliant upon the instruments to keep the wings level, he hoped and prayed they would clear Charlie's ridge and emerge from the top of the fog layer before slamming into the next mountain beyond.

Jayson reduced manifold pressure to forty-two inches for best-rate-of-climb at 2,550 rpm. Gradually, the clouds grew thinner and brighter until the crew expected at any moment they would emerge from the fog into clear sky, sooner rather than later.

Suddenly, the clouds began to break apart as they came in chunks at the windshield, reminding Jayson of a white meteor shower. Then, they burst out of the clouds, and there before them was an old, familiar sight—a mountain made of jagged rock. Jayson banked hard to the right, and as he brought the aircraft back to level flight, they all, finally, breathed a sigh of relief. There before them lay twenty miles of a beautiful valley. The Gooney Bird performed as if nothing had ever happened.

Jayson thought to himself, *I could just go on to Kunming. I could tell the story of how two men had rescued me and salvaged the airplane. I would be welcomed back with cheers and salutations, maybe even sent home with honors and medals. I would be far away from Charlie's war and would never need to fear getting shot at again. I could go to Alaska and fly for hire with my brother, Arthur. All these things I could do.*

But two things Jayson knew he could not do, two things he could never do: disobey God's calling and leave behind his family. He said to Charlie, "Okay, boss, which way to Ziyou-di?"

The Gooney Bird continued to climb until reaching an altitude that would allow them to cross through a narrow gap between two jagged peaks, protruding eleven thousand feet MSL (mean sea level) into the sky. Jayson followed the directions of Elmo and Charlie until soon they crossed another high ridge of sheer rock, where Charlie exclaimed excitedly, "Jai-sonn! Look down! Ziyou-di, Ziyou-di. There!" He pointed ahead at a large valley lying at the base of the high peaks they were crossing.

Jayson watched as the little valley grew increasingly closer, evolving into a beautiful basin of fertile land, blanketed in a forest of bamboo trees, some ten thousand feet below. He could see the thin line of the lazy river flowing through the middle and the rock wall that formed the cauldron of the ancient volcano encircling his new home. In just a few minutes, he would again hold his precious family in his arms.

Careful not to shock cool the engines, Jayson began a shallow circling descent into the cauldron. At an altitude of 1,200 feet above the basin floor, he turned to final approach. Moments later, the wheels of the C-47 softly kissed the dirt runway at Freeland. Soon, he was parking the cargo plane and eagerly going through the shutdown procedures.

The whole village had turned out, and Jayson looked for Ah-lam in the crowd of people. He saw her; Ching-Lan was in her arms, and she was running toward the airplane.

It had taken only nine days to retrieve the Gooney Bird. To Jayson, it seemed like forever. He took Ching-Lan, and together, with his wife, started for their home. For a moment Ah-lam lingered, staring at the huge and dented cargo plane. She said to her husband, "Is that the same airplane you crashed in a year ago?"

"Yes, my love."

"Indeed, it is God who has saved you and brought you here to me. It is a most incredible miracle."

The C-47 parked at the far north end of the runway for the last three days since its arrival, stuck out like the proverbial sore thumb. Jayson, Charlie, and Elmo put together a workforce to build a drive-through hangar off to the side of the runway and as close to the trees as possible, one that would not blow apart.

The crew also built platforms with ramps for raising the fuel drums to a height they could gravity feed the fuel for filling the wing tanks. One day, as the work was almost completed, Elmo called Jayson aside to talk.

"Lieutenant…excuse me, I mean, Jayson, do you mind if I call you Jay?"

"Not at all, the folks at home called me that the whole time I was growing up."

"Good, I didn't get to talk to you about this when we were in the air the other day. Charlie never left the cockpit during the whole flight. He's really excited about having you and this airplane and is anxious to get his little enterprise going."

"What enterprise is that?"

"Charlie has some connections up north, people that he wants you to get to know because you will be dealing with some of them from time to time."

"What kind of connections?"

"Well, I'm sure you realize that this whole 'save the orphans' idea is going to cost a lot of money. Nothing is free, especially in war, and the only way you get things done is through underground sources. Are you following me so far?"

"I think I get it. In other words, to get something, you have to give something, is that the way it goes?"

Elmo nodded. "That's it, my friend, you got it."

"So what does Charlie have that somebody might want bad enough they would give him the things we're going to need, like fuel or food and whatever else we might need to get this done?"

Elmo scratched the back of his neck, and looked at Jayson from the corner of his eye, nodding his head in the direction of the Gooney Bird, he said, "*You* and that Douglas."

"What about me and that Douglas?"

"We're going to be hauling some freight from time to time that will necessarily provide for our expenses. So don't overreact when you see what it is."

"What kind of freight?"

"You'll see, just don't say I didn't warn you."

"Listen, Elmo, I have a few questions about this whole thing regarding the logistics of it all. For instance, when we go get those orphans, how are we supposed to get into the Chungking airport, which I'm sure is completely destroyed from the bombings, then load up sixteen kids, without anyone asking any questions, and fly back here? Furthermore, that airplane has US Army insignia all over it, and it's just a matter of time before someone spots it and starts asking questions."

"You're right about that. Therefore, we won't be flying into Chungking. Charlie's connections have a landing strip near

Anshun, a hundred miles south of Chungking. That's what we'll be going into. Which reminds me, how are you at night flying?"

"Night flying! Is he expecting me to fly that thing at night into a remote mountain airstrip, without any navigation aids?"

"That's why I asked. How are you at night flying, can you do it?"

"I can fly at night on instruments, but without navigation aids, I won't know where I'm going. I've heard, you can get yourself killed that way."

Elmo asked again, "Do you know how to get to Chungking from here?"

"I'm not sure. On our cargo missions, we weren't allowed to carry maps with us. We had our navigation headings and coordinates jammed into our heads during the morning briefings. Without maps of some kind, we could run out of fuel before we ever find it, not to mention slam into a mountain. It's not like they're going to leave the lights on for us."

"Charlie will draw you a map, and he'll be coming along with us. He knows where to go, and as far as the army stuff all over the aircraft, when we get to Anshun, we'll have access to some tools and a hangar. We can strip the paint off and either polish it or repaint it. There are a few other modifications we'll need to make too, like an extra fuel tank and extra seating for all of those kids. The place where we're going and the people bringing those children by truck from Chungking are asking a lot in return. As a matter of fact, we may be working for them for a long time."

"What do you mean by 'working for them'?"

"Remember, we have to get those kids all the way to the US."

"Correction, Alaska, I am taking them to Alaska."

"Okay then, Alaska, anyway, we'll need help, a whole lot of help from a whole lot of people scattered all the way from here to Russia. Unless you think you can make it all the way to Alaska on one load of fuel."

"I understand that. I just don't like being left in the dark."

Elmo grinned. "That's why I asked you if you could fly at night."

"Very funny. You're a regular comedian. Just don't quit your day job."

"Don't worry. I won't. Besides, your my day job now."

At times Jayson struggled with doubts. His human reasoning screamed at him to run as fast as he could from Charlie and Elmo and their so-called *connections* to save himself and his family. It seemed he was getting sucked deeper and deeper into a trap that would inevitably snap shut.

He wasn't that concerned about his own welfare, but for the first time in his life, he had fallen in love with the most beautiful girl on earth, and together, they had made a family. It seemed like a lot for God to expect that Jayson should not only leave his family but put them at risk for an endeavor dependent upon *connections*, connections that could include everything from: underground black marketers to smugglers, killers, and who knows what else. Jayson sank to his knees and prayed, "Oh, God, my Father, my Lord and Savior. My life is not important, only your will is important. Therefore, Thy will be done. Amen."

A special calm came over him as he sensed the Lord saying to him, "My peace I give unto you: not as the world giveth, give I unto you. Let not your heart be troubled, neither let it be afraid" (John 14:27, AKJV).

At last, peace and comfort came to Jayson's mind, and a sense of confidence and assurance flowed into his heart. For the moment, all fear, trepidation, and doubt left him, for the moment.

Chapter 4

I can do all things through Christ which strengthens me.

—Philippians 4:13, AKJV

Like a neon sign, the words resounded in Jayson's mind, and with renewed energy and dedication, he threw himself into the project of saving the orphans.

What from a human perspective appeared as a daunting, even impossible task, he must necessarily leave with God to accomplish. In fact, it was not a work God had given him to do at all but a work that *God Himself*, by the Holy Spirit, had promised to do through him. Jayson's only part would be to place his complete trust in God—no matter what. Time would soon reveal how difficult that would prove to be.

Jayson finished praying and went in search of Charlie. On the way he found Elmo working with the construction crew building the hangar. He approached him.

"Elmo, have you seen Charlie?"

"He left this morning…said he would be back in a few days."

"Did he say where he was going?"

"No, but he took about fifty men with him."

"Did he say when he's planning on making the trip to Chungking?"

"I suppose we'll go when he gets back."

"Well, I need to establish an approach and departure procedure that will keep us alive if we're going to fly in and out of this basin after dark. Has the airplane been fueled yet?"

"No, but it still has plenty of fuel in it."

"I need it topped off because I need to simulate the exact weight conditions we'll have on board whenever we depart out of here in the dark. I'm assuming it will be just you and Charlie going along, is that correct?"

"As far as I know, but you know Charlie, he never lets anyone in on his plans. He makes them up as he goes along, and the only thing you can count on is that they're always nonnegotiable."

"Well, I'm going to assume it will be just the three of us, so I'll need you and one other volunteer to go with me. But first, we need to get that airplane fueled up."

"Aye, aye, Captain. I can take care of that. Go home to your family. I'll let you know when we're done."

With only two hours of daylight left, Jayson returned to the aircraft to prepare for his practice runs.

"She's all ready to go, Boss," Elmo said.

"Perfect, grab an extra passenger, and let's get going."

Jason climbed into the cargo plane and made his way to the cockpit where he wriggled his way into the left seat. Fastened to the instrument panel was a stopwatch. Jayson checked it to make sure it was working properly. What they were planning was far more dangerous than any Japanese patrol or underground desperadoes he would ever encounter. In fact, if his calculations were not perfect, he might never make any of those new acquaintances anyway.

After flying into the Freeland and seeing its location in relation to the routes he flew over the Burma Route, Jayson had a much better picture of where he lived in relation to Ledo and Kunming.

The Himalayan Mountains were the backbone of a gigantic circular cauldron surrounding the Tibetan Plateau. The lower southwestern quadrant extended in a southeasterly direction from the extreme northern borders of Pakistan and India, then east into China. From the northern border of Burma, where it meets with the southern border of China, a giant spur of the Himalayan Range extended south along the eastern border of Burma. It was the boundary of the southwestern portions of the Yunnan Valley in China that gradually decreases in elevation the closer it gets to the Gulf of Martaban east and southeast of Rangoon.

It was on the southeast side of the Himalayas, that portion extending southerly into the Yunnan Valley and the lower foothills that Jayson lived in a perfectly round volcano cauldron, some nine miles in diameter at an elevation of 5,400 feet. Many of the surrounding mountains rose to much higher elevations of 9,000 to 11,000 feet, and to cross those ridges, it would be necessary to execute a spiraling climb, circling the cauldron until reaching an altitude that would allow the Gooney Bird to safely cross the mountainous terrain surrounding their Shangri-la.

Jayson took a pad and pencil and made an outline of the notes he would need for his departure procedure. First, the time from the point where he would apply full power to the point of rotation, along with the rotation airspeed. Second, would be airspeed, pitch, and rate of climb to the point he could initiate a standard rate climbing turn that would keep them well away from the cauldron wall. Thirdly, the time from the initiation of the climbing turn, to the point where they reached an altitude of thirteen thousand feet, an altitude that would provide a minimum of two thousand feet of terrain clearance during the en route phase of the flight. Once again, he would record the time, then safely turn to a northerly heading in the direction of Chungking.

Two hours later, as the last bit of light disappeared behind the cauldron rim, Jayson and his crew of two returned from their test flights.

Charlie and his patrol were gone five weeks. When he returned, he went straight to see Jayson.

"Jai-sonn, you make airplane ready?" he asked.

"Yeah, it's been fueled and ready for several weeks, and I did a half dozen practice departures to record the flight information needed whenever we leave in the dark."

"Two days, we go. Fly away. Two hour before sunup when sun rise above mountain, we land. No later."

"Charlie, it will take a lot longer than two hours to get to Chungking."

"We no go to Chungking."

"I thought…then, where are we going?"

"Jai-sonn not to worry. Charlie show Jai-Sonn, no sweat."

At first Jayson was surprised until he remembered what Elmo had told him about the change in plans and the landing strip at Anshun. He felt somewhat relieved. At least he wouldn't be arriving at Chungking during a bombing raid.

Jayson rose early the next morning and went straight to the cargo plane looking for Elmo, and to his surprise, there was an armed guard watching the entrance. He paused for a moment a bit puzzled, wondering what enemy Charlie thought resided in Shangri-la. *Perhaps, it's me.*

He approached the aircraft and headed for the large cargo door. The guard stepped between Jayson and the ramp leading up to the open door. With his rifle across his chest and speaking in broken English, he said, "Charlie say, no can do."

Jayson looked at the boy soldier. Pushing past him, he said, "That doesn't apply to me," and proceeded to climb the ramp to the cargo door.

As he entered the cargo hold, he saw Charlie and Elmo busy securing a variety of wood crates in the back of the airplane. Jayson was not so much concerned about what was in the crates as how much they weighed. Until now, he was not interested in knowing any more than was necessary in regard to what all Charlie and Elmo were up to, but for weight and balance considerations, he did need to make sure all cargo was loaded correctly. He approached them and said, "What's going on in here?" Elmo looked startled and glanced at Charlie, who quickly slung a canvas tarp over the crates.

"Charlie, how much does that stuff weigh?" Jayson asked as he moved toward them.

"No sweat," Charlie said, waving his arm back and forth. "Jai-sonn no sweat."

"I'm sorry, Charlie, but when it comes to loading this airplane, we don't go anywhere until I know how much each of these crates weigh."

Elmo spoke up, "We don't have any way of weighing them."

"Then, I need to look inside and see what I'm hauling." Elmo looked at Charlie again, and Charlie was glaring at Jayson.

"Okay, no sweat, Jai-sonn can see."

Elmo yanked off the tarp and used a pry bar to open one of the five-foot-long crates, each measuring about two feet wide by eighteen inches deep. Jayson already suspected what was inside, and the second the lid came open, his suspicions were confirmed. Triple stacked in neat little rows alternating, butt, muzzle, butt, muzzle, lay eighteen perfectly new US Government Army issue M-1 carbines.

"Where did you get these?" Jayson asked, turning to Charlie. "Don't tell me you hijacked them from American soldiers?"

Elmo tried to move toward the cargo door directly behind Jayson. The pilot pointed his finger at him and said, "You stay put."

Both men were armed, and Charlie was once again carrying Jayson's sidearm. By now Jayson didn't care; he wanted to know what these guys were up to, and he wanted to know before he ever lifted a finger to help them.

"Japan soldier kill many Mericonn, take guns in Rangoon. Charlie find Japan soldier. China devos take guns kill all Japan soldier."

Jayson looked at Elmo, who just shrugged his shoulders.

"What are you planning to do with them, and what are in the smaller boxes?

Charlie pointed to the two feet by two feet, twelve inches high boxes packaged in burlap gunny sacks.

"Ammo, Charlie take for Chinese Army. Chinese soldier no have good guns. Charlie trade for trucks to go get orphans."

Jayson stared at Charlie and then at Elmo.

"Whose side do you think I'm on? Why didn't you want me to know?"

"Charlie think maybe Jai-sonn better off not to know."

"Charlie, we are in this together. You're my people now. I'm one of you. From now on, you don't keep anything from me, is that understood? That goes for you too, Mr. Barker. And furthermore, nothing gets loaded on this aircraft that I don't know about."

"Aye, aye, Captain, I got it.

"How about you Charlie, do you understand?" Jayson pointed toward the jungle in the direction of the mountains where he had crashed. "Out there you may be in charge, but on board this aircraft, I'm the captain, and what I say goes."

"Okay, Jai-sonn, no sweat. Outside, Charlie boss. Inside, Jai-sonn boss."

"That's right, and don't you forget it. Now, how many crates of rifles are we taking?"

Charlie pointed outside, "Fifty."

"Okay then, I want these crates moved forward to here." Jayson pointed to a location midway between the cockpit and the tail of the aircraft. "And make sure they're secured so they can't move if we get into turbulence." Turning to Elmo, he asked, "How many more of these guns do you have stockpiled here in Shangri-la?"

"A lot, Charlie and his raiders confiscated them from the Japanese a year ago and have been bringing them into camp off and on ever since. However, until now, there was no way to get them up north, until you came along."

"So how many are there altogether, a whole plane load?"

Elmo held up two fingers. "More like two loads, Captain. Most of them are still out there." He jerked his thumb in the direction of Rangoon.

"In the jungle?" Elmo nodded.

"Jai-sonn, you come look." Charlie was pointing at another box concealed in a gunny sack. Peeling back the burlap, he exposed a wooden chest approximately one foot wide by eighteen inches in length and twelve inches high.

"What's in there?" Jayson asked.

Charlie unhooked the brass hasp that fastened the lid shut and opened the old teakwood chest. It was full of diamonds. Jayson moved closer and knelt next to Charlie, who was holding a handful of the precious stones closer for him to see. Jayson exclaimed. "Wow! So what's the story behind these?"

"Diamonds come from India. We buy cheap from smuggler in Rangoon, sell to smugglers in Chungking. Make money for Chinese war."

Jayson looked at Charlie and remarked, "Are you sure you bought them, or did you steal them?"

"No, no, Charlie buy diamonds from smugglers."

Jayson looked at Elmo, who would not look him in the eye.

"Really, what else are you guys into?"

"Only one more thing," Charlie said.

"What is that?"

"Charlie, sometime take Japan prisoner, turn over to Flying Tigers."

"Do the Flying Tigers know about me or this cargo plane?"

"General, good friend of Charlie. General like Charlie very good. General help Charlie make war on Japan soldier."

Jayson looked at Charlie and then at Elmo.

"You've got to be kidding me, are you telling me that Claire Chennault knows I'm alive and that this airplane survived?"

Elmo looked away, and Charlie said, "Jai-sonn not to worry, Jai-sonn no sweat, we make airplane no more army. We make airplane hospital cross."

"You mean Red Cross?" Jayson corrected him.

"Yes, yes, then we fly Kunming get more fuel for Charlie plane. Nobody know but general."

Jayson had to sit down.

"Jai-sonn no sweat nobody know. Jai-sonn no army lieutenant no more."

"Why do you need more fuel?"

"We fly Rangoon and Calcutta, pick up more diamonds, more guns. Fly Kunming, pick up more gas for plane. We make big fuel stash at Charlie headquarter. Diamonds buy fuel, diamonds buy men, diamonds buy food for Chinese Army. Tomorrow we go Anshun, bring back orphans from Chungking and food from general to feed orphans."

"I thought we weren't going into Chungking."

"We fly Anshun. Charlie take guns in truck to Chungking."

"What time are we leaving?"

"Two hour before morning light, we go."

"Is anyone else going along, besides the three of us and this extra cargo?"

Charlie first nodded, then had second thoughts and began to shake his head.

"Is that a yes or a no?"

"Charlie, maybe say yes, but maybe mean no, twelve more devos maybe go too."

Jayson shook his head in exasperation, "Unbelievable, absolutely unbelievable."

"All right then." Jayson nodded, and extending his handshake to both Charlie and Elmo, he said, "But that's all. Then I'm done, got it?"

Charlie nodded. "Okeedokee then, Jai-sonn okay partner now."

"Only for now. Until I decide I've had enough."

Charlie stared at Jayson. A solemn look came over his face.

"Jai-sonn fly in dark okay, no hit mountain?"

"I guess, we'll find out when we get there. I already did three test runs in and out of the basin, duplicating the weight I thought we were going to have on board, and now I learn we're taking more people and cargo along, and I no longer have the time or fuel to waste on more test runs. What other surprises do you have in store for me, or do you think that's enough for one day?"

"That is all no more. We bring orphans home now."

"All right then. No more curve balls, okay?"

"Okay, Jai-sonn, no sweat."

Charlie exited the aircraft and began talking to the guard at the foot of the ramp.

Jayson and Elmo began relocating the cases of rifles. Suddenly, a shot rang out.

"That sounded like a .45 caliber," Jayson said to Elmo. Rushing to the cargo door, they both peered outside. At the bottom of the ramp lay the crumpled, dead body of the guard who had tried to prevent Jayson from entering the aircraft. Charlie was nowhere to be seen.

"Oh my Lord!" Jayson exclaimed. "Did Charlie do that?"

"No question about it, Boss."

"But why? He was just a boy."

"I imagine it was because he disobeyed orders when he let you come aboard." Elmo looked into Jayson's eyes. "Does that give you some idea about who you're dealing with?"

"It certainly does, Elmo. It most certainly does. On the other hand, it also gives me an advantage in one way."

"How's that? Boss."

"Now, I know who I'm dealing with, but Mr. Charlie Nee does not know who he is dealing with. And for now, we'll just keep it that way."

The ex-lieutenant could hardly comprehend that General Claire Chennault was aware of his survival. However, it did not surprise him to learn that he would be providing help, in the form of supplies and food, to Charlie and his raiders. After all, they did go back quite a long time to when Chennault first came to China.

The tonnages coming across from Ledo and the other bases in India were flooding into Kunming, and some of the cargo planes crossing the hump were often redirected to other bases in central China.

If Jayson was going to make regular runs into the Freeland, he wondered how long it would be before their secret Shangri-la was eventually discovered. It seemed to Jayson that there were too many what ifs, too many scenarios that could very easily end in disaster. The thought sent shivers up his spine and on the way back to the dispensary. He took his concerns to the Lord in prayer.

"Dear God, they keep throwing me more curve balls. And now I'm learning, I'm not as dead to the army as I thought I was. Only the mighty arm of God can help me. Amen."

Ah-lam held the baby in her arms as she greeted her husband at the door, and for the rest of the evening, he purposely refused to think about the orphans and the war. For the moment, he was with his family, and though it was a terrible thing that there were so many children who did not and may never have the opportunities his daughter would have, he put it out of his mind for the present. During the remaining moments of the evening, his wife and daughter smothered him with their love. Ah-lam said to him, "I love you, my husband, please come back to me." Jayson kissed her forehead.

"I promise I will," he said and fell asleep.

When Jayson awoke, it was midnight. The darkness would start giving way to light in a few hours, and it would take at least an hour before they would be ready for take off. He picked up the basket of food Ah-lam had prepared for him, kissed her and his baby, and quietly left. Ah-lam pretended she was asleep, but when he was gone, she began to cry. She gathered her little child in her arms and whispered in her ear imaginary stories of the life she would someday have in America.

The cargo plane barely noticed the extra weight, and Jayson flew the numbers he had previously established, until reaching his target altitude of thirteen thousand feet MSL. He said to Charlie, "Any particular heading you want me to fly?"

Charlie pointed out at the darkness and said, "Jai-sonn go to there."

Jayson looked at Elmo sitting in the copilots seat and said to him, "That's what I figured." Taking a wild guess, he turned to a northerly heading of 350 degrees magnetic and sat back to wait for daylight. *Lord God in heaven, I have no idea where we're going. May God help us.*

The drone of the two Pratt and Whitney's was mesmerizing. Jayson had no trouble keeping the wings level, and there wasn't much in the way of updrafts or downdrafts. For the present, at least, the flight was going well.

As far as navigation however, that was another story. There were no charts or maps, no morning briefing on weather, or enemy activity. Yet somehow, the darkness provided a degree of security, like they were in a cocoon, safe from detection, not only from the enemy, but from the previous owners of the aircraft as well.

Jayson thought about the massive undertaking he had accepted. How could they possibly expect to accomplish a task so fraught with danger and complexity? He thought about Charlie and wondered what motivated him to engage in an endeavor so daunting. Was it his hatred for the Japanese who had murdered the only father figure he had ever known? Was it because his sister asked him to do so? Was it his love for his country? Or maybe because he had been, and still was, an orphan himself.

The amazing thing about Charlie and the one thing that Jayson admired about him more than anything was his tenacity. It was as if the guy never calculated the risk of anything, as if he never considered the possibility of failure or the absolute impossibility of any task. Personally, Charlie didn't express a faith in God. And yet, the thought of failure never entered his mind. It made Jayson feel a bit ashamed of his own tendencies toward practicality and the limitations practicality had built into his personal faith.

Then he remembered the young guard. If only he had called to Charlie from outside instead of pushing past him to confront Charlie and Elmo, maybe the young man would still be alive. Jayson felt that there was a level of evil in Charlie that had yet to be completely revealed. On the other hand, he also knew the importance of strictly following orders during wartime. Jayson decided to take responsibility for the young man's demise and learn from it. Yet a subtle fear of what Charlie was capable of filled him with a whole new level of apprehension.

Jayson snapped out of his conjectures to check the time. They had only been in the air a little over twenty minutes when the aircraft began encountering turbulence. Jayson momentarily turned on a wing light and realized they had entered a cloud. Soon, freezing rain began adhering to the windscreen, glazing it over and reducing their outside visibility to zero. *Thunderstorm... we've flown into a thunderstorm.* Jayson's heart rate doubled, and his apprehensions of Charlie subsided.

The outside temperature gauge indicated eighteen degrees Fahrenheit. Jayson looked at his mechanic. He was asleep. He wanted him to keep his eye on the accumulation of ice but decided not to disturb his copilot. Deeper and deeper they flew into the worsening weather.

The updrafts and downdrafts were getting more severe. "Elmo, wake up!" Jayson yelled above the roar of the sleet and hail that hammered the airframe.

Elmo squirmed in his seat and smeared the back of his hand across his eyes.

"What's up, Boss?"

"We're in a thunderstorm. I need you to keep your eyes open for mountains while I fly this thing. Right now we're on the gauges, but if we load up with too much ice, we might not be able to maintain terrain clearance, and we'll need some outside visual reference."

"Aye, Captain, are you going to try to turn around?"

"I would have if I'd have seen it coming. But I'm not sure if we're in the center of it or flying through the fringes. If we try to turn around now, we might fly deeper into the heart of the cell or even into the side of a mountain. I think we'll keep straight ahead for now. Hopefully it won't get any worse."

"Okay, you're the boss. But if it was me, I would get the hell out of here."

"Well, if you're going to have faith in God, you can't run every time the devil throws a little something at you."

"Is that what thunderstorms are, just a *something* the devil is throwing at you? Is that like a spitball or an eraser? If I understand correctly, it's thunderstorms that kill more of your cargo jockeys than the whole Japanese squadron of Zeros combined."

"You're right, Elmo, but if we turned around and went back every time we entered a thunderstorm, only a fraction of the freight would make it through to Kunming. So if the army's freight is important enough to keep on going, then how do we compare the lives of those children? I believe there comes a time when you just have to believe, even when everything you can see and touch or feel suggest failure, even catastrophe."

"I get it, Boss, but what you call believing, I call gambling. Remember, this time it's more than just *your* butt you're betting."

"It's only gambling if there's the possibility of losing. With *Almighty God*, there is no possibility of losing."

Elmo stared at Jayson for a moment, not sure he really believed what all the lieutenant was saying and wondering if Jayson even truly believed it. Elmo had no idea that Jayson wondered the same thing.

Both Elmo and Jayson knew the C-47 in level flight could carry an enormous amount of ice before reaching its critical mass. However, any amount could affect its maneuverability at the lower elevations required for landing.

The ice was getting thicker on the windscreen, and Jayson looked out of the side window to check the leading edge of the wing. They were flying without any navigation lights, and Jayson could not even see the wing. He flipped on the inboard wing light built onto the side of the fuselage that lit up the leading edge of the wing and portside engine. His worst fears were realized. The wing's leading edge was covered with at least a one-inch-thick coat of rime ice that already had begun to distort the curvature of the leading edge, which would rapidly deminish the lift properties of the wing. He turned to his copilot and said to him, "Elmo, go get Charlie and tell him to come up here, *quickly*."

"Aye, Captain." Moments later, Charlie stood blurry eyed at the door.

"Charlie, do you know what the terrain elevations are between here and Anshun?"

"Jai-sonn, hills very low, no sweat. Maybe seven, maybe eight thousand, not so much, no sweat."

"Well, we're in the clouds, not to mention a thunderstorm, and taking on a lot of ice up here at thirteen thousand feet, and sooner or later, we need to either get out of this moisture or find some warmer air, and the only place we'll find it is down there." Jayson pointed to the mountains below.

"Jai-sonn speak to Father God, no sweat."

"Why don't you talk to him for me. I'm flying the airplane."

Charlie had disappeared back to his improvised sleeping quarters. Jayson hollered after him, "What's the matter? Do you have a guilty conscience? Don't forget, I'll need you up here whenever..." Jayson's voice trailed off, "we get out of these clouds." Charlie had left the cockpit.

The cargo plane continued to drone through the darkness and the sleet, and the turbulence continued to thrash the airplane. The ice was growing at an alarming rate. Another hour passed. Charlie and his entourage in the back were still fast asleep with their cargo of guns, ammo, men, and diamonds.

Jayson thought back to the time when he was a first lieutenant in the US Army Air Corp, flying his daily route in the very same aircraft. Hundreds of times, he had flown over the hump, back and forth from Ledo to Kunming. But never in his wildest imaginations would he ever have expected that not even a year and a half later, he would be, not only a deserter, but a gun runner and diamond smuggler, flying a cargo plane he had stolen from the US government. *Lord God in heaven, Savior, Redeemer, and keeper of my soul, just exactly what in the name of God am I doing here? And by the way, we either need to get out of this thunderstorm or find warmer air. This is all on you, Lord. I don't have a clue what I am doing. But I do know this, if something divine doesn't happen real soon, this prayer will become a moot point. Amen.*

The C-47 cargo planes were equipped with pneumatic, deicing boots along the leading edges of the wings, which, when inflated, would break up the ice and restore a portion of the lift lost by the ice. In addition, the propellers were equipped with deicing capability in the form of copper tubing leading to the base of each individual prop, which, when activated, would deliver alcohol capable of melting the ice preventing its build up on the propeller blades—an issue that could quickly deteriorate the performance of the propellers. The problem, of course, was that there was no alcohol in the deicing tanks, and the pneumatic pumps on the leading edge of the wings did not work.

The airspeed had slowed dramatically, and chunks of ice were breaking off the prop-tips and hitting the aircraft. Jayson flipped on the light again and gasped at the amount of ice that had already accumulated on the wing surface. The portside engine was so completely plastered, he could no longer see the green army color of the painted aluminum. The deadly ice along the leading edge of the wings had grown to more than four inches thick, and the airspeed had deteriorated from 180 knots to 100 knots.

The defroster had long ago lost its battle with the elements, and the windscreen was so plastered Jayson could see nothing but whiteout. There was no outside visual reference, horizon, or sky.

It was as if inside the cockpit of their airplane was the only world that existed, and outside, nothing but that god-awful ice.

The airspeed continued to deteriorate, and the aircraft began to pitch up, taking on a nose-high attitude. As the ice continued to build, the gross weight dramatically increased. The overload of ice was not the only issue; the lift characteristics known as, lift Bernoulli's law—that *phenomenon* that makes an airplane fly—were rapidly giving way to the accumulation of ice. Jayson knew it was imperative they get to warmer air, not later, not soon, but immediately.

Gingerly he pushed the nose a little lower, slightly reducing the throttle to keep the rpms in the green arc. The airplane eagerly began to descend. It had been two hours since they departed Freeland. Surely, they were getting close to the lower elevations. He yelled across the console to Elmo, "Tell me what you see out of that starboard side window."

"I see a flying iceberg. Were you expecting blue skies and tailwinds?"

"Do you know where those pneumatic boot pumps are located?

"Yeah, but they're not working."

"I know they're not working. The question is, can you get to them?"

"They're inside the wing, connected to an air compressor behind the engines. There's one on each side, but I can't get to either of them while we're in the air."

"Okay then, it looks like it's starting to get daylight out there. I think we're finally out of that line of thunderstorms, but I need you to watch for any evidence that we might be emerging out of this frozen overcast, and look out for mountains."

The C-47 was passing through nine thousand feet and descending at a rate of one thousand feet per minute. Jayson had gone back to full power in an attempt to arrest the rate of descent and keep the airspeed from getting any slower; he knew they were now flying at something only slightly above a stall, and the situation was as critical as it was ever going to get, and yet, so far, *heaven* had not lifted a finger to help. Then Jayson felt a hand on his shoulder. At first he thought it was Charlie, but when he glanced behind him, there was no one there. The pressure remained for several more minutes; although it did not interfere with his movements. A peace came over him, and the tension in his body relaxed, returning his heart rate to normal.

Suddenly, they emerged from the clouds. Tentatively, Jayson once again checked the buildup of ice, afraid of what he might see. It had grown to over six inches thick. Jayson had never known of a plane that could carry so much ice and still fly.

The air temperatures had warmed to thirty-three degrees Fahrenheit, and they were still flying well above the highest terrain. Jayson felt his shoulder where the pressure had been and whispered, "Thank you, God."

The pilot turned to Elmo, about to ask him to go get Charlie, when suddenly Charlie appeared at the cockpit door.

"Jai-sonn, no can see, too much ice."

"No kidding," Jayson retorted. "Hey, Charlie, it's been over two hours since we left, how close do you think we are?"

"Charlie no can see."

"All right then, I'll circle around for a while until we unload some of this ice. It should go fairly quickly now that the temperature is above freezing."

Jayson circled fifteen hundred feet above the highest terrain while the ice slowly evaporated into the, now, warmer air. It took well over an hour, but gradually the windscreen began resembling a window again, and Charlie pointed in a direction that put them on a heading of 020 degrees magnetic.

"Charlie not sure, look for *Hu Shan*."

"Hu... who?"

"Hu Shan," Charlie repeated.

"What's Hu Shan?"

"Tiger Mountain."

"Well, good luck with that. There's only a million mountains out there, and they all look the same to me." Jayson said.

"Hu Shan not same, you see. Turn more there." Charlie pointed ten degrees to the left, and Jayson blindly followed.

What did he have to lose? Jayson already knew he was living on borrowed time. He had come this far, and Charlie was the one God had sent to rescue him, so no matter what happened, he had no other choice but to trust that God would, once again, provide.

"There! Jai-sonn, you see there!" Looking in the direction Charlie pointed, Jayson saw a mountain at least a thousand feet higher than the surrounding hills and had to admit it did look a little like a tiger. Sprouting from another hill, several miles north, a round ridge gradually climbed like the back of a tiger several miles to its summit, abruptly ending in a round cliff face resembling the head and chest of a tiger overlooking the terrain below.

Jayson was amazed that they had actually flown directly to the destination without any flight planning aids or maps. Certainly, the Lord was directing their paths. Silently, he breathed a prayer of thanksgiving.

"Jai-sonn, go to other side, low end of ridge, then see airport."

Jayson looked at Elmo and asked, "Have you ever been in here before?"

"Nope. Never have, but I probably know some of the people there."

"I'm glad somebody knows something because I sure don't."

Charlie's voice grew excited. "There, there, Jai-sonn, look, see airport?" Jayson banked to the right in the direction Charlie was pointing. The strip lay northeast and southwest; the runway numbers were 02/20. Jayson brought in the first notch of flap slowing the airplane while he initiated a 270 degree descending turn. Rolling out on a heading of 200 degrees, directly before him lay the southwest runway. The morning sun piercing through the broken overcast was now over his left shoulder, and Jayson could finally make out the condition of the dirt runway. He estimated its length at about 4,500 feet.

The runway undulated up and down with the flattest portion in the center and the highest point at the far southwest end. Several buildings erected adjacent to the airstrip at midfield appeared military to Jayson, and one—exceptionally large structure—he immediately assumed must be a maintenance building. There were a dozen or so open hangars located in the thickest part of the trees in which were parked several P-40 fighter aircraft, apparently awaiting maintenance.

As Jayson touched down, he quickly realized the runway was a bit rough, apparently only recently constructed by the Army Corp of Engineers.

"Jai-sonn, park there." Charlie pointed at the largest building. As the cargo plane taxied toward it, two gigantic doors mounted on surplus C-47 tail wheels began to move open, and a man in mechanic overalls motioned for Jayson to keep the ship moving straight into the building.

"Who is that?" Jayson asked.

"That's Tex." Elmo answered.

"Who is Tex?"

"When he's not wrenching on broken airplanes, he flies one of the P-40s for Chennault. He's their top ace, killed more Jap planes than you've ever seen."

"You mean the Flying Tigers use this airport?"

"That's right, this is their maintenance shop. That's why they call it Tiger Mountain."

Jayson taxied the C-47 into the shop and shut down the engines. Tex closed the doors behind him and secured them with a cable. Jayson heard the rear cargo door open and moments later saw Charlie and Elmo walk around the left wing of the aircraft. He assumed everyone had departed the airplane yet suddenly sensed he was not alone. Then, from behind the flight deck, he heard a voice say to him, "How come you're out of uniform, Airman?" He immediately recognized the voice of General Claire Chennault.

Jayson froze, not sure what to expect next. If they arrested him and sent him before a Court Martial, it was entirely possible he would never see his family again. He turned to look at the general face-to-face and spoke to him in fluent Chinese. "I have no idea what you are talking about," he said.

The general looked amazed and replied, "Lieutenant Bold, I don't know what you're trying to pull here, but I already know who you are and what happened to this airplane. The thing is, this whole deal with you crashing and both you and the airplane surviving has actually worked out just right for me. Madam Chang Kia-shek has been after me to get a plane load of orphans out of China, and so far, I couldn't get the okay from the chain of command. But now, I have a way to get that job done. You don't need to worry because the only way I can do it without getting my butt in a ringer is for you to officially remain dead and this cargo plane to be made into something other than what it is, and we're going to do that right here in this shop. Do you still want to play ignorant?"

Jayson extended his hand, and in perfect English, he said to the general, "How are you, sir? Good to see you again."

"That's more like it, Lieutenant. Now listen, I need you to get Charlie Nee and Elmo Barker, and come to my office for a briefing."

"Where am I going, General?

Chennault looked at him with a puzzled expression. "You're going to get those orphans out of China for me, I thought you knew."

"I don't know anything other than what Charlie told me. He said we're taking them…" Jayson stammered as he remembered that no one was to know of the existence of Freeland. Suddenly Jayson wondered if Charlie intended on taking the children back to Shangri-la in the first place. Maybe Charlie and Chennault had some other plan for them all along. He continued, "I mean, yes of course, I know. I just don't know how."

"We have that all worked out, Lieutenant. The briefing will be in an hour. You men get something to eat."

The general turned to leave, and Jayson sat back in his pilot seat. His stomach quivered. He felt nauseated, and moisture filled his eyes at the thought of how long it might be or if he would ever see Ah-lam and Ching-Lan again. Strange men were deciding his future, men he never would have known had he not joined their war. The question was, *Exactly what* had they decided? What, if any vote could possibly exist for him and his family, if he continued to let other men decide his life? He thought to himself, *I need to come up with my own plan.*

Jayson had not eaten in over twelve hours, yet he did not feel hungry. The one thing he did feel was out of control, and reasoned that to take control, he would need all of his strength; therefore, he must eat, whether he was hungry or not. Jayson found Elmo talking to the other mechanics, and together they sought out the mess tent.

General Chennault was a no-nonsense leader of men who had bucked mainstream military idealism on more than one occasion. His previous successes in China were the result of implementing a new kind of strategy into the fighting techniques commonly used in air war. At that time, Chennault was only a captain, and his superiors scoffed at his proposals. Then, in 1933, he resigned his commission in the army.

In 1937, at the request of Generalissimo Chiang Kai-shek, Chennault agreed to come to China. The gimo had hired Chennault officially as an advisor on military strategy—yet in reality, his job was to recruit and train fighter pilots for the Chinese Air Force, where he would be working directly for the Minister of Defense: the Madam, Chiang Kai-shek.

The tactics he taught to the Chinese flyers proved so successful that by the time the United States entered the war with Japan in December of 1941, Chennault and his world renowned Flying Tigers—formally known as the AVG—had dealt decimation to the inexperienced Japanese fighter pilot forces. As a result of his successes, the army recommissioned Claire Chennault as a brigadier general and assigned him as commander of the Flying Tigers.

Jayson, Charlie, and Elmo entered a back office to the maintenance shop where the general sat looking at some documents that lay spread out in front of him. As they entered the general's office, he stood and said to them, "At ease, gentleman, please take a seat."

General Chennault extended his handshake to all three men who responded in kind. He then motioned for Charlie to follow him as the two of them moved out of hearing range of Elmo and Jayson. Their discussion was brief. In a few minutes, Charlie headed for the exit door while the general took a seat at the end of the table where Jayson and Elmo sat facing each other.

"Lieutenant Bold?"

"Yes, sir."

The general reached down beside his chair and produced a small satchel which he handed to Jayson along with an additional large manila envelope, which he slid across the table toward Elmo.

"This is your knew ID. From now on, you are Pastor Jay Baldwin. You are a civilian missionary, and you are working in China under the direction of the WWCPLC. That is *World Wide Consolidated Protestant League of Churches*. Your passport and credentials are in that briefcase, along with $10,000 cash.

"For your information, we are going to make a few modifications to your C-47 and turn it into a Red Cross DC-3. And from now on, as far as anyone is concerned, that plane has never been anything else, is that understood?"

"Yes, sir."

"My mechanics will equip your plane with an extra two-hundred-gallon fuel tank that will increase your range from ten hours

THE FRUIT OF ATROCITY

to twelve hours. You have been provided with adequate papers for getting through Russia and into Alaska."

"Alaska!" Jayson reacted with surprise. *How did Chennault know I had decided to go to Alaska?*

"Yes, Alaska. Do you have a problem with that?"

"No, sir, not at all."

"The Chinese underground will provide fuel for you until you are out of China. You can pay them with those uncut stones you got from Charlie. You will leave here with full tanks and 635 pounds of water, food rations, clothing, and blankets. It should be more than enough to get you all the way to Alaska." Chennault continued, "Because Alaska is a territory and not part of the continental United States, there will be no customs issues. You will also find in that briefcase the contact information of the people in Anchorage in charge of the orphanage. They will provide homes for the children. You are to give them whatever is left of the money when you arrive. Mr. Barker will go with you and be your mechanic. Your first stop will be Yinchuan, where you will make contact with a Major Yuan. He will arrange for your fuel. After you leave Yinchuan, you will be on your own.

"Included in the case are charts, maps, navigation aids, and I'm sure you are familiar with the most recent technology in navigation: the Automatic Direction Finder or ADF.

"Yes, sir, we have that equipment on board."

"The ground installation is called a Non-Directional Beacon. You are probably aware of the NDB installation at Ledo. It was the prototype, installed over a year and a half ago."

"That receiver will pick up any AM transmission. Your charts will show where you might expect to find some of those stations. They will be few, and far between, but there might be some that are still transmitting. There are no other places to land an airplane other than the places designated on the maps.

"Arrangements have already been made with an underground black market group in Russia. Hopefully, those arrangements will result in fuel available for purchase at Khabarovsk and Magadan. You will either need to buy or trade for it. There are no guarantees how much, or what, they will expect in payment. Don't forget to strain the fuel for contamination, and watch yourselves very carefully around the Russians. Tell them you will be making frequent trips. Maybe they will be less likely to rob you. Once you are in Russia, there will be no other sources of help or protection for you. Many of those types are extremely ruthless, and there is no telling what they might do. We will provide a secure place in the airplane for you to keep your box of diamonds and the money. We will also provide you with automatic weapons in case you need to defend yourself.

"The work on the plane will take a few days. When it's completed, I will let the Chinese know where and when they may expect you at the rendezvous points. Good luck, gentleman, and God speed…are there any questions?"

Jayson's heart was already beating out of control. "What about coming back?" Jayson asked.

"There is no coming back, son. When you get to Alaska, you start a new life, for you and for those children. When I walk out of this room, this whole thing never happened, and Lieutenant Jayson Bold is dead. According to army records, he was lost over the Burma route on June 13, 1943."

Jayson's insides felt like churned butter; he tried not to let it show.

"Yes, sir, may I ask where are we to pick up the children?"

"Charlie has taken his men and a personnel carrier, along with some other freight he brought with him, and is on his way to Chungking as we speak. He will make contact with the underground, who will meet him with the children. Your aircraft should be ready to go by the time they return."

The meeting ended, and the two men left the room. Jayson stopped for a moment and said to Elmo, "I'll meet up with you later, Barker. I need to speak to the general, alone."

"Okay, Boss. I'll be working on the airplane."

General Chennault was stuffing papers in his briefcase as Jayson returned to his office.

"Sir, may I speak with you?"

"What is it, Baldwin?" the general said without looking up.

"Sir, after I crashed in that meadow Charlie saved my life and took me to where his people live at the foot of the Himalayas. While I was recovering from my injuries I fell in love with Charlie's sister, and we now have a four-month-old child."

Chennault removed his spectacles and leaned back in his chair. "So what exactly is your point?"

"I can't do this, sir. I can't leave my wife and child forever. It is impossible for me to do that and inhumane of anyone to expect me too."

"*Your wife?* How did she become your wife?"

"We were married in the village, sir, according to Chinese custom and our faith. My wife is a Christian as am I."

The general tossed his glasses on the desk and sat forward in his chair. He studied Jay for a long moment.

"Well, young man, you have two choices. You can either take this assignment or not. If you do not, you will be miraculously brought back to life where charges will be referred against you, and you will stand before a Court Martial charged with everything from desertion to gunrunning and diamond smuggling. On the other hand, if you accept this mission, I will personally make sure that your wife and child are safe. After the war, you can come back to China and get them, but it will have to be at your own expense. Which will it be?"

"I will go, thank you, sir. There is one more thing, sir…"

"What now?"

"Sir, why can't I go back and get them now and take them with us? They are only two hours away."

"Well, Baldwin, if it was my family, I wouldn't want to expose them to that kind of risk. This is going to be a very dangerous mission, and some of those kids may not even make it. For that matter, I have my doubts that any of you will make it. Do you still want to subject your own family to that kind of danger?"

"I believe God will deliver us all safe to our destination, sir, and I'm willing to take the risk based on that faith."

"Well, if your faith is that strong, then why can't you believe your family will be waiting for you after the war just like I said they would? Consider your request denied, Airman, and if you do not show up on time at your designated rendezvous, there will be no fuel or supplies for you to continue. You're dismissed."

Jay Baldwin picked up his satchel and walked out of the general's office. He felt faint and was still quivering inside at the realization that he may never again see Ah-lam and Ching-Lan. On the other hand, what was stopping him from slightly altering the general's plans and going back to Freeland to get his family? Chennault would be gone, and aside from Elmo, who would ever know? Surely, Charlie would not object, or would he?

Jayson made his way through the maintenance shop to where the C-47—parked in a far back corner of the shop—already had a crew of mechanics working on it. In addition to Jayson's Red Cross plane, there were two other P-40s in the shop for repairs and maintenance and several more parked outside under thatched roof open hangars. Jay concluded that Chennault was probably flying one of the fighters, but he was as yet not sure which one.

Jay made his way up the ramp into the Goony Bird. Five mechanics were at work in the fuselage, and among them was his personal mechanic, Elmo.

"Barker, can I talk to you?"

"Howdy Padre, you bet, be right there." Elmo made his way down the ramp where Jay discreetly motioned for him to follow him back behind the tail of the aircraft. "What's up, Captain?"

"I need to know whose side you're on."

"What do you mean?"

"I believe Charlie knew all along that we were not going back to Freeland. I believe he never intended for my family and me to be together in the first place. I want to know if you are involved with him in this scheme, or can I trust you to be on my side?"

"Are you sure you're not getting paranoid?"

"I suppose I could be, but I need to see some evidence of that."

"Well, Padre, it's like this, you're my ticket home. I sailed over as a civilian on the same ship with Chennault when he returned with his new squadron after Pearl, and I'm more than ready to get back home. So if you're going that way, you can count on me to help you any way I can."

"Did you work for Chennault?"

"Yes, as a mechanic, only we didn't have any fancy place like this. We worked under tarps and thatched roof open hangars like the ones outside. Then one day Charlie showed up at Kunming with Chiang Kai-shek in his private Chinese Army DC-2. It looks just like this one except it's smaller and has a red star on the tail. He uses it as his own personal air taxi. So anyway, they show up at Kunming with about two dozen soldiers and a half dozen of Charlie's raiders, and the two of them get together with Chennault, real secret powwow. The next thing I know, me and fifty of Charlie's raiders along with a box of parts and tools are being parachute dropped into your meadow practically on top of this Gooney Bird where I was told to get the thing up and running. So as far as any scheme, I think you're wrong about that. On the other hand, if you are right, you can bet I'm certainly not a part of it. But I will say this, I don't trust Charlie, never have. I believe he's out for Charlie and Charlie only and is using Chennault, you, and his own emperor to accomplish his own personal agenda. He's one smart cookie and capable of a lot more than you might think, so don't turn your back on him. However, there is one thing you can be sure of. He would never let any harm come to his sister, and she is the only one who has any influence over him, and furthermore, he's not going to let you take his airplane anywhere. I'm of the opinion that when he returns from Chungking with those kids, he plans on beating it right back to Ziyou-di. That's about as close as they'll ever get to the United States or Alaska, either one. What happens after that will be up to you, but don't count on any help from Charlie or the general."

Jay actually felt a sense of relief. Surely, the Lord would provide a way to get his family and the orphans out of China at some future time.

"Elmo, I sure hope you're right."

"You also might live to regret it if I am."

"Where does the generalissimo keep his plane?"

"Do you remember that place where I told you Charlie lives, not far from where you bellied this thing in at the foot of that cliff? Well, the gimo stays there from time to time when he's not in Chungking."

"So Charlie knows all the right people, is that what you're telling me?"

"That's about it, Captain, and he knows just how to make them think whatever he wants them to think."

The picture was coming together in Jay's mind, and he knew that he would need to labor with God in prayer on a very frequent basis if he was ever going to get his family and the orphans to Alaska.

"Listen, Elmo, as soon as Chennault is gone, I want you to meet me back in that office where we can go over all the stuff in this suitcase."

"Okay, just let me know. Do you know when he's leaving?"

"I don't know, but I believe one of those P-40s outside belongs to him, so if you hear him fire up and take off, stop what you're doing and meet me in the office, okay? In the meantime, I'll be in the cockpit looking through this stuff." Jay patted the side of the satchel he held in his hand.

"Okay, Padre, I'll see you there."

THE FRUIT OF ATROCITY

"By the way, Elmo, do you know how to find that airstrip where the gimo and Charlie hang out?"

"You mean the headquarters? I think so, I've only been there once though."

"How about Madam Chiang, does she stay there too?"

"Sometimes. However, they never travel together in the same aircraft."

"Okay, thanks, I'll see you later."

"Why, are you planning to fly in to see the gimo?"

"I'm not sure yet, but as soon as I decide, I'll let you know."

Jayson made his way past the workers to the cockpit and closed the cockpit door. The first thing he saw when he opened the case was a bundle about three and a half inches wide, six inches long, and ten inches deep. He tore away a corner of the paper wrapper and found himself staring at a green bundle of good ole American cash. Jay counted it. It was an assortment of various denominations but totaled exactly ten thousand dollars.

Jay remembered Chennault's instructions to give it over to some strangers in Anchorage—strangers who were supposedly going to guarantee the American dream for all of those orphans. But something about the whole thing didn't feel right to Jayson. He was sure God was not saving these orphans so human traffickers could profit from them. Ah-lam had called them *her children*, and if they were hers, then they were Jayson's also. Therefore, they already had a foster home, and he was *not* leaving without their mother.

Jay went over the maps and flight plan that was included in all the paperwork and realized that the general's arrangements for fuel rendezvous were a bit iffy to say the least. Instructions for the first destination included flying to the city of Yinchuan—due north some 845 miles—arriving precisely at the break of dawn. There were no dates associated with any of the rendezvous.

The instructions for the first stop included: initiating a flyover at a nearby lake and landing on a dirt strip one mile to the south of that lake.

From that position, their next rendezvous would take them northeast 1,590 miles to Khabarovsk, Russia. There was no additional information provided. Jay wondered who his contact would be at that rendezvous.

From there, they would continue northeast across the Sea of Okhotsk to Magadan, Russia, a distance of five hours and 992 miles. The final leg of the journey would take them 1,958 miles and ten hours of flight time from Magadan across Siberia and the Bering Sea to Anchorage, Alaska.

The C-47 normally held a fuel range of 2,125 miles, just over ten hours of flight time in calm wind conditions. However, those numbers were published on paper in the operators handbook and therefore about as realistic as a pot of gold at the end of a rainbow. In addition, they were sure to encounter head winds, side winds, and other weather phenomenon, including frequent icing conditions. Jayson was glad for the extra two-hundred-gallon fuel tank he would have on board the aircraft. That extra fuel would theoretically give him an additional two hours of flight time and four hundred miles of range. Then he remembered the deicing problems. Pastor Jay Baldwin once again went in search of his mechanic. He, again, found him in the mess hall, eating.

"If you don't stop eating, we'll have to leave a few kids behind to make up for your fat belly," Jay said playfully.

"I've never tasted any army food this good before. What's up, Padre?"

"I wanted to remind you to check those pneumatic pumps and make sure we have an extra supply of deicing alcohol. We may use a lot of it. Also, check the oxygen supply and make sure our masks are working all right. This will turn into about a thirty-hour trip total air time, most of which will be at night and at the highest altitude we can climb up to, which will put us at about twenty-three thousand feet MSL. Make sure there are oxygen masks available for all the passengers. Also, have the other mechanics rig up a source of heat in the back of the airplane. Those blankets won't be enough at that altitude.

Elmo contemplated the Padre's request. "The heat we might be able to do, but the extra oxygen for the kids we no can do," he replied.

"Why not?" Jay said. An irritation showing in his voice.

"Because we don't have that many masks. Nor do we have any spare oxygen bottles…besides, that kind of equipment is reserved for the pilot crews only."

"I see, then that means we'll have to stay at altitudes below ten or twelve thousand feet to avoid medical issues with the passengers. There's one more thing…we can only fly at night because we have to avoid detection until we're in Russia, so while we're at our rendezvous locations during the day, we'll need camouflage material to put over the airplane."

"Aye, aye, Captain, I'll see to it."

"By the way, Elmo, I've been meaning to ask you, didn't you say you flew floatplanes when you were in Alaska?"

"Sure did, I have a civilian single-engine private license. Why do you ask?"

"I figure it might be a little tough to sleep during the day when we're hiding out, and we're going to need to keep an eye on the airplane at all times, so we'll have to sleep in shifts. Therefore, I may need you to take over flying occasionally while we're en route so I can get some sleep."

"I haven't ever flown a twin engine."

"I'll show you everything you need to know. By the time we get to Anchorage, you'll be qualified to take your test. If you have any trouble, you can wake me. Just be sure you stay on course, can you do that?"

"Yes, sir, I'm an excellent, dead reckon navigator."

"Good, that makes me feel better."

Jay paused for a moment. "Listen, do you hear that?"

"Yeah, sounds like one of the P-40s."

"I wonder if that's Chennault. Do you think he's leaving?"

"Maybe, I'll check." Jayson tugged on Elmo's arm.

"If he's gone, hurry back, and we'll go over the flight plan and course headings. We need to check them for accuracy. Any incorrect headings could cost us precious fuel and maybe even our lives. And one more thing…"—Jayson looked hard into Elmo's eyes—"in case you haven't already figured it out, I have other plans. I'll tell you about it later."

"I think I already know. And don't worry…I would do the same thing."

"I'm going to look the plane over and see if I can find anything else that we may need to fix, but more than anything, I want to keep an eye on those mechanics of Chennault's. I wouldn't put it past the general to have them install some sort of tracking device or something. I've heard they now have portable locator beacons that are set to activate on impact in the event of a crash, and some of them have recording capability and can easily be set to transmit in Morse code continuously during flight. From what I understand, they are starting to put them in aircraft now. Have you heard of that?"

"Yeah, but they're really expensive, and I don't think he would waste all of that on this ship. We're small potatoes compared to the big war. I think Chennault told you that just to cover his own butt with Madam Chiang. I don't think he cares one way or the other whether you go get your wife or not. He just doesn't want to be responsible if you get shot down while you're doing it because if the mission fails, the Madam won't be happy, and she'll expect an explanation from him."

Jayson had to admit, Elmo's logic made a lot of sense.

"I certainly hope you're right," he said.

Jayson worked closely with the mechanics assigned to his aircraft and followed every detail of their work. They were good

THE FRUIT OF ATROCITY

at what they did, and the new pastor felt relieved that his concerns were likely just his own paranoia working overtime. The more he realized it, the more he felt the need to go to God in prayer. Retreating to a quiet place, Jay prayed. The list he brought before his heavenly Father included requests for Divine protection, the Lord's provision for their long journey, and, especially, His blessing on Jayson's plans to deviate and pick up his family. Additionally, the new pastor prayed for safe traveling mercies in respect to the aircraft and in regard to weather throughout the entire trip but, most of all, the safety and future of the children, especially after arriving in Alaska.

Jay Baldwin was in the office studying the maps for his long international flight when he heard a knock and turned to see Elmo at the door.

"I just saw the general dressed in a flight suit headed out to one of the hangars outside." Jay looked surprised.

"I thought he already left."

"That was Tex, testing the airplane, but the general will be gone shortly."

"Great, check out this flight plan, and see if you agree with all of the headings I've calculated and pay attention to the notes I've included. I want us to be on the same page as far as estimated en route times and compass headings are concerned."

Suddenly they heard the rumble of another Allison P-40 engine spring to life and knew that soon General Chennault would be on his way to Kunming, 217 miles west of Anshun.

"I sure hope he doesn't come back," Jayson said.

"Me too, Padre, but I'm wondering if he assigned anyone to watch which way we go when we leave."

"That's no problem I can go north for a little way until we're out of earshot and then turn south toward the Freeland. How long will it take to finish the work on the Gooney Bird?'

"A couple more days at least."

"When is Charlie expected to be back?"

"About the same."

"Did Charlie take the diamonds and guns with him. I haven't seen them anywhere."

"Yeah, I helped him load them, but he only took a small bag of the diamonds. The box is behind the copilot seat where I put them after he left."

"Listen to me, Elmo, if Charlie isn't back here by the time these guys get this airplane finished, I'm going to take it up for a test flight, and you won't see me for about five or six hours. Can you—as inconspicuously as possible—see that it gets topped off with fuel?"

"Sure can, Captain, do you want me to go with you?"

"No, I'll go alone. You need to make sure Charlie doesn't say anything to anyone who might take off in one of those P-40s and tell the general."

"Don't worry, Padre, I got your back."

Two boring days passed since the general had departed for Kunming. Jay awoke at 0600 hours staring at the ceiling from one of six army cots, located in one of the bunkhouses. It was the third morning since their arrival at Hu Shan airbase, and Jay was anxious to get on his way to Freeland. He showered, shaved, and headed out to the mess tent.

When he arrived, Elmo was already engaged in breakfast, and Jay could tell he had gained a little weight since his discovery of the kitchen. The ex-lieutenant made his way through the chow line and joined Elmo at his table.

"Good morning, Barker, you sleep okay?"

"Sure did, how about you?"

"Okay, I guess." Jayson stared at the huge plate of food and additional side of pastry sitting in front of Elmo.

"Every time I turn around, you're in the mess hall, chowing down, are you expecting a famine?"

"I'm just an opportunist."

"Opportunism is a good thing, but what if you get so fat you can't jump on the next opportunity when it comes along?"

"Does it look like I'm not jumping on this one?"

Jay chuckled. "You got me there. How much longer before that extended range DC-3 will be ready to go?"

"They finished all the mechanical stuff last evening and spent the whole night buffing off the green army paint. Should be about ready by now, maybe by the time we finish eating."

"By the time *we* finish, or *you* finish?" Elmo stopped chewing and, without smiling, looked up at Jay. Jayson wagged his head, unable to restrain his grinning.

"Forget it, none of my business." Jay laughed out loud.

Elmo said nothing and went back to eating.

Suddenly both men froze at the sound of a truck parking by the maintenance building. Elmo looked at Jay and said to him, "I'll bet that's Charlie."

"Don't say anything about me going to Freeland. I was hoping they would not be back before I could get out of here. Let me talk to Charlie first."

Jay finished eating and gulped down his coffee, and the two men left the mess hall together in search of Charlie.

Jayson and Elmo emerged out of the mess tent door, passed by one of the P-40 open hangars, and rounded the corner to within sight of the maintenance building. There sat the deuce and a half troop truck, with the US army insignia scrubbed off the doors. Both men stopped short in their tracks.

Sixteen small children sat in front of the maintenance building pressed tightly together in a huddle, appearing totally petrified of what was happening to them.

Like hail on a tin roof, two distinct realizations occurred to Jayson: first, how Japanese their features were, but even more dramatically, how vulnerable they all appeared, so innocent looking, so small, and so terrified. Just five of them were boys. The rest were girls whose appearance struck an even greater cord of empathy within Jayson.

"My God, Elmo…if we don't get these kids out of here, they'll all be dead in a month."

"We'll get it done, Padre…don't worry. We'll get it done."

Guarding the orphans were five of Charlie's raiders. However, for the moment, Jay did not see his brother-in-law. The two men headed toward the children, and in perfect Chinese, Pastor Baldwin said to them, "Greetings, children…my name is Pastor Jay. Are any of you hungry? Would you like something to eat?" Their faces lit up with anticipation, and they moved toward him with a look of excited expectation covering their faces.

"Follow me, and I'll show you the way to the mess hall." Jayson turned to Elmo, who was staring at him with his mouth open in disbelief.

"I'm going to take these kids to get something to eat. Will you find Charlie and tell him where I am and that I want to see him."

"Aye, Captain, but where did you learn to speak Mandarin like that?"

"I took a crash course about a year ago."

"Sounded to me like you had more than a crash course!"

"You're right, it was more than that."

Pastor Jay took the children to the mess hall and, in spite of the looks of consternation from the cook, managed to get them all fed. Jay walked among the children as they ate, talking to each one of them individually, giving them the assurance that they were safe and secure and would soon see their mother—Ah-lam. Many of them understood to whom Jay was referring, and when he mentioned her name, they became very excited.

The door to the mess hall opened. It was Charlie. He motioned for Jay to step outside.

"Jai-sonn, how much general say to Jai-sonn?"

"What do you mean?"

"Where general say we go?"

THE FRUIT OF ATROCITY

"Charlie, the general left, and I have all the information I need. I'm ready whenever they finish with the airplane."

"Airplane ready, Charlie ready, we go now."

"I need to test flight it first."

"No, no test flight we go now."

"Okay, but these children need to finish eating. They obviously haven't had anything to eat in a week. Didn't you feed them along the way?"

"Charlie no have food, Charlie eat now."

"I thought you said you are ready to go."

Charlie made his way to the chow line, and Jay went in search of Elmo. Jayson walked into the maintenance building, and to his amazement, the C-47 was gone, and in its place sat a shiny new DC-3; its aluminum surface—freshly buffed and polished—glistened like a mirror. On the vertical stabilizer had been painted a huge red cross identifying it as an honest-to-goodness hospital plane. The only evidence remaining that it was the same ship they had flown into Anshun three days before was the army green interior and the damaged undercarriage incurred when First Lieutenant Jayson Bold made his fateful landing in the miracle meadow.

It was as if the C-47 had morphed overnight into a DC-3. Jay realized that he also had experienced a similar metamorphose: from First Lieutenant Bold to Pastor Jay Baldwin. Suddenly he felt a symbiotic bond with that ship that he had never experienced before. His heart felt an assurance come over him as he reflected on the metaphor, likening fallen humanity before the Spirit of God comes in and makes a new man in the image of Jesus Christ. Then it occurred to him, like the ram in the thicket that God provided for Abraham when he was about to offer his son Isaac and like the Lord Jesus Christ, who gave Himself as the ram in the thicket for humanity, Jay and his DC-3 were a God-given ram in the thicket for those children. He thought of a very familiar passage in scripture, "Fear thou not; for I am with thee:

be not dismayed for I am thy God: I will strengthen thee: yeh, I will help thee; yeh, I will uphold thee with the right hand of my righteousness" (Isaiah 41:10, AKJV).

Elmo was in the D3 checking the new rigging that would provide secure seating for the children.

"Elmo, is this ship ready to go?" Jay asked, as he entered the cargo hold.

"I believe so, as far as I can tell."

"Did you get it fueled and check the oil?"

"Yesir...did that yesterday."

"Are we ready to roll it out?"

"I reckon so."

Several of the mechanics helped roll the ship out of the door and turn it in the direction of the runway. Jay checked the finished work and rigging.

"Elmo, do we have extra oil if we need it?"

"Yesir, I brought a fifty-five-gallon drum, but the oil that's in it will be fine for at least a hundred hours."

"Well then, let's get Charlie and those kids and get out of here."

Jay was getting anxious to see his beautiful wife and child, yet he wasn't sure if Charlie knew that he had no intention of heading to Yinchuan until he first returned to Freeland to pick up his family. He decided to wait until he was in the air and let him find out for himself. *Hopefully he won't shoot me in the head.*

Elmo said to him, "Here they come."

Jay looked up from where he and Elmo stood by the tail and saw the children following Charlie toward the airplane.

"Let's set up that ramp, Elmo."

Together Jay and Elmo lifted the ramp into place, and the children cautiously entered the huge cargo door. They paused at the top of the ramp, curiously looking at the interior of the big metal bird. Pastor Jay spoke to them in their native tongue, "Welcome aboard, boys and girls, let me show you to your seats."

The children were very cooperative and polite. Jay could see the visible influence that Ah-lam had had on them.

"Is that everyone? Are we ready to go?" Jay looked first at Elmo, then at Charlie who nodded. Elmo gave Jay a thumbs up.

"Elmo, shut that door and fasten it," Jay said. Then he inconspicuously whispered in his ear, "Stand in this cockpit door until we're on the way. Don't let Charlie come through. After we're in the air, you can take your seat." Elmo nodded. He knew that the moment of truth was near, and they were about to find out who Charlie really was—friend or foe.

Captain Jay Baldwin fired the two Pratt and Whitney 1,200 hp Wasp engines and went through the required pretakeoff checklist. As he released the brakes, the Douglas began to roll. Jay taxied to the east end of the airstrip where he began his run up. It was still early in the morning, but the sun was to their backs, and the wind was calm as Pastor Jay Baldwin shoved the throttles forward until achieving thirty-six inches of manifold pressure. The shiny new Red Cross plane rattled and bounced over the rough runway before lifting into the air. As the airspeed increased to 105 k, Jay raised the nose establishing a climb rate of eighteen hundred feet per minute, at 2,350 rpm. Finally, Jay turned to a southerly heading that would take them directly to Freeland.

Charlie stepped up to the cockpit door where Elmo was standing.

"Barker, you sit."

"I will in a minute."

"You sit now." Charlie took Elmo by the arm and physically shoved him into his copilot's seat.

I just wanted to see how the kids were going to do during the takeoff."

Charlie stepped up to the door looking intently out the front windshield.

"Jai-sonn no-go Yinchuan, okay? We go Ziyou-di."

"We will, Charlie, but I'm going to pick up my family first, and don't try to stop me because—what did you say?"

"Charlie say...no go Yinchuan. We take orphans, go Ziyou-di...Freeland."

"That's what I thought you said. Well, then I guess we're on the same page after all." Charlie was silent.

"We should still have time to swing by Freeland and pick up my family and make it to Yinchuan before dark. We should be in Freeland in a little under two hours."

Charlie said to him, "We no go Yinchuan. We go Freeland."

Suddenly, Elmo pointed out the portside window and exclaimed, "Look! There's one of Chennault's P-40s!"

Jay snapped his head around to look out of his portside window, and there, in stride along side of the Douglas, was not only a Tiger P-40 but General Claire Chennault manning the controls. Jay's heart jumped into his throat as a sudden burst of pure adrenaline shot through his body.

Jay looked at the general as though nothing was wrong and saluted him.

General Chennault returned the salute and moved in behind the Red Cross plane.

Jayson said, "What's he going to do, shoot us down?"

Charlie said to him, "General, escort my personal airplane."

"So, Charlie, what's the big hurry anyway. Why didn't Chennault want me to divert to pick up my family?"

Charlie was quiet for a long time, then said to Jayson, "General do only what Madam Chiang say. Charlie work only for the Generalissimo. Charlie say...if Jai-sonn take family, go Alaska, Jai-sonn no more come back to China."

"What's wrong with that? I thought that was the plan."

"Charlie must have airplane for fighting Japanese. Jai-sonn take family and children, go to Alaska, Charlie no have airplane no more."

"Charlie, if you want me to bring this airplane back, I can do that, that's not a problem, but I have to get these children and my family to Alaska where they'll be safe. It won't take that long. I can be back here in two weeks, three tops."

Charlie thought again but for only a moment.

"Two weeks too long. Charlie must have plane now."

"What about the rendezvous and the arrangements that have been made with the underground for our fuel?"

"No sweat. Charlie know many people, fuel no sweat."

"So if we stay and help you with your war, how long will you need me to fly for you and when will I be able to finally get out of here?"

"Two more month, then Jai-sonn go before winter come."

"That's too long, Charlie. The weather will be too dangerous by then. We'll need to go as soon as Ah-lam and the village women can prepare food and clothing for the children."

Elmo looked at Jay. He said to him, "We already have a truck load of rations and blankets."

"I know, but they need different clothes than what they have on and their own kind of food. I'm sorry, Charlie, but this is the way it has to be. Me and Elmo will be back in less than two weeks. Do we have a deal?"

Charlie was silent for a long moment. Finally, he said to him, "Jai-sonn, work for Charlie two week, then go. Then come back before winter, okay?"

Jayson reached back over his shoulder and shook hands with Charlie to seal the deal.

"You got a deal, Charlie, two weeks it is. See, all you had to do was ask me. I would have given you my word. Anyone can tell you, my word is as good as gold."

Charlie was quiet again and moments later retreated to the cargo hold.

Jay said to Elmo, "What do you think, Barker, do you believe he'll keep his word?"

"I think I could do a better job of predicting the weather than predicting what Charlie will do. But my gut feeling says, not in a million years."

Thirty miles out, Jay began to let down for his approach into the cauldron. The P-40 behind them, pulled out in front, wagged its wings, and made a steep turn in the direction of Kunming.

Jay breathed a sigh of relief. Though he never saw Claire Chennault face-to-face again, he already regretted he had ever met him at all.

Chapter 5

The freshly polished aluminum glistened in the sunlight as the DC-3 circled the cauldron encompassing Freeland. Jay slowed the airplane in preparation for the final approach. As the wheels touched the runway surface, he glanced at the small band of villagers gathered alongside the airstrip in the hopes that he would see his wife and child.

Jay taxied the airplane to the far end of the crude runway maneuvering the aircraft in a clockwise circle, parking it under the newly constructed drive-through hangar. Again he looked for Ah-lam in the throng of people but could not find her.

Moments later, the cargo door opened, and Charlie along with his raiders set about helping the children out of their seat harnesses. Jay finished his shutdown procedures and one more time scanned the crowd for any sign of his family; there was none. Concern began to pave the way for the panic trailing close behind until he heard a familiar voice. His heart practically stopped as he whirled around to spot Ah-lam, with Ching-Lan, coming through the cargo door. His cheeks were already wet with his own tears as he took them both in his arms and held them for a long and precious moment.

Groans and gasps for air escaped his lungs as he struggled for control of his feelings. For a time, he had thought he might never see them again, but now they were once again in his arms; overcome with emotions, his body shuddered. "Thank you, God, in heaven," he whispered.

Ah-lam said to him, "You came back to me, my husband, like you said you would."

"Yes, my love, Lord willing I will always come back for you."

Looking around at the orphans, she remarked, "Thank you for bringing my children to me."

"You can thank the Lord. I have accomplished it only by the grace of God."

"Will you hold Ching-Lan while I go to them?"

"I would love nothing more."

Pastor Baldwin gingerly took his little daughter in his arms and followed Ah-lam as she went from one to another of the sixteen five-year-old children that she had nurtured since the day they were born, first in Nanking and then too in Chungking. They knew her instantly and flocked around her constantly.

Jay longed to be alone with his wife, but the children consumed all of her time, and he knew that their emotional needs were more important than his. He held his daughter and followed the children and his wife everywhere they went. Ah-lam appeared to him as an angel that God had sent for them, even as the heavenly Father had sent His only Son into this world for the salvation of all men. If only the world flocked around the Lord Jesus Christ the way those children crowded around Ah-lam, then there would be no more wars, and tears would come only from hearts filled with joy.

By the end of the day, Ah-lam finished treating the children for their nicks and bruises, and the woman in the village contributed to their care and nurturing. Jay looked on wishing they could all stay in the Freeland the rest of their lives.

Finally, he was once again alone with his own family, and as they lay beside each other, he said to Ah-lam, "We will be leaving for Alaska in a couple of weeks. Can the women of the village find some winter clothing for the children and prepare some travel food for them?"

"Yes, I will see to that right away, but I thought we would be leaving in a few days."

Jay thought for a minute, not sure at first if he should tell his wife about his agreement with Charlie. Yet Ah-lam was the only reliable confidant he had and he valued her advice.

"Charlie wants me to fly for him a while before we go. He say's he has things he needs me to do with the airplane."

"What kind of things?"

"I'm not sure, but I agreed to stay for two more weeks before we go. As soon as I get you and the children settled in Anchorage, I will come back and work for him until the end of the war."

"My husband, I don't want you to come back here. What will we do in Alaska until you return, and what if you never return?"

"You're sounding just like your brother. He doesn't believe I'll return either."

"I am so sorry, my husband. If that is what you must do, then I will trust in God to keep you safe until you come back to me."

Jayson rose up on one elbow and looked softly into her eyes.

"It's important that we go before the bad weather comes, and if we don't go in the next couple of weeks, we might be stuck here until next year. Sooner or later, the Japanese will find this place, and I can't take the chance on you and Ching-Lan still being here when they do."

Ah-lam was quiet.

"I suppose it is for the best." She said, "I am surprised my brother agreed to this. It is not like him."

"I'm not even sure he did. He might have just been blowing smoke at me. I told him we needed to leave in two weeks at the latest, so we'll need to have everything ready by then. Even then, we'll probably have to sneak out of here in the middle of the night."

Ah-lam asked her husband, "How much food should we prepare to take?"

"The army provided rations and other provisions, but you and the ladies of the village might want to put together some travel food that the children are more accustomed to. We'll be flying mostly at night and sleeping during the day."

"What about water?"

"We have enough."

"How long will the trip take?"

"About thirty hours of flight time, but we could be a week to ten days getting there if we have to wait out weather conditions."

"What about fuel for the airplane?"

"There is supposed to be fuel available at several prearranged rendezvous along the way. Claire Chennault wanted me to take the children and go immediately and leave you and Ching-Lan behind, but I wouldn't do it. Charlie said he would make new arrangements for fuel if I would wait and work for him for two more weeks.

"What if something goes wrong with the plan?"

"Something already has, but we'll trust in God to provide for that."

"What is it that has already gone wrong, my husband?"

Jay was quiet for a moment. Ah-lam sensed there was something he did not want to share with her, and she rose herself up from the mat on one elbow to look into his eyes. He looked at her and touched her cheek with his hand; then gently stroking her silky black hair, he said, "I am being used by Madam Chiang Kai-shek and General Chennault to fly these children out of China to Alaska under threat of Court Martial if I refuse."

"Why would you refuse?"

"I haven't, it's just that they wanted me to do it immediately, and I wouldn't leave without first coming to get you and Ching-Lan. The general ordered me to leave at once and come back to China after the war to find my family. He said he would see to it that you remained safe. I agreed, then diverted to come for you anyway."

"Oh, my husband, does he know?"

THE FRUIT OF ATROCITY

"Oh, he knows all right, he followed us all the way here. I'm sure he knows a whole lot more than me or Elmo put together. In fact, I'm sure he and Charlie have manufactured a scheme of some sort, and I'm smack-dab in the middle of it. And just like a patch of mushrooms, they're keeping me in the dark and feeding me a load of fertilizer."

Ah-lam laid her head on Jayson's breast and snuggled closer to him.

"I will pray for you continuously, my husband."

Jay Baldwin awoke to the sounds of morning. He lay listening to the birds chirping their elation over being alive for another day, along with the sounds of children already at play in the village. He grinned at the thought of how many parents had kicked their children out of the bungalow at such an early hour so they could be alone with each other for a while.

Jay studied his wife sleeping beside him. Her beauty mesmerized him. He purposely snuggled against her. She moaned and turned toward him, pressing herself against him.

Jay's body began to respond, and he rolled over on top of her. Her arms embraced his thighs, and she began to move against him.

Suddenly, Jay heard footsteps and voices at the entrance of their home. Charlie began calling, "Jai-sonn, you come...we go."

Jay was shocked. He did not expect Charlie to be up so early in the morning. He whispered to Aha-lam, "We may need to put this off until tomorrow. I'll see if I can get rid of him."

"Go away!" Jayson hollered back at Charlie.

"Jai-sonn come, we go now."

"Go where?"

"Charlie coming in now."

"No, stay out, go away!" Jayson's voice grew louder.

Charlie entered through the curtain into their bedroom.

"What're you doing? I didn't say you could come in."

"Jai-sonn, come now, we go Charlie headquarter."

"What do you mean...where's your headquarters?"

"We go see President Chiang Kai-shek."

Pastor Jay Baldwin sat straight up in bed. Ah-lam was clawing at him to stay while at the same time in her native language—forgetting that Jayson could understand—heatedly scolded her brother for intruding into their privacy.

Charlie paid no attention to his sister.

"You come. We go. Charlie men load guns onto hospital plane. We go Charlie headquarter. Charlie take guns Chinese Army. Jai-sonn come back, two, maybe, three hour, no sweat."

"Why don't you ever tell me anything in advance?"

Ah-lam tugged at Jay's arm.

"My husband, do not go. It is not good. You must not go."

Jay turned to his wife. He said to her, "It's okay, it won't take long. You and Ching-Lan can come along."

Charlie retreated through the curtain to another room, and as Jay finished dressing, he asked Charlie, "I thought you traded the guns to get the children out of Chungking."

"Trade only few."

"So this is only going to take a few hours, is that right?"

"You will see. We go now. Bring Jai-sonn family. We all go now."

Jayson remembered the awful feeling that had come over him when he had returned from Anshun and after landing did not see Ah-lam in the gathering of people. His heart had filled with panic, and he dreaded that something terrible might have taken her and his child away. Jay was not completely comfortable with taking his family along to Charlie's headquarters but even more uncomfortable leaving them behind.

Pastor Baldwin and his family, along with Elmo, his copilot/mechanic, Charlie, and fifteen of his bodyguards boarded the hospital plane and prepared themselves for the one-hour flight to Charlie's headquarters. According to Elmo, it was located only ten miles from where First Lieutenant Bold, in his C-47, had met his demise only the year before.

THE FRUIT OF ATROCITY

The morning sun was already rising above the cauldron rim as the Douglas DC-3 lifted into the air, spiraling upward to clear the high terrain that guarded the Freeland. Barely over an hour later, Charlie poked his head through the cockpit door to vector Jay into the headquarters airstrip. It too was so secluded; Jay would never have known it was there were it not for Charlie's directions.

The village was located at the foot of the same mountain Jay had practically met head-on the year before, only from the opposite side. He could see why Charlie did not want to pack all those crates of guns through the jungle and over the high mountains.

Another thought had occurred to Jayson, that when he took his family and the children to Alaska, Charlie would probably never see his sister or niece again for the rest of his life, so it did not surprise him that he might wish to postpone that day as long as possible. He had already mentioned to his brother-in-law that he should retire from his job and come along with them, but his conviction that China needed him, along with his pursuit of revenge, had become a matter of honor. Family ties and friendships were insignificant compared to the debts that he must necessarily settle, as well as his country that he had resolved to defend at all cost. In spite of his deceitful and manipulative ways, Jayson admired the jungle fighter for his patriotism, although he did fear for his soul. At that moment, he sent a prayer to heaven on behalf of his professional killer and brother-in-law.

The shiny new D-3 settled onto the turf strip, and as Pastor Jay Baldwin taxied to the far end of the field, he took in as much of the surrounding area as he could. Long thatch roof huts setting well back into the trees lined both sides of the runway. To Jay, they appeared to be barracks. Armed guards, some carrying Japanese 7.62s and some carrying American-made M-1 carbines, were everywhere, which with Jay served as a testimony of how many Japanese soldiers had met their demise at the hands of Charlie's killers and how many American arms, stolen by the Japanese had ultimately been recovered by them.

Their variety of weaponry included not only rifles and pistols but knives and hand grenades manufactured everywhere from America and Japan to Germany and Russia. He wondered how the raiders managed to find German-made weapons.

They were all a motley looking bunch, wearing those Akubra jungle hats and every description of trousers from stolen Japanese britches to GI fatigues. They appeared at first glance to be undisciplined, but Jay knew it was in appearance only. These were the fiercest fighting men he had ever seen and not only their lives but their country was dependent upon that ferocity. Jay felt fortunate that he was not a Japanese soldier in China.

Tucked away under a drive through hangar, nearly completely out of sight, sat an army green DC-2, with a red star painted on the tail. Jay wondered if the generalissimo was home alone or if the Madam was with him.

"Charlie, is that the gimo's private plane?" He pointed to the Douglas DC-2 (prototype to the DC-3) secluded under the open hangar.

"Maybe President, maybe Madam boss."

"Where do they stay when they're here? All I see is these barracks scattered around in the jungle."

"Jai-sonn see very soon, bring family, we go see now."

"I thought we were going to unload this airplane and head back to Freeland?"

"No sweat, Madam Chiang want see Charlie new niece."

In a few minutes, a two-ton truck with four armed soldiers on board arrived at the hospital plane to escort Charlie, Elmo, Jay, and his family to the headquarters. Jay was surprised to see the soldiers salute Charlie as if he were a high-ranking officer. He had never seen any of the other raiders do that before.

Jay sat on a bench in the back of a canvas covered troop truck with Elmo on one side and Ah-lam on the other. Beside her, on the far side, sat Charlie. The army truck, with the Chinese Nationalist red star painted on the doors, headed down a narrow

THE FRUIT OF ATROCITY

dirt road concealed under a thick canopy of bamboo trees, the tops of which weaved their branches together to provide perfect concealment from above.

The road was a bit rough, but compared to a few thunderstorms Jayson had been in lately, it was a reasonably smooth ride. In a mile, or so, the truck came to a stop in front of a gated steel fence and large stone and mortar guard shack.

"Jai-sonn, we walk now," Charlie said as he motioned with his hand for everyone to disembark.

Jay said to Charlie, "I don't see anything that looks like a headquarters building."

"You come, you see." One of the guards opened the door of the guard shack, and they all followed Charlie down an underground narrow stairway completely encased in concrete with electric lights mounted into the ceiling every fifteen feet. At the bottom of the stairway, they came to another door and another guard, who opened it and saluted Charlie as the procession passed through. Charlie returned the salute.

From there, they traveled along a hallway approximately fifty feet below the surface of the ground through yet another door that led to a large concrete-enclosed room, dimly lit by a lone light bulb in the center of the ceiling. A long table and a dozen chairs, positioned directly under the light, were the only furniture in the twenty-by-thirty-foot waiting room—or was it a holding cell?

Charlie turned to Jay and said to him, "Jai-Sonn stay. Charlie go see boss, come back for Jai-sonn." He pointed to a hinged steel door at the far end of the room.

Jay and Elmo along with Ah-lam and the baby all took a seat at the table except the two armed guards that had accompanied them, who remained standing at attention against the walls.

Charlie pushed a button on the steel door; in moments, the door opened, and an American man in a civilian, dark-gray suit greeted Charlie and stepped aside as he entered. For a moment, he looked at the remaining occupants in the room, then, without expression, closed the door. A hollow metallic click suggested to all in the room that he had bolted the door from the other side.

Jay looked at Ah-lam and said to her, "Are you cold?"

"A little," she said, rubbing her hands up and down her arms. Jay took his fleece-lined leather flight jacket and placed it around her shoulders.

He looked at Elmo and asked, "Do you know what any of this is about?"

"I don't know for sure, but I have an idea."

"What's your idea?"

"I think maybe Charlie is a lot more connected to the big brass than either of us imagined. Did you see those soldiers saluting him?"

"Yeah, what do you suppose that means?"

"I told you, he's a big shot around here."

Jay thought about that a moment and asked, "Do you think we're here because it's Charlie who wants something, or are we here because it's the *boss* that wants something—from us?"

"I'm not sure, but it's probably a little of both."

"By the way, Elmo, are you a praying man?"

"Not normally, but I've been in a few rough spots before where I hollered out at God for some help or whoever it is that's up there."

"Did He holler back?"

"I didn't hear anything. On the other hand, I'm still above ground, so I guess maybe it worked."

"Well, that's good. Actually, there is no right or wrong way. The fact that you looked to God when you were in the rough spots was the main thing."

Elmo studied Jay for a moment and queried, "Why did you ask?"

"Because I think we're about to find ourselves in a rough spot, maybe even several of them, and I think we should pray now so we won't have to holler later."

"I'm with you on that one, Padre, you go first."

Jay took Ah-lam's hand and reached across the table to take Elmo's. The mechanic paused briefly feeling a little strange at the idea of holding hands with another man but then relented by firmly grasping Jay's hand and bowing his head.

"Father God and Jesus Christ our Lord and Savior, lead us according to your will and way into the unknown and unexpected things that are before us. Whatever we must face, we trust it will make us stronger and serve to advance the work of the Lord in the lives of all men. In Christ's name we pray, amen."

The door clicked like a prison gate as someone on the other side slid the bolt and opened the steel door. Jay, Elmo, and Ah-lam all turned in unison to see who would be coming through the door next. The man in the gray suit stepped through, and behind him stood a captain of the US Army Air Corp. Jay gasped and stood so fast he knocked over his chair.

"Carl!" he said in elated surprise, "Carl Prichard! What on earth are you doing here?"

Captain Prichard stepped toward Jay, his hand outstretched in greeting. "Hello, my friend. I guess I can't call you lieutenant any more, can I?"

"No! Matter of fact, as far as the military is concerned, I'm officially dead, or so I've been told. But it looks like you are doing well for yourself. I see you finally made captain, which comes as no surprise to me. So what are you doing here, or did I already ask that question?"

"Why don't you folks come in and join us. We're in the process of discussing your future." Carl patted Jay on the back and smiled as if there was something humorous about his statement.

"We'll see about that. Who is *we*? You got a mouse in your pocket?" Jay said returning the grin.

"By the way, Carl, I'd like you to meet my wife and daughter. This is Ah-lam."

"I heard you were married now, congratulations, and the little one, boy or girl?"

Ah-lam gleamed as she spoke for the first time, "Girl, her name is Ching-Lan."

Carl paused to admire the precious package and said to them, "Beautiful, absolutely beautiful." Jay beamed with pride.

They all followed the man in the dark-gray suit through a modestly furnished but well-lit apartment—apparently a guest room—through to a set of double doors opening into an adjoining conference room furnished with another long table providing seating for at least twenty-four people.

"Have a seat here," Carl said, pointing to the closest end of the table. Captain Prichard politely seated Ah-lam and asked, "Can I get anything for you or the baby?"

"I need to feed her. Should I do it here or in there?" She nodded toward the room they had just passed through.

"If you can wait a moment, our host will be here any minute. After the introductions, you can excuse yourself for that reason."

Jay asked, "Who are our hosts?" Carl was about to answer when they all heard voices coming from another room past the far end of the table and on the other side of a sliding door.

Moments later, the door to the adjoining room opened and in walked none other than Generalissimo and Madam Chiang Kai-shek.

Everyone stood and bowed appropriately as the president and his wife, the Minister of the Chinese Air Force, entered the room. The informality associated with their introduction put Jay at ease, and Ah-lam was soon proudly showing her baby to Madam Chiang.

Then, in perfect "Wesleyan" English—tinted with a Dixie Land accent—the Madam asked, "How old is she?"

"She was born on May 19 at five o'clock in the morning."

THE FRUIT OF ATROCITY

"She is so beautiful," Madam Chiang said as she stroked the baby's cheek.

Ah-lam smiled and graciously thanked the Madam.

"Are you comfortable? Would you rather sit on a couch in another room?"

"As a matter of fact, I do need to feed her."

"Of course, let me show you to where you will be more comfortable."

The Madam led Ah-lam through the next room to an adjoining sitting room and seated her on a couch next to a reading lamp. From a cupboard, she found a shawl and covered Ah-lam and the baby for privacy. "Thank you, Madam President."

"You are very welcome. But it is I who must thank you for what you have done for those poor children. I had no idea there were babies born out of the atrocities in Nanking until Charlie brought it to our attention. I immediately felt concern for their welfare and yours. I am going to help your husband and you get them out of China and provide a sanctuary for them."

"Oh, thank you, Madam, thank you so very much."

"There are towels in the cupboard if you need to change the baby, but now I must talk with these gentlemen that are waiting for me. Your baby is so beautiful."

"Thank you, Madam, you are so kind, and it is such an honor to meet you."

The man in the gray suit talked privately with Generalissimo Chiang Kai-shek. Jay began to get the impression that he possibly represented the US government in some capacity. He knew that Carl obviously represented the army but was no longer sure in what capacity. All he had ever known about Carl was his role in the war effort that consisted of flying freight over the hump, as Jay had done during the fifteen months before his life-changing mishap. Except, Jay did recollect that he had not seen Carl for the last four months of that time.

Jay and Carl chatted about old times and *Lieutenant Bold's* bumpy landing in the meadow.

Charlie listened intently to the conversation between the gimo and the gray suit. Speaking only when spoken to and much more respectful, polite, and subdued than Jay had ever seen him. It was completely obvious that Charlie was, as well as a man of many faces, a man of many hats, one of which was a major player in the fight for Nationalist's China's future.

Madam Chiang returned to the conference room and moved to the head of the table to sit next to her husband. The mystery man in the gray suit sat directly across from her on the opposite side. Carl seated himself next to him, and the man handed Carl a large pad and pencil. Charlie sat next to the Madam, and Jay and Elmo sat at the far end facing the dignitaries.

The man in the gray suit was the first to begin speaking, "Ladies and Gentlemen, if there are no objections, I suggest that this meeting be conducted in English." The man waited a moment as everyone agreed. "My name is William Cheney. I am the National Security Advisor to the President of the United States of America and head of the Office of Strategic Services, most recently designated the OSS.

"Thank you, Generalissimo and Madam Chiang Kai-shek, for your hospitality as host nation to the United States Army Air Corp and your cooperated efforts with the army in ridding China of its invaders. We both know of course that the success of that endeavor will be dependent upon your continued cooperation. Furthermore, let me assure you that, united, we shall prevail.

"Now, allow me to introduce Captain Carl Prichard, representing the Army Intelligence unit stationed in Ledo, India. Captain Prichard is the liaison between US Army intelligence and China intelligence, and because this meeting classifies as *Top Secret*, Captain Prichard will serve as the recorder. All determinations and agreements arrived at here today shall be made an official matter of record."

THE FRUIT OF ATROCITY

Suddenly it hit Jay like a bolt of lightning. *Captain Prichard, US Army Intelligence. Charlie Nee, China's head of Intelligence. They've all known all along what happened to me—that little worm.*

Cheney continued, "We have special guests here with us today, which include Charlie Nee, the head of China's Central Intelligence, who is our source for frontline knowledge of troop movement and activities of the Japanese operating in Burma and Western China."

Everyone applauded and Mr. Cheney continued, "Approximately one year ago, Mr. Nee sadly informed us of the tragic loss of one of our pilots. I would like to read you the report at this time.

> On June 13, of last year—1943—First Lieutenant Jayson Bold, while flying his C-47 transport over the hump from Ledo, India, to Kunming, China, was in fact fired upon by a Japanese Zero. That engagement resulted in his crashing into the jungle of Burma. Charlie Nee and his patrol of resistance fighters were witnesses to the event. Mr. Nee reported the loss of the American transport and its pilot to Generalissimo Chiang Kai-shek, who subsequently reported it to General Claire Chennault at the Kunming airbase in the Yunnan Province.
>
> The US Army officially documented the loss of that aircraft and its pilot and declared the aircraft unsalvageable and the pilot as MIA (missing in action). Lieutenant Bold's body has never been recovered.
>
> On that same day and aboard that same aircraft was a Protestant minister, a missionary, by the name of Pastor Jay Baldwin, who the resistance fighters found still alive and whom they rescued from the crash site. Charlie and his men carried Mr. Baldwin across the border into China to a place of safety where they provided him with treatment for his injuries and recovered him to health.

"This account is the army's official record of the fate of First Lieutenant Jayson Bold. We would like to welcome Mr. Baldwin here today, and thank you, sir, for coming. Also, we all care to congratulate you on your marriage to Charlie's sister Ah-lam and your recently newborn child."

Jay acknowledged the meager applause from each of the government officials with thank-yous and gestures of appreciation but was somewhat taken aback by the carefully manipulated scheme that the two intelligence agencies had cooked up. He actually felt like he had just attended his own funeral.

Cheney continued, "America is now at war with the Japanese and has been since December 7, 1941. However, we are in China at the request of Generalissimo and Madam Chiang Kai-shek, and the future of China is dependent upon the successful outcome of our combined efforts in ridding China of its aggressors. Due to the United States's huge investment of men and equipment in the European theater, President Roosevelt has extremely limited resources to lend to the war in China. The president of the United States deeply regrets this unfortunate circumstance and has asked me to convey those regrets to the General and Madam Chiang Kai-shek."

Madam Chiang glanced at her husband who sat expressionless and unresponsive. Then gracefully she acknowledged the US president's gesture.

"Please tell Mr. Roosevelt we understand fully. The war has practically engulfed the entire world. It is so terrible."

Cheney continued, "The president also would like me to make it perfectly clear that this decision in no way implies that China's distresses are of any less importance in the eyes of America or her allies. Therefore, the president is committed to ramping up the flow of cargo and supplies from India into China in support of the Chinese Army and its air force.

In addition, the efforts of the Flying Tigers and their unprecedented accomplishments in achieving so much, with so little, have inspired us all to match their example in resourcefulness. Therefore, Mr. Baldwin, we have asked Charlie Nee to bring you here today for a reason. Madam Chiang Kai-shek, would like to appeal to you for your help in a certain matter at this time."

Cheney sat down, and the Madam stood up; she began to address the group, "Please let me, on behalf of the people of China, thank you, Mr. Cheney and Captain Prichard, and especially you, Mr. Baldwin, for accepting our invitation to meet with us today."

Suddenly, Jay noticed the chair beside him was still unoccupied and wondered what was taking Ah-lam so long. He thought maybe the baby was feeding longer than normal or maybe had fallen asleep, and Ah-lam didn't want to disturb her.

The Madam continued, "I also would like to extend China's special thanks to Charlie Nee, who has, much like General Chennault, accomplished so much, with so little…"

Elmo leaned against Jayson. Whispering into his ear, he said, "How come she has a southern accent?"

The madam continued, "Several years ago, Charlie informed me of his sister's efforts to care and provide safety to sixteen, mixed race, Chinese/Japanese orphans, housed in an orphanage in Chungking.

Jay whispered back, "She was educated in the United States, went to a Methodist College in Georgia."

"These children, through no fault of their own, are the product of the terrible atrocities in Nanking by the Japanese soldiers during which time they murdered and raped over eighty thousand Chinese women and girls in a span of only three weeks time…"

"You're kidding! Is she Christian?" Elmo whispered again.

The madam did not hear them and continued, "These orphans have little chance of a future in China and certainly none in Japan. They are children, born without a country, and the morals of both China and the United States demand that we provide for this unfortunate circumstance… "

"Yes, so is the gimo. At least he professes to be. Now, sh," Jayson answered.

"When Charlie informed us of the downed aircraft and the pilot that had survived, we immediately informed Captain Prichard who in turn passed the information on to Mr. Cheney. In spite of our limited resources, we saw an opportunity to provide a way to get those orphans, victims of the Rape of Nanking, out of China to America where they could live in safety. It is certain that were they to remain in China, their lives would not only be constantly at risk but most surely lost.

"We would like to officially express our gratitude to General Claire Chennault for his part in salvaging the downed aircraft and converting it into a private hospital plane no longer affiliated with the military. Also, through the ingenuity of the Intelligence people involved, the missionary pilot rescued from the crashed transport plane has accepted the mission of flying the orphans out of China to the territory of Alaska." The Madam looked at Jay and smiled. Jay thought there was something facetious about it, but nonetheless, he smiled back—facetiously of course.

The Madam continued, "Earlier this past week, General Chennault provided this pilot the opportunity to participate in an immediate plan that would have gotten the children already on their way to Alaska with the help of the Chinese regulars and some underground affiliations. Had Mr. Baldwin followed the general's instructions, we would not be having this meeting today. However, Mr. Baldwin chose to divert from his mission, to Ziyou-di, not wishing to leave without his family.

"Today, China's head of Intelligence, Mr. Charlie Nee has informed me that he wishes to use the hospital plane and its pilot for covert operations into Burma and India, which is, deemed by all here, vital to China's National Security and success in the war against the Japanese. Lieutenant...excuse me...I mean, Mr. Baldwin, we desperately need your help. My proposal to you, sir, is this: if you will agree that after you return from delivering the orphans to Alaska, you will work with Charlie toward the accomplishment of these National Security operations, we will reestablish the connections necessary for you to take the orphans to Alaska within the week. During which time, I will personally see to it that your family is protected and cared for until your return and during your service to China. After the war, when Mr. Nee no longer is in need of your services, you may take your family and return to America."

Jayson was shocked, and along with his heart rate, his blood pressure was shooting through the roof. Glancing again at Ah-lam's still vacant chair, he stood to excuse himself.

"With all due respect, Madam Chiang, I need to be excused from this meeting for a moment."

Jayson turned toward the door of the conference room and hurried into the adjoining room where he had last seen Ah-lam and Ching-Lan—they were gone. Hurriedly he checked the adjacent rooms: bedrooms, bath, closets, and the sitting room— there was no sign of his family.

First panic set in, then anger. Infuriated, he returned to the conference room; standing before the high-ranking officials, he demanded, "What have you done with my wife and child?"

Charlie stood and said to him, "Jai-sonn, no sweat, sister and niece okay. Charlie take very good care of sister and niece. Jai-sonn not to worry. Jai-sonn work for Charlie, family still here, no sweat."

Jayson's heart was pounding in his chest. How dare they hold his family hostage? Incensed and indignant, the normally affable, amiable, genial, and all-around good-natured country boy from Sikeston, Missouri, recently designated as a missionary to China, felt betrayed by not only his brother-in-law but his own country, the country for whom he had practically lost his life while serving.

Struggling to regain control of his emotions, Jayson, still standing at the end of the table, paused to survey the panel of government officials.

Elmo saw the rage that had welled up in his pilot and imme-diately became concerned that he might retaliate and do something unforgivable, something that would make matters much worse for not only Jayson, who was his ticket home, but Elmo as well. For that reason, he tugged on Jay's coat sleeve in an effort to restrain him until he could get control of his anger.

Every person in the room waited in silence to see what would happen next. Then, Carl stood along with Charlie, and the two began to make their way toward the ex-lieutenant. Jayson pointed his finger at Charlie and said to him, "You, sit down. If you come any closer to me, I'll tear you apart." Charlie froze and said nothing, but a dark scowl covered his countenance.

Carl Prichard moved next to Jay and placed his hand on his friend's shoulder.

"Jay, listen to me. It's actually better this way. Charlie will be gone a lot from Freeland, and most of his men will be gone with him. Freeland will be virtually unprotected while they're out on patrol. Your family will be much safer here in the headquarters bunker."

Jay slowly turned his head to look at Carl. "So you have been in on this with them all along, is that right?" He jerked his thumb toward Charlie. "My family can go with *me*. They don't need to be held hostage to guarantee my return. They'll be safe when I get them to Alaska where they can stay with my brother until I return, which I have already given my word that I would do. And I have already agreed to work for Charlie as soon as I return for as long as he needs me. Turning to Madam Chiang Kai-shek, Jay continued, "Don't misunderstand me, Madam Chiang, I appreciate what Charlie and his men did in saving my life. I certainly would not have lived through that ordeal without their help. I am deeply indebted to China for that. But I must protect my family at all cost. I am at your service and am willing to help in whatever way I can. However, I cannot, under any circumstances, leave my family behind. I must insist that they be allowed to go with me. Once I have them settled and have provided for them and the orphans, I will be glad to return and serve China in whatever capacity I am needed.

William Cheney rose from his seat and said to Jay, "Lieutenant, let me remind you of something General Chennault already brought to your attention. This is not an option for you. You are still under orders from the United States Army Air Corp, and if you refuse to follow these orders, you will be returned to your original identity and rank and potentially brought up on charges of not only disobeying a direct order but desertion. I suggest you accept these terms, and in return, I will provide the proper passports and documents for your wife and child that will secure their safe and unrestricted international travel as soon as your commitment with the Chinese government is completed. At such time, you will be free to take your family and return to the United States.

"Mr. Baldwin," Madam Chiang said to him, "I know this is very difficult for you, but this war has been difficult for everyone. Let me say, it is my personal opinion that your family would be at greater risk if they go with you when you take the orphans to Alaska. If something were to go wrong, your wife and child may be lost forever, and I would personally regret that very much. Therefore, China would like to harbor them for you in the event of that worst-case scenario. If you are lost during this very dangerous endeavor, I pledge to you that your family will be provided for and your child will be given every educational opportunity China has to offer. I will also see to it that *you* are honored as a hero in the war that saved China, and your memory shall be preserved in perpetuity."

Jay thought carefully for a long moment and said to her, "Madam, it would have been nice if you could have put it that way in the beginning instead of assuming that I would not keep my word and presuming to kidnap my family. However, because you have already presumed to kidnap my family and intend to hold them hostage, I must insist that you release them immediately and let me take them with me to Alaska. I will return as soon as I can and agree to work for you until the end of the war. Those are the only terms I can agree to." Madam Chiang turned to face Charlie.

"Mr. Nee, I am inclined to believe this young man. Personally, I do not see what difference two more weeks could make. Would you be willing to let Mr. Baldwin do this?"

Charlie watched Madam Chiang closely as she spoke to him. He said to her, "Charlie no can do."

"How about you, Mr. Cheney, would you be willing to trust Mr. Baldwin?"

Cheney looked at Charlie and back to Madam Chiang. "No, madam, I'm sorry, but it is a matter of the utmost importance that we begin these operations as soon as possible."

Jayson glared directly at Charlie, who glared right back. Jayson said again to the Madam, "May I see my family before I go?"

Pausing briefly while glancing first at Charlie, she answered, "Of course you can, Mr. Baldwin, I will see to it."

Generalissimo Chiang Kai-shek rose from his position at the end of the table and followed William Cheney into the next room from which they had initially emerged. The Madam lingered, talking to Captain Prichard and Charlie.

As far as Jay was concerned, they had all conspired together to kidnap his wife and child, initiating an additional war along with the one they were already fighting, only the new war was personal for Pastor Jay Baldwin.

Jay struggled with deep feelings of betrayal and resentment. He could think of nothing else but how long it would be until he would see his family again. Anger had taken control of his mind and would not let him go anymore than he wanted to let the anger go. Somehow, he knew *that* terrible anger would play a vital role in his survival. He vowed to keep it for as long as it took to win this private war with Charlie that had officially begun.

Although, Jayson knew, for the time, he must cooperate with Charlie for the sake of his family's safety, a ruthless vengeance had already began to smolder within him. For a brief moment, he thought of the prayer he had prayed earlier as he sat hand in hand with Elmo and Ah-lam. His prayer for God's provision and strength for any potential *rough spot* suddenly seemed surreal and long ago. Unexpectedly, in an effort to make room for his rage, he had shoveled his faith in God into the dark recesses of his consciences where it no longer had control or influence over his reason.

Jay rose from the table and turned to retreat to the room where he had last seen his family. There, standing in the doorway of the next room, was Ah-lam, guarded by two armed soldiers. The gimo and Cheney stood behind them conversing together. Ah-lam had realized that for some reason, she would not be going home with her husband, and tears were already streaming down her face.

Jay went to her and wrapped her in his arms.

"Where is Ching-Lan?" he asked.

"She is sleeping in another room. What is happening, my husband, why have they separated us?" Jay pulled her to the side where he would not be overheard.

"They want me to take the orphans to Alaska and then come back and fly for Charlie. They are afraid I might not come back so they are going to keep you here while I'm gone to make sure I do come back. Ah-lam, I want you to know that I love you and our child more than my own life. I will come back for you no matter how long it takes. You must believe that. If I cannot find you in Freeland, I will look for you in Chungking. Go to the airport and leave me a clue how to find you. I will be back before winter, and at every opportunity, I will look for you."

"I love you too, my husband, be careful. I too will look for you. I will always wait for you, and God will keep us safe until we are together again."

Jay felt a hand take hold of his arm. It was Charlie. Spinning around, he deliberately broke loose from his grasp.

"Jai-sonn, we go now." Jay clenched his fist and, before he could consider the consequences, planted a left cross squarely on Charlie's chin, knocking him backward onto the floor.

Charlie landed on his back and in an instant was back on his feet with Jay's own Colt .45 out of its holster and aimed directly at Jay's head. Jayson turned back toward Ah-lam, reaching out to her in a final gesture of affection. She ran to him, sobbing.

"No, my husband, do not fight them. God will bring us together again. Do not fight them." Jay opened his mouth to speak...when suddenly, everything went black.

Chapter 6

Jay awoke to the noise of jeeps, army trucks, and a canopy of trees against a background of blue sky and fluffy clouds. He was lying on the wooden floor of a Chinese Army troop truck, bouncing relentlessly over a bumpy road. Someone had placed his flight jacket under his head. His neck felt as if it had been broken. He would have slipped back into unconscious, but the jostling over the rough dirt road brought him fully awake.

Around him, sitting on the truck benches, were five of the armed guards that worked for Charlie along with Elmo and Captain Carl Prichard. From his prone position, he could not see for sure but assumed that Charlie was riding in the front seat. Jay expected they were on the way back to the airstrip.

He tried to get up, and both Elmo and Carl reached for him to give him a hand.

"What happened to me?" Jay asked, rubbing the back of his neck.

Elmo spoke first, "Charlie laid some of that Chinese kung fu on you when you turned your back to him."

"That little snake, where is he?"

Carl spoke up, "You'd better leave it alone, Jay. If you escalate this any further, you could jeopardize your mission to the point you may never see your family again, much less get those orphans to Alaska. I know you're angry, but right now, it would be better to be smart. I suggest you apologize to Charlie, work something out with him, and get on with the business at hand.

Jayson realized his actions had been irrational and the direct result of his failure to trust in God, and if he didn't get back to trusting Him immediately, it would only get worse. The rest of the way to the hangar, he prayed, "Lord God, I have made a huge mistake. I feel like Moses, when he struck the rock out of frustration. Give me back my right mind, I pray."

The deuce and a half halted in front of the DC-3 hospital plane, and Jay and Elmo disembarked and conferred together over the present circumstances while Captain Prichard conversed with Charlie.

Soon Carl called to him, "Pastor Baldwin." Jay had not yet grown accustomed to his new name and hesitated before answering. Slowly he turned around and faced his one-time friend.

"What do you want?"

"Your trip to Alaska is postponed for a while due to your irrationality. We are all going with Charlie to Ledo tonight. This will be a very important mission, and the first of many. I suggest you do not let your personal feelings get in the way. Charlie is the boss, and that comes from higher-up, not only from the Chinese government but from our government as well. He is a bigger fish than you think he is, and although you don't realize it, right now, he's your best insurance for getting your family and those kids to Alaska successfully.

"Furthermore, I want you to know one more thing. I was not in agreement with this plan. This came from Cheney, Charlie, and the gimo. They are the ones who didn't trust you. I tried to talk them out of it. I tried to tell them that you were a man of your word, and if you said you would come back, then you would. But you have to understand, in this war, there is too much at stake to take somebody's word for something that involves national security. They need insurance. So there you have it. Let's just get this thing done and get this war over. As far as Charlie is concerned, when he's in the field, he works for me. I'm the only one who has any influence with him. I'm the one who tells him what we need of him, and he is the one who gets it for us. He will be far more effective with you and your airplane than ever before.

Jay, you do this for me, and I'll take care of you and see to it that you get your family back. You have my word, and anything else you need, just let me know."

Jayson looked at the captain. A sinister expression came over his face. "Your word or Charlie's word, neither one means a bag of squat to me anymore. You say my trip to Alaska is postponed? I say, none of you had any intention of letting me go in the first place. So don't insult me with that *postponed* business. Let's just get this show on the road—what is it you want me to do?"

Prichard studied Jay for a moment. He glanced toward the ground as a look of disappointment came over his face. He said to him, "There are several missions you need to do before you go that cannot wait. I'll fill you in on them when we get to Ledo."

"You guys have already failed to follow through with everything you've ever told me. How do you expect me to trust anything else you say?"

"Jayson, it will only take a couple of weeks. Don't worry. Sometimes things change, and we can't predict when that's going to happen."

"I'm not the least worried! Do you know why?"

"Why?"

"Because I have my own agenda, and nothing is going to stop me from getting *that* done, not you, not Charlie, and certainly not this war. If you guys can change the rules any time you want, so can I."

"Jayson, I'm begging you, don't go there."

"Tell Charlie I want my Colt .45 back, or I am not going to fly that airplane tonight or any other time." Jay turned and headed up the ramp into the freighter.

A couple of the ground crew personnel were working inside the plane as Jay entered the cargo hold. Making his way to the cockpit, he checked the secret compartment behind the copilot's seat to see if the box of diamonds was still where he had hidden it. He found it still intact and unmolested along with the ten thousand dollars Chennault had given to him and the five thousand that belonged to Elmo.

He then checked his briefcase to make sure his maps and rendezvous information was still there. Breathing a sigh of relief, he went in search of Charlie.

Jay could not remember ever exhibiting any violent behavior before and was as surprised at himself as everyone else. The anger that had driven him to react the way he did toward Charlie had diminished a great deal until he was actually feeling a bit ashamed. Both Madam Chiang and Carl had made perfect sense, and it occurred to him that it was actually the Lord, who was behind the decision to hold his family in protective custody until his return, maybe even the end of the war. A terrible dread come over him at the thought of not seeing Ah-lam or Ching-Lan for possibly several more years.

It was late in the afternoon when Jay found Charlie. He was in one of the barracks talking to some of his men. Jay noticed immediately he was not wearing the sidearm.

"Charlie, what is the plan, are we going back to Freeland or staying here tonight?" Charlie slowly turned to Jay, his face set like stone and his eyes glaring into his.

"We go at dusk, go Ledo, India, take Captain Prichard and Mr. Cheney to army headquarters. Then we load airplane and come back here. Jai-sonn live here now. Stay in barracks with Charlie's men."

"You want me to land here at night?"

"We leave Ledo early morning, land here twilight tomorrow morning."

"Why can't I stay with my family in that underground bunker?"

"Sister and niece leave morning light with Madam Chiang, go Chungking."

"Who is flying the Madam's aircraft?"

"Chinese pilot fly for Madam boss."

"Why don't you get a Chinese pilot to fly for you?"

"All Chinese pilots fly for Chinese Air Force, no pilots to spare for Charlie. Besides, Chinese pilots no fly nighttime."

"What makes you think I want to fly at night?"

"No can fly in daylight, enemy can see, only fly night. Fly day-time...maybe get shot down."

"Really? I have news for you. Confucius say, 'Fly night, hit mountain.'"

Charlie thought a moment and replied, "Chinese pilot fly night hit mountain. Jai-sonn fly night, no hit mountain."

Jay's face lit up in surprise. "Charlie, was that suppose to be a compliment?"

Charlie pointed to Jay's neck and said, "Jai-sonn okay?"

"Yeah, it's okay, you got me pretty good though."

"Charlie so sorry, Jai-sonn hit Charlie pretty good too."

"Yes, I did, except you didn't stay down as long as I did, plus you deserved it. But I apologize anyway. I was kind of mad at you, still am for that matter."

"Charlie understand, but sister and niece no safe Freeland, no safe here, family safe Chungking with Madam Chiang, safe from Japanese and safe from communist party."

"Charlie, you won't ever get me to believe that, so if I were you, I'd give up trying."

"Jai-sonn make plane ready, we go soon. Charlie make sure everybody ready to go."

Jay turned and headed toward the airplane. He felt a little better about getting his hard feelings squared away with Charlie but still did not trust him or Cheney or anyone else for that matter, except maybe Elmo.

Jay entered the cargo hold and made his way to the cockpit. Elmo sat in his copilot's seat going over some charts and making notes in preparation for their night flight over the mountains.

Elmo said to Jay, "Did you make peace with Mr. Nee yet?"

"Yeah, we're real good friends. Why do you ask?"

"Well, I don't want him to leave us hanging anywhere just because you guys can't get along."

"He won't do that. He needs us too much to leave either one of us hanging. We did settle up, but he only apologized because he knew he had to. If he didn't need us, we would be dead by now. At least I would. Do you have your numbers all lined up for getting us to Ledo?"

"Yeah, we'll depart northwest, straight ahead until reaching six thousand feet, then make a left turn due west until we get to fifteen thousand feet. We'll maintain that heading for about three and a half hours until we start picking up the NDB (non-directional beacon) signal from our ADF (automatic directional finder). Those numbers will give us a good three thousand feet of clearance above the highest terrain in that part of the Himalayas. From there, we can adjust our heading to the northwest again and proceed direct to the station. Have you ever landed in Ledo at night before?"

"Yeah, about a hundred times. I don't have the approach plate, but I remember the procedure and the radio frequency. I'm not sure if anyone will be on duty in the tower or not and don't know what our designation is, but I can ask Carl when he comes on board. I'm sure someone will be expecting us. It seems to me they've had this whole deal worked out from the very first day Charlie stole my Colt .45."

"Speaking of that, look behind you."

Jay jerked his head up to look at Elmo, who was pointing at the cockpit wall behind Jay's head. There, hanging from a coat hook, was the ex-lieutenants 1911 Colt .45. Jay climbed out of his seat and belted the weapon around his waist. It felt good, and suddenly he felt as if he was in the army again and back in the war.

The two pilots heard voices outside and footsteps on the ramp. Looking in the direction of the cargo door, Jay saw Charlie and Captain Prichard coming aboard the plane.

"Carl, I have a question. What's our designation, and will there be anyone in the tower when we get to Ledo?"

Captain Prichard reached into the breast pocket of his flight jacket and pulled out a folded piece of paper, which he handed to Jay.

"Your designation is 'R-C-347,' and your call sign is 'D-C-3.' They're both written on this paper."

Jay looked at the paper; it read: "Radio Charlie 347 / Delta Charlie 3."

"You and your navigator should memorize them, then burn the paper. You will monitor and transmit on the CTAF (Common Traffic Advisory Frequency), which is secure. When you are approaching the airbase, you will make your initial transmission from ten miles out and the last transmission when you're on a two-mile final to land. At that point, you will get either a green light to land or a red light signal to not land. If you get a white light signal, you're to circle the field until you receive further instructions, be it a red or green light. As soon as you get the green light, the runway lights will turn on and stay on until you have finished your taxi to the hangar. A pilot car will be there to guide you in. At no time will you audibly speak into the microphone. Your transmissions will consist of microphone clicks in Morse code, for both your initial and final transmissions. If you are having an emergency, you will add the Morse code emergency signal SOS, to the tail of each transmission. Are there any questions?"

"Yeah, while they're loading the aircraft for the return flight, where will my navigator and I go?"

"There's a secure briefing room where you can get some rest or food, whichever you prefer. Also, I have secured your personal items from your barracks, and they will be available for you to take back with you, or if you wish, I can mail them to your family, just let me know."

"I'll take the stuff with me when I go, and when I get to Anchorage, I can leave it with my brother. What all will we be loading for the return trip?"

"You will have two jeeps, a small pallet of medical supplies and a medic whose only other option is going to the brig, I hope you don't mind."

"Is he going to be part of our flight crew?"

"Yes, I'm giving him to you. He'll be your man, not Charlie's, so you can use him anyway you want. He's extremely resourceful, which is why he's in trouble so much. If you need anything else, let me know before we land."

Jay patted his Colt .45.

"Thanks for getting this back for me."

Carl's face reflected a puzzled look, and he said to Jay, "I forgot to say anything to Charlie about that. I thought maybe you had."

Five of Charlie's raiders were ready and waiting for the captain and Mr. Cheney to take their seats. Jay turned to his brother-in-law.

"By the way, Charlie, thanks for returning my weapon. However, I also need a box of ammo and extra ammo clips. And could we get a couple of carbines with ammo for Elmo and me up front?"

Charlie looked at Jay and smiled. "Jai-sonn ready now for war. Charlie can do carbines for Jai-sonn, okay."

Jayson felt a small sense of guilt at the thought that Charlie could see the self-preservative war like nature emerging from within him that he had kept invisible for so long. He had even sensed it himself. Yet no matter how hard he tried, he couldn't check it. The more of the war he saw, the more he felt compelled to pick up his end of the sword. Right or wrong, he now realized that his family, the orphans, and China itself were dependant upon him never hesitating to pull a trigger again. He wondered, *Did Charlie kidnap my family on purpose to bring this side of me to the surface? God help me.* He prayed silently.

Tar pots, lined each side of the runway, spaced a hundred yards apart, and men with torches ran from one to the other, lighting them as darkness fell upon the raider's base camp headquarters. Jay let the two 1,200 hp Pratt and Whitney engines warm as he and Elmo went through the before-take-off checklist.

"Elmo."

"Yeah."

"While we're climbing out, I need you to keep an eye on the engine instruments for me. Call out oil temperatures and pressures every few minutes, okay?"

"Aye, aye, Captain. I can take care of that. You just keep this tub right-side up, okay?"

"Don't worry, I've flown this thing through IMC [instrument meteorological conditions] for hundreds of hours as a single-man crew. It's the takeoff and landing part that makes me sweat. Prichard said they have electric runway lights at our destination. I sure hope he's right. We didn't have that when I used to fly in and out of there. They must have hooked up generators or something. I wonder what other amenities they have now."

"Are you worried that anyone will recognize you?"

"I doubt anyone I knew will even be awake. The 47s worked mostly in the daytime. Only the C-46 Commandos worked around the clock."

The last of the runway lights flickered to life as they cast their yellow and orange hue across the dimly visible dirt strip. The surrounding mountains were swallowed up in the darkness of night as the ground crew signaled to Jay they were cleared for takeoff.

The Douglas DC-3 lurched over the runway as the two P&Ws roared to full power. Soon the tail lifted off the ground, and Jay transferred his attention from the view outside of the windshield to the instrument panel inside. Carefully but with determination, he pulled Radio/Charlie 3-4-7 upward into the blackness of the night sky.

The only light in the cabin come from the glow of the instruments, which provided just enough light to make out the dim profile of his copilot/mechanic/navigator sitting across from him.

"Have you ever been to Ledo before?" Jay asked without taking his eyes off the instruments.

"No, I came by boat to Rangoon and was trucked up country to Lashio, where I boarded a transport just like this one, only on that trip I sat in the back. From there, I went to Kunming and wrenched on P-40s for a living."

"Sounds like you've come up in the world, in more ways than one."

"Yeah, well the only problem is, I don't know if I'm still working for a living or working myself into an early grave. By the way, we're passing through five thousand, only one thousand to go before you begin your first turn. Your initial heading is 3-1-0 degrees. From there, you'll take it on up to fifteen thousand, where you will level off and turn to 2-7-0 degrees. Maintain that heading and fifteen thousand until the ADF needle begins to wake up, should be about a three-and-a-half-hour ride all together. After you get a lock on the station, it's your airplane. You can fly the approach whatever way you want to."

"Thanks, Elmo, there are actually two stations. One is located on top a mountain above the Assam valley about seventy-five miles northeast of the field. That's the one we're heading to now. Once we cross it, we'll be able to pick up the second station, which is the initial approach fix, located five miles west of the airfield."

"So we're going to cross the airfield and then come back to it?"

"Yes. Our crossing altitude at the initial approach fix is six thousand feet. From there, we'll fly outbound from the station for two minutes and initiate a procedure turn that will put us inbound back to the same station. After we complete the procedure turn and are established on the inbound course, we can make our initial transmission. When we cross the station the second time, inbound, we'll descend to the MDA [minimum descent altitude], make our final transmission, and wait for them to turn the lights on for us.

"I need you to clock the time after station passage, should take about four minutes at twenty-nine inches MP. Hopefully, they'll give us a green light, and we won't have to climb back up and do the whole thing all over again."

"Sounds like you've done this before."

"Yeah, a few times. The stars are out, so without a cloud cover, the fog sometimes sets in but tonight, the air seems fairly dry. Hopefully, it will stay clear. However, when we go to leave in the morning, fog could definitely be a factor."

Elmo thought about that a minute and said, "What about the end we just departed from, what if it's all socked in when we get back?" His pilot did not answer.

The drone of the aircraft engines was mesmerizing, and the conversations between Jay and his navigator soon fell quiet. Jay's mind envisioned what Ah-lam might be doing. He wondered if she had heard the airplane when they departed from the headquarters airfield. He wondered also if she was asleep by now or lying awake thinking of him as he was thinking of her. Jay wondered what time the gimo's plane would depart in the morning and would there be a chance he might be able to see his wife and child one more time before they were taken away.

He could feel the adrenaline surging through his heart and sensed the anger rising once again.

"Why God, did it have to happen like this? I would have come back, why did you let them do this?" he cried out.

"Did you say something?" Elmo asked. Jay did not answer.

"Your needle is coming alive."

Jay checked the activity on his ADF and saw that the indicator was starting to move and would soon settle on the heading that would take them directly to the first navigation station known to all the pilots as the *Burma Fix* NDB.

With little wind to consider, they would be able to fly a direct line to the station. He said to Elmo, "Keep your eye on that dial, and read me the new heading whenever that needle quits flickering around. We're still a little too far out to get a solid fix, but we should have it in another thirty miles or so."

"Too bad we don't have two of these instruments. They're a real neat deal. Them poor flyboys dropping bombs in Germany could probably use one of these NDB stations set up smack-dab in the middle of Berlin."

Jay glanced at Elmo. "I'm sure that would go over real well with the Fuhrer."

"It sure would cut down on a lot of the Allied losses. A whole lot of flight crews have gone down from just plain getting lost and running out of fumes," Elmo replied.

"Definitely a novel idea, which makes me wonder why *this* facility hasn't been destroyed by now."

Elmo pointed to the ADF indicator. "Charlie has a hundred of his men guarding it. That's why."

"Really? I knew someone had to…but I didn't know it was Charlie."

Elmo continued, "Yeah, Charlie is a real live, walking war hero. After this war is over, he'll probably get a shrine or something built in his honor."

"If he crosses me again, he might not live long enough to see it."

"There's your altitude, Padre. Turn right sixty degrees to 3-3-0. I'll let you know when the needle swaps ends indicating station passage. From there on, it's up to you, but at that point, you should be able to descend all the way to your crossing altitude. What did you say that is?"

"Six thousand feet over the initial approach fix."

"Will you begin your descent out of six thousand after crossing the fix or after you come out of the procedure turn?"

"We'll maintain six thousand until we have completed the procedure turn and are established on the inbound course. Then we'll start letting down to our crossing altitude over the final approach fix. From there, it's a good seven miles to the airport, so we'll have plenty of time to get down to the MDA.

Elmo, what was the name of that town in Alaska where you said my brother is living?"

"It's not a town yet, just a roadhouse, but it's called the Wasilla Junction."

"I need to send my brother a post card. Can I address it to General Delivery Wasilla Junction, Alaska?"

"That should work. How long will it be before we pick up those kids and head that way?"

"I'm not sure, but it sounds like Prichard has a few things for us to do before we go."

"Are you planning on dropping sixteen kids off on your brother's doorstep and then hightailing it back here before winter?"

"I'm going to send him a letter and give him a heads-up that we're coming. Maybe he can make some arrangements before we get there. I'll tell him we have money, but I'm not going to try to send him any."

"Maybe he could get some church group to take them."

"I don't know. Sixteen kids are a lot of kids. I'm not sure how this is all going to go down. I was counting on Ah-lam to help me with this whole deal, but she's no longer part of the equation. For that matter, my brother might tell me he doesn't want anything to do with it. If that happens, we might be there too long to make it back before winter. This whole thing is getting more and more complicated. So, Elmo, are you going to come back with me or stay in Alaska?"

Elmo did not reply but pointed to the ADF indicator and said, "There goes your needle. We just crossed the Burma Fix. What's the frequency for the next one?"

Jayson looked at his notes. "Five, two, three."

As Elmo dialed in the new frequency, the ADF needle immediately spun in the direction of the next station associated with the NDB approach to the Ledo Army Air Field.

Jay banked the airplane to his new heading and reducing manifold pressure to twenty-nine inches, initiating a five-hundred-foot-per-minute rate of descent from fifteen thousand to six thousand feet. Other than a faint glow of light from a crescent moon now behind them in the southeastern sky, his memory of the eighteen months he spent flying the Hump, along with that one little needle pointing toward the station, was all the eyesight he had. Through the windshield he could see nothing but darkness, and with every tick of the clock, the ground was growing closer.

"How's it going up here?" Jay recognized the voice of his one-time friend Captain Prichard. He no longer was sure that Carl had the same priorities as Jay but knew that for now he was about his surest bet. Also, Jay was not convinced that Charlie really did take his orders from Carl. His impression was that Charlie was his own boss and used everyone he come in contact with, including Carl, to advance Charlie's own agenda. It seemed to Jay that anyone that thought Charlie was working for them only thought so because Charlie wanted them to, as part of his agenda. Jay was sure that Charlie was smarter than all of them, which made him the most dangerous. On the other hand, Charlie just may be reliant enough on Carl and his resources to reciprocate in the interest of his own cause. Jay only wished he understood better *his* role in that cause, or for that matter, the cause itself.

"We're dialed into the initial approach fix," Jay answered in response to Carl's question. "We have just begun our descent."

Prichard tapped Elmo on the shoulder.

"Barker, I hope you don't mind, but I'd like to trade places with you."

Elmo seemed surprised; he wasn't sure if he should be offended that he was being replaced or happy that there would be two competent pilots at the controls in the event of a problem.

Jay interrupted, "Not happening, Captain, this is my airplane, and I want Elmo to stay right where he is. If you wanted to sit there, you should have said so before we left. I'm about to begin this approach, and I need you to go sit down and fasten your safety harness."

Carl stared at Jay with a shocked expression on his face but, without saying anymore, returned to his seat in the cargo hold.

"Thanks, Padre, I think we'll make a pretty good team."

Jay grinned back and said to Elmo, "I think it's time we let them know who's really in charge."

The hospital plane emerged from the procedure turn and began its descent to the assigned crossing altitude. Pastor Jay Baldwin repeatedly clicked his microphone as he sent his call sign "DC3" in Morse code, then crossed the final approach fix, and began his descent to the MDA.

Leveling off at the minimum descent altitude, he sent his last transmission. Seconds later, a green light flashed from the control tower. In only a few moments, the runway edge lights lit up, and there before him lay a very familiar ten thousand feet long concrete runway.

Jay slightly corrected his flight path to align with the center of the runway where he gently set designation Radio/Charlie, 3-4-7 firmly onto the runway.

"Welcome to India, ladies and gentlemen," he said.

"Good job, Captain, that's five times I've survived flying with you. I hope that's not some kind of record."

The aircraft rolled freely to a taxiway exit from the runway where a jeep sat awaiting their arrival.

Slowly he taxied the hospital plane toward the vehicle that led them to a large enclosed hangar where ground personnel signaled him to continue his taxi into the huge structure.

Jay went through his shutdown procedures, and as the large hangar doors rolled closed behind him, the lights suddenly flooded the interior of the building and the aircraft cabin.

It had been almost a year and a half since he had been in Ledo, and for a moment, he felt the nostalgic feeling that he was home again. He thought of Ah-lam and his little child Ching-Lan and reminded himself that now, *they* were his home, and until they were all together in Alaska, he would never truly have a home again.

Jay and Elmo disembarked the aircraft behind their passengers while the ground crew personnel began preparing the aircraft for loading.

It was a new facility built since Jay had left Ledo to begin his odyssey. It was the largest and longest hangar he had ever seen. There was room for at least four more cargo planes of just about any size. The jeeps, intended as their cargo, were sitting in close proximity to the aircraft along with what appeared to be a small pallet of medical supplies. The Red Cross emblems plastered all over the intended cargo appeared to Jay to be more for the purpose of appearance than cargo identification. Jay thought, *First, they make my C-47 into a hospital Red Cross plane that is actually used for underground resistance warfare, and now they are giving us Red Cross Jeeps, a pallet of medical supplies, apparently, and a medical corpsman whose only other option appears to be life in prison.* Jay wondered where he was going next that would necessitate these deceptive tactics.

"Pastor Baldwin?" Jay turned around to see an army enlisted man approaching him and Elmo.

"Yesir, that's me. What can I do for you?"

"Where do you want me to stash my gear?"

"What gear, who are you?"

"I'm your new corpsman, Corporal Raylan Jaworski. I've been assigned to your crew."

Jay looked at Elmo, and Elmo looked at Jay and said, "Maybe it's going to be three against the world instead of just us two."

"Still doesn't sound like very good odds. Well, Corporal, you're not a corporal anymore. From now on, you're just Jaworski, and I'm your boss, and this is Elmo your other boss. Do you have any civilian clothes?

"Yesir."

"You'll need to give me your military ID. I'll get Prichard to get you some Red Cross ID or something."

"The captain already did that, sir." Raylan handed Jay a passport identifying him as a Red Cross volunteer worker.

"Did Prichard give you any other instructions besides reporting to me?"

"No, sir, Captain Prichard just sprung me from the brig and said to report to a Pastor Baldwin in building B, so here I am."

"What were you in the brig for?"

"AWOL. I missed my flight back to the base from Calcutta."

"They put you in the brig for that?"

"Well, it was the third time in six months."

"Join the club, Jaworski. Shucks, I've been AWOL for a year and a half. Let me make one thing clear, however, you will be working for me from now on, and I expect your undivided devotion to my orders, or I send you right back to Captain Prichard, is that understood?"

"Yes, sir."

"If anyone else associated with this mission tries to abscond with you, you will report it to me, is that understood?"

"Yes, sir. May I ask where it is we're going?"

"I don't know for sure, but in a couple of weeks, we'll all be going to Alaska, and you'll be doing some babysitting for me."

"Alaska? Babysitting?"

"That's right, now stow your gear in the tail of that Red Cross plane. That's where you'll be living from now on. Are you a good medic?"

"Yesir, the best."

"Why do you keep going AWOL?"

"I keep falling in love with girls when I go to town."

"I see, well, we're all done with girls for a while. From now on, you belong to me and to this man right here. His name is Elmo and he's our copilot, navigator, and mechanic. You'll help him with whatever he needs your help with, got it?"

"Yesir."

"Okay, hurry up and stow your gear and come with us. One more thing, corpsman, do you know how to shoot?"

"Yesir, I am a very good marksman."

"Can you shoot the enemy if you have to or did you become a medic because you're a noncombatant?"

"Actually, they made me a medic as part of my all-around specialized training."

"Specialized, what is your specialty?"

"Sniper, and other stuff that might come in handy."

"Sniper?" Jay looked at Elmo.

Elmo said to him, "That could come in handy, Padre." Jay didn't reply.

"Okay then, is the chow hall in the same place it used to be?"

"Yes, sir."

"All right then, let's get some breakfast."

Raylan Jaworski stowed his gear. Both men grabbed a few extra pairs of mechanics coveralls from the shop and, together with Pastor Jay Baldwin, found their way to the mess hall.

"Raylan, find the head chef around here and get us a bunch of sandwiches to take when we go, while I find you an army issue sidearm."

"Yesir, but I already have a sidearm, sir."

"Good I want you to wear it at all times."

"Yesir."

"You too, Elmo, you need to keep yours on also."

"Aye, aye, Captain."

The growing crew of the Red Cross plane sat at a table, chowing down in the mess hall when Captain Prichard entered through the bomber-hinged double doors.

"Mr. Baldwin, I see you've met your medic," Carl said.

"Yeah, we've met."

"He should come in handy for a variety of things. Did he tell you he speaks fluent Japanese and Russian?"

Jay's eyes opened wide, and he remarked, "Really? No, he didn't mention that. No wonder the ladies keep falling for him."

"Let me give you a heads-up into what you will be doing for the next month."

"Month!" Jayson exclaimed with his mouth full.

"That's right, first, you will fly back to Charlie's headquarters, where you will unload one of the jeeps that are on your aircraft. Then you will fly Charlie, and a dozen of his men, to Lashio, Burma, where you will unload the men and the remaining jeep. Next, you will fly back here, to Ledo, and pick up a load of fifty-five-gallon drums of aviation fuel, which you will also take back to the headquarters. There you will unload the fuel and reload the other jeep, along with another pallet of medical supplies and another dozen of Charlie's men. Then you will return to Lashio and disembark both the men and their jeep.

"Charlie and his men will still be there waiting for you. However, keep your eyes open. After that first incursion, the Japs may be watching the place. As soon as Charlie's men unload the jeep, you guys slam that door shut and scram. From there, you will return back here to Ledo, but stay low until you are well into India.

"As long as Charlie is in Burma, I want you to keep hauling fuel from Ledo to Charlie's headquarters for the next several weeks, around the clock, as many trips as you can make. I will let you know when to go back into Lashio to pick up Charlie and his men. Are there any questions?"

Jay asked the captain, "Yes, I have a couple. I thought I would be leaving for Alaska in no more than two weeks."

"Sometimes things change. It's the army way, next question."

"Will we make two extractions to get the men and the jeeps back out or will we just take Charlie and his men and leave the jeeps?"

"We'll cross that bridge when we get to it. There are two deuce and a half troop trucks on the way to Lashio as we speak. They are also disguised as Red Cross trucks. They will be loaded with Red Cross people and supplies. Their job is to set up a temporary medical aid station at the grass field airbase. If all goes well when Charlie and his men return, they will leave the jeeps at the aid station and come back in those troop trucks.

"This cover operation will come in handy because there will be more incursions yet to come. This is mostly a fact-finding effort. We will formulate the plans for our next move when Charlie brings us the information we need. However, I can tell you this. It's all part of a strategy to take Burma back and reopen the Burma Road. Charlie and his men will be working together with a British squadron called Merrill's Marauders. As soon as they have gathered the intelligence we need, we will bring in the P-40s and B-26 bombers and hit them where it hurts. You guys are our secret agents so to speak. We are depending on you to get this fighting unit into Burma without raising a lot of interest from the Japanese command, therefore giving us some element of surprise."

"What if we run into resistance at Lashio while we're waiting for Charlie?"

"I'll provide you all with BAR 7.62 automatic weapons, ammunition, and grenades for that very scenario. Whatever you do, do not let Charlie or any of his men confiscate those weapons. They are for you. Your orders are to protect that airplane at all cost, and just between you and me, that means at *all cost*. Do I make myself clear? I do not want any Jap soldiers left alive to tell their people

THE FRUIT OF ATROCITY

some story about a hospital plane dropping off Chinese *Militia*." Jay looked at Elmo, then at Raylan, and back to Carl.

"Okay, I think we got it."

Carl handed Jay a brown hard paper file folder. "Here are papers documenting your affiliation with the Red Cross and your work as aid workers from the United States. Your cover work is primarily to provide medical treatment to civilians and rescue orphans.

When you go back to pick up Charlie, he will bring with him some Burmese woman and children. Keep them on board and take them with you when you return to Lashio. They will help to legitimize your cover as Red Cross volunteers working in Burma. You will be in and out of there frequently, so make it look real. You men try and get some sleep. You'll need to be airborne by 02:30. Good luck, gentleman." With that, Captain Prichard turned and walked out of the mess hall.

Elmo studied Jay.

"Did you write that letter to your brother yet?" Jay paused for a moment before answering.

"No, I think I better hold off for a while."

The Red Cross transport plane taxied its way toward the warm-up area just shy of the hold short markings to the active runway. The time was 0225 hours military, and Jay with his copilot/navigator were once again about to be airborne for their return trip to Charlie's headquarters base.

"Elmo, it's time you got some stick time on this freighter. I'll manage the power settings, and you pull this tub into the air for me. You have ten thousand feet of concrete in front of you, so just let it fly itself off the runway."

"Are you sure?"

"I'm sure. Maintain runway heading until you reach five thousand feet, then turn a right crosswind to seven thousand, then another right to the downwind Continue your climb to eight thousand feet. When you reach eight thousand turn northeast to

191

cross the airport at midfield. You should be at ten thousand feet by the time you get to that point. After that, just keep climbing to fifteen thousand direct to the Burma Fix, the same NDB we crossed last night up on that mountain. I'll call out your altitudes to you."

"Aye, aye, Captain, are we cleared to go?"

"Watch that tower. As soon as we get a green light, you can taxi into position and take off at your discretion."

"Padre, there's a vehicle coming toward us on the taxiway, looks like it's in a hurry."

"Jai-sonn, no stop." Jay looked over his shoulder to see Charlie standing in the cockpit doorway. "Jai-sonn fly now, fly now." Jay and Elmo both reached for the throttle controls and shoved them forward to full power; the freighter immediately lurched ahead.

"He's pulling out onto the runway. What should I do?" Elmo yelled.

"Keep going. I'm betting he moves before he lets us run over him."

"It's the military police. Elmo cried out."

"Dang it! Charlie, what did you do? Did you steal something from the base?"

"Charlie no take, Jai-sonn take."

Closer and closer the hospital plane came to the four MPs seated in their jeep, broadside on the runway.

Elmo screamed, "They're trying to move, but it looks like they killed the engine, and they're pointing their weapons at us."

Jay yelled, "Pull up! Pull up!" Elmo hauled the yoke all the way back to his chest, and the transport lifted off the ground. Jay watched the jeep disappear from view under the nose of the DC-3 as four Military MPs scattered in as many different directions.

As the plane passed over the jeep, Jay felt a bump against the left main landing gear.

"I can see why you wanted me to do this instead of you," Elmo said, his eyes bulging half out of his head.

"Sorry, buddy, I wasn't expecting anything like that. You did just fine. The tower will probably give you an alternating red and white light. That will mean, circle and return for landing. Don't do it, just keep going. That little bump didn't feel like it could have caused much damage. We'll keep our eyes on the hydraulic fluid pressure gauge. We can check for any gear damage when we get back on the ground in China.

"What do you suppose that was all about, Padre?"

Jay looked behind him to see if Charlie was still in the cockpit; he was gone.

"I don't know, but I'm going to find out. Do you have this ship?"

"I got it, Captain."

Jay unbuckled himself and exited the cockpit to find Charlie. He was talking to one of his men. Both of them were sitting in the forward jeep that they had loaded back at Ledo.

"Charlie, what do you mean 'I take.' What did I take that would bring the military police down on our heads?"

"You take prisoner." Charlie pointed at Jaworski sitting in the aft end of the fuselage. "Captain Prichard no tell military police he take medic. He take prisoner from brig for questioning, then no bring back."

"Oh great, I suppose when we come back, we're all going to get arrested?"

"No sweat, Captain Carl fix by then, no sweat. Jai-sonn do good, no stop for police. Charlie no have time for police."

Jay returned to his seat and said to Elmo, "The cops were after Jaworski."

"That sounds just like the government, the right hand doesn't know what the left hand is doing."

"Yeah, and we're the left hand. In other words, the ones that get *left—hanging*. Hopefully Carl will have that all cleared up by the time we get back."

"Yeah, and while you're hoping, you can add that landing gear to the list."

Daylight was breaking and casting its twilight shadows across the Yunnan province, revealing a million pockets of fog lying in the many canyons and ravines of the Himalayan foothills. Elmo turned toward home and began his descent into the headquarters base camp.

"You did a great job, Elmo, let me take it from here. I'm going to do a flyby and see if I can see the runway from directly above. Look for a tree sticking up through the fog, near the end of the runway. When we begin our approach, we won't be able to see the airstrip, and we'll have to let down into the fog. We need a landmark to tell us where the tree line ends, or we might bump that landing gear again."

Jay passed over the base camp area and could see the tops of the trees that outlined the perimeter of the camp. There, at the northeast end of the strip, was one lone snag sticking out of the fog.

"We'll come back around and let down just inside that snag. Elmo, did you say you are a float pilot?"

"Yesir, sure am."

"Well then, you should be familiar with this, it's what you float pilots refer to as a glassy water landing."

"Oh yes, I'm very familiar with it, and that's what scares me."

"The rest of us cargo jockys call it a carrier landing. I expected we might have to deal with something like this, and before we left, I memorized exactly where the edges of this runway lay in relation to the barracks on both sides of the field. I also remember that snag."

Elmo stared at Jay like a sane man stares at someone who appears to be a full cup shy of half full. He said to him, "If that was supposed to make me feel better, it didn't."

Jay slowed the Douglas to just above stall speed and brought in enough power to control the descent as the overloaded freighter crossed over the snag and descended into the ground fog. Once again, forward visibility disappeared, and both members of the flight crew held their breath for what seemed like an eternity.

Jay's grip tightened on the yoke in anticipation of what might happen next in the event that his judgment had been off just a little. He felt the aircrafts descent rate slow as they entered ground effect and reduced power while raising the nose for the final time. Finally, *thunk.* the freighter was on the ground.

Jay chopped the power and let the tail settle to the turf. The forward visibility was not much better than zero, but they could see the outline of the edges of the runway through the side windows. Jay let the airplane coast to a stop and went through the shutdown procedures.

Elmo exhaled. "Whew, I hadn't even realized I'd stopped breathing."

"The good news is we're alive and the gear held up," Jay said.

"I'll jump out and check it," Elmo said, breathing a sigh of relief.

Jay remarked, "I never thought I would be elated to see fog in here, but it means that the boss's plane probably hasn't taken off yet, and I might be able to see my family before they go."

"You want me to park this thing while you go watch for them?"

"No, I am going to leave it right in the middle of the runway until the fog clears. I'm sure they won't be leaving before then anyway."

Charlie and his men had the cargo door already open and had disembarked the aircraft by the time Jay worked his way around the jeeps and other cargo.

Jay exited the cargo door as Charlie and his men returned with a flatbed truck hauling a loading ramp for removing the jeep.

"Charlie, has the general left yet?"

"Boss all gone, Jai-sonn family all gone."

"I thought you said they weren't leaving until morning?"

"Boss fly away early morning."

"Did they go to Chungking?"

"Charlie not know, boss no say. Charlie work now, unload jeep, gas up airplane, then we go. No time for family, family wait for after war. Jai-sonn must now move airplane to fuel dock."

Jay was extremely disappointed but not surprised. As yet, no one had ever kept their word with him, and he knew that from now on whenever he thought about his wife and daughter, he would have to put them in the hand of God until His almighty hand gives his family back to him. Until then, there was only one thing he could do, and that was his part in getting the war over, getting those orphans to America so he could return to find his family, no matter how long it would take. Oh, how he wished he had taken them along when he left for Anshun. They would all be together in Alaska by now. The anger that had welled up in him the day he knocked Charlie to the ground had returned, this time to stay. At that moment, Jay came to a final conclusion: Someday, Charlie would cross him for the last time; someday he would go too far, and Jay would put an end to Charlie's interference in his life. The thought sent a cold chill up his spine.

Chapter 7

In the fall of 1935, Jayson Bold along with a Christian youth group from Sikeston attended a baseball game in St. Lewis, Missouri. The hated New York Yankees were in town for a three-game set against the St. Lewis Cardinals. Dizzy Dean had hit Lou Gehrig with an errant pitch. Casey Stengel was so furious he kicked dirt from the home plate all over the umpire's shoes, a childish reaction that got him tossed. That was the only game St. Lewis won in the series. Jay remembered wondering how a person could ever get so mad he would be capable of such immature behavior.

Jay had seldom heard a cross word or seen such dysfunctional behavior from any of his immediate family. Jay's father was the epitome of patience and maturity; his mother, of kindness and pleasantness. On the other hand, Arthur, Jay's older brother, was not only capable but often guilty of becoming irrational under duress. Even Jay himself, when circumstances seemed to give a fellow no other choice, could get angry enough to throw down a tool or kick something and walk away from a project until he cooled off enough to think straight. On a farm in the Midwest during the depression, it was not wise to get mad and break things. It cost too much to replace or fix them, and all the equipment was vital to the farm's function.

Jayson's Christian experience was very real. His heart and mind had settled into the truth of the Gospel, and he lived each day as though his actions might make a difference in what someone else should think of his Lord and Savior Jesus Christ.

The challenges of everyday life cemented his trust in God as he sought the Lord for the solution to every problem, watching the hand of God at work and the arm of God move in answer to all his prayers.

To Jayson Bold, Christianity was an experience, not a religion. As he visited the variety of denominations around the area, he noticed that most held to the position that theirs was the only True Church; *their* take on the doctrine of God was the best and only *true* take.

Jayson did not believe that way. To him, all the various Christian faiths contained gems of the gospel, certain unique understandings contributing to that more complete and thorough whole. He realized that God did not care what church a man joined or had affiliation with or what doctrine he held too as opposed to his neighbors. To God, only one thing mattered: *What have you done with My Son?* Those, were the words Jayson imagined the Divine God in heaven had to say to every soul.

Is the Son of God your Lord and Savior? Is *He* your life, hope, substitute, and surety? Those were the questions Jayson considered as the most important for every man to consider.

Jayson also observed that about the only thing organized religion had actually accomplished was denominationalism, a form of separatism which had done more to divide the *body of Christ* than it had to unite them. Only the gospel of the Lord Jesus Christ and His sacrifice on behalf of all mankind was truly able to unite the people of God or, for that matter, the human race.

Jayson had pondered these and many other questions until he arrived at the conclusion that all true Christian believers were bound together by the Spirit into one body—*the body of Christ*—and *that* is what comprised the *one and only Church*, by which all believers are united by the one common denominator, that threefold work of Christ on the cross: redemption, reconciliation, and propitiation accomplished on behalf of *all* humanity through Jesus Christ the Divine Son of God.

But like Christ's disciples whose faith was tested in the fires of doubt, while they witnessed their Messiah and King, hanging on a disgraceful Roman cross, like the Christians of Martin Luther's time who sang songs while their bodies burned at the stake, Jayson too would find his metal tested in ways he could never imagine. His early lessons of trust in God and faith would ultimately be his only tangible connection to the hope that he someday would eventually be reunited with his family.

With his new name, Pastor Jay Baldwin, Jayson Bold found he had not only a new identity but a strange new intention that had come over him as well. Once amiable by nature, he suddenly had taken on a definitive determination. Suddenly, he had a new purpose for his life. It wasn't just about himself anymore or, for that matter, just his family. It was bigger, much bigger. It was about winning a war that would ultimately save thousands upon thousands of lives. It made him feel alive, alive without fear or doubt about what he should or should not do or even if he would survive. Faith in God had risen to a new level. He thought of a scripture his mother had taught him from the time he was a small boy. "Whatsoever thy hand findeth to do, do it with thy might; for there is no work, nor device, nor knowledge, nor wisdom, in the grave, whither thou goest" (Ecclesiastes 9:9–11, AKJV).

Who were these *Japanese* that they should assume to destroy the people of China as though they were any less human than they? So they could lay claim to their country and resources? What incredible arrogance.

Who do the Germans think they are, that they should condemn every other race to extermination for the sake of single-handedly ruling the world uncontested?

Jay thought back in time to the prophecies of Daniel and how history had fulfilled so accurately the biblical predictions.

The book of Daniel chapter 2, the dream of Nebuchadnezzar: The great image with a head of Gold, representing the kingdom of Babylon; the chest and arms of silver, representing the joined kingdoms of the Medes and Persians; the thighs of brass, representing the mighty Alexander the Great and the kingdom of

Greece. Finally: the legs of iron, the Roman Empire, all of which aspired to the same common goal—one-world government, one-world power reigning alone and uncontested without share of kingdom or rule.

Then, the feet, a mixture of iron and clay with the ten toes representing the ten kingdoms Rome eventually was divided into. And ultimately, the great *Stone* cut out of the mountain without hands, representing the Kingdom of the Son of God coming down from heaven and smashing the image in the feet, demolishing and grinding and destroying every other kingdom of the earth that has set itself against the Most High God and His Divine Son Jesus Christ.

Methodically, Jay traced the history of nations since Daniel's day to see the repeated attempts of man to achieve the thing God had said would never again be—one-world government.

He reflected on a book he once read about the history of the American Indian and its many tribes, each tribe viewing the other as if they were not human, a view that gave each tribe the right to slaughter their neighboring tribes without conscience. Such thinking destroyed any chance of their collectively succeeding against the European incursion of white men.

Years later, after WWII, Jay talked with a Japanese soldier still living in China who was part of the atrocity in Nanking, China, in December of 1937. He asked him why and how could a people with families of their own, living in their homeland, invade another country and justify the terrible atrocities that took place. The old Japanese soldier confessed that they had all been brainwashed into believing that the Japanese were the only true humans on earth, that the Chinese people were only so much livestock and like cattle or pigs or the water buffalo should be slaughtered to make way for the real human beings from Japan. What a striking similarity to the mentality of the Native American Indian in their relationships between the tribes of their own culture. Similarly also was the view of the colonist's as they slaughtered their way across America, stealing it from the Native American Indian whom they had labeled subhuman savages.

What nation has the right to judge another as nonhuman and slaughter them until they are no more?

What church has the right to claim that they are the only *true church* and condemn all others to the flames?

What religion has the right to declare all others as infidels and declare holy war for the purpose of the ultimate extermination of all people who are not of their persuasion?

When will mankind understand that from God's perspective all men are in Christ, all men are saved in Christ, all men are human, because Christ is human, that all men, through Christ, are both human and divine because Christ is both human and Divine, and all men are in Him? *Maybe, Jay thought, when they have seen enough, of the fruit of atrocity. Until then, as long as there are men whose ambitions are to rule the world, the righteous, of a necessity, must take up arms against them. The responsibility lies with the ones who see and understand the insanity behind the ambitions of governments and nations seeking power and control of the masses through one-world government. The Bible has predicted it would never again be until the Kingdom of God would reign supreme on the earth.*

Jay breathed a sigh of conscience revelation. "I see," he said. "I see…God has placed the burden on those who are willing to pick it up, those who will stand to fight and sacrifice even their very lives against tyranny and oppression so that succeeding generations of all nations may live free. I understand better who Charlie is. I now understand who I am and to what purpose the Lord has called me."

Pastor/Pilot/Jay Baldwin turned south as he crossed the Burma Fix NDB and descended to a few hundred feet above the terrain.

The DC-3, designation R-C-347, carried a jeep, a dozen more of Charlie's men, their equipment, and medical supplies along with its crew.

"How far is it to Lashio?" Elmo inquired.

"I'm not sure. It may be a little hard to find. I hope we don't wake up too many Japanese looking for it. Watch for an area about thirty acres square with a dirt road running alongside the turf airstrip. I think maybe sixty or seventy miles from our present location."

"Are we going to unload and get the heck out of there or stick around to see if company shows up for dinner?"

"You heard the captain. He said unload and go regardless of what Charlie wants."

"Where's Raylan?"

"Right here, sir."

"Raylan, will you go get Charlie for me."

"On my way, Boss." Raylan poked his head through the cockpit door into the cargo area and hollered for Charlie, motioning for him to come to the flight deck.

"Jai-sonn find Lashio okay?" Charlie asked, as he leaned into the cockpit.

"Not yet, but we're getting close. Listen, Charlie, when we get on the ground, we need this thing unloaded as fast as possible. We're running a little late, and it's already daylight. Every Jap in the country will have either seen us or heard us fly over their heads by now, so we need to get going quick."

"No sweat, can do."

Elmo pointed straight ahead at a patch of clearing with a road running along side of it.

"There it is, and I see a truck and some people."

Jay slowed the D3, lowering the gear and extending the flaps in preparation for landing. "It looks like the Red Cross volunteers have shown up already. Uh-oh! It looks like we got company. There's Japs down there."

THE FRUIT OF ATROCITY

"Jai-sonn no land."

"They've already seen us, Charlie. If I don't land, it will blow the cover for the ground personnel, and they'll probably all be killed, and besides, there's only about seven or eight of them."

Elmo said to Jay, "There might be more in the jungle. Don't forget what Prichard said, '*Protect this plane at all cost.*' Are you sure you want to get in the middle of this?"

"Charlie, as soon as the tail is on the ground, you and a couple of your men hide behind the pallet of supplies. I'll park just short of the volunteers on the ground. Elmo and Raylan, you two, open the cargo door as if you're going to unload the jeep. All those Japs will come over to see who we are and what we're up too. When there's enough separation from the Red Cross people, lay it on them. Elmo, get our BARs ready by the cargo door and take off your pistol belts, you too, Raylan. If they see you have guns, they might start shooting before we do."

"Aye, aye, Captain."

As the big DC-3 settled onto the turf runway, the Japanese patrol dove for cover behind the deuce and a half Red Cross troop truck parked next to the medical aid tent still under construction. Jay nonchalantly taxied toward the aid station.

The Japanese soldiers waited behind the truck, watching the hospital plane and studying the pilots for any sign suggesting they might be more than just civilian Red Cross volunteers. The airplane came to a stop, and for a long moment, nothing happened.

Jay let the engines run in case he might need to take off in a hurry. Elmo unlatched the cargo door and swung it open, expecting gunfire to ensue any second.

"Cut the engines, Jay. They're not going to come out as long as those engines are running." Jay knew he was right and reluctantly cut the fuel to the two Pratt and Whitney's. Jay emerged from the cockpit to help Elmo and Raylan who were already removing the tie-downs from the pallet.

"Here they come," Elmo said, continuing what he was doing as if nothing were wrong.

Jay remained out of sight until the soldiers were in closer proximity to the cargo plane.

"There are only five..." Raylan whispered. "Three are still behind the troop truck"

"Get ready, Charlie," Jay said as he picked up the Browning Automatic machine gun. "Raylan, use your best Japanese and tell them we are Red Cross volunteers, and we're here to set up an aid station to help the Burmese people. Tell them we have medicine and food."

Raylan stepped to the door and waved at the Japanese soldiers. In their native tongue, he repeated what Jay had said. The soldiers were tattered and dirty from obviously many weeks or months in the jungle but were not about to be caught off guard.

With their rifles pointed at Raylan and Elmo, the leader of the patrol, a particularly stout-built soldier, stepped forward to reply.

"Americonn, get down from airoplane, everyone off airoplane, now."

"Okay, were getting down," Raylan answered. Then whispering to Jay, he said, "It's now or never, Boss."

Jay replied, "When I holler at Charlie, you two drop to the floor...now!" Jay shouted.

Elmo and Raylan both dropped to the deck at the same moment Jay poked his BAR into the door opening and pulled the trigger. He did not hear the eruption of automatic fire that emerged from behind him as Charlie and three of his men popped up firing from behind the pallet of medical supplies or the return fire coming from the five Japanese soldiers who fired blindly as they stumbled backward in shocked surprise. For a brief moment, bullets were whizzing by in opposite directions within a foot of Jay's head. Jay's finger continued to squeeze the trigger against the metal guard until the forty-round 7.62 Nato magazine was

THE FRUIT OF ATROCITY

completely emptied. Jay yelled, "They're down, Charlie, but there are three more behind the truck."

Charlie and his men poured out of the cargo door, scattering two by two in different directions. The six Red Cross volunteers, cowering in the half-erected aid tent emerged pointing in the direction that the remaining soldiers had retreated. Jay reloaded a fresh magazine into his weapon and jumped from the cargo plane. The dead bodies of five Japanese soldiers lay scattered about, within thirty feet of where he stood.

"Elmo, you and Raylan help me get these bodies out of sight until we get that plane unloaded. Turning to the volunteer workers, he said, "Can you guys come help us?"

Other than the heavy breathing coming from the men carrying the dead bodies, the Red Cross aid station and airstrip had fallen silent. Only ten minutes passed, however, before automatic fire once again erupted within fifty meters of the perimeter of the camp.

Soon Charlie and his men returned, dragging the last three dead soldiers from the Japanese patrol.

"Jai-sonn, we unload plane lickity-split, put dead soldiers in plane, Jai-sonn take off Ledo. Hurry up."

Jay turned to the oldest man of the group of volunteers and said to him, "My name is Pastor Jay Baldwin. Are you the only people who will be manning this aid station?"

The man extended a quivering hand to Jay, "I am Dr. Wilbur Stanton. Yes, we are, for now. However, there is supposed to be another truck load of supplies on its way to us, along with a couple more volunteers. We sure are glad you fellows showed up when you did. We think those Japs were going to kill us."

"What makes you think that?"

"They wanted the truck, and they wanted us to take down the tent and reload it onto the truck. I can't imagine what might have happened if you hadn't shown up when you did…" Dr. Stanton shook his head and stammered. "Well, it was just a miracle that's all."

"Do you see that squad of Chinese militia fighters?" Jay pointed to Charlie and his men who were loading the dead bodies into the cargo plane.

"They will stay with you for a couple of days and help you get set up, while my crew and I return to Ledo. We will be back tomorrow morning with another jeep and more supplies for your station plus some additional men for Charlie."

"What will they do after you get back and resupply them?"

"They have their own agenda, but you can be sure of one thing, every day they're in the jungle, the safer the jungle will become."

"Thank you, Mr. Baldwin, did you say you were a pastor?"

"That's what I've been told, gotta go, see ya."

"Wait, Mr. Baldwin." Jay turned around to see what more Dr. Stanton wanted.

"Sir, you are bleeding! Were you hit by a bullet?"

"Just a scratch, Doc, I'll have my medic take care of it. Right now, we have to get out of here."

Jay headed to the D3, motioning for his crew to climb aboard, then saw Charlie coming toward him.

"Charlie, we should be back by this time tomorrow. Try to make this place a little safer, will you?"

"Jai-sonn, you are wounded! Charlie pointed to Jay's left midsection where the blood stains on his shirt was growing larger.

"I'm okay. Take care of those RC workers. They need some help. we'll see you tomorrow."

Raylan poked his head into the cockpit door and reported the cargo area secured. Jay shoved the duel throttle controls to full power and lifted the empty freighter into the air. Barely two hundred feet above the trees, he banked hard left and headed direct to India eighty miles to the west.

Once across the border, the Douglas turned north-northwest to Ledo.

THE FRUIT OF ATROCITY

"Well, boys, I guess we're about to find out what those MPs wanted the other night." Neither Raylan or Elmo said a word.

"By the way, Elmo, did you check the landing gear?"

"Yeah, it looked okay as far as I could tell. It wouldn't hurt to have it checked again when we get to Ledo. Maybe they can fix it while we rot in jail. By the way, Captain, did you know you're bleeding? You got blood all over your shirt."

"Yeah, I know, take over this thing for a minute while I have Raylan check it out."

Jay turned the airplane over to Elmo while Raylan went to get his medical bag.

"It's just a flesh wound, Boss, just missed your bottom left rib. I'll patch it up for you, but you should go to the dispensary when we get to the base and get it stitched up."

Jay gritted his teeth while his medic disinfected the area and dressed the wound.

"So, Raylan, what else have you been into besides AWOL once in a while?"

"I don't know what you mean."

"I think you do. Those MPs were after you for more than just going AWOL. I've known Captain Prichard for over two years, and he's not the kind of officer who neglects to take care of a detail as significant as clearing your release with the cops. There's something else you're not telling me, and I want to know what it is. Either you tell me or I'll kick you off this crew and give you back to the MPs as soon as we touch down." Raylan did not answer for a minute while he finished binding Jayson's wound.

Then, he said, "Captain Prichard selected me for more than just my ability to patch people up after they get shot."

"What else do you do?"

"I steal."

"What do you steal?"

"Whatever I'm told to steal."

"Why did Captain Prichard think I would need someone who could steal?"

"I don't know, I'm just telling you what my skills are if you don't have any use for them, then don't use them."

"I can't imagine I would ever need someone to steal anything."

"I do other things too."

"Like what? On second thought…forget it, I don't even want to know."

"I'm a sniper."

"You told me that already. You mean like, a rifle sniper that kills people from some hiding place."

"Yesir."

"Do you have a sniper rifle?"

"I have one back at the base."

"Well, leave it there. I don't see why we would need that either. You still haven't told me what those MPs want with you."

"I brought something back with me from Calcutta that they confiscated from me, only they didn't secure it very well, and it turned up missing. They may think that I took it."

"What did you bring from Calcutta?"

Jaworski muttered something under his breath.

"Say again, I didn't get that."

"Stones, I brought back some stones."

"What kind of…you mean diamonds?"

"Yesir."

"How many diamonds?"

"A small sack full…maybe a couple hundred, cut and polished."

"Two hundred! Cut and polished? How much are they worth?"

"I'm not sure, maybe a half million dollars."

Jay held his breath for a minute. "So did you or did you not take them from the MPs, and don't lie to me."

"I did, I have them in my bag, but they're mine."

THE FRUIT OF ATROCITY

"All right then, you can give them to me. I'll put them where those MPs will never find them, and you have my word I will return them to you."

Raylan dug through his duffle and produced a black velvet bag, tied with a string at the top and bulging with the polished diamonds. Jay reached into the bag and let the brilliant-colored stones drift though his fingers. "Are there more where these come from?"

Raylan studied his boss who went by the name of Pastor Jay Baldwin, wondering why he would ask such a question.

"Yesir, but I stole them, and if you want any, I would have to steal them as well."

Jay was silent as he closed the cockpit door behind him and stowed the polished diamonds in the same chest with the uncut diamonds and cash. When he had them safely hidden, he returned to Jaworski.

"Raylan, I need you to go through the pockets of these dead soldiers and see if there's anything we might be able to use. I'm sure Charlie's men have already picked them clean of their valuables, but there might be some sort of equipment left, or even maps."

"Yesir, Captain, I'm on it."

Jay returned to his pilot's seat to prepare for landing. Elmo said to him, "You're going to need to make your Morse code transmission soon."

Pastor Baldwin looked at his copilot. "Thanks, Elmo, I'll take the airplane now."

Elmo removed his hands from the controls and gave control of the airplane over to his chief pilot. Jay transmitted his first coded message and began the initial phase of the approach; finally crossing the final approach fix, he began his descent to the threshold.

It was a sunny day, and it felt good to be alive. In spite of the skirmish with the Japanese, Jay's mission had been successful, and it seemed to him that the worst danger was over. Charlie and his men would clear the area of enemy threat, making every other mission thereafter safer and much less likely that he and his crew would get involved in another firefight.

There had been no time to reflect on what happened back at Lashio, or Jay's part in it. Furthermore, he did not want to recall it. The less he could keep that moment from replaying in his conscious mind, the better. He had just taken the lives of men, real live men, human beings. Sure, the deadly shots may or may not have come from his gun; then again, maybe all of them died from his bullets. Actually, the most probable conclusion was that Charlie and his men, men who were professional killers, men who seldom missed their targets, were the ones who fired the fatal shots. That was the most feasible, and as far as Jay was concerned, that is, in all probability, where those fatal rounds had come from. On the other hand, he knew, in all likelihood, that would not be the last time he would find himself in a gunfight, raising a deadly weapon against other men just as desperate to kill him, as he would be to kill them. Where would Charlie be then? Maybe, ultimately, he would find it necessary to believe; he had killed already, therefore, could kill again.

Chapter 8

Two military police vehicles sat on the tarmac waiting for the shiny allunninum DC-3, to escort it from the active runway. Once again, Jay taxied through the huge doors into the maintenance building. Jay and his crew of two stood on the flight deck talking when suddenly they heard pounding on the cargo door from outside.

"That's the cops," Jay said. "Don't give them any information about our operation. If Captain Prichard wants them to know anything, he can tell them. We're flying support for a Red Cross aid station in Burma. That's all they need to know. Everything else is classified, got it?" Both men acknowledged. "In the mean time, Jaworski, you stand over there out of sight. Elmo, you can open the door. I'll do the talking, is that clear?"

"Yesir." Both men answered simultaneously.

Elmo moved toward the cargo door, released the latch, and swung the door open. There, standing below them were six very burly MPs. The ranking NCO (non-commissioned officer) ordered a ramp to be set in place. Jay moved Elmo aside and stood in the doorway as Master Sergeant First Class Clifford Anderson sauntered up the ramp.

"Who's in charge of this Red Cross plane?" he said in a demanding tone.

"You're looking at him, Sergeant." Jay extended his handshake as a matter of professional courtesy, which the master sergeant ignored.

"And who might you be?"

211

"I am Pastor Jay Baldwin, and this is my crew. We are ARCVs, American Red Cross Volunteers, working directly for Captain Carl Prichard, the head of Army Intelligence."

"I don't care what you're doing or who you're working for. I want to know who was flying this airplane the other night when my men tried to intercept it before it departed."

"You will need to talk to Captain Prichard about that. We work for him and answer only to him. Besides, we didn't see your men until it was too late to abort. Furthermore, that was a bonehead move your men made. They could have destroyed an airplane and killed the whole crew. For that matter, why in the sam hill were you attempting to intercept us in the middle of our takeoff run?"

"I'm looking for someone, and I think he might be aboard this aircraft."

"Who are you looking for?"

"A prisoner of mine by the name of Raylan Jaworski. Is he on board or not? And don't lie to me 'cause I'm going to search this airplane, and if he's here, I'll eventually find him anyway."

"I'm not harboring any prisoner of yours, and nobody is coming aboard my aircraft without Captain Prichard's authorization, so get off my ramp. We have work to do."

"What's the problem here?" All eyes turned to see who was asking the question. Jay's face lit up with a grin.

"Aha, there's the captain now."

The master sergeant and his five MPs turned and saluted Prichard. Jay spoke first, "Captain, these men want to board my aircraft. The sergeant is accusing me of harboring some prisoner."

"Don't worry, Mr. Baldwin, I'll handle this." Prichard took the master sergeant aside, leaving his men at the foot of the ramp.

Jay immediately turned to speak to his copilot, "Elmo, help me drag a couple of these bodies to the doorway. Jaworski you stay out of sight."

Jay and Elmo grabbed the first dead Japanese soldier and dragged him to the door, then returned for another, which they stacked on top of the first corpse. Suddenly, Prichard and Sergeant Anderson stopped talking and stared in astonishment at the two dead bodies.

"What the—" Captain Prichard immediately came up the ramp. He asked Jay, "Where did you get this cargo?"

"They're trophies from Lashio. We met up with some resistance. The other ARCVs arrived in the truck ahead of us, and while they were setting up their tent, these Japs showed up with plans to confiscate their truck and equipment and leave the ARCVs in the same condition these guys are in." Jay pointed at the dead bodies. "There are six more still in the rear."

Prichard turned to the MPs. "Sergeant Anderson, get these dead Japs off my airplane, and don't let anyone see them. I want you to give my airplane and my crew your support and protection from now on. They work directly for me, and you are not allowed to question them or board their airplane without my permission, is that understood? As far as your missing prisoner is concerned, he doesn't exist anymore."

"Yes, sir, Captain." Sergeant Anderson motioned for his men to remove the dead bodies; then, together they left the hangar.

"Pastor Baldwin, I want you to report to my office for a debrief. I have given the shop crew instructions to do a maintenance inspection and provide any necessary repairs to your aircraft. It looks like you picked up a few bullet holes. Also, it will be loaded with drums of aviation fuel for your return trip to China." Captain Prichard glanced at Jay's midsection. "I see blood on your shirt. Did you catch a bullet?"

"Yes, sir, just a scratch. My medic took care of it."

"Go to the dispensary and have that looked at. You men get something to eat and report back to me."

"I need my mechanic to stay with the aircraft during any maintenance if that's okay with you."

"That will be fine, but bring Jaworski with you."

"All right."

Jay turned to Elmo. "One of us has to stay with the airplane at all times from now on, and don't let anyone on board except the mechanics, and never leave them alone."

"Aye, aye, Padre."

"Jaworski, you come with me."

Pastor Baldwin and Raylan Jaworski set their food trays on a table in the officer's mess hall. Raylan studied the pastor for a long moment, then asked, "You said you knew the captain for two years. How did you two come to know each other?"

"We joined the Army Air Corp together."

"How come you're not in the army anymore?"

"Because I work undercover for Army Intelligence now. That's all I can tell you, so don't ask any more questions."

"Where does Charlie fit in to all of this?"

"All of what?"

"This hospital plane that used to be a C-47 for one thing. I wasn't born yesterday. Anybody that knows anything about DC-3s can tell that the cargo door is almost twice the size of a D3. How else would a jeep fit through it? Not to mention the fact that it's still army green inside."

"Maybe it was modified or something. I told you not to ask me anymore questions."

"What about the part numbers on the backs of the pilot seats, aren't they military?"

"I told you…all right then, it *was* a C-47 at one time, and Intel wanted to use it as a special ops airplane for this big Burma thing."

"Was it wrecked at one time?"

"Why do you ask?"

"If you look under the floor deck, you can see some extensive damage to the underbelly of the aircraft that has been recovered from the outside."

Jay considered for a moment. "What were you doing looking under the floor deck?"

"I was checking to see what you did with my diamonds."

THE FRUIT OF ATROCITY

"Why, are you planning to steal them again?"

"Only if I think someone else may be stealing them from me."

"No one is going to take your diamonds. I put them where it will be most unlikely that anyone will ever find them. Except you, of course, I guess you've already figured it out, is that right?"

"Yup, what all is in that teak chest?"

"Elmo and I have some documents and papers we keep in there that could blow our cover if the Japanese were to find them. Listen to me very closely, Jaworski, if you steal from me, you can kiss your carcass good-bye. I'll leave you someplace you won't want to be, is that understood?"

"Yesir, I understand, but I would still like to know what the story is behind this converted C-47 and your dealing with Charlie."

"Okay, I'll tell you, but you have to keep this to yourself, understand? Only Elmo and Prichard know."

"Your secret's safe with me, Boss."

"A year ago, I was a first lieutenant, flying out of this same base and eating my meals in the very same mess hall we're in right now. That Red Cross plane was my freighter until the day I met up with a Jap Zero and had to belly into a mountain meadow not far from Charlie's headquarters. I survived, and Army Intel decided to change my status to MIA and gave me a new identity. They salvaged my airplane, restored it, and now I work for them, except I'm on temporary assignment to Charlie so to speak. Any more questions?"

"I knew you weren't no preacher, but how come you and Charlie hate each other so much?"

"I don't hate Charlie, besides, that's none of your business, and I'm not answering any more of your questions, so finish eating. The captain is waiting on us. By the way, when we're done with Prichard, I want you to take Elmo a tray of food and get us resupplied with army rations. Also, be sure you have plenty of whatever medical stuff you might need."

"Yesir."

"And I'll tell you what else you can do since you are so gifted. Get your sniper rifle and any more BAR clips and ammo you can find. Also, I need topography maps of China including a map of Chungking."

Raylan stopped chewing as he stared at Jayson.

"What's in Chungking?"

"None of your business."

"Elmo told me you're married to Charlie's sister and you have a daughter. He also said he had your wife and kid kidnapped, is that right?"

Jay was stunned, mostly at the realization that Elmo had been so reckless with his personal information.

"Elmo doesn't know what he's talking about, and like I said, it's none of your business. Eat your chow."

"I bet I can help." Jay stopped eating and looked straight into Raylan's eyes.

"Help with what?"

"I've been paying attention to what's going on around here, and I think Charlie and Prichard are holding your wife hostage to get you to do something for them, am I right?"

"Prichard wasn't in on it, but go on."

"I'm just telling you what all I've been figuring out, but if you give me more details, I bet I can also figure a way to get her back."

"On what condition?"

Jaworski laughed. "What makes you think there's a condition?"

"Because nobody, especially someone with your specialties, would want to risk their life unless there is something in it for you, so what is the condition?"

"Okay, you said you were going to Alaska, and you wanted me to babysit some kids, what kids?"

"I have to work for Charlie until just before winter, then take sixteen orphans to Alaska, and then beat it right back here to work for him again until this war is over. I think they expect me

THE FRUIT OF ATROCITY

to win WWII for them with one Red Cross plane, a mechanic, and a criminally insane medicine man."

"See there, I hear it in your voice."

"Hear what?"

"Resentment. It's written all over your face." Raylan scooted his chair closer to Jay.

"Listen, here's my deal. I get your family back, and we go to Alaska and never come back to this hellhole again, forget those orphans."

"Not a chance, leaving those orphans is not an option, but taking my family when I go is precisely what I've wanted to do all along."

"What does Prichard have to do with all of this?"

"Charlie is the head of China's National Intelligence and Prichard of course is US Army Intelligence. Charlie works directly for, and with, Prichard. This whole idea of holding my family hostage was cooked up between Charlie, William Cheney, and Generalissimo Chiang Kai-shek."

"Cheney! You mean the National Security Advisor to the president?"

"That's right. He's a worm, and I don't trust any of them to keep their word. I'm just biding my time until I figure out what to do. Now, I want to ask you a question for once. Why did Prichard assign you to this detail? Have you worked for him before?"

"I've been working for Army Intel since before either one of you came over here." Jay felt a surge of anticipation. Maybe there was more to this little thief than he thought.

"What kind of work?"

"Let me put it this way. To get anything, anything at all, you have to pay for it. Army Intel doesn't have a budget to work with, so they use me to rob from Peter to Pay Paul, if you know what I mean. The medicine man is my cover, sniper is my forte, and stealing is my job."

Jay's mouth fell open, and a look of something between astonished and impressed appeared on his face.

"I think you might come in handy after all. Consider yourself hired, soldier."

"Does that mean you want my help?"

Jay tried to keep it from happening, but hope, once again, began to rise within him. Maybe Jaworski was right, maybe there was a way to get his family and get out of this God-forsaken place and never come back.

"Let me think about it. Right now we have to see Prichard."

Pastor Baldwin knocked on the steel door to Captain Prichard's small office. The voice on the other side said, "Come in." Jay and Raylan Jaworski entered.

Prichard was reading an article in the *New York Times* on the accomplishments of Franklin D. Roosevelt over his first three terms, as well as outlining his proposals for a United Nations Council where "…difficulties between nations could be resolved peaceably through negotiation."

Jaworski took a seat, and Jay leaned against the wall waiting for the head of Army Intelligence to finish reading.

Captain Prichard looked up from his newspaper to study the two men before setting it aside. He looked first at Jay, then at Jaworski. "Haven't either of you soldiers ever heard of military courtesy?"

"What do you mean?" Jay said.

"I mean…have you forgotten how to salute a ranking officer?"

"I'm dead, remember?" Jay said.

Raylan immediately snapped to attention.

"Sorry, sir."

"At ease, soldier. You too, Baldwin. I need a detailed statement from each of you about what happened back there at Lashio. So before we talk about anything else, have a seat at that table

over there and write it up for me. I'll be back in fifteen minutes."
Captain Prichard left the room.

Raylan said to Jay, "We should have dumped those Jap corpses
out over the jungle before we got here. We wouldn't be doing this
paperwork if we had."

"I don't do things like that. After the war, those bodies will
be returned to their families in Japan for a descent burial. It's the
Christian thing to do. The hardest part of war is to keep from
descending to the same depths of moral bankruptcy that led your
enemy to start the war in the first place."

Raylan looked up from his paper.

"Is that what's happening to you?"

"What do you mean?"

"Elmo said you were a real choirboy until they took your family. He said you couldn't shoot anyone if your life depended on
it. Now all of a sudden, you are mowing down Japs with a BAR
machine gun without out even blinking."

"Just shut up and finish your report. I told you this is none of
your business."

"Actually, I think you were a preacher or, if not a preacher,
at least a religious person. I think the reason you're changing is
because you've lost all hope of ever seeing your family again."

"I told you to shut up."

Jay's hand was shaking as he finished his report. From the corner of his eye, he kept checking to see if Jaworski would notice.

Secretly he knew Raylan was right. He knew too that the
Lord's arm was moving in his behalf in spite of his lack of faith.
At least that is what he wanted to believe, but was it really? Jay's
faith had actually deteriorated to the point he wasn't sure of anything anymore.

Had God sent this killer/thief to help him recover his family, or was it a trick of the devil to raise his hopes and have them
dashed again? Would an attempt to find and take back his family
only end in disaster? Silently, he prayed, *Oh God, forgive me for*

loosing faith, forgive me for giving up so soon. If the Lord has sent this man as a means of accomplishing your will, I pray that I will know for sure beyond even my own doubt. The office door burst open.

"Have you men finished yet?"

Jay stood and handed the captain his report. "Got it right here. Carl. Can I talk to you alone when we're through here?"

"Sure, Jay, I have something I need to give you anyway. But let me give you guys your assignment first. Are you finished yet, Jaworski?"

"Yesir." Raylan handed his report to the captain.

"All right, gentlemen, listen up. There are 360 of Charlie Nee's raiders still at Generalissimo's headquarters. These men are trained paratroopers, and your mission will be to drop them into Lashio in groups of twenty at a time.

When you leave this place and get back to the headquarters camp, unload the fuel drums of gas, and refuel your airplane. Then, load twenty of Charlie's men and their gear and fly back to Lashio. Only instead of landing, you will drop those men over the airstrip in the dark from twelve thousand feet and return to Charlie's headquarters for another load of paratroopers. You'll need to do a low pass over the headquarters' airstrip to let them know you're back so they can fire up those tar pots. Make three drops each night for six nights until all 360 of them are out of that door. Now listen up. Every morning, after you've finished your last drop, return to Ledo, and we'll reload you with more fuel to take back to the gimo's headquarters. Are there any questions?"

"Yeah, I thought we were supposed to drop off that other jeep and pick up some Burmese people."

"Change of plans. After that little skirmish you had with the Japanese, I don't want to risk the aircraft by putting it back on the ground."

"How am I supposed to find Lashio in the dark? It's hard enough to find in the daytime."

THE FRUIT OF ATROCITY

"You will cross the Burma Fix at fifteen thousand feet MSL and pick up the 176-degree bearing, outbound from the station. Track it for exactly one hour at 175 ktas [knots of true air speed]. Then, kick those men out of the door. Calculate for wind correction the best you can, and don't worry about where they wind up. They're jungle rats and will find their way just fine."

Jay asked, "What if the Japanese ground troops hear us and send Zeroes out to meet us on the next trip."

"They've already done that. We've had a C-47 flying that same route duplicating your course three times a night, every night, for the last three weeks. They sent out Zeroes for the first five nights, then give it up. They actually almost got one of our freighters, but he managed to give them the slip. Hopefully, you won't have any trouble, but keep your eyes open. Remember, those guys can't see at night any better than you can. However, if the moon is out, you could have trouble. Then again, if they see your polished aluminum and that big Red Cross on the tail, you might get lucky, and they'll leave you alone. As far as sleep is concerned, you will have to trade off with your mechanic during the en route phase of your flight."

Prichard turned to Jaworski and said to him, "By the way, Jaworski, what did Sergeant Anderson want with you?"

"He thinks I took something that belonged to him…sir."

"Well, did you?"

"No, sir."

"Do I want to know what it is?"

"No, sir."

"Am I ever going to hear about this again from anyone other than Sergeant Anderson?"

"No, sir."

"All right then, if there are no more questions, that will be all. Good luck, gentlemen. Corporal, you're dismissed. Baldwin, you stay." Raylan saluted the captain and shut the door behind him on his way out.

"Jay, you wanted to see me alone. What can I do for you?"

"Carl, I need to know the real reason you assigned Jaworski to me."

"What makes you think there is any other reason?"

"Because it seems illogical to me that you would give me someone with his specific qualifications unless you expected those qualifications to be put to good use."

"Do you have a particular use in mind?"

"I do, but I'm not sure I would be helping or hurting my cause—that is, making the situation better or worse."

"I understand your dilemma, Mr. Baldwin, but if I thought that a man with Jaworski's unique qualifications would have made matters worse for you, I would never have assigned him to you in the first place." Prichard handed Jay a manila envelope filled with papers.

"By the way, you dropped this earlier."

"That doesn't look like…oh, I see, I guess I did. How careless of me, thank you."

"Will that be all, Mr. Baldwin?"

"Yes, sir. Thanks again, Carl."

"Finish this Burma project for me, will you?"

"You bet I will, Carl, and look me up after this war. I won't be far from those orphans."

"If I knew what you were talking about, I probably would, but I don't, so get out of here."

On the way back to the maintenance facility, Pastor Baldwin was walking on air. He had gotten all of the confirmation he would get from Carl and all he would need to take Jaworski up on his offer. Although, he now realized it had nothing to do with any generosity on the part of Jaworski. Prichard had obviously thought the plan through in advance and assigned Raylan to him to help him retrieve his family before he left for America with the orphans.

THE FRUIT OF ATROCITY

Jay felt guilty for doubting Carl in the first place and was elated that Carl had not held it against him. Indeed the Lord was at work; indeed, the Lord had provided an opportunity for him to recover his precious wife and daughter. *Thank-you, oh, God. Thank you, thank you.*

After a quick shower and shave, Jay headed back to the maintenance facility where he found Elmo working in the cargo hold, securing the load of freight. "Did you check that left main gear?"

"Sure did, Boss, the gear was fine, but there was a crack in the sidewall of the tire where it hit the jeep, so we replaced it."

"Good, I see we're all loaded up. Are we refueled too?"

"Yes, sir, but I haven't seen Raylan."

"He's picking up a few items for us."

"What's in the envelope?" Elmo asked.

"I don't know. Captain Prichard gave it to me, and I haven't looked inside as yet. I'll let you know in a minute."

Jay made his way to the cockpit where he spread his flight jacket across his lap, opened the manila envelope, and dumped the contents onto his coat. There he found citizenship papers and new names for Ah-lam and a birth certificate for his daughter Ching-Lan. Also included were papers identifying himself, Elmo, and Raylan as doctors from the United States, along with teaching certificates and a letter from Madam Chiang Kai-shek. The letter, addressed to the International Red Cross, requested help in an advisory capacity at the University of Chungking School of Medicine, Chungking, China, along with a hand-sketched map of the city and brief instructions for finding the university.

Jay looked inside the envelope for anything he might have missed, hoping for some additional information as to where he might find Ah-lam, but there were none. The sound of footsteps on the ramp told him Jaworski was back, and it was time to go.

D.L. WATERHOUSE

✪ ✪ ✪

The polished aluminum hospital plane climbed into the eastern sky, once more, on its way to Charlie's headquarters airbase. Again, Jay was flying a load of extremely flammable aviation fuel.

The overloaded freighter climbed slowly in the hot afternoon air. Ahead, towering cumulus nimbus thunderheads loomed high in the sky that extended fifty thousand feet upward from the land surface where they enveloped the towering peaks of the Himalayas, far above the climbing limits of the Douglas DC-3. Elmo looked at Jay and said to him, "Are we going to bore straight through?"

"Don't have much choice, watch for lightning strikes so we can avoid them if possible. Maybe we can find a cell that has already matured and is dissipating, but either way, we're in for a wild ride.

"What was in that envelope the captain gave you?" Elmo asked curiously.

"I'll show you later. Get Jaworski up here."

Elmo made his way to the cargo hold and hollered for Raylan to report to the cockpit.

"What's up, Boss?"

"Get yourself strapped in. It is about to get plenty rough."

"Will do, Boss."

"Did you get everything?" Jay asked.

"Yesir, even a little extra."

"Like what?"

"I got us a few boxes of *dynamite*."

"Dynamite!"

"Yesir, figured it might come in handy."

"Is it fastened down good? We're about to penetrate a line of thunderstorms a hundred miles long, and who knows how many pieces we'll be in by the time we get to the other side, not to mention that full load of fuel we got onboard."

"It's okay, Boss, if that fuel goes for some reason, it won't matter at that point if the dynamite goes with it."

"Very comforting, Corpsman. Did you get those maps I asked for?"

"Yesir, that and more."

"More, like what?"

"More as in the latest updated runway conditions at Chungking."

"How old is this *latest* information?"

"Don't know, sir."

"Well, I guess it will have to do. Good job, Doc. So tell me about these runway conditions?"

"The main airport has been bombed to death, so we can't land there. But there is a road on the southwest side of the city."

"Is it somehow connected to the airport?" Jay asked.

"No, it's a road leading from the hill country to the city, which is about three miles away from the tree line. There's no report as to the condition of the road, just that it's open, could be a little bumpy, not to mention narrow."

"Does this road ever get used by anyone else, say for instance the generalissimo?"

"Don't know, sir, but I would bet it does because we know that he comes and goes from Chungking occasionally, so he has to land and take off from somewhere."

"Well then, as soon as we get the rest of these Chinese paratroopers dropped into Lashio, we're going to make a side trip."

Raylan asked, "What paratroopers?"

"We got a new job. We'll be dropping 360 of Charlie's men into Lashio. Three drops per night for six nights. Then, during the day, we'll swing by Ledo for another load of fuel."

"Sounds like fun. Are they real paratroopers?"

"Prichard says they are."

"Sir, did Prichard give you any other information that might come in handy?" Jay's brow wrinkled as he looked at Raylan.

"Like what?"

"Like about where we look for your family."

"How did you know about that?"

"We figured this all out before I came to work for you. He said when the time come, he would give you a heads-up."

Jay grinned facetiously and said, "I figured you knew more than you let on."

"The captain suggested a few things, and when you're ready, I can pass them on to you."

"Does Prichard recommend we land on this dirt road at Chungking, or should we take a chance on going into the Flying Tigers base in Anshun and absconding with one of their troop trucks?"

"Anshun would not be a good idea. Captain Prichard, the Madam, and the three of us are the only ones who know anything about this operation."

"What operation?" Elmo asked.

Jay ignored his mechanic and continued.

"How about this letter we have from the Madam. Evidently, we're the doctors she's expecting, so why not land this hospital plane in broad daylight, like we don't have anything to hide?"

"What letter?" Elmo asked.

Jay handed the envelope to his copilot. Raylan answered, "We could, I suppose, but we would risk detection by the Japanese bombers. And we don't know who may be watching from the city."

"You mean like Japanese spies?"

"Something like that. The Jap's usually do their bombing runs around midnight so they can arrive back in Hanoi by sunup. I think if we go in at dusk, like five minutes before dark, we could see the road well enough to land and camouflage the aircraft. That should give us time to find my wife and daughter and get to Freeland by dawn where we would have enough daylight to land. What do you think, Elmo?"

Jay's copilot, chuckled, and wagged his head from side to side as he glanced at his senior pilot. "Nobody lives forever, Padre, count me in."

Raylan said, "There is just one thing missing. We need someone who is familiar with the city, someone who can get us to the university and back as quickly as possible. The less people we encounter along the way, the better."

"I know Chungking a little," Elmo said. "I went there at least a half dozen times when I worked for the Tigers."

"Perfect," Jay said. "Do you know where the university is?"

"No, but according to this sketch, it shouldn't be too hard to find."

"I hope you're right because we'll need to get out of there before midnight, or we might risk losing the aircraft if those bombers happen to show up." Elmo scowled and looked back at Jaworski.

"That would mean we would be flying around for several hours waiting for it to get light enough to land at Freeland. If we do that, we would have to take extra fuel with us and refuel the airplane before leaving Chungking."

"Where is this Freeland you keep talking about?" Raylan asked.

"You'll see," Elmo said, "if you're lucky."

The Red Cross plane entered the clouds in which were buried several dozen embedded thunderstorms and immediately lurched as the violent up and down drafts wasted no time in beginning their torment of the aircraft.

"You better get yourself fastened down, Jaworski," Jay ordered.

Elmo paid no attention to the turbulence, fascinated with the documents he had found in the envelope, his facial features lighting up in surprise when he saw his new identity.

"Wow, I'm two people at once and a doctor no less."

Jay turned to his copilot. "Now you know how I feel. Listen up. This turbulence is going to get severe through here. Are those drums secured well enough?"

"I'll go check."

Elmo left his copilot's seat and made his way to the cargo hold where fifteen fifty-five-gallon drums of fuel strained hard against their bindings as the aircraft bucked and lurched in the rough air. As Elmo passed through the cabin door, he immediately became alarmed.

"I smell gas!" he hollered above the noise of the sleet and rain.

"Jaworski, do you hear me? I smell fuel!

"You don't have to yell. I'm right here. We got a leak in one of the drums," Jaworski answered back.

"How did that happen?"

"I don't know. Haven't found it yet." Elmo's face went ashen.

"I'll tell the boss." Quickly he returned to the cockpit. "Padre, we got a fuel leak."

Jay's grip tightened on the control wheel. "How bad, and where's it located?"

"It's one of the drums. Jaworski is checking it out now. Try to find some smooth air, or we might have some drums breaking loose and more of them start leaking."

"There isn't any smooth air for another hundred miles. You guys find that leak pronto and turn the drum upside down and get some more bindings on the rest of the load."

Raylan worked his way around from one gasoline drum to another looking for the source of the fuel that was now spreading throughout the cargo deck.

"Did you find it yet?" Elmo yelled. Panic was telling in his voice.

"Maybe, I think it's one of these top ones. Whichever one it is, the boss said turn it upside down."

"Yeah, I know! What did you think I would do with it? The problem is, we have to take the blinders off to do that, and in this turbulence, the other drums on top could get away from us."

"Keep trying to find the one that is actually leaking," Elmo hollered.

Raylan answered, "I'll need you to give me a hand."

Elmo made his way to where Raylan wrestled with one of the drums. Raylan said to him, "I think it's this one. Help me turn it over."

"I'll get another binder in case we need it."

The plane continued to lurch up, down, and sideways in the violent turbulence as the two men tried desperately to manhandle the drum of fuel. Carefully, and under extremely adverse conditions, they managed to get the drum of aviation fuel turned upside down.

Finally the gasoline stopped leaking, but by then, it had thoroughly saturated the cargo deck. With the leaking drum turned upside down and resecured, the two men finished checking the rest of the load and returned to the flight deck.

"Shut that cabin door before I pass out…" Jay hollered. "And open your vents on that side…we need some ventilation up here before those fumes get under the instrument panel and an electrical spark turns this ship into a ball of fire." Elmo opened his side window to let the rushing air dissipate the flammable fumes.

The hospital plane tossed and lurched for an additional hour as it churned its way through the line of thunderstorms; the giant clouds had become so dark it was as though nighttime had arrived two hours early. The lightning and thunder crashed around them in blindingly bright flashes, illuminating the inside of the black clouds and the aircraft cockpit. What had started out as rain turned to ice pellets that soon grew to the size of golf balls, smashing against the airframe and windscreen.

Pastor Jay Baldwin in all his missions across the hump as First Lieutenant Jayson Bold had never been in weather so violent. The powerful updrafts lifted the DC-3 to climb rates of six thousand feet per minute, only to catch a down draft that would hurl the flying bomb toward the mountains below at equal velocities.

Jay Baldwin silently prayed. *Father God, we are all only mortal sinners, saved by Grace and Grace alone. May God be with us to see us to a successful end. Amen.*

Jay said to Elmo, "It seems like the worst is behind us. Maybe it's going to smooth out a little."

"Maybe, and maybe not. If we're between thunder cells, there might still be more ahead of us."

"Could be, except, it is getting lighter. It looks like we're still on course, but I have a feeling we've been carried past our destination. As soon as we get out of this soup, we'll have to drop down and backtrack underneath the cloud layer, if the ceiling is high enough, that is.

Soon the clouds broke apart to reveal a high thin overcast above the Yunnan Valley. The crew of the Red Cross Volunteer hospital plane backtracked under the cloud deck that encompassed the foothills wherein lay the headquarters airstrip.

Jay let the freighter full of fuel, dynamite, and frightened airmen settle gently onto the turf runway. Applause erupted from his one-passenger and single-crew member. "Okay, men, let's grab a couple hours of sleep. In the morning, we'll load up, and do it all over again."

Chapter 9

Pastor Jay Baldwin awoke from a sound sleep, lying on one of the vacant army cots in Charlie's barracks. It was 2000 hours (8:00 p.m.). And he had only been asleep for two hours. Remnants of a recent dream were still clear in his mind—a dream he did not want to end.

In it, he and his wife and daughter sat playing on the bank of the river that ran through the center of Freeland. The cool breezes swirled Ah-lam's satin black hair around her face as she held their child. It was like heaven. When Jay awakened, his cheeks were still wet. It was moments like this that revived in him his resentment of Charlie.

Jayson had settled in his mind that this mission that Captain Prichard had assigned to them would be the last. All other obligations that Charlie required of him would have to wait until he returned from Alaska—if he ever did.

Together, Carl Prichard and the Madam Chiang had provided a window of opportunity for him to smuggle his family and the orphans out of China.

Jay knew too well that Charlie *never* had any intention of letting him see his family again, ever. Were he to leave without them and then return to work for Charlie as he had agreed, his family would be hidden where he could never find them, and Charlie would tell his sister a story of how the great Lieutenant Jayson Bold died valiantly in battle defending their mother country. He now realized that Carl and Madam Chiang also knew it as well.

Jayson suspected that Charlie would even go so far as to build a memorial to the great American hero and place it next to the Flying

Tigers memorial for the succeeding generations of Chinese to visit in honor of all the brave Americans who helped save China from the hated Japanese.

Still sluggish from far too little sleep, he gathered his flight gear and made his way toward the Douglas.

Raylan called to him, "Boss, the paratroopers are ready to go."

Half asleep, Jay replied, "Are we fueled up?"

"Yesir, Barker is counting heads now."

"Did you remove the cargo door?"

"Yesir, we stowed it in the rear of the plane."

"Okay, let's get them onboard." Jay and his medic followed the twenty Chinese paratroopers as they boarded the Red Cross plane.

Standing in the forward area of the cargo hold, Jay addressed the soldiers in their native language.

"You men listen up. When we're five minutes from the drop zone, we will turn on a red light. That means stand and form a line to the door. When it's time to jump, a green light will flash on, and then off again, for each jumper. Do not delay going out of the door. I trust you all have been trained enough to know what you are doing, is that correct?" Jay waited for a reply, but there was none. He repeated, "It is my understanding that you all have parachuted from an aircraft before, is that correct?" Again, no one responded.

One of the raiders sheepishly raised his hand and said to him, "Excuse please, sir, Charlie Nee show how to count 1, 2, 3, pull cord." The man gave an imitation of yanking a ripcord, then nodded his head and smiled, revealing a mouthful of teeth stained with betel nut.

Jay sighed, shook his head, and turned to Raylan.

"Raylan, these guys have never even done this before. Let's get them lined up. We're going to go through a drill."

Jay turned to Elmo. "Barker, when I stand in the door, you flash that green light." Then he turned to address the group of would-be paratroopers.

THE FRUIT OF ATROCITY

"I want everyone to watch me. Each of you will do exactly as I do, is that clear?" The paratroopers all nodded and smiled.

Jay grabbed an extra chute, strapped it on, and stood in the cargo bay doorway with his back to the outside; the green light flashed, and Jay fell backward down the ramp. One by one, the rookie paratroopers imitated exactly the same procedure.

"Don't forget to pull that rip cord as soon as you clear the door, but whatever you do, do not pull it before you go out the door, is that clear?" Jay watched as all twenty men nodded. "Okay, get strapped in, and let's get airborne."

The Douglas DC-3 rumbled down the runway, then climbed into the night air, disappearing into the overcast. Elmo sat in his copilot seat. Glancing sideways at Jay, he began to chuckle.

"Who told you those guys were paratroopers?"

Prichard, he also told me a lot of other things which I am beginning to wonder about."

Elmo replied, "This is going to be a fiasco. Half of those guys won't make it to the ground alive, and the other half will probably get lost."

"Well, I do imagine there will be a few losses, but I think the ones that can still walk after they've landed, I'm sure will find their way okay. They're a whole lot more at home in the jungle than you are with your head in a cowling or I am in this left seat."

"I hope you're right, Padre."

The plane full of paratroopers droned on through the night sky.

Jay heard someone behind him and turned in his seat to see Raylan sitting behind him on the flight deck.

"Jaworski, you said Prichard had some suggestions for us. What are they?"

Raylan rose from his seat and moved closer to his pilot.

"Well, it has to do with when we get to Chungking. He's a little concerned about how we plan to handle any resistance if we encounter it, wants to know if we have anything to buy our way in and out as opposed to using deadly force. He doesn't want us shooting any Chinese regulars."

"We have your polished diamonds. We can use them."

"I don't think so, Boss. Those are my nest egg for when I get back to the world. Besides, don't you and Elmo have a little something in that teak chest we can use?"

"What I got in there is for getting us through China, Manchuria, Russia, and Siberia. And by the time I do that, there probably won't be much left. If there is, I'll need it to find housing for those orphans."

"Well, that just leaves one option."

"Which option is that?"

"We need to make a side trip to Calcutta."

"What's in Calcutta?"

"Diamonds, both cut and rough diamonds. The latter are not worth a great deal but serve as very reliable currency in all of those countries you just mentioned."

"How do we get them?"

"You don't get them, I do. That's *my* job. All you have to do is fly me there and leave the rest to me, and if you don't want to know anymore than that, don't ask me anymore questions."

Jay stared at Raylan wondering how he could be so matter-of-fact about his profession. There was not a hint of conscience in him, and it seemed that he actually enjoyed *robbing from Peter to pay Paul*, as he put it.

"I'm not sure we'll have time for a side trip to Calcutta, but I'll keep it in mind."

Jay stared into the night sky; the line of thunderstorms that a few hours earlier tried to kill them had dissipated, and in their place, a hundred million stars speckled the sky.

"Elmo, keep your eyes open for Zeros. We'll be sitting ducks up here until we get some more cloud cover."

"Captain, I have a question. I'm wondering if we could persuade a couple of those raiders to give us a hand in Chungking?" Jay's mouth dropped open.

"Hey, that's an incredible idea. While we're waiting in the airplane, they could be alerting the general who would put us in jail, and we wouldn't have to fly any more of these dangerous missions." Jay glanced at Elmo with a facetious grin on his face.

"Maybe, then again, maybe not, Padre. Depends on who we get. If we approached it the right way, we may find a couple of them that would rather live in an airplane, with us, then die in a jungle, and if we put a few diamonds in their pockets, they might come over to our side. We could parachute them onto that dirt road in the middle of the night along with Jaworski and me, find your wife and kid, and bring them to the landing zone. You could go to Anshun and wait twenty-four hours until the next night, and when you get back, we could meet you on the road."

Jay thought about it a minute and turned to his medic.

"What do *you* think about that, Raylan?"

"I like it, Boss. Elmo and I can keep tabs on them and not let them out of our sight."

"Do either of you speak Chinese?" Both men were silent. "That's what I thought. I think you have a great plan as long as we select the right people, but I'll have to be the one who goes with Raylan. Elmo will have to fly the airplane. So from now on, Elmo, I'll sit in the right seat while you get some left-seat time. By the time you land at Ledo and the headquarters a half dozen times, you should have the hang of it."

"Okay, Padre, if that's the way you want it, so how do we go about picking out our guys?"

"I think we should wait until we have dropped all but the very last group. Then I can ask for two volunteers for a special mission, and we can keep them separate from the others until the last of them are out of the door. That way they won't be apt to spill the beans to the wrong people."

"Captain, even if it did get back to Charlie, we would already be out of the country by the time he could do anything about it."

"I'm not so sure. He has more connections than Ma Bell. It wouldn't surprise me if he even had the Japanese working for him."

"How long will he be in Burma?"

"I don't know. Prichard wouldn't say what their mission actually is, but I'm hoping it keeps him tied up a while. He'll be expecting us to lift them back out of there, and when he realizes we're not coming, he might get suspicious. Hopefully, we'll be long gone by that time."

The cockpit fell silent as they neared the Burma Fix.

"I'm going to slide southwest a little and pick up that 176-degree outbound bearing from the NDB so we won't have to reintercept the course after we cross the station. That way when we start our one-hour countdown, it will be more accurate. When I say *ready*, turn on that red light."

"Ey, ey, Captain."

"Raylan, you're in charge of getting those men out of the door."

"Okay, Boss."

The time passed quickly, and Jay called out, "Ready! Five minutes to jump time!" Elmo turned on the red light, and Raylan supervised the men as they stood in line awaiting their first ever parachute jump. Raylan pointed to the first man who stepped to the door facing the outside—eyes closed. The corpsman turned the man around and slapped his face. "Keep your eyes open, no close eyes." Jaworski hoped he understood, but it was too late to worry about it; the green light came on, and Raylan pushed the man backward out of the door. He watched for a few moments until the soldier disappeared into the darkness; his chute never opened.

"Next." He grabbed the second paratrooper and pointed his finger at the ripcord handle. "Don't forget to pull this." The man reached for the handle to pull it. "No, not now, after you jump. Pull after you jump." The green light again blinked on, and

Raylan pushed the man out into the darkness. This time, he did not watch. One after the other, they went out of the door. Finally, there was only one that remained. The soldier paused as if he was afraid to go.

"Get up here," Raylan shouted. The soldier hesitated, then stepped to the door. Before Raylan could stop him, he had pulled his ripcord and fallen backward out of the opening. The parachute had already hit the cargo deck by the time the jumper was outside, and the corpsman saw the lines wrap around his legs before he disappeared.

From up front in the cockpit, Jay felt a tug on his rudder pedal. Astonished, he hollered back at Raylan, "What was that!" There was no response.

"Elmo, go see what's going on." The copilot unfastened his harness and made his way to the rear of the plane. Soon he returned with Jaworski trailing behind. Raylan's eyes were bugging out of his head.

Elmo spoke first, "Captain, the last man opened his chute prematurely, and he's hung up on the left horizontal stabilizer, trailing like a banner at an air show."

"Oh no, God help him. I'll see if I can do some maneuvering to try and cut him loose."

Jay slowed the airplane and executed a steep turn to the left in an effort to allow the parachute to disengage itself from the stabilizer.

"Well, that didn't work. You guys get buckled in. I'm going to do a hammerhead tailslide stall. Maybe that will get him off of us." Jay applied full power to the two big P&W 1,200 hp engines and raised the nose straight up to the sky. Quickly the airspeed dissipated to zero, and the aircraft entered the stall.

Jay reduced the throttles to idle as it slid backward, tail first toward the treacherous mountains below. Suddenly, Jay saw movement out of his side window. It was the Chinese soldier. Terror covered the poor man's face as their eyes briefly met. Jay looked toward the rear to see if the chute had come free. He could not tell but had only a moment to spare as the nose of the aircraft began to fall sharply forward. He stuffed opposite full rudder and let the stalled aircraft pivot to the starboard side, nose downward; earth replaced the night sky in the windscreen, and as the airspeed increased, the wings eventually redeveloped their lift properties, and the airplane once again began to fly. Quickly Jay applied full power and lifted the nose of the aircraft back to level flight; he asked, tentatively, "Did he get off?"

"I can't tell, Boss, but I think so," Raylan answered. All three men were silent. For several long minutes, no one spoke a word. Finally, Elmo broke the silence.

"Padre, is it true that you go to heaven when you die?" Jay did not answer immediately. Elmo continued, "There sure is a lot of dying going on in this war, and sometimes I wonder how God keeps track of who goes to heaven and who goes to hell."

"I've wondered the same thing, Boss." Raylan interjected, "Those poor bastards don't have a clue about religion other than their Buda stuff. What chance in hell do they have of ever going to paradise?"

Jay recalled the time in his own life when he considered the same questions. There was the time his childhood friend, Bookter Portwood, drowned in the local swimming hole. The boys were only five years old and were playing on the banks of the town reservoir, only a half mile from their home. Jay's older brother, Arthur, had gotten too far ahead and left them alone. Jay didn't see Bookter go in, but he heard the splash, and by the time he turned around, Bookter had disappeared into the muddy water. He screamed, and Arthur came running, but it was too late— Bookter was gone.

Even as he sat in his pilot's seat flying his Red Cross plane back to Generalissimo's headquarters for another load of para-troopers, Jay could vividly remember the horrible experience.

THE FRUIT OF ATROCITY

Reminding him once again of the loss of his parents, the horrible memory, revived in him the terrible feelings of sadness.

Jay remembered clearly the day the police arrived at their home in Sikeston, Missouri. It was late in the evening. Jay and Arthur had been repairing farm equipment all day while their mother and father were out of town. It was a Sunday, and Mother had wanted to attend the wedding of her best friend's niece. The police said they were on their way home when a drunk driver ran a stop sign and hit the family car, broadside, at over sixty miles per hour. Both his parents had died instantly.

At the funeral, Jay remembered the preacher telling them his parents were already happily in heaven and looking down at the congregation, thinking that the thought would comfort them in their hour of bereavement.

Jay went home and searched the scriptures to understand what happens to a man spiritually when he dies.

Elmo interrupted his thoughts. "I think we're already in hell, because...well, this war is hell."

Jay thought a moment and answered, "As far as the scriptures are concerned, the Bible says: 'For the living no that they shall die: but the dead know not anything...their love, and their hatred, and their envy, is now perished... for there is no work, nor device, nor knowledge, nor wisdom, in the grave wither thou goest'" (Excerpts taken from Ecclesiastes 9: 5–10, AKJV).

"So are you saying that people don't go to heaven when they die or only certain people go or what?"

"I only know what the scriptures say. I haven't been there or done that as yet, so I have no firsthand experience, and outside of the story of Lazarus and the Lord Jesus Christ in the scriptures, I don't know anyone who has. However, I do know this: If a man is a believer in Jesus Christ and that man dies, it is his body that deceases and goes into the dirt. His 'Soul,' the breath of life, departs to be with Christ [Philippians 1:23, AKJV]. The confusion begins with what happens after that. In 1 Thessalonians 4:13

[AKJV], it says: 'But I would not have you to be ignorant, brethren, concerning them which are asleep, that ye sorrow not, even as others which have no hope.' It is clear, from this passage, that the soul which has *departed* in Phillipians 1:23 *is 'asleep in Jesus'* in 1 Thessalonians 4:13.

"Any man who believes in Jesus Christ, that He 'is the Son of God; And that He… died for our sins… was buried, and that he is risen the third day according to the scriptures' [1 Corinthians 15:1–4, AKJV] is saved immediately. From the very moment he truly believes in his heart that Jesus Christ is Lord and Savior, his salvation is instantly in place. As far as the body is concerned, the Bible says: 'His breath goeth forth, he returneth to his earth; in that very day his thoughts perish' [Psalm 146:4, AKJV].

"It is my firm conviction that the Spirit of God has been poured out upon all of humanity. 'That was the true Light, which lighteth every man that cometh into the world' [John 1:9, AKJV]. However, not all men have received it—that is to say, have benefited from it. To those who have, it is said of them, 'Know ye not that ye are the temple of God, and that the Spirit of God dwelleth in you?'" (1 Corinthians 3:16, AKJV).

Elmo shook his head as though he were confused.

"So if everyone has this Spirit, why are we fighting a war, why do human beings slaughter one another like they were only so much cattle?"

"As these scriptures say…just because the Spirit is poured out, does not necessarily mean it has been received. The Spirit of God is only received by faith and faith alone. The Bible says, 'Faith cometh by hearing, and hearing by the word of God' [Romans 10:17, AKJV]. That is the whole purpose of preaching the Gospel to the world.

"God created humanity for one express purpose: to be the temple of the Holy Ghost, the residence of the Divine God. Unless a man has that understanding, unless he believes by faith, that 'God so loved the world that He gave His only begotten Son, that

THE FRUIT OF ATROCITY

whosoever believeth in Him should not perish but have everlasting life' [John 3:16, AKJV] and that by that faith and by virtue of the Gift of God, he has received the indwelling Holy Spirit, then he will be nothing more than an empty vase for satanic spirits to occupy. Moreover, if the atrocities of war are any indication of that truth, then it is clearly evident that the real war, the real controversy, takes place between God and Satan over the *habitation* of all human beings, and the *souls* of mankind are the prize. It is also true that the work of the Spirit of God in the earth is to reveal the horrible depths of all that the human nature is capable of apart from the Grace of God, and *that*, my friends, is why God permits war."

Elmo and Raylan contemplated the things Pastor Baldwin had shared with them. Raylan said, "It seems to me that the devil is way ahead on that score."

Jay thought for a moment and answered, "Actually, it is the very opposite. The Lord Jesus Christ won *that* war on the cross of Calvary where he took the sins of all mankind, past, present, and future upon Himself, paying the ultimate price to satisfy not only the law of God and the government of heaven but God Himself. Where also, He not only 'became sin for us' but made us—that is, you and I—'the righteousness of God in Him.'"

Elmo turned to look at his chief pilot. "What does that mean?"

"It means that it is impossible for the devil to win *that* controversy. In fact, it means that he has already lost. It means that by the blood of Jesus Christ, shed for the sins of all humanity, through all the ages, and by the righteous life of Jesus Christ given as a 'propitiation,' substitute, for man [1 John 2:2, AKJV], humanity is no longer under the condemnation of the law [Romans 8:1, AKJV]. Think about it, the law is divine. How could unholy humanity who are not divine keep a Holy and Divine law? It is impossible. Therefore, '*God sent His Son* [who *is* Divine] *into the world that the world through him might be saved*'" (John 3:17, AKJV).

Jay was quiet. He knew that what he had told them was a lot for them to understand. Yet he also knew that it was not his responsibility that they understand it, only that he plant the seed. It would be up to the Holy Spirit of God to bring that seed to germination (understanding) in the Lord's own time.

"Jaworski, we better let the Padre pay attention to his flying. Padre, are you going to be able to get back into that headquarters field in the dark?"

"I think so. I just want to say one more thing if you don't mind."

"What's that?" Elmo asked.

"It's about all of those people that we see dying and even— unfortunately—the men that may yet die, whether by our hand while we're defending ourselves or those that jump out of our airplane. I believe it is God's will that evil be stopped, and that not only the world but most especially the Japanese and Germans understand clearly the effect they should expect from the atrocities they have incurred upon humanity. The souls of all mankind are in the care of God and God alone. However, Godly men have the God-given responsibility to protect themselves, their families, their communities, and their country from un-Godly men whether at home or abroad."

"I agree with that, Padre."

"Me too," Raylan said.

"So then, we will keep dropping these men into Lashio, and for the ones who live to fight, they may, God willing, return home. For those that die, we will commit to God. Our job is to get them out of that door as close to the drop zone as we possibly can."

"Hey, Boss, I got an idea that might help with that."

"Good, Jaworski, what is it?"

"We should tie a ten-foot-long rope to the door hinge and tie a carabineer to the other end. We can hook the carabineer to the rip cord of each jumper, and the rope will pull their cord for them. We should be able to retrieve it and get the next guy hooked up in time for his turn out the door."

THE FRUIT OF ATROCITY

"Great idea, Raylan. See if you can find anything back there that will work for that, and be careful you don't lose yourself out of that door in the process. If there's enough rope make several so the men can get out the door even faster."

Raylan unbuckled his harness and proceeded to the cargo hold where the vacuum from the open jump door tugged at his body. Carefully, he hung onto the webbing alongside the fuselage wall as he worked his way to the tail section. Suddenly, Raylan saw movement. He reached for his sidearm, pointing it at the dark corner of the baggage area, the same area where the crew kept miscellaneous equipment. Raylan switched on his flashlight, and there in the tail cone of the airplane was one of the Chinese paratroopers. From his expression, the man appeared terrified. His parachute was missing, and he made no move to stand or defend himself in any manner. Raylan hurried back to the flight deck. "Boss, we still have a jumper on board."

"What jumper?"

"One of the soldiers, only he doesn't have a parachute."

"Go get him and bring him up here."

"Yesir."

Again, Jaworski worked his way to the rear of the aircraft. The Chinese soldier sat on his haunches, knees tucked against his chest, violently shaking.

Raylan tapped him on the shoulder.

"You come with me," he said, motioning for the man to follow. Slowly the soldier stood up and, still quivering, followed Raylan to the flight deck.

Jaworski took the man to the cockpit and sat him behind the copilot's seat where Jay could talk to him from over his shoulder. In perfect Chinese, he said to him, "Why didn't you jump back there with the others, and where is your parachute?"

The man stared at Jay in silence. Jay turned in his seat to get a closer look at the man in the dim light, immediately he rec-

243

ognized him as the same paratrooper he had seen from his side window while executing the hammerhead tailslide stall.

"My God, I recognize this man. That's the guy who got hung up on the horizontal stabilizer. He floated by my side window while we were in the tailslide."

"You're kidding. How did he wind up back in the airplane?"

"He must have fallen back in through the door when I kick right rudder to break the slide. That's why he doesn't have a chute. When he found himself back in the plane, he probably disengaged from it to keep from getting sucked back out."

"Padre, this guy is shaking like a leaf. He must be freezing cold."

"I see that. Get a blanket around him, and give him something to eat."

Once again, turning to the soldier, Jay said to him, "Listen up, my friend, you don't have to worry about ever jumping out of an airplane again. We're going to make you part of our crew. Do you understand?"

A slight expression of understanding began to show in the man's face. "Thank you, mericonn pilot, thank you. Mericonn pilot...put Chi-shoo back in airplane." Elmo looked at Jay and grinned.

"He thinks you did that maneuver intentionally to get him back on board. He doesn't know—"

"He doesn't need to know either, Barker." Jay interrupted.

"Yes, sir, Captain."

Jay said to him, "Is that your name, Chi-shoo?"

"Chi-shoo, yesuh, mericonn pilot."

"You can call me Jayson. This is Elmo, and that guy behind you is Raylan. You are one lucky guy, do you know that?"

"Chi-shoo studied Jayson's lips as he attempted to repeat what he said, "Wonlukeegye?"

THE FRUIT OF ATROCITY

"That's right. Let's just make it Wonlukee. From now on, that will be your new name—Wonlukee. Elmo and Raylan, meet Wonlukee, the latest addition to our crew."

✪✪✪

Fog shrouded the headquarters, but once again, Jay Baldwin reunited the landing gear with the turf airstrip, in spite of visibility so poor even the birds could not fly.

"Let's get this ship fueled and loaded up with jumpers. We got thirty minutes."

"Yesir, Boss." Elmo answered.

"Wonlukee, you stay here I want to talk to you."

"You betcha, mariconn pilot, Jaysonn-sonn."

Jay finished his shutdown procedures and said to his new crew member, "Wonlukee, I need your help."

"Okay, you betcha, Wonlukee help Jaysonn-sonn."

"I have to find someone."

"Wonlukee help Jaysonn-sonn. Wonlukee life all gone now. Jaysonn-sonn give back life. Wonlukee live new life for Jaysonn-sonn for all of Wonlukee new life."

"I can relate to that, Wonlukee. I belong to someone who saved my life also."

"Who person Jaysonn-sonn want to find?"

"I have a wife and daughter. They were kidnapped from me and are being held hostage. When we get through dropping all of your buddies into Lashio, we're going to go find my family and take them back to America. Would you like to go along?"

"Wonlukee go with Jaysonn-sonn you betcha. Wonlukee help Jaysonn-sonn find family you betcha."

"Okay, I appreciate that, and from now on, you are also part of our family."

Wonlukee believed Jay had saved him from a fate worse than death and repeatedly bowed to him out of respect and honor.

Jayson added, "We'll be making a lot of trips back and forth to Lashio, and I need you to find some people with torches who will line up along the sides of the runway when we come back in the dark. When they hear the airplane overhead, I want them to light those torches so I can see to land. Do you understand?"

Wonlukee nodded. "Yes, master Jaysonn-sonn, Wonlukee can do."

"Also, help Elmo and Raylan get those jumpers loaded up so we can get out of here on time."

"Yesuh, master Jaysonn-sonn."

"And one more thing. I don't want anyone else to know that we're going to go find my family. Do you understand?"

"Yesuh, master Jaysonn-sonn."

Jay and his crew made two more night drops into Lashio before returning to Ledo for another load of fuel—fuel they once again unloaded at the headquarters before starting another round of parachute missions.

Several hours had passed since the Red Cross plane touched down at the headquarters airstrip. Jay had gotten a couple hours of sleep at Ledo, trading watches with Elmo. Raylan fixed sleeping accommodations for himself on the flight deck expecting to grab some nap time on the return trip from Ledo with the next load of fuel.

More and more, the freighter was becoming their only home. However, there was still one problem that everyone was acutely aware of, the reality that inside the aircraft was nothing that remotely resembled a hospital plane—no litters, field dressings for serious wounds, plasma, or IVs. Only the backpack of medical supplies for superficial wounds that Raylan had confiscated from the aid unit along with some morphine and a lab coat. This factor was constantly on everyone's mind. With each round-trip, the number of soldiers at the headquarters declined, leaving less and less men to defend the base. They never knew when they might land at the headquarters and find the place completely overrun with Japanese.

On the last pass of the night over Lashio from ten thousand feet MSL, Jay said to Elmo, "Is the last man out the door?"

"I'll check with Jaworski." Elmo made his way to the back to see if all the jumpers had gotten out. When he returned to the cockpit, Jay was flying the airplane from the copilot's seat.

"Have a seat, Barker. You can fly that approach into Ledo from the left seat. Fly direct to the Burma fix and begin the approach there, just like we usually do."

"Okay, Boss, I'm on it."

"Wake me up if you have any questions."

Trip after trip, Elmo became more and more comfortable flying the DC-3. The jumps were going much more smoothly. Raylan's idea had made a huge difference. All of the Chinese soldiers were inexperienced at jumping from an airplane, and many more lives would have been lost were it not for Raylan's improvised static lines.

It had been a long week. The crew was returning to Charlie's headquarters airstrip from Ledo when Elmo said to Jay, "Three more trips tomorrow night, and we'll be done. I'm ready for some R&R. How about you?"

"As soon as we're finished with this operation, we'll make that trip to Calcutta and then go find my family. You can get some R&R in the back of the airplane on the way to Alaska."

"We haven't even started the trip yet, and I already need a vacation."

Jay didn't answer, and Elmo gathered that he wasn't in the mood for humor.

Still in the right seat where he had been since handing the left seat over to Elmo four days before, Jay looked out over the starboard wing into the darkness. Instantly he realized that something was wrong. Quickly he slid open the side window to see more clearly. A knot appeared in his stomach as his suspicions were confirmed.

Black smoke poured from the engine cowling, a shiny sheen of oil plastered the surface of the wing streaming from the trailing edge of the ailerons directly behind the engine. He barked an order to Elmo, "Shut down that starboard engine."

Elmo looked shocked. "What's up, Captain?"

"We got trouble. Shut it down before it catches fire."

Elmo carefully reduced the manifold pressure, letting the exhaust gas temperatures cool and then shut down the crippled engine.

As thrust from the dead engine deteriorated, eventually disappearing altogether, the aircraft increasingly yawed to the right. "What do you want me to do, Boss?"

"That depends on what the problem is. We have a bad oil leak coming from under the cowling at about the ten o'clock position on the engine. What do you think that is?"

"Could be a broken oil line or a cracked cylinder, won't know for sure until I can get the cowl off and see inside."

"We're still an hour away from Charlie's headquarters." Jayson commented, "If it's one of the jugs, would they have a spare?"

"I seriously doubt it, and even if they do, it would be for the general's plane, which is a DC-2, and obviously the jugs aren't the same, but there might be one in Anshun at the Flying Tigers's maintenance facility. It might be a little tough maintaining our altitude, but we should be able to make it to Tiger Mountain on one engine."

"Okay, keep going on to Anshun, trim that left rudder for single engine operation, and increase the manifold pressure on the portside engine to forty-eight inches. Try to maintain your altitude if you can. If it starts getting hot, reduce the MP back a little, and let it down to twelve thousand feet MSL.

"What about the rest of the paratroopers waiting for us at headquarters? Shall we do a low pass to let them know we're thinking about them?"

"No, right now the only thing we're thinking about is that left engine and maintaining terrain clearance. If we give up our present altitude, we would never get it back with this load on. We have enough fuel, and it should be daylight by the time we get to Tiger Mountain, so hopefully, we can get this thing fixed and get back to business. This should only cost us a day at the most. If things go too bad for us, we can unload some of those drums of fuel out of the door."

Over three hours had passed since Jay first noticed the oil leak requiring the engine shut down. Raylan and Wonlukee lay sound asleep directly behind the cockpit on the flight deck floor. Elmo, still flying the airplane from the left seat, was struggling to maintain what bit of altitude they had left, which had gradually deteriorated from fifteen thousand feet to ten thousand feet while still flying over terrain elevations that averaged nine thousand feet and more. He said to Jay, "We're burning extra fuel by weaving our way around these higher peaks and ridges. How much farther do you think it is to Tiger Mountain?"

"It should be coming into view soon. I was hoping it would be a little lighter than this, but we'll still be able to see its outline against the night sky. However, it will probably be dark down in the jungle where the airstrip lies. If we get there before daylight, we may need to circle a while until it gets light. I'm not familiar enough with that airstrip environment to attempt a landing in the dark."

For thirty more minutes, the crippled DC-3 droned its way toward Anshun on one engine, narrowly missing many of the higher ridges that were sill undetectable in the darkness.

Finally, Jay pointed straight ahead. "I see it," he said.

"Elmo, let me have the airplane. When we're established on final approach, I may need some help with the left rudder to get this thing lined up. We're already practically out of trim. It will take a lot of rudder pressure, so be ready in case I need you."

"Okay, Boss, you have the airplane. Do you want to fire that engine back up just for the landing?"

"No, the airstrip is long enough. We should be able to get in there all right."

"I was thinking more in terms of having to make a go-around."

"Loaded on one engine...a go-around is not an option," Jay replied.

Jay headed directly to Tiger Mountain, silhouetted against the sky and towering well above the lower ridges.

"I can't see anything down below. Can you make out the airstrip yet?"

"Not yet, Captain, maybe we should go away and come back later when it gets daylight."

"I don't want to get too far away. We'll circle for a while and wait until it gets lighter."

The Red Cross special ops DC-3 circled for an additional forty-five minutes waiting for the horizon to slowly grow lighter in the east. Finally, the outline of the runway below them began to appear. Jay muttered under his breath as if he were talking only to himself, "I think I see it. I'm going to circle one more time and then start down."

"What if there are obstructions down there, like a downed tree or something?" Elmo asked. The anxiety he was feeling was beginning to tell in his voice.

"We'll look it over on the way down. If it looks good, we'll go on in. We should be able to determine all of that before we get too low."

Jay continued his counterclockwise circling with his eye on the dim outline of the airstrip below. Suddenly he stopped the descent and applied full power. "Something doesn't look right down there."

"What is it, Padre?"

"I'm not sure, I still can't see too good. There, I see now. It looks like the maintenance shop has been demolished, and there are huge potholes on the runway. I think the Japs have bombed the place. I see several trucks on their sides too, and the chow hall has been blown up."

Elmo stiffened; a shocked look came across his face. "What do we do now?"

"Kunming, we'll have to push on to Kunming."

"Padre, I hate to remind you, but these fuel gauges haven't worked right since your off-airport landing in that meadow a year ago, and I don't think we have enough fuel to make Kunming."

"Why? Didn't they top us off before we left Charlie's headquarters last night?"

"Not all the way."

"Why not all the way?"

"Because I told them we had enough to get us to Lashio and back with an hour of reserve, and we were short of time."

"Did you physically check the fuel to see exactly where it was on the stick?"

"Nosir."

"Well then, do you remember the day I taught you to pray?"

"Yesir."

"I hope so, because you need to get started right now."

"Aye, aye, Captain, Padre."

Jay knew their chances of making Kunming were slim at best. He also knew that God had delivered him from predicaments much worse. Although he had made his point with Elmo, he added his own prayer as well.

Father in heaven, the forces against us and our mission are greater than we can overcome with our limited human strength. We call on you, oh God. We call on Your power and arm to make a way for us. May all of this, somehow, someday, bring glory and honor to God's name. Amen.

The fully loaded DC-3 with its single engine handicap and motley crew of four tried in vain to gain additional altitude. Without which they would not be able to clear the mountainous terrain separating them from the Flying Tigers airbase in Kunming. Even if they could gain enough altitude to get above the lower ridges, circumnavigating around the high ridges and peaks was burning extra fuel they could ill afford to spare.

"Padre, what about Chungking?"

"What about it?"

"We have fuel onboard. Maybe we could find a way to get it into our tanks after we get on the ground."

"That would be fine, except we don't know how long it would take, and if we're on the ground too long, we might be detected."

Elmo thought a moment and replied, "Generalissimo flies that DC-2 in and out of there. He must refuel while he's there, so surely we can too, and it's considerably closer than Kunming."

"That doesn't solve the engine problem."

"No, it doesn't, but we aren't sure that it is an engine problem. That oil could be coming from a cracked oil fitting or a ruptured line. If that's the case, I could fix it, and if we can find enough fuel to get us back to headquarters, we could still finish our job."

"The Japs bomb Chungking every night, so I think the gimo probably fuels either at his headquarters or Kunming. On the other hand, if there is fuel, it would have to be someplace away from the city out of harm's way."

"There is one other consideration, Padre."

"What's that?"

"We could send Raylan and Wonlukee to look for your wife and kid while you and I work on the airplane."

Jay was silent, but Elmo could tell by the expression on his face that he liked the idea.

"Get Wonlukee up here."

Elmo climbed from the left seat, awoke the slumbering ex-paratrooper, and returned to the cockpit. He was not surprised to

THE FRUIT OF ATROCITY

see that his pilot had switched seats again and was now flying the airplane from the left seat.

"Here he is, Captain."

Jay looked over his shoulder to see his new recruit staggering toward him still half-asleep.

"Wonlukee, how well do you know Chungking?"

"Wonlukee know Chungking very well. Wonlukee live all of life in Chungking."

"Excellent, we have a problem. We had to shut down the starboard engine due to an oil leak, and we understand that Generalissimo Chiang Kai-shek keeps his personal aircraft somewhere near Chungking. Do you know where?"

"Yesuh, master Jaysonn-sonn, big boss keep airplane, no at big airport, big boss keep airplane, secret airport outside city."

"Secret airport? Do you know where it is? Can you help us find it?"

"Yesuh, master Jaysonn-sonn, master Jaysonn-sonn turn to there."

✪✪✪

The hospital plane was on a northwesterly heading to Kunming when Wonlukee pointed out of the right side window to a north by northeasterly heading. Jay carefully banked the airplane to track in the direction Wonlukee indicated.

"Elmo, do some navigation calculations and tell me how far we are from Chungking. Wonlukee, you stay up here with us and make sure we don't get off course. We're short on fuel."

Suddenly, from the cargo area, Jay heard a shout, "Boss, we got company!" Raylan yelled.

"Elmo, forget that for now. Go see what's going on."

Elmo put aside his maps and navigation utensils and made his way to the back of the transport. Jay looked over his left shoulder behind the freighters wing and gasp at what he saw. There, flying abeam the open cargo door, was a Japanese Zero fighter plane;

the huge red sun painted on the top of each wing glistening in the morning sunlight.

Raylan burst through the cockpit door. "We got trouble, Boss, a Jap fighter is parked on our left flank."

"What's he doing back there?"

"Nothing, Boss, just looking at us."

"Can you get to your sniper rifle without him seeing you?"

"I can try."

"Good, get your rifle, and position yourself out of sight by the door opening. Wait until you're sure you can get him before he turns away. If you think you can make the shot, go ahead, but don't try shooting through the propeller. I'll try to keep this thing as still as I can."

"Okay, Boss, here goes."

"Tell Elmo to put on that lab coat and let the pilot see him. Maybe it will distract him long enough for you to take your shot."

Elmo yelled from the back, "He's gone. He moved up on top."

"He'll be back. Raylan, now is your chance, get ready by the door."

Jaworski quickly positioned himself by the cargo door out of sight from the outside. Elmo grabbed a white coat from among the stash of medical supplies and stood in the doorway. He said to Raylan, "Tell the Boss the zero is hanging out behind the tail. I think he intends to follow us."

Raylan rushed back to the cockpit and repeated the information to Jay.

"He's just sitting back there behind us, Boss, looks like he is going to follow us to Chungking."

"That's not good. He knows the main airport is out of commission and figures we have some alternate place to land, so he's not going to shoot us down until we lead him to the generalissimo's airstrip."

"Maybe we should change course again and head to Kunming. He won't want to go there all by himself."

THE FRUIT OF ATROCITY

"If we do that, we will no longer be of any use to him, and he might shoot us down. Besides, we don't have enough fuel to make it to Kunming and maybe not even enough to get to Chungking."

"This day just keeps getting better, doesn't it? I have an idea, Boss, if he doesn't come back along side of us, where I can get a shot at him, maybe I can take him out with a hand grenade?"

"That's a long shot, Raylan, if it hits the prop before it gets to the cockpit, it won't do enough damage to put him down, and he'll shoot us down in retaliation. However, a couple of those sticks of dynamite might work. You would need to let the fuses burn a little low before you sling it. How close is he to us anyway? If he's too close, it might damage our plane, and if he's too far back, you might miss him altogether."

"I'll go check, Boss, but it looks like we're running out of options anyway, so we got nothing to lose?"

"Use your best judgment, Raylan. I'll say another prayer for us."

Raylan picked three sticks of dynamite from the crate and taped them together. He braided the fuses into one and scrambled to the door.

Elmo watched him in astonishment. "What do you think *you're* doing?"

"I'm going to blow me up a Jap."

"You may be going to blow us up with him."

"Part of the cost of doing business partner, stand back." Raylan lit the fuse and started counting.

"Hang on to me so I don't throw myself out of the door."

Elmo grabbed Raylan's belt from behind and braced his shoulder against the hinge side of the cargo door.

"One, two, three, four, five, six, seven." The ten-inch-long fuse burned quickly, and with only two inches of fuse left, Raylan heaved the package of explosives as hard as he could straight up into the air. The two men turned and ran toward the cockpit. A moment later, a violent explosion rocked the cargo plane. The compression of the blast pushed the tail of the airplane straight down, placing the aircraft's attitude into a full stall.

Jay was already operating on a wing and a prayer trying to keep the aircraft above the terrain when suddenly he realized the aircraft had entered an abrupt stall that was about to result in a unrecoverable spin due to the lack of altitude over the terrain. Instantly he reduced power to the portside engine with one hand while struggling to pull the plunging aircraft out of its nosedive with the other, all the while applying opposite rudder application to counter the developing spin. Frantically he hollered for his copilot, "Elmo, get up here…fire up that starboard side!"

"Yes, sir, Padre." Elmo piled into his seat and fired the crippled engine, and as Jay neutralized the downward spiral, simultaneously the two pilots slammed the throttles to full power.

"Pull it up! Help me pull it up!" Jay yelled.

Desperately they fought to keep the craft above the treetops that were now but a few feet beneath the underbelly of the airplane.

Elmo's voice was quivering when he said to Jay, "That was a close one, Padre. We almost bought the farm that time."

"Give me thirty-six inches on both engines until we get some of our altitude back and then shut that right side back down."

"Aye, aye, Captain," Elmo said.

"What happen back there? Did Raylan score?"

"I guess he did. I haven't seen any bullets coming our way."

With both engines performing once again, the DC-3 was soon climbing high above the terrain.

"How's the oil leak?" Jay inquired.

"It's still there, and the smoke is getting worse. I better shut it down. I think it's more than just a fitting too. It wouldn't be smoking that bad if it were only in the line, so I'm sure it is one of the jugs."

Elmo once again shut down the starboard engine, and turning to Jay, he said, "Maybe the general is home, and we can use his plane. I could have his pilot fly me to Kunming and get another jug while you and Wonlukee go look for your family. Raylan could stay and watch the airplane."

"Right now, the general is the last person I want to see."

"Hey boss…" Raylan said, pointing out of the windshield. "We got Chungking, straight ahead and ten miles."

"I see that. Get Wonlukee up here."

Raylan retreated to the rear of the plane and soon returned with the new crew member.

"Wonlukee, where did you say the general parks his airplane?" Wonlukee pointed to the far west side of the city, at the thick bamboo forest beyond.

"Master Jaysonn-sonn go past city. You see dirt road running straight through middle of two big rice paddies. Road disappear into jungle. Master Jaysonn-sonn land aeroplane on road, drive aeroplane into jungle out of sight."

"Are you sure?"

"Yesuh, master Jaysonn-sonn, Wonlukee very sure. Drive into jungle, you see."

"Elmo, as soon as we reach the center of the city, I need you to fire up that starboard engine one more time. We're going to need it. If we don't get this right the first time, we won't stand a chance at making a go-around without the extra thrust."

"Aye, aye, Captain. What if there isn't enough oil to keep it running and the whole engine seizes?"

"Then I guess we'll be toast, but we have to take the chance. We'll keep an eye on the oil temperature gauge. If it approaches redline, we'll shut it down again."

The starboard engine once again sprung to life. Jayson immediately climbed to two thousand feet above the city of twenty-nine million people. The huge city of Chungking spread out over fifteen miles across. As the central portion of the city passed below, Jayson lined up with where he anticipated the centerline of the dirt road would most likely be, still more than ten miles away.

As they peered down at the city below, Jayson could see the extensive damage from the frequent bombings. Thousands of people scattered and ran as the ship passed over their rooftops. Jay said to Elmo, "As soon as we get past the edge of town, we should be able to see the dirt road. We'll carry power until we clear the city. As soon as we touch down, shut that engine down again."

"Aye, aye, Captain."

Suddenly, both engines began to sputter. With one last cough, they backfired and expired. For a long moment, the shocking sound of silence took the breath from the two pilots, while the silent whistling of the rushing wind over the wings sounded like ghost breathing down their necks.

"We just ran out of fuel, Captain."

Jay didn't answer. The aircraft was sinking fast, and it was obvious that within seconds, they were going to crash straight into the middle of the densely populated city below them.

Jay shuddered as the view through the windscreen seemed remarkably reminiscent of another time and place, a time when God had moved his arm to save Lieutenant Jayson Bold from certain disaster, and a place where He had created a meadow (lamb) out of a mountain (thicket) in the final seconds of his life. Once again, Jay prayed. *Oh God, send us a miracle in Jesus's name.*

Chapter 10

Like a dose of anesthesia, the grotesque silence benumbed the crew of the doomed aircraft as they held their breath in anticipation of their mortality. Broken only by the sound of the wind over the surface of the wings, the silence filled the cabin of the Douglas DC-3 as it plummented faster and faster toward the densely populated city of Chungking. Until from but two hundred feet above the buildings, the pilot could vividly see the expressions of terror on the faces of the people as they scattered, running in every direction.

The moment the engines quit, the hospital plane had become a gliding bomb. As if in slow motion, it dropped from the sky toward the masses of people, threatening the innocent citizens of Chungking, with even more death and destruction—citizens who were completely unaware that their end was mere moments away.

Elmo cried out, "We're going to hit, Padre. We're going to hit! Holy Jesus!"

Suddenly, like rays of the sun piercing through the center of a thunderstorm, both engines began to cough and backfire; smoke poured from the exhaust as they came sputtering back to life. Pastor Jay Baldwin shoved the dual throttles to full power only an instant before the aircraft crashed into the sea of tin roofs, barely twenty feet below the aircraft. The huge propellers clawed at the late morning air, and in the final seconds before impact, the terrifying free fall was arrested. Slowly at first, the aircraft began to climb, gradually rising up and away from the crowded city.

"Where...did that come from?" Elmo stuttered.

Jay breathed for the first time in what seemed like hours.

"I just remembered that long-range fuel tank we had installed in Anshun. I thought now might be a good time to try it out."

"Ya, think!" Elmo's voice trembled with credulous exasperation.

Jay said to him, "Maybe you shouldn't have waited so long to pray to *Jesus*."

"What do you mean?"

"Well, just when you thought we were goners, I heard you call out to Him."

"I didn't realize that was a prayer."

"*He* must have thought it was."

The landing gear rumbled along the rough dirt trail as the aircraft slowed to a taxi. Used mostly for water buffalo and single axle carts hauling firewood to the city, Jay taxied the Douglas to the far end of the dirt trail into the dark canopy of bamboo trees. Finally, out of the sun and under the shade of the dense forest, his eyes slowly adjusted to the lesser light. The Red Cross crew quickly realized they had entered a completely different world, another city that no one was aware existed, secluded from the sky, the sun, the outside world, and, most importantly, the war.

Hundreds of people scurried about like ants. A large contingent of greeters gathered around the aircraft. Jay could hear them clamoring against the fuselage.

A dozen, or so, WWI Russian biwing, single-seater Polikarpov E-15 fighter aircraft sat in a line along the left edge of the improvised runway, along with several two-seater, low-wing monoplane Polikarpov E-16s—all WWI vintage aircraft.

To the right, farther back in the trees, Jay could see a city of bungalows constructed on stilts. He continued his taxi straight ahead into the middle of the village.

Raylan shouted, "Boss, they're coming aboard."

"Let them. Remember, we're doctors. Make sure you have your new identities with you." He turned in his seat and said to Elmo, "Go see if they have a maintenance shop."

"Aye, aye, Captain."

"If they don't have what you need, take one of those monowings and go to Kunming. Chennault will have it. If he won't give you what you need, then steal it and hightail it back here."

"I don't know how much hightailing I'll be able to do with that thing, but I'll do my best," Elmo replied.

Jay breathed a sigh of relief that they had made it to the ground in one piece, and now he needed a minute to be alone and not only give thanks but make further request to God in heaven for the parts they now needed to fix the airplane. He had just begun to pray when he faintly heard a familiar voice.

"My husband, is my husband here?"

Jay's heart leapt within his chest. His breath stopped, and he would have cried out were it not for the golf balls in his throat. Frantically he unhooked the safety harness that held him in his seat. As he burst through the cockpit door, a blur the shape of the woman he loved rushed through the opening, slamming against him so hard he nearly fell backward into the instrument panel. He grunted as the impact forced the air from his lungs; tears of joy flooded his eyes, and he gasped. "Ah-lam, Ah-lam, oh my dear God in heaven, Ah-lam *it's...it's* you."

For several minutes, they embraced each other, quietly sobbing and gasping for air as their lips pressed together in a prolonged and passionate kiss.

"My husband, I love you. I have missed you so much. I knew you would come. I prayed you would come. I knew that somehow God would bring you to me."

"Ah-lam, I love you too. Yes, God is good. He has seen fit to once again bring us together." Her face was buried against his neck; he pulled her away to look into her eyes.

"Where is Ching-Lan?" Ah-lam was quiet. Jay repeated the question more fervently, "Where is Ching-Lan?"

"She is at home with Madam Chiang Kai-shek."

"Home! Where is home? Do you live with Madam Chiang?"

"Yes, I will take you there. The air escaped from his lungs as if he had just resurfaced from a dive.

"Ah-lam," he said softly, "tell me what all they have done with you, and how is our daughter? Is she well?"

"Yes, she is well. We live with the Madam, and she is very good to us, but we are well guarded. Our apartment is underground. I am forbidden to bring the child with me when I go out." Ah-lam lifted her head and looked into her husband's eyes.

"How did you know I was here?"

"I didn't. I was told you were living at the university in the city. We would have looked for you there were it not for our engine trouble."

Jay briefly explained the circumstances that led to their finding the secret city in the jungle. Ah-lam took his hand and led him away from the crowd of people. He said to her, "What do you call this place?"

"It is called Chiang Kai City. It is a subterranean city of over two thousand. Mostly soldiers and maintenance personnel live here with their families. The generalissimo and his wife live in a separate underground apartment. It is a safe place concealed from the war."

Jayson looked around at the secret airport. Besides the old Russian fighter aircraft, which were apparently still airworthy, he saw several troop trucks, but he could see no indication of a maintenance facility.

"Where does the general keep his airplane?"

"When the general is home, it is kept in the maintenance facility, which is also underground. However, he is gone today, as are many of the army personnel."

"Will you take me there?"

"Yes, but won't you come and see your daughter first and stay with me a while?"

"Of course I will, my love. I'll go with you right now."

Jay followed Ah-lam to a long building built far back into the forest, similar in construction to the barracks where he had stayed back at Charlie's headquarters. The floor level was raised six feet above the ground and accessible only by a long pole eight inches in diameter with notches cut into it that provided steps. He followed his wife as she led him along a porch, its roof covered with bamboo thatch. Soon they came to a room on the back side of the building.

There were no windows, and the door was merely a curtain. Inside was a bed made of bamboo poles and a large floor mat, woven from bamboo leaves. Ah-lam paused outside the opening to remove her sandals. Jay did the same.

"What is this place?"

"I often come here during the day to be alone. We will have privacy here." She turned to her husband and melted her body against his. Jay felt strange at first, as though he was doing something illegal.

"Take me and have me, my husband." The human passion for love burned like fire within him. She took him by the hand and pulled him toward her.

For a brief period, Jay Baldwin had again become Jayson Bold. More and more he felt the confusion of the dual personalities which he lived. He longed for the life they first had in Freeland. How naive he had been to think that their Shangri-la could last. Yet here, and for a few brief moments, he was in her arms again, and she was in his. What the next hours or days or weeks would bring for the present moment did not matter. He clutched his precious wife against him and was unable to think of anything but her stunning beauty and the smoldering passion of her love.

An hour had passed, and in that time, their love had reached its crescendo three times. Exhausted, they lay together, their needs for the time fullfilled.

"How long can you stay with me, my husband?"

"Do you mean here in this bed, this afternoon?"

"No, silly, how long will you be here before you go away again?"

"I will never go away. I will never leave you again." Jay paused as he heard the drone of a Polikarpov E-16 take to the air.

"Who is flying away?" Ah-lam asked.

"That's Elmo, taking off for Kunming. As soon as we get that engine fixed and get fueled up, we're going to finish our commitment with Charlie, then, pick up those kids and head for Alaska. You and Ching-Lan are going with us."

"How will I get the baby past the guards?"

"What guards?"

"There are guards at the entrance to the underground apartment."

"I'll figure a way to do that. Do the guards know about us, or are they just posted at the door?"

"I am not sure exactly what they know. However, they do know I am not allowed to take the baby out alone."

"Do they work for the general, or are they assigned exclusively to Madam Chiang?"

"The generalissimo assigned them to her, but they do whatever she says."

"Good," Jayson said, relieved. "I got the feeling during that meeting back at the gimo's headquarters that she was somewhat sympathetic to our situation."

"Yes, she is my very good friend, and I am sure she will let me go with you. But if you take us with you, we must go straight from here to America. Otherwise, Ching-Lan and I must stay here with her."

"We only have three more parachute drops to make, and I'll be done with Charlie. I was planning on dropping you off at Freeland until I finished the drops and then take us all to Alaska from there. I certainly don't believe the Lord arranged this set of circumstances so I could leave you behind again. The only reason I did before is because they kidnapped you away from me."

"My darling, if I go with you now, the Madam may be at risk. The generalissimo does not know that his wife is helping us. If she is discovered, she could be charged with treason."

"So you know about that?"

"About what?"

"I received a message from Captain Prichard that came from Madam Chiang, which he passed on to me. She is the one who provided the information that you were in Chungking. She also provided you and Ching-Lan with new passports."

"So that is how you knew where to find us. She has said that she wants to do everything she can to help us get to America. However, my brother, Charlie, and the generalissimo do not intend to let us go. They only do what they must to make it appear they are helping. If we go to Freeland and my brother finds us there, he will take us, and you will never find us again. He intends on using you as his personal pilot long after the war is over in his fight against communism. He believes you belong to him for the rest of your life because he saved you after you crashed."

"I got news for him, as I said before, the only one I belong to is God and you, and if I leave you here, I may never see you again. You can tell the Madam I appreciate all that she is doing for us, but you're going with me, and that's final. You and Ching-Lan can live with us in the airplane until we're through with the drops. Then we have to make a quick trip to Calcutta, and from there, we'll pick up the orphans in Freeland and head northeast to Manchuria. Besides, Charlie is in Burma fighting the Japanese. By the time he gets back, we'll be shoveling snow and warming our toes in front of a cozy fireplace in Wasilla."

Ah-lam snuggled against her husband and smiled. She could feel his strength once again prodding against her, and for the first time since their separation, she felt safe. She turned her face to him and said, "Soon I will take you to see Madam Chiang, and you can tell her yourself. But first I desire that you make love to me again."

Two hours later, Jay and Ah-lam were silently making their way through the jungle to a secluded place where two armed guards stood before the entrance of a small bamboo-thatched roof hut. They paused just out of sight of the guards, who, as yet, were not aware of their presence.

"Are you sure the general is not here?"

"I am sure. I rarely see him."

"Is the Madam home?"

"Yes, she is taking care of Ching-Lan."

"Does she know I'm here?"

"Yes, she is the one who told me you were coming just moments before you arrived."

"Then someone must have alerted her before we landed. How could anyone have known?

"There is a two-way radio communication from the city only three miles away. They received messages transmitted from an AM radio transmission outpost ten miles east of Chungking. Everyone knew of your coming long before you passed over the city. The last message received said the engines were no longer working and the airplane was going to crash into the city. Then, miraculously, the engines restarted. Everybody now believes you have great favor with Buddha."

"Did you know it was me?"

"Yes, my husband, I knew. I also know that it is our God who brought you back to me, not Buddha, and I was not afraid."

"Is Madam Chiang expecting me?"

"Yes, she said you must show your new identification to get past the guards. She has already informed them that you are a doctor and the Madam has sent for you. They do not know you are my husband. Ah-lam glanced at the army issue Colt .45

strapped to Jay's waist. "You should take that off. The guards will not let you pass if you are armed."

Jay stashed his sidearm close by and followed Ah-lam as they approached the guards. Surprisingly, neither of them paid much attention to his fake ID. A brief phone call—apparently to the underground bunker—and the guards let them through the bolted door to a long passage where they came to a second heavily bolted steel door.

Ah-lam reached for the light switch on the wall and flipped it up and down several times. Madam Chiang opened the door to her apartment and greeted them heartily.

"So nice to see you again, Mr. Baldwin."

"It's my honor, Madam Chiang. I hope we didn't disturb you."

"Not at all, come right in. Can I offer you anything?"

"I'm a little thirsty for water if you have any."

"I will get it for you," Ah-lam volunteered.

"Mr. Baldwin, I assume that your wife has informed you of the precarious position I am subjected to by extending you my help?"

"Yes, she has, and I understand, but I fear that if I don't take my family with me now, I may never see them again."

"Mr. Baldwin, I assure you that if you do take them now, neither they nor you will live to spend your lives together and neither will the orphans."

"Why do you think that? I can take them with me in the hospital plane, finish my parachute drops in Burma, and swing by Freeland to get the children. Then, we'll all take off for Alaska."

"It would be a swell plan, Mr. Baldwin, except for one detail."

"What would that be?" Jay asked.

"As soon as the generalissimo returns and finds your family gone, he would immediately put out an alarm. Besides, the children are no longer in Freeland where you left them."

Jay looked stunned. "No longer in Freeland? Then, where are they, and when were they taken away?"

"Immediately after you left for Ledo, the general sent his plane to Freeland and brought them back to Chungking because he and Charlie both anticipated that you might renege on your obligation. They also destroyed the airstrip you built there so you would be unable to land. Charlie and the generalissimo are together frequently, and I expect that he may be with my husband when he returns."

"I dropped Charlie off at Lashio nearly three weeks ago. He's supposed to be running around in the jungle of Burma, killing Japs."

"Mr. Baldwin, you do not know Charlie and my husband very well. Chiang Kai-shek sent his plane back to Lashio the next day and brought Charlie out. He has been here at least once since that day and is monitoring your movements from a distance."

Jay rolled his eyes.

"I should have known. Does he know I'm here?"

"It is very possible, and even if he doesn't because you missed your scheduled parachute drops, he will soon find out, so if you are going to do this, you must do it quickly."

Jayson's head swirled with concerns and speculations as to what to do. The safety of his family was top priority, but not losing his family to the scoundrel Charlie and the generalissimo—who was turning out to be an inconsistent ally at best—was an even higher priority.

"Madam Chiang, whenever we get this ship airworthy, I'll be ready to go. Can you get those children here by then?"

"Mr. Baldwin, what about your commitment to Charlie and the generalissimo and your last parachute drops?"

"What about it? They aren't keeping their commitments to me, so why should I keep mine to them? I stand to lose my family, and the only promise I made, that was not under duress, was to you and my wife, which is to get those children out of China."

"Please remember, Mr. Baldwin, just because Charlie cannot be trusted does not mean he is not effectively fighting the

Japanese in Burma. If the Japanese win there, all of China and India will be lost, and the United States will be hard pressed to win the war in the Pacific. This is a very important campaign, and I wish you would at least finish the paratrooper drops."

"I am more than glad to do that, but I need to get my family and those kids somewhere safe until then."

"Why don't you take them to India?"

"You mean Ledo?"

"Yes, wouldn't they be safe there until you are ready to take them to Alaska."

Jay thought for a minute about the reaction he would receive from Captain Prichard. Maybe the Madam had a point. After all, how could they say no to sixteen orphans?

"Madam, I think you have a good idea, so how soon can you get those children here?"

"When will your airplane be ready to go?" the Madam asked.

"I don't know for sure. My mechanic took off to Kunming in one of those old E-16s to find a cylinder. Whenever he gets the new one bolted back on, we'll be ready to go."

Madam Chiang paused for a moment, considering the situation. She said to him, "We should not use the radio, so I will write a note and send a courier to Chungking. We will have the children here by tomorrow morning, first light. Will that be soon enough, Mr. Baldwin?"

"It'll have to do. I just hope the plane will be ready by then. Well, Madam Chiang, I appreciate your help, and I hope you won't suffer any consequences for this."

"Don't worry about me, Mr. Baldwin. My life has always been, and will always be, a sacrifice for the cause of China. In our country, each generation lives for the prosperity of the next. That is how we have survived for these many thousands of years."

Jay turned to Ah-lam who had been listening while holding the baby.

"Ah-lam, take everything you need for the baby, and I want you in a safe place close to the aircraft so we can go at a moment's notice."

"Are we going to Alaska when the children arrive?"

"No, I am going to leave you and the children somewhere safe, and after I finish that last airdrop over Lashio, I'll return to get you, but I'm not going to leave you here. However, we need to get going first thing in the morning, by daylight at the latest. Madam Chiang, we need a couple of men we can trust. Do you have any to spare?"

"Yes, you can take the two men that are guarding this bunker. I will inform them."

"Thank you, Madam Chiang. This might be the last time we ever see each other, and I want you to know that I hold you in the highest esteem."

"Thank you, Mr. Baldwin. I have told your wife many times that she has chosen her husband well. I will make your name a monument to China's victory for many years to come."

Jay retrieved his weapon and carried his daughter as he followed Ah-lam through the thick forest of bamboo. One of the guards led the way and the other followed behind Jay.

Ching-Lan, oohed and ahhed and tugged at her daddy's lips and ears as if she had never missed a day with her father. As they walked, Jay frequently stumbled over the roots and rocks in the path as he nuzzled and kissed his little girl.

Suddenly, the lead guard stopped, and Ah-lam stopped, and Jay didn't stop, almost knocking her down as he bumped into her.

"What is it?" he asked in a low tone.

"Sh, I hear something," Ah-Lam said. "Don't let the baby cry."

Jay rocked the child.

"I don't hear anything?" he said.

Ah-lam held her finger to her lips.

"Sh, sh! Listen." Finally, Jay began to hear the faint drone of an airplane coming closer, and it was not the monowing.

"That's the general's DC-2!" Jay exclaimed. "We need to hurry and get you hid. Can these guards really be trusted?

"Yes, I think so."

"I hope you're right. I want you to go stay in the bungalow where we spent the afternoon." Jay took his wife in his arms and held her close to him. "As soon as it's safe, I'll come for you."

"I'll be waiting there for you, my husband. I love you."

Jay kissed his wife and daughter and turned to the two Chinese guards. Speaking to them in their own language, he said to them, "Take my family to her bungalow and keep her safe. I'll be back for them in the morning. If I'm not here by daybreak, you two bring them to me. I'll be in the Red Cross airplane. It will be parked on the runway." Jay looked intently into their eyes. "You do that for me, and I'll take you with us, okay?" Both men grew excited and vigorously nodded.

Jay turned to leave not knowing for sure when, where, or if he would ever see his family again. The familiar sickening feeling in the pit of his stomach returned, as well as the hurt in his heart. He could feel the panic setting in that he had felt when Charlie first separated him from Ah-lam almost a month before. He clenched his fist and set his jaw as he hurried along.

Quickly, Jay made his way back to where he had parked the converted C-47. As he emerged from the forest of trees in the staging area; the sound of the incoming DC-2 increased as the airplane came closer. Jay looked out through the opening in the forested canopy above and watched the camouflaged airplane with the red star on its tail as it touched down only moments before it entered under the canopy of the forest.

Jay whispered a prayer, "Lord God in heaven, I'm certain I know who that is, and I desperately need your help."

It had been over eight hours since he had landed and followed Ah-lam to her bungalow. Jay looked to see if the hospital plane was still where he had parked it—it was gone. *Elmo probably put it in the maintenance facility, wherever that is*, he thought.

Jayson crept out of sight toward the general's plane. He looked around for any sign of Raylan but did not see him. He kept along the edge of the tree line to remain as undetectable as possible, working his way to the far side of the cart trail he had used as a runway. Jayson glanced all around to see if anyone had spotted him, then made his way around the tail of the gimo's DC-2, still parked on the road facing into the forest.

Several minutes had passed since the propellers had stopped. Yet the side passenger door remained closed. Jay could see movement through the cockpit window, but it was so badly glazed he was unable to recognize who was there.

Suddenly, the side door opened, and to his surprise, Elmo stood in the doorway. Jay moved out of the shadows toward him. "What the…Criminy Christmas Elmo, what are you doing in there?"

Elmo placed his finger over his mouth as a warning gesture to keep quiet. Then he let down the boarding ladder and motioned for Jay to stay back. To Jay, it seemed that Elmo was acting strangely suspicious. He unfastened the strap securing his pistol and started up the ladder.

As he reached the top, a familiar figure pushed the mechanic aside and took his place in the doorway while holding a German Luger, pointed at the back of Elmo's head. Jay hesitated as he looked into the deadly, black eyes of his brother-in-law.

"Charlie…what are you doing here, and what's with the gun?"

"Charlie come, help Jai-sonn fix Charlie's airplane, make sure Jai-sonn keep promise to Charlie."

Jay stepped into the DC-2 as Charlie moved back against the far wall, dragging Elmo with him.

"We had a cylinder go bad on us. We're trying to get it fixed. Besides, how is threatening us with a gun helping us get our job done?

Charlie pushed Elmo aside and pointed the gun at Jay's belly.

"When Jai-sonn finish parachute drops, Charlie have much more work for airplane to do."

"Charlie, this is the second time you've pointed a gun at me. I told you the last time that if you ever did that again, I would make you sorry. Now you're doing it again."

Charlie raised the gun and pointed it at Jayson's face.

Jay ignored it and said to Elmo, "Did you find the parts we need?"

"Yeah, that and more." Jay noticed Elmo had picked up a one-inch diameter pipe about eighteen inches long, which he was holding behind his leg, out of sight from Charlie. Realizing his copilot was waiting for a chance to hit Charlie from behind, Jay frowned at him and discreetly shook his head.

He said to Elmo, "More, as in what, and how much?"

Elmo pointed to a large crate.

"I got a whole engine, a 1,200 hp Pratt and Whitney."

"A whole engine is a lot of weight. We need to lighten it up a bit. Can you remove what parts we might need and leave the rest here?"

"Not a problem, Boss."

"I hope those cylinders aren't too worn out.

Charlie interjected, "Jai-sonn take one cylinder only, leave rest of motor at old headquarters when we go to get paratroopers. No can come back here no more."

"Listen, Charlie, I intend to get our ship flying again and make those last few parachute drops. Then, me, my family, my crew, and those orphans are leaving China and going to America. And you, my dear brother-in-law, would be making a big mistake if you try to get in the way of that."

Charlie stepped forward and pointed the gun just inches from Jay's forehead. He said to him, "Charlie, shoot you right here and make the fat one fly my plane for me." Charlie gestured toward Elmo.

Elmo replied, "Good luck with that. You'll have to shoot me too, buddy, because I ain't working for nobody but the Padre."

Then, from the open doorway, another voice joined the conversation.

"Nobody's going to shoot either one of you, and whoever you are that's holding that gun on my boss, you have two seconds to drop it before I waste your brains all over the inside of that piece of crap DC-2."

All eyes turned to see Raylan Jaworski, standing at the foot of the ladder, his sniper rifle aimed squarely at Charlie's head.

Jay slowly reached for the nine millimeter Luger. "I'll take that." Charlie, still glaring at Jay, reluctantly released his grasp of the weapon.

Elmo said to Jay, "What do you want to do with him, Padre?"

"Gag him and tie him up. We'll leave him in the back of this airplane for now. Oh, by the way, how did you wind up with the general's plane? I heard you when you left in that old monowing shortly after we arrived. What did you do with it?"

"It's still in Kunming, parked on the ramp. When I got there, I went looking for the parts I needed and ran into a guy I knew in maintenance. He's the one who told me I could have this engine. I saw the general's plane parked nearby, and we decided to borrow it for a few hours. Then just as I was about to leave, Charlie showed up with his German Luger and insisted on coming along."

"So is the generalissimo still in Kunming?"

"Oh yeah, probably mad as a hornet and wondering where his ride went."

THE FRUIT OF ATROCITY

Jay took Elmo aside where Charlie could not hear and said to him, "Is there enough fuel in that monowing for me to get back here?"

"There should be. It was full when I left."

"Good, okay listen up, Elmo. I'm going to take Wonlukee with me, and if we're not back by daylight when those kids show up, then I want you and Raylan to get them to Alaska without me. Do you understand?"

"The orphans are coming here?"

"Yes, they'll be here in the morning, so will my wife and child. Are you going to do this for me?"

"Padre, what makes you think you won't be back by then? It's only two hours each way, and you have all night."

"I know, and I'm sure I will be. I'm just saying that if something goes sideways, and I don't make it back, I want to know that my family and those kids made it. Are you going to give me your word or not?"

"You have my word, Padre. We'll get it done. But if you don't make it back here in the morning, you can bet I'll hoof it right back to China and find you one way or the other."

"Good, that's what I wanted to hear. Now, go get Wonlukee and send him to me, and you get started on that engine repair."

"Aye, aye, Captain."

Jay made his way back to where Raylan was still holding his gun on Charlie.

"Raylan, I want you to gag him and tie him up, then inject him with something that will keep him quiet. I want him to forget about us for a while. After that, get him into a parachute, bundle him up in a tarp, and secure him in the back of this DC-2, until we're ready to go."

"How am I supposed to do that and hold a gun on him at the same time?"

Jay slowly pulled his Colt .45 from its holster and cocked back the hammer. Pressing the muzzle against Charlie's belly, he said,

275

"Okay, Charlie, I don't want to have to put a bullet in you, but I will if you try any of that kung fu crap. Do you understand me?" Charlie stared at Jay without expression and said nothing. Jay backed away until he was a safe distance from Charlie and raised the gun, aiming it at his head.

"It has come to my attention that you think I belong to you for the rest of my life because you saved me out of that high meadow. Well, let me straighten you out about that. It was my God in heaven that saved me. He only used you at the time because you were handy, and if it had not have been you, it would have been someone else. He could have used a gorilla for that matter. Do you get it?"

Charlie continued his expressionless stare, never averting his eyes from Jay while Raylan tied his hands behind him.

Jay continued, "I was more than happy to help you with your covert operations and would have continued to do so as long as you needed me. All you had to do was let me get my family and those orphans to Alaska. But no, you had to hedge your bet by kidnapping my wife and child. Who would do that to their own sister and niece? So now, here we are, and you're still trying to force me to do something that I already told you I would do willingly. Well, now I got a headline for you. The deal is off, and I'm making a whole new deal. Do you want to hear it?" Charlie glared even more fiercely at Jay, his black eyes cold and unblinking and seething with hatred. "I guess you don't have anything to say. Well, you're going to hear it anyway: Good news, bad news. The good news is, I'm taking my wife and family, which includes all sixteen of the orphans living here in Chungking, and we're leaving you and your war behind. The bad news is, you're not going to be able to do anything about it. And right now, Jaworski is going to make you comfortable in the back of the airplane. Then, we're all going for a ride. How do you like them apples?"

Charlie's stare bore completely through his brother-in-law as if he were not there.

"Raylan, when you're done with that, see me up front, will you?"

"Okay, Boss."

Raylan tied Charlie's hands behind his back and bound his feet. Then secured him in the far back end of the general's plane where he covered him with a tarp. He then searched through his bag of medical supplies and found a vial of morphine, which he injected into Charlie's arm. Raylan was amazed that it seemed to have no effect on him at all. He checked the vial to be sure it was not merely saline. Then, assuming that Charlie would pose no further threat, went to the cockpit to see what more his boss wanted of him.

"I got him all squared away, Boss."

"Are you sure? Did you give him something to put him out."

"I gave him morphine, but it hardly fazed him."

"It will. Listen, Raylan, I need you to stand by Elmo in case he needs any help. I'm going to take Wonlukee with me and take this plane back to the general." Raylan looked surprised.

"Why?"

"Why what?"

"Why take Generalissimo's plane back. He can fly one of those bucket of bolts back here and get it himself. I'd just leave it here."

"I thought about that, but what if they come looking for us? When they see that the DC-2 isn't back yet, won't the general get suspicious and come looking for it?"

"Maybe, and maybe not. Wouldn't it be worse for you to go to Kunming and risk getting arrested? Didn't I hear you tell Charlie that we're taking those kids out of here in the morning?"

"Yeah, but I plan on being back by then."

"You don't have to worry about making it back if you don't go in the first place. Why take the chance? We're this close"—Raylan held up his thumb and forefinger with barely any daylight between them—"to getting this deal done. The last thing we need is to lose you. That would totally jeopardize the whole mission."

Jay thought for a moment. He said to him, "What about going to Calcutta? If I don't take that plane back, they will come after us, and we won't be able to get to Calcutta and back before we go."

"We'll have to go with the resources we already have. If you're having doubts, maybe you need to pray more."

Jay stared at Raylan with his mouth open.

Pray more? He's right. I do need to pray more. Obviously, God has opened a door of opportunity here, and I'm worried more about the generalissimo's inconvenience than I am about getting through that door before it slams shut.

"You're right, Jaworski."

"Good, so now, what are we going to do with your brother-in-law?"

"We'll take him with us. But we need to get him out of this airplane and hide him somewhere until Elmo has the Douglas ready to go."

"Why don't we just kill him?" Raylan asked.

Jay looked at Jaworski, shocked that he had such disregard for human life.

"Long story short, primarily, because he's my brother-in-law for one thing, and for another, he saved my life and my wife is his sister. Besides, there's enough killing going on in this war."

"Okay, whatever you say. You're the boss."

Jay looked at his watch. *Only two hours till dark.*

"Has anyone seen Wonlukee?"

"Wonlukee here, Master Jaysonn-sonn."

Jay looked up to see Wonlukee coming through the door.

"Wonlukee, we have a prisoner we need to keep out of sight. Do you know of a place around here where we can keep him until we're ready to leave in the morning?"

"Wonlukee know good place. Where is prisoner?"

Raylan led Wonlukee to the rear of the airplane and jerked the tarpaulin off of Charlie. Wonlukee gasp.

"Aah! It is Mr. Nee! Very important soldier. Why Mr. Nee prisoner?"

Jay turned to look into Wonlukee's eyes.

"A long time ago when I was badly injured, Mr. Nee gave me a potion to drink to ease my pain. It also sent me on a trip to lala land. Do you know how to make it?"

"Aah, yes, Wonlukee know. It is mixture of opium, marijuana, and Ginseng, mixed with rice milk. Very good for pain and for healing."

"Will you make enough to keep Mr. Nee intoxicated for a week or so? Then put him where he won't be discovered. We need to keep him alive but harmless."

"Yes, Master Jaysonn-sonn. Wonlukee can do."

"When you have it ready, come and get me before you try to give it to him by yourself."

"Okay, can do, Master Jaysonn-sonn."

"While you're doing that, I'm going to go get my family, I'll be right back."

Jay returned to the bungalow where the two Chinese soldiers stood guarding his family.

Speaking to them in their own language, he said to them, "Change of plans, fellas."

Ah-lam appeared in the doorway.

"What are we doing now, my husband?"

"We're going to spend the night in the gimo's plane, or until Elmo finishes the repairs on the Douglas. Should be done by morning. We'll leave as soon as the DC-3 is ready."

"I don't understand…"

"I'll explain later. Get Ching-Lan."

"What about—"

"Not now, Ah-lam, I'll explain later."

Ah-lam realized that something drastic had occurred that demanded the change of plans but knew not to inquire further. She accepted that her husband knew what was best.

Pastor Jay Baldwin, his family, and Wonlukee spent the night in the general's DC-2. Raylan and Elmo worked through the night, replacing the cracked cylinder on the DC-3. Charlie spent the night in a bomb shelter, guarded by the two soldiers Madam Chiang Kai-shek had donated to the cause.

✪✪✪

The light of another day had barely penetrated through the canopy of trees when Jay awoke, entwined in his wife's arms. He relished the quiet serenity of the moment and studied his wife's perfect beauty as she slept.

Suddenly he heard the voices of many people outside the aircraft. Someone was coming up the ladder.

"Padre!" Elmo hollered.

Jay quickly put on his pants and went to open the cargo door. There, at the foot of the ladder, were the sixteen orphans, Elmo Barker, and Raylan Jaworski. Jay said to Elmo, "Is the Douglas ready to go?"

"Aye, Captain, she's ready."

"Is anybody at that maintenance facility suspicious of us?"

"Not in the least. They all think we're a hospital plane full of volunteers working for the Red Cross."

"Good, is it fueled up?"

"Yesir."

"Are you absolutely sure this time?"

"Supervised it myself, Captain."

"Excellent, take Raylan and bring the airplane up here, and we'll get loaded up."

"I don't need him just for that. Maybe he can see to some of these other people that are outside."

"What other people?"

"There's a lot of the village people out here that think we're doctors, and they're seeking medical attention. And Raylan is the closest thing we have to an actual doctor."

Ah-lam, who had been listening, said to her husband, "I will take care of them."

"Thank you, dear, but Elmo is right. Raylan can do it.

"Raylan, take all those people over to the maintenance building."

Ah-lam took her husband's arm and looked into his eyes.

"I will help Raylan with the people. He will need a translator. Do you have food and blankets on board the plane for the trip?"

"We haven't had time to—"

"We have everything we need," Elmo interrupted.

Jay looked surprised. "Where did it come from? We didn't have anything when we arrived."

"I'm not sure, a bunch of people started bringing food and blankets along with children's clothing and piled it all up beside the DC-3 while I was working on it."

"What about fresh water?"

"We have a fifty-five-gallon drum with a hand pump."

Jay looked at his wife and smiled.

"I'll bet Madam Chiang had all that provided for us. Okay, Elmo, just leave the Douglas where it is, and we'll go over there and load it all on the plane while Raylan and Ah-lam see to these people."

Ah-lam said to him, "I hope the Madam doesn't get into trouble for this."

"I have a feeling it might be the gimo that would be in trouble if he tried to stop her," Jay replied.

"Padre, what about Charlie?" Elmo asked.

Jayson glanced in the direction of the bomb shelter.

"As soon as we're loaded, we'll get him and his two bodyguards on board. And be sure we have a parachute for him."

"A parachu—"

"That's all, Elmo, you're dismissed."

Ah-lam looked carefully at her husband.

"For what is the parachute, my husband?"

"For an emergency."

"Only one parachute for all of us?"
Jay didn't respond and left to go see the children.

Brigadier General Claire Chennault stood in the door of his office looking out on the flight line where eighteen P-40s and nine C-47s sat parked at attention. The P-40s were out of service due to a shortage of both parts and aircraft mechanics, and the C-47 pilots were getting much-needed sack time in the barracks before returning to Ledo.

Generalissimo Chiang Kai-shek sat in a chair behind General Chennault, complaining of the lack of resources President Roosevelt had committed to China's war effort with Japan. Chennault had already explained to him the president's predicament, several times, but Chiang did not seem to understand or didn't care to. In an attempt to change the subject, Chennault said to him, "Wasn't that your airplane out on the ramp yesterday morning?"

"Yes, Charlie Nee took it to Chungking. I am waiting for his return. He should have been back by now."

"Who flew that old monowing in here yesterday afternoon? Was that one of Charley's men?"

Chiang looked concerned.

"I thought he was one of yours."

"What made you think that?"

"He was American, and I know I have seen him before somewhere. I thought it was here."

Chennault turned around to face Chiang.

"What did he look like?"

"He was heavy-set, looked like the American baseball player… Baby Ruthy."

"You mean *Babe Ruth*?"

"Yes, that is the one."

"Where did you see him?"

THE FRUIT OF ATROCITY

"He was with one of your mechanics, and they were loading a big engine into my airplane. Charlie Nee was with them."

"Where do you think they were planning on going with that engine?"

"I assumed Charlie had made some sort of deal for it. I did not ask."

General Chennault lit a cigar and looked back at the flight line where the old Polikarpov E-16 sat parked, precisely where Elmo Barker had left it. He began to chuckle.

"Generalissimo, I believe that pilot and the mechanic I gave to your man Charlie has made off with your airplane."

Generalissimo stood and quickly made his way to stand beside General Chennault.

"Charlie would never allow that."

"Charlie may have met his match. Don't forget, that man was trained by the United States Army Air Corp. And I understand that your man Charlie kidnapped his wife and kid. If I were you, I'd be on my way to Chungking."

"Charlie has my airplane. I am stuck here until he brings it back."

"Can't you take that monowing sitting out there?"

"No can do, monowing too old and too slow, not enough protection for the generalissimo. I must wait for Charlie."

Chennault turned to look at the gimo. "If you want my opinion, I'm guessing Charlie doesn't have that DC-2 anymore, but if you want, I can grab one of my C-47s out there on the line and give you a ride back to Chungking."

"Yes, General, the generalissimo would be most grateful."

General Clair Chennault sent a lineman to prep one of the C-47s while he paid a visit to the maintenance building, where he soon found the mechanic who donated the old Pratt and Whitney engine to Elmo.

"What's your name soldier?"

"Corporal Jameson, sir."

"Did you see Elmo Barker in here yesterday?"
"Yes, sir."
"What did he want?"
"He needed a cylinder for a Pratt and Whitney, said he was the mechanic on a Red Cross hospital C-47 that you had assigned to him. So I gave him a whole engine. It needed overhauled anyway, thought he might need more parts from it sooner or later."
"Good man, Corporal. Did Barker say where this C-47 is parked?"
"No, sir, I helped him load it into the gimo's DC-2. Charlie Nee was with him, so I went back to work."
"I figured that. As you were, Corporal."

The two men saluted, and Chennault headed to the ramp where his C-47 and both the lineman along with Chiang Kai-shek stood waiting.

"General, I'm ready if you are. Let's go find your ship."

Pastor Jay Baldwin slowly made his way from the tail of the DC-3 forward to the cockpit as he checked the harnesses that had been put in place to secure the children. He paused next to the cargo door where Charlie sat on a grass mat between his two guards. Jay knelt beside the guard sitting nearest to Charlie.

"How's he doing?"
"Prisoner sleep. Sleep all the time."
"That's good. Keep your eye on him. He could be faking it."

The pastor moved over to his wife and child and kissed them both; holding them close to his breast, he said a prayer, "Loving God, go with us and keep us and make a way for us. In Jesus name, amen."

Ahlam said to him, "My husband, are we still going to India?"

Jay looked into her eyes as he swept her hair away from her eyes.

"I'm afraid something has come up, my love. It is now or never for getting these children out of here. I hope the Madam will understand."

"I'm sure she will, my husband. As a matter of fact, I'm sure she has understood all along."

Jay slid into the left seat of his DC-3 hospital plane and secured the safety harness. Elmo sat in the copilot's chair and Raylan sat behind Elmo.

"Are you boys armed?"

"Yes, sir."

"All right then, let's get out of here."

Jay and Elmo quickly went through the pretakeoff checklist and, one at a time, fired the two Pratt and Whitney engines.

"Did you check the compression in that new cylinder and run the engine to check for oil leaks?

"All taken care of, Padre. This ship is ready to go."

Jay increased power and quickly did a run-up on each engine.

"Sounds good, feels good, everything seems to be in the green, so I guess we're ready."

The converted C-47 began to move toward the daylight from where they had entered the hidden city in the jungle.

"How much runway do we have out there?"

"I don't know, Padre. I guess we'll find out. One thing for sure, we better do this before that road fills up with carts and wagons going back and forth to the city."

Jay looked across at his mechanic.

"All right then, let's get out of here."

The polished aluminum glistened in the morning sun as the McDonald Douglas DC-3 emerged from the forest into the daylight. Jay let his eyes adjust to the brightness of the light and called out to his copilot, "Full power and lock down the throttles."

"Aye, aye, Captain, locked and loaded," Elmo answered as he shoved the throttles forward.

Reluctantly, the aircraft lumbered along the dirt road, bouncing and lurching as it gained momentum. Finally, it lifted into the air. Jay maintained a level flight attitude in ground effect long enough to achieve the aircraft's best rate of climb airspeed, then raised the nose to establish climb out. Suddenly, he heard his name, not his new name but his old name.

"Lieutenant Bold. This is General Chennault. I want you to set that airplane back down on that goat trail."

Elmo's face turned white. Jay's face turned red. He started to pick up the microphone but paused for a moment before setting it back down, deciding not to respond. *What was Clair Chennault doing in Chungking, and how did he know—*

Jay's thoughts were interrupted. The general's plane was now alongside; he could see it in his peripheral vision yet continued to intentionally disregard it.

"They're alongside, Padre. What are we going to do?"

Jay turned off the radio.

"Who is alongside? I don't see anyone."

"What if he sends one of his P-40s after us?"

"We'll deal with that, if and when it happens. Besides, do you really think they'll shoot down this plane full of orphans? Chennault is just humoring Chiang Kai-shek. He probably got concerned about his airplane and talked Chennault into flying him over here to find it."

"What about when the gimo discovers we have his man Charlie?"

"Chennault will still have to take the president back to Chungking and drop him off, and by then, we'll have too much of a head start."

Elmo reached over to turn the radio back on.

"We better listen to this. We might miss something important."

General Chennault watched the Red Cross plane lift off from the dirt runway and adjusted his throttles to match airspeed with it until it gained enough altitude for him to pull alongside. He knew his empty C-47 would have no trouble outrunning the loaded hospital plane if he actually intended to follow them.

Chennault was nobody's fool. He understood exactly what was going on. He had known all along that Charlie and Chiang Kai-shek had intended to use Lieutenant Bold and his salvaged C-47 for their own purposes. He also knew they had no intention of letting that opportunity slip by over a few orphans that nobody wanted. General Chennault knew just as well that, officially, he worked for the Madam Chiang Kai-shek and not the generalissimo, and he certainly didn't work for Charlie Nee. As far as Lieutenant Bold was concerned, his only crime was that he survived an extremely unfortunate incident, only to find himself under the control of Charlie and his devious plans. Chennault himself considered Lieutenant Bold to be as fine an Army Air Corp Officer and pilot as he had ever seen. He only wished the young man had followed his advice back in Anshun. But then, how was he to know the lieutenant had married Charlie's sister? How was he to know that they had had a child. It isn't any wonder he didn't follow orders. *I don't blame him, I would have done the same thing*, the general mused.

It was clear to Chennault that the young lieutenant had made every effort to cooperate with both Chiang Kai-shek and his man Charlie. It was the two of *them* who had manipulated and deceived the young pilot until he no longer could cooperate with them, save his family, and, at the same time, fulfill his agreement with Madam Chiang. Charlie and his boss had shot themselves in the foot, and it was because they knew it, that they hated the lieutenant so much.

"Looks to me like they picked up those kids and are on their way to Alaska," Chennault said to the gimo. "I'll see if I can get him on the radio. Although I doubt he'll answer me. Hell, if I were him, I sure wouldn't."

Generalissimo frantically answered, "Yes…make pilot land… now!"

General Clair Chennault reluctantly pressed the mike button and said, "Lieutenant Bold, this is General Channault. I'll be pulling up on your starboard side." There was no response from the Red Cross DC-3.

The general waited a few moments and tried again, "Lieutenant Bold, AKA Pastor Jay Baldwin, I order you to answer me." Again, there was no reply.

"Mr. Baldwin, I see you're determined to do this the hard way, so I'm not going to stop you. I do hope you have a safe trip, son, God help you."

"Why did you tell him that?" the Generalissimo asked. His frustration turning to panic. "The man is a traitor to China. He must be captured and put in prison."

"Good luck with that, Chiang, as far as I'm concerned, he's doing just what your wife asked him to do, and I'm not lending any more of my resources to this project. Furthermore, it appears to me that you have forgotten who your real enemies are. Your plane is probably parked in that hidden city back there where they just come from, waiting for you. But to make you happy, I'll try one more thing before we turn around.

Go into the back of the cargo area. There is a grenade launcher back there. Then, open that cargo door and point it at them. Maybe that will intimidate him into turning around.

A huge smile came across the generalissimo's face as he retreated to the rear of the airplane. One last time, General Chennault spoke into the microphone.

"Pastor Baldwin, you may see the gimo pointing a grenade launcher at you shortly. Don't worry, it's not loaded. I just wanted to get him out of the cockpit for a minute. Listen to me. When you get to Yinchuan, go into town and find a man named Major

Yuan. He'll be able to provide you with everything you need. Tell him Clair-sonn sent you. One more thing, when you get to Russia, watch your six. There is no one there you can trust, absolutely no one."

Pastor Jay Baldwin finally broke radio silence.

"Like I told you once before, General, I guess we'll just have to trust God. Thank you, sir. Consider yourself saluted."

General Claire Chennault returned the young airman's salute and the polished aluminum Red Cross DC-3 dipped its wings one last time. Suddenly, in a very aggressive maneuver, Chennault initiated a steep 180-degree bank turn to starboard.

Generalissimo Chiang Kai-shek, slowly made his way to the rear of the cargo plane where he located the grenade launcher, soon realizing with great disappointment that it was unarmed. *They will not know the difference*, he thought as he opened the portside cargo door. He had barely put the weapon to his shoulder when the C-47 banked steeply to starboard. The generalissimo tumbled into a heap against the cargo hold wall. Staggering to his feet, he made his way back to the cockpit. Angry with Chennault, he said to him, "My man Charlie will bring them back. They will not get far without fuel."

"Suit yourself, General, but Charlie has enough on his plate. You can chase Mr. Baldwin all you want, but it seems to me that you have more important priorities. You should be ordering Charlie to get back into the war where he could be a lot more useful to you than he is chasing a plane load of orphans all the way across China."

Pouting, the generalissimo said, "Drop me off at Chiang Kai City."

"Be glad to, Mr. President."

Chapter 11

Elmo Barker stared thoughtfully out the copilot's side window as the Douglas DC-3 continued its climb north by northeast toward Yinchuan. Turning to Jay, he said, "It's a good thing I turned that radio back on when I did. You would have never known the general was rooting for you if I hadn't. Isn't that right?"

Jay grinned and looked across at his mechanic.

"Yeah, good thing. Just don't let it go to your head."

Elmo turned the volume down on the transceiver and leaned back in his seat. He yawned and rubbed his eyes.

"What was the name of our contact there?"

"Some guy named, Yuan…Major Yuan."

I wonder who this Major Yuan is, and how do you suppose Chennault knows him?"

"I don't know, but it sounds like they might have been friends at one time."

"Speaking of friends, what are we going to do with the one we got tied up in the back?

"I'm not sure yet. I'll let you know. Did you bring a parachute?"

"You bet. I got one that will be just perfect for him."

"What do you mean by that?"

"It wasn't packed just right, kind of all wadded up, and since I don't know how to pack one, I stuffed it back in as best I could. I hope it works. Oh, and I should mention, it had a few rips in it, but it was the only one I could find."

Jay stared at Elmo apprehensively, not sure what to make of Elmo's comments.

"Is it going to open all right?"

"Oh sure, no problem, heck I'd use it myself…if I didn't have anything else…and if the engines had quit…and the plane was on fire…and the wings had fallen off."

"In other words, if we shove him out, he's going to fall to his death. Is that right?"

"Maybe, maybe not, what do you care? Tell the Lord you did the best you could under the circumstances and let the big guy in the sky worry about him."

Jay looked at Elmo. First, he felt consternation, then compassion, not for Charlie, but for Elmo.

"How can you be so careless when it comes to taking a life?"

"It's a self-defense mechanism because I know that if he gets the chance, he'll not just kill you and me but everyone on this plane, and I don't want to see him get that chance."

"It's our job to make sure he doesn't get that chance. Besides, he's not going to kill his sister, and I don't believe he would kill those orphans. Remember, he started out as an orphan himself."

"I think those orphans are a big pain in his posterior. In fact, I think he would waist them and not even blink. Charlie is about Charlie and nobody else. For that matter, he may be capable of sacrificing his own sister for his precious cause. But whatever you want to do with him is up to you. I'll tell you this much, if he gets loose and so much as blinks wrong, I'm going to take him out. You can count on that."

"Maybe we should take him with us to Alaska."

Elmo gasped and dropped his head into his open hand.

"Padre, sooner or later he's going to find a way to get loose. If we don't get rid of him while we have a chance, he'll ruin our whole vacation."

"Maybe this Major Yuan will have a better parachute, or maybe he will take him off our hands."

"I hope so. If he goes with us all the way to Alaska, I'll have an ulcer by the time we get there."

Pastor Jay Baldwin considered carefully Elmo's perspective on the matter. He knew, of course, that from a practical standpoint, the solution was staring him square in the face: strap the parachute on Charlie's back and push him out of the door. Problem solved. Though Jay knew he wasn't really a pastor, nonetheless, he was still bound to the principles of everything he believed in his heart, everything he knew to be right and righteous. Elmo's way would be murder, plain and simple.

Jay did not condemn Elmo for his view of the situation, nor did he consider him as having a murderous spirit in his heart, at least no more so than comes naturally by virtue of the fallen, sinful nature inherent in humanity. He understood as well that in times of war, men resort to extreme measures to survive, measures they would never in a million years consider under normal conditions. But isn't that what Charlie was doing too, resorting to whatever extreme measures he felt would salvage his China out of the grip of the Japanese? Or line his pockets? Who even knew for sure what Charlie's real motives were?

As far as Jay was concerned, it was not about *who* is right or wrong but rather *what* is right and wrong. For that matter, it always had been.

Elmo's time and distance calculations from Chungking to Yinchuan indicated close to five hours of flight time in the ten to fifteen knot winds coming out of the northeast. Getting there was not the concern; finding the place, however, was a huge concern. Nobody on board Jay's airplane, except possibly Charlie, had ever been to Yinchuan before, and locating it, in that maze of mountains, ridges, and valleys, would be like looking for a needle in—forget the haystack—China.

On the bright side, at least it wasn't nighttime, and they had plenty of fuel. Jay turned the ship over to Elmo.

"I'm going to the rear to check on our buddy."

THE FRUIT OF ATROCITY

"You mean Jaworski?"

"Yeah, him too."

The sixteen orphans—fruit of the 1937 atrocities of Nanking by the Imperialist's Japanese army—were finally on their way to freedom.

Most of them lay in a heap, huddled against each other on the cargo floor to keep warm. Some hung from the canvas harnesses provided in Anshun when the C-47 underwent its alterations. Ah-lam lay among them. By her side, sound asleep in a basket, lay Ching-Lan, cradled by one of the orphan girls whose name was Jai-Ling.

Jay approached his wife and inquired, "How is everyone doing?"

"We are all fine so far, my husband. The children will probably be hungry when they wake up. How long before we land again?"

"It's five hours to Yinchuan, and we've been in the air about an hour and a half. Did you all find the facilities okay?"

"Raylan showed us...*unique* was the word that came to mind."

"It's called a *tail wheel toilet*, in case you're interested."

"Thank you, we are forever in your debt," Ah-lam said facetiously.

"Don't mention it."

Ah-lam looked pensively at her husband.

"What do you plan to do with my brother?"

"I'm not sure. I'm sort of waiting on the Lord to see what he provides. My crew wants to toss him out the door in that parachute, but I'm not sure it's packed correctly."

"Then it is not your intention to kill him?"

"No, my dear, it is not. However, he *has* become a serious problem. He threatened to kill us to prevent us from going on this trip, so I had no choice but to restrain him to keep him from calling down the entire Chinese army on our heads. Chiang Kai-shek is hand in hand with Charlie to keep us in China. Even General Chennault had to stand against him because he was aiding Charlie in his attempts to stop us. If the gimo had known we were holding Charlie prisoner, he would have continued to follow us. In fact, he may still come after us when he figures out we've kidnapped his top intelligence man."

"Are we going to run into more trouble before we are out of China?"

"I hope not. Chennault gave us the name of someone in Yinchuan who might help us with getting fuel. If that works out, we should be on our way by morning."

"What is the name?"

"Yuan, Major Yuan."

"I am not familiar with the name, but I am so glad the American general is still willing to help us. Maybe one day we can thank him personally for what he has done. And I want to thank you, my husband, for all *you* are doing to save these children." Ah-lam placed her hand gently against Jay's cheek and smiled at him.

Jay leaned close to his wife and kissed her. Then speaking softly into her ear, he said, "There is nothing I wouldn't do for you my precious, and whatever happens, remember, I will always love you no matter what."

"I love you too, my husband," she said, pressing her cheek against his."

"Now, I need to go speak to Raylan a minute, and then I'm going to take a nap. Try to get some sleep if you can. I'll check on you later. Whenever you and the children get hungry, let Raylan know."

Raylan Jaworski had wrapped himself in a blanket and was sitting on a box of ammunition on the portside of the aircraft, facing the tail of the airplane with his back against the bulkhead separating the flight deck from the cargo area. His rifle lay next to him. He appeared at first glance to be asleep, but as Jay approached him, it was apparent that he was not only awake but diligently keeping a critical eye on Charlie.

Jay's brother-in-law sat cross-legged, tied against the aircraft wall less than a dozen feet away. The two Chinese guards took turns napping while they too watched him. Jay slid another ammo box next to Raylan and sat down beside him.

"When we get to Yinchuan, I'm going to take Wonlukee and go into town to try and find a man named Major Yuan. I need you and Elmo to stay with the ship. If we don't come back, you guys are going to be on your own. You will still have about seven hours of fuel available. Not enough to make Khabarovsk, Russia, but enough to make it back to Chungking."

"Why won't you be back?" Raylan asked.

"You never know. Life is full of surprises, or haven't you figured that out by now?"

"So why would we go back to Chungking? We just came from there?"

"Because...at that point, you would be out of options. It's eight hours to Khabarovsk, and there's absolutely no place to land between Yinchuan and Khabarovsk, so don't even try. I would rather you scrapped the trip altogether, then crash into the mountains."

"Okay, Boss, we'll take care of it. But you speak Chinese, so why don't you take me with you instead of Wonlukee?"

"I think the people in town might talk more freely to Wonlukee than to me, or you. It will give us a better chance of locating this Major Yuan fellow. I need you here to keep my brother-in-law secure and under the influence of those drugs, also to protect our cargo. Don't forget what this load of kids—mostly girls—would mean to black marketers if they could get hold of them."

"Do you mean human traffickers?"

"That's exactly what I mean. We have to keep that from happening, and you have my permission to kill whoever tries, or so much as intends, on taking these children to do them any harm. So keep those Browning Automatics handy."

"Don't worry, Boss, we'll handle it."

"Another thing, I've been talking to Elmo, and we've decided to take Charlie along with us to Alaska."

"I figured that out already. You're too soft, Boss. Are you forgetting that this is war, and the rules of war are kill or be killed?"

"Don't forget, my friend, there isn't any reason to survive if the cause is lost…"

"What cause is that?"

"The cause of human decency and integrity, without which we are nothing more than beasts. One more thing, when those kids wake up, they might be hungry. You can have Wonlukee distribute some of the rations to them. I'm going to take a nap."

Raylan sat silent for a long moment, staring into the blank eyes of the *beast* tied against the wall. "All the more reason to kill him now, Boss."

Jay contemplated Raylan's reply and said to him, "I think you missed my point, Jaworski."

Jay returned to his pilot seat. Elmo had a concerned look on his face.

"What's up, Barker? You look worried."

"The farther north we get, the higher these mountains get. We're already at twelve thousand feet. I'm getting concerned about the children and this thin air."

"Nothing we can do about it, Elmo. The winds are light, so keep it as low as you can over the ridges but be safe. Remember those kids are more adapted to this high country than we are. They'll be fine. Just try not to go above fourteen thousand feet for very long periods."

"Roger that, Padre."

"How's our time and distance looking?"

"We're still about three and a half hours out."

"Okay, I'm going to get a nap. Wake me in three hours, and I'll help you find the place and take over the landing phase."

"Have you figured out how you're going to find the major?"

"Me and Wonlukee will go into town to look for him," Jay repeated the instructions he had given to Raylan, "if we're not back by morning, scrap the mission and take those kids back to Chungking."

"Are you sure about that?"

"I'm sure."

"Are you worried about the gimo loading up some of his troops and coming after us?"

"That certainly crossed my mind."

"Well, you can relax…I removed a fuel line on his ship. That should cost him a little time. He'll have to get Chennault to take him to Kunming to get another hose. By then, we'll be well on our way to Russia—Lord willing."

"Good job, Barker, but I still want you out of here by daylight if we're not back. If they had an extra fuel line in their maintenance building, they'll have that fixed and could be here shortly after daylight in the morning. So I want you all gone at daybreak, no later."

"Aye, aye, Captain."

Pastor Jay Baldwin unfolded an army cot and placed it on the flight deck floor directly behind the cockpit. He was asleep in seconds and soon began to dream. When he awoke, the dream was still vivid in his mind. Startled and affected emotionally by its vivid reality, he climbed into his pilot seat; in a very faraway tone of voice, he said to Elmo, "How close are we to Yinchuan?"

"Forty-five minutes, Padre. You want the airplane?"

"Not just yet. I'm recovering from a dream I had."

"Was it a good one?"

"I hope so."

"What was it about?"

"I'm not sure, but I'll never forget it as long as I live."

"You want to tell me about it?"

"Well, it was really strange. It seemed like I was making my way through a boggy marsh of some sort, all full of dead falls and brush, like the Everglades or something. Only it was also covered in dense fog. It was so spooky it made my skin crawl.

"At any rate, I had been groping my way through the fog for what seemed like an eternity. It was like I was lost and all turned around. I didn't have any idea where I was going. Then, suddenly, I emerged from the fog and realized I was standing on the bank of a wide river.

"On the other side was sunshine and blue sky with green rolling hills and lush meadows. Children played and scampered, chasing butterflies and chirping birds. It was a beautiful scene and very pleasant to behold. The incredible, peacefulness of it all is still vivid in my mind."

"Was there anyone else in the dream?" Elmo asked.

"Yes, on the far shore of the river stood the most incredible man I've ever seen. He was so impressive to look at, at least twelve feet tall, with blue eyes that I could clearly see even from where I stood on my side of the river, which was like a mile wide, yet I could see him perfectly. He was so powerful in appearance. And yet, I could detect the gentleness in his eyes. He wore a robe, a white robe. It hung all the way to the ground. His hair was as golden as the sun and hung softly over his broad shoulders.

"The man looked into my eyes, and in that moment, I knew I wanted to spend the rest of my life in his presence. Then, he raised his right hand and gestured for me to approach him. I stepped out to wade across the river, and instantly, it narrowed into a small rippling brook that I easily stepped across. As soon as I did, the brook widened again into a river.

"At that point, I was standing directly alongside this man who now towered almost four feet above me. I have never felt such peace and comfort and security in my entire life. It was truly amazing. I turned to him to inquire who he was.

"Slowly the man turned to look at me. He gazed right into my eyes. It was like he was looking directly into my heart, even into my soul. Then he pointed back toward the river. Somehow I knew that I was expected to go back.

"A terrible sense of dread came over me as I looked back at the bank of fog where I had come from. Furthermore, on the far shore where I had stood only moments before stood an old man. He was bent over and crippled, with a long flowing gray beard that hung all the way to the ground, his long hair drifted in the breeze, and he clung to a gnarly old wooden cane, and he was beckoning for me to come back.

"Panic struck straight through my heart at the thought of leaving that paradise. Fear and dread, like I have never known gripped me. Frantically, I clung to the garment of the man at my side. It was then I realized who he was. I clearly knew that I was standing next to none other than the Lord Jesus Christ, our Savior and Redeemer—and I was actually with him in Paradise."

"What happened then?" Elmo asked eagerly.

Then, he slowly turned to look into my eyes and nodded. His mouth said nothing, but His eyes spoke volumes. *It will be okay*, I thought. Instantly a great peace flooded into my heart as I understood that I had received a vision of my eternal destiny. A tremendous gladness filled my soul.

I stepped out into the broad river. Once again, it became a small stream. I stepped across into the fog, and it was at that moment I awoke."

Elmo looked across the console that separated him and his captain. He said to him, "Do you think it's a prophesy?"

"You mean a prophesy of our mission?"

"Yeah, do you think it's a prophesy of the success of this mission, or is it a prophesy of the doom of this mission?"

"I think it doesn't matter one way or the other. I think it's a prophesy of not only *this* mission but our whole lives. In fact, the whole experience of humankind in general on this earth. Think about it, life is such a struggle. It's like groping through a fog, stumbling over everything in the path. We go through this life with blinders on, staggering our way through. Isn't that the way it's been on this mission? We don't even know if we'll live through the night from one day to the next."

"So you're saying that we could meet with disaster during this mission and still come out on the other side?"

"Exactly, I mean it doesn't matter what happens here. God is always in control. Our only responsibility is to keep on moving forward with whatever the Lord has given us to do, to meet every obstacle as though it were already conquered. I have realized that to expect defeat is the prequel to failure. The Lord has given us the victory already."

Jayson looked over at his mechanic. "Don't worry about leaving by daybreak. Wonlukee and I will find Major Yuan and get the fuel in time." Elmo nodded and checked his watch.

"My time and distance calculations indicate we should be within twenty minutes of Yinchuan. But there are so many mountains around here I don't know how we'll ever find it."

"I'll take the airplane, you look. I'll climb up a bit and see if we can get a better view."

Elmo said to him, "I see a lake, but then I've seen a million lakes since Chungking, except this one is a bit bigger, and there's a village about a mile north of it."

"How about a runway? Is there a runway somewhere?"

"You'll have to come back around again. It's behind us now."

Jay slowed the aircraft and banked to the portside. He held the turn until once again the aircraft was positioned where he could now see clearly the terrain directly below him.

"I see something that could be a runway. Looks more like a round clearing, but it should be long enough to land. However, I'm not sure about getting back out."

Jay began a descending circular spiral until he was able to determine if the clearing was adequate for landing or, more importantly, taking off again.

"I see what appears to be a road through the middle of it, actually a cart path like the one back at Chungking," Jay said.

"Is it wide enough, straight enough, and long enough?" Elmo asked, a bit wide-eyed.

"You're asking an awful lot, Elmo. It does look straight enough. I don't know about wide enough. As far as long enough, that's going to depend on a whole lot of additional factors that include: elevation, temperature, and weight, not to mention the condition of the runway."

"What do you want to do?" Elmo asked eagerly.

"Doesn't matter, we'll make one more pass and take it in."

Elmo remarked, "It looks to me like it will be a 'one way in and one way out' deal, land north, take off south."

"I usually only go one way at a time anyway."

Elmo looked at Jay, not sure if he was supposed to laugh or take him seriously.

"Was that a joke? Did that vision skew your sense of humor or your sense of reality?"

"Neither one, it just turned my sense of fear into an adventure of faith. You should try it."

"I'll stick to the sense of reality for now if you don't mind. Just for balance, if you know what I mean."

The polished aluminum Douglas DC-3 settled below the tree line as pilot Jay Baldwin let the wheels softly touch the dried dirt surface of the narrow cart path.

The available runway looked much shorter from the air, and Jay breathed a little easier as he realized it was longer than it had appeared.

The Lord must have stretched it out for us just as we touched down. Kind of like when the widow and her son fed Elisha from the last store of meal she had, only to discover the next day and every day thereafter, there was always enough for them to eat.

Jay spotted a flat portion of the clearing that appeared solid where he could park the aircraft away from the landing zone. He spun the tail around in a takeoff direction next to the trees and left the engines running.

"Elmo," Jay hollered, "let those radials cool a while before you shut them down, I'm going to the rear."

"Aye, aye, Captain."

Jay walked through the flight deck aisle and entered the cargo hold. He looked immediately at the place he had last seen Raylan. Jaworski was not there, and Ah-lam and the children were all lying on their bellies facing the rear of the aircraft.

Jay froze as he realized the two guards that were supposed to be guarding the prisoner were standing by the cargo door. There was no sign of Charlie.

Suddenly, he felt it—cold mettle pressed against the back of his neck. He started to turn but a strong hand gripped his neck. He heard Charlie say to him, "Jai-sonn, kneel on floor."

In spite of the iron grip around his neck, Jay continued struggling to turn around where he could face his nemesis. In the next instant, he saw a bright, white, and red flash of light, only a millisecond before he completely lost consciousness.

Pastor Jay Baldwin awoke. His head throbbing with pain. He could taste the blood that had trickled down the side of his face from his forehead and into his mouth. He was sitting on a thin grass mat in the corner of a bamboo cage, his arms bound to the uprights of each wall—cold, bleeding, and naked.

Jay tried to open his eyes but could not. Then he recalled something. There was the light; he remembered the red and white flash of light and a terrifying thought occurred to him. *Where is Ah-lam and Ching-Lan? Where are the orphans? And where is Elmo, Raylan, and Wonlukee...for that matter...where am I?*

Jay tried to move again and realized his legs had been bound together.

He could feel his back pressed against the bamboo poles. He tried to call out only to realize a gag was in his mouth. *Charlie must have gotten loose. Raylan and the guards must have fallen asleep. The altitude...it must have been the high altitude that put them all to sleep...how stupid of me.*

He listened to see if he could hear any sound that would identify his location. Thoughts swirled in Jay's mind like clouds in a tornado. *I wonder if I'm somewhere in Yinchuan, Charlie must have connections here. My family...where are they...are they okay? Got to get this blindfold off.*

Jay wriggled against his bindings until he felt one of the bamboo sticks against the side of his face. He began working his head up and down until the blindfold slid a fraction below his left eye. Finally, he could see slivers of light, but the cloth tied around his eyes kept sliding back up, hampering his vision. *Got to turn more.*

Jay continued to struggle eventually working the blindfold below his nose. It was dark, but for the first time, he could make out some of his surroundings. He was in a bamboo-thatched hut. It was night, but there was light coming from somewhere, and it leaked through the cracks between the bamboo slats. The cage he was in looked to be about six feet by eight feet in size. There was no furniture, only the grass mat he was sitting on. Jay's rear end was completely numb from lack of circulation, and his feet were tingling for the same reason. He tried to wriggle and squirm in an effort to get the blood moving. It helped some, but the leather that bound him cut deep into his wrists and ankles causing them to bleed.

The gag consisted of a wad of cloth stuffed in his mouth, held by a leather thong tied across his mouth and around the back of his neck to prevent him from spitting it out.

Jay tried to chew the thong, but it made him gag. He could only breath through his nose, and now, because he had worked the blindfold down below his nostrils, breathing had become even more difficult.

Got to get this gag off, but how? he thought. He tried again to chew the leather, but the gag was so fat he couldn't touch his teeth together. *Maybe I can work the wad of cloth under the leather thong and spit it out.*

Jay had lost track of time. He knew it was now dark but had no idea what time of the night it might be. He had already wet himself once, while he was asleep, and had to relieve himself again. There was no option but to let it go. The smell quickly became unbearable, and combined with the gag in his mouth, he soon began to dry heave. *Lord, please don't let me vomit.* He laid his head back to rest and soon passed out.

When Jay awoke the next time, someone was slapping him in the face. Semiconsciousness returned a little more with each slap.

"Wake up, Jai-sonn, wake up." It was Charlie. Someone was with him, but Jay did not recognize him.

Charlie reached out and yanked the gag out of Jay's mouth. "Jai-sonn, traitor, Jai-sonn, traitor and liar. Charlie save Jai-sonn…Charlie make Jai-sonn safe…give Jai-sonn job…let Jai-sonn have sister for wife. Jai-sonn give Charlie word, then no keep. Jai-sonn, deserter. Jai-sonn no have honor. Now, Jai-sonn pay with life."

Jay could hear the words Charlie was saying, but it was as if they had no meaning. What Charlie was accusing him of made no sense to Jay. Struggling to speak, he said to him, "My family, what have you done with my family."

"All die, Charlie kill them all. That fat mechanic...Elmo, and Jai-sonn bodyguard—Joborsee...." Jay knew Charlie was referring to Jaworski. "... And the traitor, Wonlukee, not so *lucky* anymore. All die. Now, Jai-sonn work for Charlie. No more anything else to do. Jai-sonn work for Charlie for the rest of Jai-sonn life. Now, Jai-sonn have time to think. Jai-sonn think now how Jai-sonn made this bad thing happen. Bad thing did not need to happen. Jai-sonn could have family and work for Charlie too. Jai-sonn no will do. Jai-sonn want be hero, want save orphans. Orphans, no real people, orphans no human being. Orphans, Japanese dung. Orphans, now all dead. Orphans, now no more. Jai-sonn now have much time to think...Jai-sonn think until ready to work for Charlie. No more run-a-way. Jai-sonn run-a-way more, Jai-sonn die." Charlie ran his finger across his throat as if he were slashing it. Jay knew what it meant.

"Someday, Jai-sonn work for Charlie, no more run-a-way."

Jay was confused. He could not fathom the idea that Charlie had murdered his family and crew and all the children. Elmo and Raylan were right. He should have thrown Charlie out of the airplane from high above the mountains. Again he strained against the leather bindings.

"Go to hell," he said. The words sounded strange and evil coming from his own mouth—had Charlie murdered his soul too?

The man standing behind Charlie handed him a large stick and watched as Charlie began to beat Jay's feet and legs.

Thirty, forty, fifty times he whipped them until the skin tore and chunks of flesh and blood splattered against his face. He writhed and grimaced in pain but refused to cry out.

Every muscle in his body quivered. He stared at his brother-in-law, without whimpering and without blinking. Then he closed his eyes; his head slumped against the bamboo wall.

Dead! My family...the orphans...all dead! Oh, my God.

Oh God, how could that be? The words kept resounding through Jay's brain. *Dead...dead...all dead. Oh, my God in heaven.*

Unable to endure it any longer, he cried out, "No…no…it can't be. Oh God…oh God…no, don't let it be. Why? Why?" Again and again, Jay slammed his head against the bamboo sticks behind him until the warm blood trickled down the back of his neck. Then, he remembered. *The dream…the fog…the river…the Lord Jesus…Paradise. Is this the fog?* he thought. *If this is the fog, then it is also my journey, which means all is not lost. I must trust the Lord…I must not let my faith be stolen from me.*

Another thought occurred to Jay…a thought that tore at the only thread of faith he had left. *Maybe it was the lack of oxygen, maybe the dream was only an hallucination. But,* he thought, *I hadn't been off of the oxygen that long. Surely, it truly was a vision from God…of course it came from God. He gave me the vision to strengthen me for this…this evil that has befallen me. Oh God, strengthen me.*

Suddenly the voice of the Lord came to him, clear and remarkable like a rainbow in a rainstorm: *"For my thoughts are not your thoughts, neither are your ways my ways, saith the Lord. For as the heavens are higher than the earth, so are my ways higher than your ways, and my thoughts higher than your thoughts"* (Isaiah 55:8–9, AKJV). *"I will never leave thee nor forsake thee"* (Hebrews 13:5, AKJV).

Tears flowed down his cheeks mixing with the dried blood as Pastor Jay Baldwin lifted his eyes upward. Again he prayed, "God in heaven, not my will, but Thy will be done." Once again, consciences slipped away as his chin fell against his chest.

The horrible night of shivering and writhing in pain finally gave way to the light of another day. However, for Pastor Jay Baldwin, the only thing that ended was the darkness.

The ex-lieutenant awoke shivering in the Fall air, his legs ached and twitched from the lack of exercise, every muscle screamed to be let loose. The numbness had crept all the way up to his waist until he no longer had any feeling from his belly to his toes—toes, feet, and legs that were already turning blue and purple.

THE FRUIT OF ATROCITY

Jay tried to focus on his surroundings. He tried to think clearly, but his wounded body had had no treatment, and every laceration that had not turned numb stung fiercely. The blood had dried and caked in his hair and on the side of his face. More dried blood stuck to the back of his neck, and like scabs, caked against his skin.

As effect follows cause, the days turned into nights and the nights into days. Occasionally, Jay could hear birds chirping, and from time to time, a parrot would screech at its neighbor. Jay counted, trying to keep track: three days and three nights now; he had been without food or water. Three days and three nights, no one had come. Since his last beating, he had not heard a single sound that suggested the presence of another human being.

Jay lay in his own filth; his body excreted its waist without him any longer being conscience of it. He could no longer feel his arms, his hands, or even his face. Infection had set into the wounds in his head, but he could no longer feel his scalp. Black and purple streaks ran from his feet up his legs.

I will never leave thee or forsake thee. Jay could no longer speak, but over and over, he repeated the words in his mind. *I will never leave thee or forsake thee.* Jay had been left to die, and those words were all he had left. He clung to them, hoping that somehow they would give him the will to stay alive.

Chapter 12

Arthur Bold, stood on the porch, waiting and watching as the taxi turned into the driveway from the gravel road marked LL. Nostalgically he studied the land where he and his younger brother, Jayson, had been born and raised, where they had lived their entire lives together until the war began. For the last time, he looked out at the fifteen hundred acres of prime farmland. It had only been two days since the sale had closed. Tears formed in the corner of his eyes as he stared across the fields the two brothers had worked with their father since they were ten years old.

Since the folks had died, Arthur and Jayson had struggled to keep the place up. Each year they planted what few fields they could manage by themselves. Some with soybeans, others with feed corn, and together, along with the crop dusting business, they managed to stay afloat. Then, Jayson enlisted in the Army Air Corp.

Many of the farm boys they had grown up with were already fighting on various fronts from Europe to the South Sea Islands. Most of them were foot soldiers, grunts, killing and getting killed. Some of the boys, who had since been sent home in coffins, were boys he and Jayson had gone to school with.

After Jay joined the Air Corp, he had gone to North Carolina for officer cadet and flight training. Before he left, he said he wanted to go to China to fly C-47 transports. Arthur knew of two other young men the same age as his brother from just across the river in Illinois who went to Europe to fly those cargo planes, and both of them now occupied the cemetery in Peoria.

"What makes you think they're any safer than the bombers or fighters?" Arthur asked Jayson before he left.

"Don't worry, Art," Jay had said, "the Lord will bring me back."

Jayson took after his mother when it came to religion. Arthur took after his dad. To Arthur, religion was too incomprehensible, too many different opinions and interpretations of what the Bible said and taught. Arthur, and his father, left all that to those who felt they could understand it. For them, work is what life is about; a man is born to work and raise a family.

"Well, Jay, my brother, I suppose someone has to fight that damn war. So if that's what you feel you need to do, then I'm not going to try to stop you. But you better pray your ass off while you're over there, or you might come back like those two red-headed kids from Peoria."

"Don't worry, brother, I do pray, every day, mostly for you."

"Hell, you don't need to pray for me. I can take care of myself."

"Yeah, that's what those two red-headed kids thought."

Arthur squinted and looked carefully at his brother.

"How do you know?"

"'Cause I knew one of them. Carl, remember him? Well, I had a similar conversation with him one time, only I didn't pray for him. Now I wish I had."

"You better get on board, or you'll miss your train, and I'll have to put you back to work."

It was the last time Arthur saw, or heard from, his younger brother.

Arthur's bags sat on the porch beside him. He returned to the front door and took one last look inside the house that had been the only home he had ever known. For a brief moment, he could see his mother standing behind his father as he sipped his morning coffee and read the newspaper, her hand resting on his shoulder as she refilled his coffee cup. A tear escaped the corner of his eye and traveled down his cheek as he slowly pulled the door closed behind him.

There was no need to lock the house. The paperwork was already completed, and the new owners would be moving in within the week.

Arthur didn't have the heart to tell his brother he had sold the farm. He didn't want to distract him from his training. However, he did leave a letter with the nearest neighbors, the Williams, down the road, addressed to Jayson. He knew that if his brother made it back from the war, he would go to the Williams first.

Mr. Williams had purchased the two Puffers and the crop-dusting business, and Arthur had sold the farm to a fellow with eight kids, three of which were teenagers—none of which felt the same calling to go get themselves killed that Jayson had felt. Then, Arthur shipped his belongings to Anchorage, Alaska.

The taxi driver closed the lid on the trunk of the 1940 Packard and said to Arthur, "Where to, mister?"

"Cape Girardeau, bus station," Arthur replied.

"I'm Ralph," the driver said, looking at Arthur through the rear view mirror.

"Arthur Bold."

"You sellin out too?"

"Yeah, just did."

"Lot's of folks gone broke these days, say you're that crop duster feller, aintcha? Yeah, I know you. I've seen your poster at the granary before. My brother-in-law works over there. I gotta tell ya, I don't know how you guys fly them…"

The taxi driver talked nonstop all the way to the bus station. Arthur tuned him out. His mind overflowed with nostalgia of the life he was leaving behind and optimism for the life he anticipated. At Cape Girardeau, he paid the cabbie and bought a bus ticket to St. Lewis.

Commercial air travel did not truly get going until after the war ended in 1945, and what air travel that *was* available was extremely expensive.

THE FRUIT OF ATROCITY

At St. Lewis, Arthur boarded a train for Portland, Oregon. Two weeks later, he was walking into the office of flight operations at Pearson Field, across the Columbia River in Vancouver, Washington.

A tall, slender-built man of about forty years got up from his desk and approached the counter with his attention focused on the five-foot-eleven powerfully built man who had just walked through the door.

"Can I help you, sir?"

"Maybe, I'm looking for an airplane."

"We're not in the business of selling airplanes, but I can give you a number to call. Are you looking for new or used?"

"Used. Going to fly it to Alaska and use it to make my living."

"My name's Winslet, Larry Winslet, I run the FBO, and you're…?"

"Arthur Bold. Glad to meet you. I just got off the train yesterday from St. Lewis."

"Welcome to the Pacific Northwest, Mr. Bold. Here, give this man a call. You can use that phone on the outside wall. There's a lot of airplanes for sale these days, but some of them are not in too good of shape…been sitting for a long time what with the depression and all. Ask for Bill Matthews. He's got a Stinson he wants to sell…probably give you a good deal."

"Thanks, Mr. Winslet, I will."

One week later, Arthur Bold was pushing the power forward on a 1931 Stinson SM2AA. A five-seater, monoplane powered by a 215 horsepower R-680 Wright radial engine.

Arthur was pleased with the price. Fifteen hundred for an airplane that only eleven years before—in 1931—had sold for $4,995.

Bill Matthews had bought the Stinson new and flown it primarily for business between Seattle and California. Evidently, his business had grown, and he had upgraded to a larger plane that could haul more passengers.

Arthur Bold had dreamed of this day since he read a magazine article featuring the bush pilots in Alaska. He had missed the initial surge of aviation into the far north; the great bush pilots of Alaska were already making their names household familiar, from New York City to Bettles, Alaska. Names like, Noel and Sig Wien, Bob Ellis, and Joe Crosson etched forever in the history of aviation, north of the 54th parallel.

It was February of 1942 when Arthur Bold left Pearson Field in Vancouver, Washington. He had equipped the Stinson with a set of skis and set out for Alaska at the first sign of clear skies.

Arthur followed the roads through British Columbia and the Yukon to Dawson Creek. Then, relying on the Corp of Engineers maps of the proposed Alaska Highway, he continued on to Alaska.

Since the attack on Pearl Harbor, Canada had relinquished their objections and finally agreed to plans by the US Army Corp of Engineers to build a highway connecting the lower forty-eight, and Canada, to the far north. And on March 8, 1942, construction officially began. However, in reality, preliminary work had already begun. At that time, Tok Junction, Alaska, was a road commission camp servicing the construction engineers building the Alaska Highway.

In spite of obstinate weather conditions, three weeks after leaving Vancouver, Arthur Bold landed his Stinson at Tok Junction, Alaska. Immediately, he offered his aerial services to the Army Corp of Engineers, who as yet had not officially began hiring.

Arthur soon realized that at least a hundred pilots and their airplanes, like himself, were in line before him, so he loaded his Stinson with supplies and left for Anchorage with the intention of buying a piece of land where he could build a shelter for the winter.

Arthur found a ninety-acre piece just west of the growing town of Wasilla Junction and began to look for help to build a hangar for the Stinson, a structure that would also serve as a temporary home for himself.

THE FRUIT OF ATROCITY

One day at the Wasilla trading post, Arthur met a man named Elmo Barker, a mechanic, pilot, and dozer operator.

"I'm looking for some help," he said to Mr. Barker.

"Help doing what?" Mr. Barker asked, never in a hurry to commit himself too soon, especially to a project that might involve hard work and low pay.

"My name is Arthur Bold. I bought a piece of land out of town and need to put up a building."

Barker shuffled his feet and kicked at the ice-covered dirt.

"It's a little early to be doing earth work. The ground is still frozen at least four feet down."

"That's okay. I'll build on top of the permafrost for now. I can shore it up later if the ground ever thaws out. But I have to put up a place where I can live and keep my airplane out of the weather."

"Yeah, sure, I can help you do that."

And so, Elmo Barker and Arthur Bold went to work in the middle of winter, building a structure. Arthur bought a dozer, and Elmo ran it. Arthur bought the materials, and they both cut and sawed and nailed them together. By the end of April, Arthur's place sported an eighteen-hundred-foot airstrip and hangar for the Stinson. Incorporated into the hangar was a small apartment—Arthur's new home.

"What are you going to do now?" Arthur asked Elmo.

"I'm headed to China with Clair Chennault's group of Flying Tigers."

"Are you going to fly those fighter planes?"

"No, I'm a mechanic. I worked for him when he was over there in 1937. So he wants me back."

"So you're not a part of the army, just a civilian hire?"

"That's right. However, I signed a contract, and if I breech it, I won't get my bonus money."

"Well, good luck, stay safe, and if you make it back, look me up. I'm going to be flying this Stinson around trying to make a buck. I'll probably be able to put you to work."

"I appreciate that, but I got other plans after the war."

"Like what?"

"Like getting rich, that's what."

"Okay, well good luck with that. Let me know how that works out for you."

Arthur did not realize it at first, but his timing for arriving in Wasilla with an airplane that had plenty of cargo space and that could haul a 900-pound payload could not have been better.

The Willow Creek Mining District along with at least fifty mines in the Talkeetna and Kantishna areas around Mt. McKinley was desperate for a regular air service that could provide supplies and provisions to their communities.

In addition—beginning in 1935 and due to the depression of the 1930s—the US government created an agency called The Alaska Rural Rehabilitation Corporation that set up yet another agency known as The Matanuska Colony of Agricultural Development of Alaska. As a result, hundreds of families— mostly farmers from the Midwest—began flowing into the area, along with as many more, who would provide goods and services. By spring breakup, Arthur Bold was in business.

Soon the ice-covered runways gave way to mud-rutted roads or gravel bars, and Arthur soon learned to adapt to the frequent transitions from skis, to wheels, and then to floats. By the end of 1942, Arthur had purchased an adjacent property, on which he built a small cabin.

Growing up in Sikeston, Missouri, had its limitations as far as options for romance. The boys learned early on that work came first and the girls came…well, last, on a list of higher priorities that included: scholastic education, agricultural environmental studies, flight training, and of course farm chores—chores that did not, necessarily, fall under their parent's definition of work.

However, Arthur managed to create enough spare time to occasionally court a pretty young girl named Loretta. They had been sweet on each other since grade school, and Arthur still

THE FRUIT OF ATROCITY

thought of her frequently. He began sending letters shortly after arriving in Wasilla. She wrote back, oohing and aahing over his fascinating descriptions of Alaska. When he had finally finished building the cabin, he wrote to her once more. It read:

> Dearest Loretta,
>
> I have finished the cabin. My business is thriving, and only one thing is missing. I have never been good with romantic words, but it doesn't take a Hemingway to say I love you, especially when that love is bursting at the seams to spend my life with you. If you say yes, I will love you and provide for you and take care of you for the rest of your life and won't charge you a penny (ha, ha). Will you marry me???"
>
> Yours to love forever,
>
> Artie

The private wedding took place at Loretta's parent's home in Sikeston, Missouri. The reception at the VFW hall was standing room only.

Most folks wanted to know two things: What was life like in Alaska, and what have you heard from your brother? The answer to the first was "Like *nothing* you have ever seen," and the answer to the second was "*Nothing.*"

Arthur thought about Jay occasionally but always with a pang of dread that he would eventually learn his brother was missing or killed in action or, worse yet, a prisoner of the Japanese. The remedy: don't think about him at all. Arthur was living the good life—the American dream. Jay was fighting for his right to do so. Deep inside, Arthur could feel a sense of guilt over it.

Married life suited Arthur to a tee. Loretta loved Alaska and loved her new home. She easily made friends with the other ladies of Wasilla who all loved her to pieces.

Arthur flew his airplane relentlessly during the long days of spring and summer. In the winter when the days were shorter, he hunted or worked on his airplanes. He had two planes now; a new Waco on floats had joined the fleet.

It was the fall of 1944. Arthur was in his hangar working; suddenly, he stopped what he was doing to listen. An airplane was coming his way, growing louder the closer it came. It sounded military. Arthur stepped outside, and to his alarming surprise, a polished aluminum McDonald Douglas DC-3 was on final approach to his eighteen-hundred-foot-long airstrip. A huge bright red cross painted on the vertical stabilizer glistened in the evening light. He thought, *What the hell is a Red Cross plane doing landing on my runway?*

Loretta had come out of the cabin and was shielding her eyes from the setting western sun as she too watched the incoming Red Cross plane. She hollered at her husband, "Is the runway long enough for that thing to land?"

"I guess, it depends on who's flying it," Arthur answered, absentmindedly.

Suddenly, the portside engine began to cough, sputtering twice, then quit altogether. At the same moment, the DC-3 settled onto the grass airstrip.

The pilot had done a fine job in approaching the short strip at barely above a stall, maintaining power on approach all the way through the touchdown. The huge airplane rolled to a stop less than ten feet short of Arthur's hangar. Moments later, the pilot shut down the starboard engine.

Arthur could see movement through the window on the copilot's side of the cockpit, but none on the pilot's side. Loretta came down from the cabin, her eyes the size of saucers. Soon the cargo door opened. Standing in the doorway was none other than Elmo Barker the mechanic Arthur had hired when he first arrived in Wasilla. Then Loretta cried out, "Arthur, Arthur, that man is hurt, and the plane is full of children!"

"I see that. What have you got going on there, Barker?"

THE FRUIT OF ATROCITY

Elmo did not hear. His vision had blurred, and the loss of blood had finally overwhelmed him; he collapsed at the door and fell forward unconscious to the ground, several feet below the belly of the aircraft.

Arthur rushed to Elmo's side and rolled him onto his back. His face was ashen from lack of blood and dried blood caked his shirt and coat. Someone had let down a ladder, and Arthur looked up to see who it was. A beautiful Chinese girl stood in the doorway holding a baby.

"Is he alive?" she said, concern telling in her voice.

"Just barely, how the hell did he land that plane in his condition? And who are you people?"

"Are you Arthur…Arthur Bold?" she asked pensively.

Arthur looked at her again, this time with consideration.

"Yeah, that's me, why do you ask?"

"I am your sister. How do you say? Sister-in-law?"

Arthur froze, his mouth fell open. "Sister-in-law…what the hell do you mean?"

Loretta tugged on his sleeve. "Artie, we have to get this man to the doctor now."

Arthur shook his head to clear the confusion in his mind and said to the woman still standing in the cargo door.

"Has this man been shot?"

"Yes, he was shot saving me and my children." Ah-lam waved her hand toward the group of children standing behind her.

"We expected to crash in the ocean long ago. I tried to doctor his wound while he continued to fly the airplane, but I could only do so much. It was God who kept him alive, and now he needs a hospital."

"Okay, we'll get him to a doctor. Who did you say you are?"

"I am your brother's…I mean, Jayson Bold is my husband. My name is Ah-lam, and this is your niece, Ching-Lan." She thrust the baby toward him as if to prove to him that what she said was true.

Loretta gasped and put her hand over her mouth.

"Oh my God, Artie, it's your brother's family."

Arthur was stunned. He tried to understand, but nothing made any sense. He wanted to know more, like where in God's name was his brother, Jayson, but there was no time; he had to get medical attention for Elmo. Arthur hurried to get the old four-wheel-drive army jeep that served as their work truck and family car.

The closest medical attention was a family practitioner clinic in Wasilla. Dr. Harvey B. Brown had founded the clinic, and Arthur had flown him into the bush country on many an emergency, transporting patients, both sick and injured.

Suddenly, Arthur realized that there was a problem. Quickly he turned to Loretta. "Take the truck and go get Doc Brown. Tell him it's an emergency and come alone. Tell him a man has been shot, but don't let anyone else hear you. We don't want any authorities out here. Tell him to hurry, and I'll explain when he gets here."

"Okay, Artie." Loretta ran to the jeep and soon was speeding over the dirt road toward town.

"Who are all those kids? Are they Japanese or Chinese?"

"Both," Ah-lam replied. "They are orphans from the 1937 Rape of Nanking and are my responsibility. I must find a place for all of us to live."

"What kind of a place?"

"A safe place. They are refugees. They have no home, no country, and no people. China does not want them, and the Japanese would have killed them if they had the chance. Please, sir, you must help us, please I beg of you."

"So where is my brother? Why isn't he here? I thought he was flying C-47s in China?"

"As far as the US Army is concerned, my husband is listed as killed in action. However, he is still alive, at least I hope he is. They gave him a new identity when he worked for army intel-

THE FRUIT OF ATROCITY

ligence. His name is no longer Jayson Bold. It is Pastor Jay Baldwin." Ah-lam handed Arthur her husband's Red Cross ID and passport."

"Aw, hell, I don't understand any of this. This is totally confusing, too much for me to digest all at once. When was the last time you saw my brother?"

"Two days ago."

"Where did you see him?"

"It is a long story, Mr. Bold. We are all so tired, and the children are very hungry. Is there a place we can go to bathe and rest?"

"We'll get to that as soon as we get Elmo to the doctor."

Arthur climbed into the cargo hold and started counting heads.

"My God, you got sixteen kids in here. I got to have some help with this."

Arthur was about to jump down when he heard a groan. He moved farther into the rear of the plane, and there on a pile of parachute silk was a Chinese soldier, lying on his side holding his belly.

"Who is this? He doesn't look like no orphan kid, that's for sure. Looks like he's full grown, I think."

Ah-lam approached him and knelt down beside the soldier. "His name is Wonlukee. He is devoted servant to my husband."

"How come?"

"My husband saved his life in a most remarkable way, and they named him Wonlukee."

"Lucky eh, looks to me like all of you have had some luck of some kind. I'm just not sure if it was good or bad. What's wrong with him?"

"He is sick. He was given a massive dose of morphine by my brother. It almost killed him."

Arthur could hear vehicles coming down the road. He turned around and descended the ladder as Loretta and Dr. Brown pulled alongside the DC-3. Dr. Brown hurried to the wounded man still lying unconscious on the ground. After examining his wound, he said to Arthur, "We have to get this man to the clinic, fast…he's been shot."

"Yes, I know, and there's another man inside the airplane that, evidently, overdosed on morphine."

"Who gave him morphine?"

"I'll have to explain on the way."

"Do you know how this man got shot?" Dr. Brown inquired as Arthur helped him load Elmo and Wonlukee into the Jeep.

"Your guess is as good as mine, Harvey. I don't know much of anything, except his name is Elmo Barker, and he just flew that DC-3 all the way across the world from China, then passed out shortly after he landed."

"Then I take it that none of those Orientals that came along for the ride are US citizens? Am I right?"

"That's it, Doc."

"What's their story?"

"You'll have to get it from the Chinese girl. She's their guardian. She tried to explain it to me, but I'm not sure I followed it all."

"Who is she, and why did this man bring them all to your place?"

"She says she's my brother's wife, says he's listed as KIA by the US Army, but for some reason, he's still alive, at least she thinks he is. Evidently he was alive the last time she saw him, which was two days ago…that's what she says anyway."

"Do you believe her?"

"Don't have any reason not to. You need to get this Barker fellow patched up so we can talk to him and get this all straightened out. But right now, I have to do something about those orphans. They need food and baths and clothes and beds, and I'm going to need some help with all that."

"Call Bishop O'Reilly, maybe he can help."

"He'll probably call the authorities, and I don't want them in on this just yet. If we get too many people involved, soon enough, they'll be separating those kids and parting them out to different families all over the place, and I'm not so sure that would be the right thing to do.

"I'm going to fix them up in my hangar for tonight. It's heated, and with the airplanes out of the way, there should be room enough for everybody for right now."

"Okay, Arthur, sounds like you got a plan for the night at least. Order takeout from the Wan Chu's Chinese Palace. I'll pay for it."

"Don't worry about it, Doc. I can get it. You're going to be busy enough tonight, trying to keep that pilot alive."

Doc Brown took the wounded Elmo Barker to his dispensary and, with a handpicked medical staff, discretely attended to his wounds.

The velocity of the rifle bullet had slowed significantly as it passed through the exterior of the airplane cockpit. Then entered the right side of Elmo's bottom rib cage at a steep upward angle, smashing two ribs and penetrating through the bottom portion of his right lung, where it remained lodged until Dr. Brown removed it.

The doc called Loretta to let her know that Elmo would recover, and they could visit him in a few days.

Two days later, Arthur entered the private room where Elmo lay. Color had returned to his face, and though medicated, he was now lucid enough to talk.

"How ya doin', buddy?" Arthur asked.

"Hey, don't I know you?"

"Yeah, do you know where you are?"

"The last thing I remember I was running out of fuel on final approach to your place when that portside engine quit. I don't remember much after that. But I guess this must be Wasilla."

"Wasilla it is, and you're in a clinic run by Dr. Harvey Brown. He's everything from a bumps and bruises family practitioner to the general surgeon for the whole Matsu Valley. And he's all there is for what ails you, unless you're in Anchorage or Fairbanks."

"What about—"

"Oh, the gunshot wound? The doc says you'll recover just fine. As a matter of fact, I'd like to hear more about that when you're feeling better."

"What about the orphans?"

"The kids? They're fine. I got them put up in my hangar for now. I've been trying to get another open hangar built alongside the runway for the other airplanes until we can make other arrangements for the kids. That girl—"

Elmo interrupted, "You mean the Chinese girl...your sister-in-law?" Arthur stopped in midsentence.

"Is that true?"

"It's true, she's your brother's wife, and that baby is your niece. She must be about eighteen months old now."

"Loretta will be happy to hear that. Listen, Elmo, I got a million questions, but Doc says I should wait until you're on your feet. By the way, when he lets you out of here, you can stay at our place. We got a spare room you can have. Loretta tried to give it to the girl...I mean my sister-in-law, but she wanted to stay in the hangar with the kids."

"Who's this Loretta you keep mentioning?"

"My wife, we went to school together, and when I got the cabin finished, I sent for her, and we got married."

"I never figured you for a family man."

"I never figured you for a pilot either, but you sure set that Douglas down like you knew what you were doing."

"Actually, the only thing I had ever flown was floatplanes until your brother taught me to fly that cargo plane. He could do anything with that airplane, why you should have seen him—"

"I think that's about enough for now, Arthur," Dr. Brown interrupted as he entered the room. "Mr. Barker needs his rest. You can visit him again tomorrow."

"Okay, Doc. I need to talk to you anyway. Seeya later, Elmo. I'll be back tomorrow."

Arthur followed his friend Harvey into a small office next to the nurse's station nearby the entrance to the clinic.

Dr. Brown began by saying, "It appears to me that your friend was shot from the outside of that aircraft while he was flying, or perhaps while the plane was on the ground. I'm not sure which, but judging from the angle of the bullet, he might have even been standing up at the time. Maybe you could check the outside of the airplane for any exterior damage that would substantiate that.

"Furthermore, I'm not sure what the circumstances were, but it appears to have been a rifle bullet. It was significantly distorted before it ever entered Mr. Barker's body, therefore caused a lot of damage. He is very fortunate to be alive, and how he ever stayed conscience for all the time it took to fly that airplane from wherever they came from is beyond anything I've ever seen. We'll keep him here for a week or so, and then you can take him home…he does have a home, doesn't he?"

"He'll stay with us, Doc. I'll take good care of him. I'm going to need him to take me back to China to find my brother."

"Find your brother? I didn't know you had a brother."

"Yeah, he's three years younger than me. Joined the Army Air Corp in '42 and went to China to fly transports for Chennault."

"Why do *you* have to find him. Doesn't the army know where he is?"

"I don't know the details, Doc. All I know is that four days ago, they were all together somewhere in China, and now that plane, along with Elmo, those kids, and my brother's wife are all here, and he's still over there. So something bad must have happened, and his wife doesn't even know if he's still alive, so I'm going to go find out. However, we still need to find a place for those kids. Like I said, I need your help with that, and my…my sister-in-law won't let them be separated. I guess they've been through too much together."

"Don't you worry about it, Arthur. I'll handle that for you, but I want to talk to…what is her name?"

"Ah-lam."

"Yes, I would like to talk to her. Maybe you could bring her tomorrow when you come in."

"I can do that. Evidently, she's a nurse, at least that's what she told my wife. I understand she was studying medicine at the university in Nanking, China, wanted to be a doctor. It was about the same time the Japanese invaded the place and started making babies, which is how those kids came to be. They're half-Chinese and half-Japanese in case you hadn't noticed. She said their birthdays are all within three weeks of each other."

"My God, man, how horrible."

"Can you believe it? She actually saved all those kids out of Nanking, China, by herself when they were only two or three years old and took them to Chungking, where she kept them in an orphanage. That's where they came from, in that same airplane that's parked at my place. She's a pretty tough little nut, don't you think?"

"She sure is, as well as beautiful. I can see why your brother fell for her. Also, I think she might be the solution to your other problem, Arthur. I'll get with my attorney, and we'll start the paperwork to form an orphanage right here. It could be non-profit, and an extension of the clinic. Ah-lam could run it, and if she wants, she can work for me in the clinic when she has time."

"Where is the funding going to come from for that?"

"Well, between you, me, and a few others who might contribute to the cause, we could at least get it started. Things like that have a way of supporting themselves after they get going. We can worry about that later."

"Thanks, Harvey, I don't know how to thank you."

"Think nothing of it, Arthur, without your air taxi service and generosity, I would've never kept this clinic open in the first place.

Winter came suddenly to the Matsu Valley in 1944, and Arthur had to scramble to keep up with the growing demand for provisions to his customers that lived and worked in the many remote villages.

At night, Arthur worked to make the hangar more comfortable for the children, providing separate quarters for the girls and the boys. Regardless of their efforts to keep the children hidden from the public, word soon got out, and generous supplies of food and clothing began to show up at the hangar door. Many of the women—and older children from the local church groups—offered their help in caring for the orphans. Arthur and Loretta sustained a constant barrage of offers to give the children up for adoption, but Ah-lam would not agree to it and argued vehemently against it.

Rumors began to swirl that the war in Europe might end soon, possibly by spring, and people seemed to be more optimistic about their future life, especially business life.

The Alaska Highway—now completed—provided road access to the north country, from the contiguous United States, and the smaller communities were beginning to show signs of growth and prosperity.

Gold from the mines had also contributed to the local economies of Anchorage and Wasilla. However, the influx of farming since 1935 directly led to the greater growth of Palmer over Wasilla until the town of Palmer quickly became a city hosting a small hospital, grade school, and high school that offered academics to the citizens of both Palmer and Wasilla.

The word was out that Arthur and Loretta had sixteen children—children that had arrived all in one day and none of which looked a thing like Arthur or, Loretta either one. People from as far away as Palmer, Anchorage, and even Fairbanks stopped in to drop off clothing and food. Some felt the need to donate hard-earned cash, which went into the orphanage's general fund.

A large old home with twenty-four rooms and indoor plumbing sat vacant on the outskirts of Wasilla. At one time, it had been used as a bed-and-breakfast rooming house before the farming boom when travelers on their way to the gold fields traveled by train. But with the war almost over and soldiers returning home and looking for work, there was no money to spare, and the owner could not keep it up, nor could he sell it. So like a great white elephant, it waited for the time it could once again be useful.

Dr. Brown and Ah-lam approached the owner with a proposition. She said to him, "Gift us the property for our orphanage, and we will maintain it and pay the taxes on it until prosperity returns to the region. When the children are grown and are on their own, we will bestow it back to you. In the interim, we will use it for home and school for my children, as well as outpatient housing for the clinic, and maybe even convalescent care for the senior citizens of the community." The owner agreed, and they finalized the deal. Ah-lam Nee Baldwin finally had her own orphanage.

Dr. Brown filed the paperwork, creating a nonprofit entity. He was proud of Ah-lam, and when he learned that she was also an orphan, he not only filed papers to adopt her but all sixteen of her children as well.

Ah-lam applied for American citizenship as Mrs. Jay Baldwin. Proof of birth for her and all the children, including Ah-lam's marriage certificate, was manufactured by Loretta Bold, who at one time was an art major at a satellite extension of the St. Lewis Institute of Arts and Science, located in Cape Girardeau, Missouri. In those days, ingenuity and self-reliance were natural survival traits learned from childhood, requisite skills for living in harsh times.

Never again would Ah-lam or her children need be concerned over where they belonged or if they had a country. At last, they were American citizens; it said so on the paperwork. Wonlukee, fully recovered, helped care for the children in the orphanage.

After Elmo recovered from his gunshot wound, he began working for Arthur. When he wasn't wrenching on the airplanes, he was flying the Waco on floats. Business continued to grow, and Arthur began considering adding another plane to the fleet. Then one evening at Loretta's dinner table in the cabin, Arthur said to him, "Elmo, if I thought you were going to stick around for a while, I might buy another airplane. The government is pouring money into the fisheries to put people to work, and they need both fish spotters and fish haulers. We could put that DC-3 to good use hauling fish to the canaries in Seattle and San Francisco. There's loads of money to be made."

"Sounds like a lot of fun, but I'm leaving the first of July."

"Leaving for where?"

Elmo was quiet for a moment before speaking.

"I'm going back to Russia."

"What's in Russia?"

"I left a friend back there, and I told him I would be back to get him."

"What friend, you mean my brother Jayson?"

"No, but when I find my friend, if he's alive, we're going to go back to China and find your brother."

"Hell, I'm going with you if you're going to do that. I told Doc Brown six months ago I wanted to go with you to find my brother."

"No, you can't go. I won't take you."

"Why not?"

"It's too dangerous. I can't guarantee this beautiful lady of yours"—Elmo indicated toward Loretta sitting next to her husband—"that you would come back, standing up. Can't take the chance. You folks have done too much for me. I wouldn't feel right taking you off to China to get you killed."

"I can take care of myself."

"Yeah, I know, but I'm going to be involved in some things that you wouldn't want to be associated with."

"What kind of things?" Arthur asked through squinted eyebrows.

"Me and my buddy, providing I can find him, will have to resort to some illegal activity to sustain the expenses of our trip."

"You mean like smuggling?"

"Something like that."

"Where do you think Jayson is, if he's alive?"

"Well, if he hasn't let his hard head get himself killed, he won't be far from Ah-lam's brother."

"What does Jayson have to do with his wife's brother?"

"I guess I better tell you the story from the beginning. The month before Jayson met his wife, he was flying that aircraft that is sitting on your airstrip. It was a C-47 at the time and..."

Elmo proceeded to relate the sequence of events leading up to when they left Chungking with the children and headed for Yinchuan.

Loretta started crying before Jayson crash landed in the miracle meadow and never stopped throughout the rest of the story. Sometimes, she sobbed so hard Elmo had to stop to let her catch her breath. At which time he would begin where he left off. Of course, Loretta would start crying again.

Elmo felt bad that he had to tell the story. He knew it was hard on Jayson's family. Elmo himself had become so hardened and insensitive to suffering and killing that watching Loretta cry caused him to take pause at what had happened to his own emotional well being; watching people suffer and die had become no more dramatic than watching them eat a plate of food.

"Good God in heaven!" Arthur exclaimed. "My brother did all of that? And you say this Charlie is the head of China's National Intelligence?"

"Yes, it's all true. Charlie Nee works as Generalissimo Chiang Kai-shek's right hand man, and because he saved your brother's life, he considers him and that airplane to be his own private property for the rest of his life."

"So what happened after you landed in Yinchuan?"

"Well, about twenty minutes out, Jay took over the airplane and landed it. He taxied to the far end, spun around, leaving the aircraft in a takeoff position. I don't know why, but for some reason, he left both radials running when he got up from his seat to go to the cargo area. That was where his family and all the orphans were sleeping. The last thing I heard him say was, 'Elmo, you can shut this thing down if you want, I'm going to the rear.' I said to him, 'Aye, aye, Captain,' and he left. The next thing I knew, I saw him out of my right side window, being dragged across the clearing toward the trees by two men, with Charlie not far behind, yelling something at them. At that time, your brother appeared to be unconscious. Then I saw Charlie turn and head back toward the airplane. At the same time, Raylan Jaworski staggered through the cockpit door, holding his head, with blood running down the side of his face."

"Who's Raylan?" Arthur interrupted.

"He's my friend I left in Russia."

"How come you left him in Russia?"

"I can only tell one story at a time, wait till I finish the first one."

"Honey, let him finish," Loretta said between her sobs.

"Anyway, Raylan staggers into the cockpit like he had just woke up from a drunk and was hollering, 'Go, go, go, let's get out of here.' So I didn't wait to ask questions. I just slammed the power forward and headed for the other end of the field. Well, believe me, I was sweating bullets. That was the shortest strip I'd ever been into, and we were still loaded. I thought for sure we were going into the trees, but we only took the tops off of two or three of them on the way out. Dang, I'm sweating all over again just telling it."

"Why was Raylan in such a hurry to get out of there? Why didn't you guys go help my brother?"

"Well, I wasn't privy to what had gone on in the back of the airplane, but we had taken Ah-lam's brother, Charlie, captive back at Chungking and had him tied up in the back of the airplane the whole way to Yinchuan. Me, and Raylan both, had tried to talk your brother into letting us kill him, but Jay wouldn't go for it. He told me to find a parachute to put on him so we could throw him out over the mountains, somewhere to get him out of our hair while we got out of China."

"Why didn't you?"

"I did, but the parachute was so old and torn and hadn't been packed right, and since none of us knew how to pack one correctly, your brother wouldn't take the chance on his brother-in-law getting killed, so he wouldn't let us toss him out."

"So did he get loose or something? Didn't you have someone watching him?"

"Yeah, we had the two guards that Madame Chiang gave us. They were guarding him. But we had to climb up to fourteen thousand feet to get over some of those mountains on the way to Yinchuan, and no one had oxygen except the pilots, so everyone fell asleep including your brother."

"Why wasn't he on the oxygen?"

"He wanted to take a nap because he knew he would be up for a long time after we got fueled at Yinchuan. I remember him telling me about a dream he had. It was about—"

"So why wasn't Charlie asleep too?" Arthur interrupted.

"We think that Charlie wasn't as susceptible to hypoxia as everyone else because he has spent so much time in the mountains. We think he kept the guards awake and talked them into turning him loose."

"I still don't understand why you left Jay there. You guys obviously had automatic weapons, and it was just the three of them."

"I know, we thought about that later, but the Padre had given all of us specific orders that if anything happened to him, or anything went sideways in any way at all, we were to put the children and his family first before him and get them to safety. So we did. That's why I'm going back."

THE FRUIT OF ATROCITY

"Do you think that Charlie guy killed my brother?"

"No, not at all, he has probably beat him up a little to teach him a lesson, but I'm sure he's still alive, and we'll find him if it takes us the rest of our lives. The war in China is starting to wind down a little, and Charlie will be looking to line his pockets with diamonds. We got away with his most valuable resource, that airplane sitting out there. That's the one Jayson was flying when he went down, and like I told you before, it was Charlie who made the deal with army intelligence to salvage it and convert it to a hospital plane. He had planned all along to make Jayson his private pilot and that plane his personal freight hauler so he could supply his own army of smugglers and black marketers. Anyway, what I'm saying is, if we hadn't have gotten the hell out of there when we did, we might have lost our only opportunity to get Jayson's family and those sixteen children out of China."

"Where did you get the fuel to make it this far? I thought you didn't have enough to make it to your next rendezvous."

"Our next fuel stop was in Russia, a place called Khabarovsk. It was our designated rendezvous on the original orders we got from Chennault. The problem was: we were running about three weeks late."

"Did you stop anywhere for fuel to get you the rest of the way to Khabarovsk?"

"Hell…I mean, heck no. Sorry, the Padre always gets on me when I swear. He's real religious."

"I know he did me too. Mother was even worse."

"Anyhow, we just pointed it to our heading and leaned those radials back so far the cylinder heads almost melted. In fact, both engines quit while I was landing at Khabarovsk too."

"You do that a lot. You must like living on the edge. Who did you get fuel from in Khabarovsk?"

"Everybody in Russia is either smugglers or middlemen, but they're all involved in the trade of stolen goods, one way or the other. Everything went well in Khabarovsk. The underground people were good to work with. They didn't have the appearance of gangsters at all. We paid them generously, told them we'd be back, and headed to Magadan."

"Magadan! Is that Russia or Siberia?"

"I'm not sure, probably Siberia. It's on the coast, a fishing village, but there is a runway there, built by the underground—"

"You keep saying 'underground.' What is the underground? Militia, Mafia, military, what?"

"Russian Mafia. These guy's are bad, real bad. It's where I took my bullet. I came in low, located the airstrip, and circled the village looking for anyone who might be expecting us. But at first no one came out, not a soul. So then, I circled around to land.

"As soon as I touched down, I taxied to the far end of the strip and spun the tail in a takeoff direction. Before I could get it shut down, all of a sudden here come about thirty men out of the trees armed with major weapons, mostly 7.62 caliber BARs and rifles. They surrounded the airplane.

"I stayed at the controls on the copilot's side. That's the side I learned on. Raylan opened the cargo door to talk to them. I didn't hear everything that was said, but pretty soon he came back in and told me I could shut it down. He said they would sell us fuel but wanted to know how much money we had. I guess they got mad when he wouldn't tell them. Finally, they gave him a price for the fuel, and he agreed to pay them with diamonds, which amounted to all the diamonds we had other then Jaworski's personal stash."

"Do you still have Jaworski's diamonds with you?" Arthur asked.

"Yes, sir…anyway, they brought a deuce and a half tanker truck out onto the field that had a pump driven by a diesel engine mounted on the back of the rig. Real neat deal, I just hope it's still there when I get back.

"Anyway, I went to the rear of the plane with Raylan to watch while two of their people climbed onto the wings to refuel us. We noticed the ringleaders talking among themselves. Once in

THE FRUIT OF ATROCITY

a while they would look our way and point. Raylan and I both knew something was up."

"Sounds like they were making a spur of the moment plan to hijack your airplane."

"I'm sure of it, and I'm sure also that their intentions were to traffic those kids. So Raylan and I made a quick plan of our own. I gave Raylan the diamonds he had agreed to give them, and I went back to the cockpit. Raylan took his sniper rifle and slung it over his shoulder. Then, armed with his sniper rifle and a grenade launcher, he waited out of sight by the cargo door. As soon as they finished refueling the plane and were off the wing, Raylan fired the grenade launcher and jumped to the ground while I was starting the engines."

"What did he fire the grenade at, the fuel truck?"

"I'm not sure...I hope not. I think he just fired it into the ground to scatter them while he headed for cover. Anyhow, the radials were still warm, so I slammed the throttles to the wall." Elmo paused to sip the last of his coffee.

Loretta went to the kitchen and returned with a fresh pot.

"Mr. Barker, would you like more coffee?"

"Sure, thank you, ma'am."

Arthur had a stern look on his face. He said to Elmo, "What was the plan that you and Raylan made? It seems like you keep running off and leaving your partners everywhere you go."

"It was his idea. He told me to get going as soon as he jumped out. He said he would hold them off until I got airborne. He didn't say what all he had in mind to do, but you have to understand that Raylan is special. He shoots people like they are bottles on a stump. He's like a ghost, he just disappears, eliminates the threat and shows up again."

"Sounds like there's a good chance he might be alive. So when did you get shot?"

"When Raylan fired off that launcher, everything went crazy, and I could hear a lot of shooting. Bullets were hitting the side of the airplane, so I crossed my fingers hoping I wouldn't hit Raylan and spun the tail around in a full 360-degree turn to clear the area. When I straightened out, I stood up in my seat to see out of the portside window. That was when I took the bullet.

After we got into the air, I started feeling woozy and discovered I was leaking blood all over the floor. I hollered for help, and Ah-lam came and managed to slow up the bleeding."

"How long did it take you to get to Anchorage from Magadan?"

"A little over ten hours. I didn't think I was going to make it, but your brother taught me to pray, so I did, and I doubt we would have made it otherwise. Ah-lam helped me fly the airplane. She kept it straight and level so I could take breaks. But I still had to stay conscious enough to do the navigating.

"Goodness gracious, God Almighty. That's the scariest story I guess I've ever heard. Hell...I mean, danged, if my hands aren't shaking too. So you're sure you want to go back there all by yourself?"

"Well, I have to find out what happened to Raylan."

"Listen, I have an idea. There are a hundred ex-GIs around here that are out of work. Why don't we see if any of them were infantry? If we could find a half dozen guys that can handle weapons, maybe you could pay them with some of those diamonds."

"Actually, that's a good idea. I never would have thought of it. Yeah, I got diamonds. They all belong to Raylan though, but I'm sure he won't mind if I cash a few of them in to get him home. Do you think there's a black market jeweler in Anchorage? Those diamonds are probably worth five to ten grand apiece."

Arthur sat back on his chair and stared at Elmo, shocked. Loretta inhaled deeply, and her eyes got big as saucers. Arthur said to him, "I don't know if we'll be able to get that much for them, but we can try. We'll fly over to Anchorage tomorrow and check it out. There might be a few places on the south side that would have those type of connections. Some of them deal in gold

THE FRUIT OF ATROCITY

and precious stones, and I'm sure we'll run into a few ex-military while were there."

"That's great, it won't matter if I can't get full price as long as I get enough to pay our way. I also need money to fuel the DC-3 before I leave, which reminds me. I forgot something in the airplane. I'll be right back." Elmo excused himself and hurried out of the door.

Loretta looked fiercely at her husband. "You scared me when you told Elmo you were going with him."

"Well, he's right. I probably would get my head shot off over there. But that's my brother you know! I understand more about why they left him behind now, but at first, it was sounding like Elmo had just run out on him."

"Here he comes," Loretta whispered.

Elmo had a package under his arm as he shut the door behind him.

"Remember when I told you how Chennault ordered your brother to take those children and get out of China immediately after the airplane modifications were completed?"

"Yes, you said Jayson wanted to go get his family first."

"That's right, well, evidently there was supposed to be an orphanage in Anchorage all ready to take those kids off his hands and the general gave him $10,000 cash to give to the people running it."

Elmo handed the package of money to Arthur.

"Wow, are you telling me there is $10,000 in here?" Arthur tossed the package up and down in his hands as if he were weighing it.

"There sure is, and Jayson said he didn't want the children to wind up in an orphanage where they would be sold off like so much beef, so he told me to give it to you and ask you to provide for them."

"Why didn't you give us this before?"

"I totally forgot about it until now."

"Well, I guess if there was any question in my mind about your story, there isn't anymore. Put it there, partner." Arthur extended his handshake to Elmo, who eagerly accepted it.

"All right then, let's throw enough fuel in that DC-3 to get to Anchorage. We can fill it up over there."

"Why do we need to take the Douglas? I'm not leaving for another month. We can wait until a week or so before I leave to pick up those army guys."

"Well, because there's some equipment that I need to get to some miners up at a place called Porcupine Creek. I was wondering if you could help me with that?"

"Absolutely, but there is one more thing I want to do." Elmo reached into his shirt pocket. "These are for you." Elmo reached one hand toward Arthur and the other at Loretta.

"What's this?" Arthur asked. Elmo dropped a beautifully cut and polished diamond into each of their hands simultaneously.

"Oh my god." Loretta gasped.

"What are these for?" Arthur said.

"They're for the two of you. When I get back, I'll bring you some more."

"But I thought these belonged to Raylan?" Loretta objected.

"They did, but they're yours now. Someday, they'll be worth a lot more than they are right now, so save them for your retirement or something. And I won't take no for an answer."

"Thank you so much, Mr. Barker, you are very generous." Loretta rushed around the table and gave Elmo a huge hug.

"Thanks, buddy, we'll get you fueled up and stocked with food and supplies before you go, and Lord willing, we'll find some competent help so you can find Raylan and my brother and bring them both home—alive. And I have no doubt you will succeed."

"There is one more thing, Ah-lam has your brother's passport and Red Cross ID. I may need that to get him out of China."

"Actually, I have that," Loretta said. "I'll get it for you." She scurried off to another room. Moments later, Loretta returned with the documents in her hand. "I used them when I forged Ah-lam's documents so they would match."

Over the next three weeks, Elmo and Arthur made a dozen runs into mining camps and villages hauling the kind of equipment that could have never been hauled in either of Arthur's smaller aircraft: huge generators, light plants, water pumps, sluice systems of every make and design, as well as building materials. Arthur and Elmo made the last delivery and were on their way home.

"You be sure and bring this airplane back with you when you come, ya hear? We can join up and make a killing hauling this kind of freight."

"When I get back, we'll be able to buy as many of these airplanes as you want. Maybe even a couple of C-46s. There's already a surplus of C-47s and C-46s available. And the more of them the government turns loose, the cheaper they'll become. As a matter of fact, I'll give you a few more of those diamonds, and you can pick up two or three of them while I'm gone."

"That's okay, keep the diamonds. I'll make do with what I got until you get back. Maybe then we can do something together."

Elmo sold ten diamonds while he and Arthur were in Anchorage. Due to the tough economy, he only got three grand a piece for them. But thirty thousand dollars was a lot of money, and Elmo was satisfied that it would be more than enough.

It was the third week of June, and the news was spreading that the war in Europe had ended. It was nearing time for Elmo to go. Elmo and Arthur headed back to Anchorage.

The streets were filled with out-of-work men, women, and teenagers standing in soup lines and labor halls looking for any relief they could find from the devastated economy.

Arthur had been there before, looking for labor help on his many projects, projects that very often happened miles away in some remote village where manpower was scarce. Most of the labor men they encountered were not labor ready, either they were too old, too young, or too drunk.

Many of the servicemen who had returned from the military still wore uniforms with the insignia of the outfit to which they belonged. Elmo and Arthur looked for the infantry patch that would identify the soldiers as competent with weapons. There were a few, but Elmo was looking for men who were physically fit, and so far, the only ones they had found were physically disabled, more than likely, wounded in action.

"Let's try the USO," Arthur suggested. "The soldiers we are looking for will be hanging around the nearest dance club."

"Good idea," Elmo said.

Arthur continued, "As a matter of fact, I believe there's a USO show scheduled for tomorrow at Fort Richardson.

The USO—Uniform Service Organization—had been founded in 1941, at a time when just about every corner of the world was involved in, or directly affected by, war. From the European Theater to the western fronts of Russia and the Baltics, to China in the Far East and South Sea Islands, war raged from one corner of the earth to the other.

The human resources available in the United States for military duty had been exhausted to a critical point. Moral was becoming an issue that clearly could determine the successful or unsuccessful outcome of the war.

On May 6, 1941, Bob Hope and a small group of professional entertainers from Hollywood, California, performed before the troops at March Field in Fairbanks, Alaska, only three months after the Uniform Service Organization came into existence. And throughout the remaining war years, hundreds of singers, dancers, and famous entertainers donated their time and talents to the active duty servicemen stationed all around the world, some even gave their lives.

Arthur turned to Elmo. "That's where we'll find our men."

THE FRUIT OF ATROCITY

The next day, they flew the DC-3 into Merrill Field and took a car to the Fort.

They were there all right, about 150 of them, along with the Andrew Sisters and Marlene Dietrich.

"Wow, Arthur, you should have brought Loretta."

"Are you kidding, I wouldn't let her anywhere near all these young bucks."

"I suppose most of the men in uniform are probably all active duty, do you think?" Elmo said.

"Maybe, maybe not, but we can start with the men in civilian clothes if you want. You do the talking. You might want to start by putting some cash money in their hand—like maybe, a hundred bucks. Most of the underranked-enlisted men live on less than seventy bucks a month, so a hundred spot ought to get their attention."

"I'm going to need more than just enlisted men. I need another pilot, or two, in case I get shot again."

"I doubt if you'll find any of them. They're all still flying for the ERP."

"What's the ERP?" Elmo asked.

"The European Recovery Program. All the officers and higher ranked–enlisted men have been diverted to the ERP project while the grunts that fought in the trenches are gradually getting discharged and coming home. So if you want people that know how to fight and stay alive, these guy's are your best bet. You'll find everything here, from snipers to ordinance to explosive experts. As a matter of fact, you might want two of each."

"You make a good point, Arthur. I'll go see what I can come up with."

It was both a sad and exciting day when Elmo Barker and his thirteen mercenaries departed from Arthur Bold's grass airstrip.

Ah-lam and all the children were there, bidding Elmo and his crew farewell. Tears of both joy and sadness watered the grass— sadness because Elmo Barker had succeeded in saving them all out of a country torn by war and a past that could only be forgotten by starting over in a new country and joy because Elmo was going back, back to that dangerous God-forsaken place in search of a lost husband, father, brother, and friend, who desperately needed help getting home to his family. "Greater love hath no man than this, that a man lay down his life for his friends" (John 15:13, AKJV).

Elmo shook hands with Arthur and hugged Loretta, Ah-lam, and all of the children, including Wonlukee; even Arthur wiped a tear from one eye.

"We will pray for you," Ah-lam said through teary eyes. "And we will pray for your men."

Elmo closed and latched the door and waved at his adopted family from the copilot's window. Soon the Red Cross DC-3 roared westward toward the far end of the short grassy field until it lazily launched into the Alaska sky, slowly melting into the western horizon.

Chapter 13

Elmo Barker climbed into the copilot's seat of the Red Cross DC-3 wearing his leather, sheepskin flight suit and cap. In the left seat sat his new pilot, Captain Richard Wilson. Wilson was an ex-B-17 driver with a purple heart, who had received a hardship discharge after his two younger brothers died in action at Guadalcanal in the 1941 to 1942 campaign.

It was already after ten, yet the sun was still high in the western sky. Elmo peered out his window and saw Arthur and Loretta standing alongside the runway. He waved to them. Ah-lam and the orphans were there too, and they all returned his farewell. Then shoving the throttles forward to full power, the hospital plane began to roll.

As the DC-3 lifted into the night sky, a strange kind of anticipation came over Elmo. He could not put it into words or even into a tangible thought, but he could definitely feel it: a reservation, a dread, or, possibly, fear associated with a cold shiver that traveled all the way up his spine. Elmo shrugged it off and concentrated on his navigation.

"Wilson, do you think you can fly this bucket of bolts?"

"I suppose, then again, I'm not sure I'll be able to stay awake without someone shooting antiaircraft guns at me."

"How many missions did you go on before they sent you packing?"

"One."

"*One*? I thought you said you got a purple heart?"

"I did. I was flying one of twelve B-17E's with the first group of bombers to enter the war in May of 1942. We were on a diversionary mission, flying out of Wycombe England over France. Our commander, Major Paul Tibbets, was in the lead plane, and I was flying right wing. We started getting into antiaircraft flak, and a lot of tracers were coming up at us. Major Tibbetts and his crew were getting beat up pretty bad, so I broke ranks and ducked under the major's plane to take some of the hits for him.

"Well, we took one too many, and my ship was one of only two bombers lost on the mission. As a matter of fact, it was the success of that mission that sold the USAAF [United States Army Air Force] on the B-17 as their bomber of choice. That was when they really started cranking them out, wound up building over twelve thousand. One of the greatest airplanes ever built."

"What happened after you went down?"

"We were hit pretty hard but still had one engine running at about half power, so I headed for the coast and put down in the water next to a British battleship that was pounding the beach with its twelve-inch guns. It was on that ship that I learned of my two brothers and received my ticket home."

"I thought you had to be wounded to get a purple heart."

"I *was* wounded. I caught some shrapnel in my rear end. It come up through the floor and the bottom of my seat. I never had anything hurt so bad in all my life. I still walk with a limp."

"Well, we're glad you made it, Captain. Welcome aboard."

"Glad to help, Barker. Say, what did you say this fellow's name is, the guy we're looking for?"

"He's a missionary pastor named Jay Baldwin. We had to run off and leave him in China, on account, we had to get a planeload of orphans out of there before they all got killed. His wife and child were on board too, so he ordered us to leave him there."

"Well, anything I can do for you just let me know."

"I hired you to back me up flying this crate. I took a bullet on the way home to Anchorage, barely made it. I almost bled to death on the way back. In fact, the pastor's wife had to fly the airplane half the time because I kept passing out. It was a miracle we even got there."

"What are all those ex-infantry guys with guns doing in the back? Are you expecting trouble somewhere?"

"Yeah, we're expecting trouble all right. We'll run into that at our first fuel rendezvous in Magadan, Russia, provided we make it that far before running out of gas. Looks like we got some headwind. We'll need to take it up to about twenty thousand feet." Wilson eased back on the yoke and added power, the DC-3 began to climb.

"I see you '47 drivers got an oxygen system all set up in here like the '17s."

"We just installed this system back in Anchorage. We only had enough for the two pilots before that. That's the reason we burned so much fuel. We had to stay low, even got into a bit of rough weather that almost put us into the surf. So I'll feel a whole lot better up at altitude."

As the DC-3 climbed through twelve thousand feet, Elmo left his right seat and worked his way back to the cargo area where he could speak to his crew.

"You men listen up. We're going on up to twenty thousand feet, so get your oxygen masks ready. There's plenty to go around. We're about ten or eleven hours out of Magadan, Russia, depending on what kind of winds we encounter. I'll let you know when we're getting close, should be a couple hours after dawn. Have your parachutes ready. You'll be jumping from twelve thousand feet into the woods around the airstrip. Be sure and get a good visual of the complex and the perimeter on the way down. If it's light enough, try to locate the fuel truck if you can. The complex is about a mile from the runway, so don't linger over it too long, or you may not make the landing strip, or even worse, if the Mafia sees you, they might shoot you while you're suspended in the air.

"After the last man is out of the aircraft, we'll keep going as if we're not landing. When we're out of sight and out of earshot of the compound, we'll turn around and head back. I'll make a straight in low approach. As soon as you have the perimeter secured, send up a flare. If we don't see a flare, we'll assume that the airstrip is not secure and keep circling, but remember, we'll be very low on fuel at that point, so get the perimeter secured as quickly as possible. And one more thing, watch for an American by the name of Raylan Jaworski. I left him there last year, and I'm not sure if he's still alive. If he is, you probably won't have much to do. If he isn't, the Russian Mafia may even be expecting you.

"If you do run into resistance, engage them only in the area of the airstrip. Don't pursue them very far into the woods. We'll need your protection when we get on the ground. After we land, five of you stay with the airplane, and the other seven take off toward the compound. You guys can decide who does what. Try to find that fuel truck and bring it to the airstrip.

"That's about all, gentlemen, now get some sleep. I'll wake you an hour before jump time." One of the men in the group spoke up.

"What does this Jaworski look like?"

"What's your name, soldier?"

"Leo...Leo Sanders, from Wichita."

"Well, Leo, he's about five feet, ten inches, 180 pounds, and carries one of those Russian SVT-40 sniper rifles with a scope. You'll know he's not one of the Mafia if he gets within a hundred yards of you and you're still alive. Believe me, those Russian Mafia guys will shoot you the instant they see you."

"What's their beef with you? Did you guys take off without paying them for the fuel?"

"That too, but mostly because they were about to hijack the airplane. They wanted the orphans for the underground sex traders, and the next time we meet, they will try to take the airplane. That's why I hired you men."

"So are these guys smugglers?" Leo asked.

THE FRUIT OF ATROCITY

"That's right. They trade in diamonds mostly, but also in guns, gas, munitions, and human trafficking. They'll take anything from anybody and think nothing of leaving you dead if you get in the way."

"How many of them are in that compound?"

"I'm not sure. There were about thirty that met us at the airport when we landed. Raylan took out at least a dozen of them with that grenade launcher before he jumped out of the airplane and ran for the woods. That's the last time I saw him. It's also when I took my bullet."

"So what are we going to do once we neutralize the threat?"

"We'll get fueled up and leave half of you men there to keep control of the place while Raylan and I and the rest of the men go on to China. I just want to know I can count on you guys to pull this off for me."

"You can count on us, Mr. Barker, as long as your money's good."

"The money's good, but it won't do you any good if you don't kill them before they kill us. You're going to have to hit the ground running and stay spread out, shoot any man who doesn't look like he's from Georgia. And I don't mean the middle east."

✪✪✪

The Red Cross plane droned on through the night. Elmo calculated and recalculated their course, using magnetic headings adjusted for wind correction and magnetic deviation. At times, whenever the sky was clear, he would recalculate with celestial navigation using a sextant, shooting angles off Polaris, the north star, to calculate the aircraft's altitude against the horizon—a way of determining the aircraft's latitudinal and longitudinal position over the northern hemisphere. It worked beautifully, and as always, Elmo kept the DC-3 on a perfect course.

"You're a pretty good navigator," Captain Wilson said to him. "I've known guys that were good at dead reckoning, but I think you're the best I've ever seen." Elmo glanced over at the new captain in the left seat and smiled.

"Thanks, just comes natural I guess. It's a fascinating science to me. I love it.

Elmo looked at the clock mounted on the instrument panel. It read oh-six-thirty. He said to Wilson, "We're about two hours out. I'll go wake the men. How are we on fuel?"

"It's going to be close. We've bucked a headwind all night."

"Those main tanks will run dry shortly, and you'll need to switch to the auxiliary. You have another two hours of fuel after that. Stay at this altitude for another hour and a quarter, and then let it down to twelve thousand. Hold your present heading. I'll be back in a few minutes."

Elmo returned to the rear of the plane and woke up the men. After briefing them one more time on what to expect, he returned to his seat.

Wilson said to him, "How come you fly from the copilot seat?"

"The Padre trained me from here. Before flying for the Red Cross, I was a float pilot in Alaska, all single-engine stuff. I became a DC-3 pilot out of necessity."

"Are you saying you've never actually been professionally trained in multiengine?"

"I guess you could put it like that."

"No wonder you were looking for a real pilot."

Elmo got the impression the captain wasn't too confident in his abilities. He decided to ask him a few questions to find out how much *real* experience his new copilot actually had.

"So, Wilson, how are you with landing in the fog?"

"Landing in the fog? You mean on instruments?"

"Yeah, can you set this thing down in the fog if you have a decent point?"

"I guess, but I would like to do it a few times in the daylight without the fog first so I could make a note of the time, distance, descent rate, and airspeed. I would have to know all of that before going in blind."

"No time for that. You'll have to go in blind and get it right the first time because there will be a layer of coastal fog over the runway. Also the runway is a bit short. You'll have to set it down like those aircraft carrier drivers do. Bring it in under power, about 1.3 over stall speed—in the fog. Do you think you can do that?"

Suddenly, the color drained out of Captain Wilson's face. His mouth was open as if he wanted to say something, but nothing was coming out. Then, sheepishly, he said, "Is that what you went to the back for, to tell those guys they would be parachuting into the fog?"

"That's right."

"How can you tell that from way up here?"

"See that pink circle around the moon, that means fog on the ground along the coast and at least ten miles inland, especially in the lowlands." Captain Richard Wilson was quiet.

Elmo said to him, "If you're not comfortable with it, I'll take over after the men have jumped. I'll probably have better luck finding the place if *I'm* flying than if I were trying to describe it to you."

"Good idea," Wilson replied. "By the way, is there an extra parachute in this crate?"

"No, the parachutes are all spoken for, sorry."

Captain Wilson didn't say much for the next hour and a quarter. Finally, Elmo said to him, "You can start down now. We need to come in steep, so maintain this heading and give me about a fifteen-hundred-foot rate of descent. When we arrive at twelve thousand, I'll take it from there." Wilson remained silent.

Finally, the airplane leveled out at twelve thousand feet, and Elmo took over the controls.

"Go to the back, and when I turn on the red light, help them get that door open. I'll blink the red light three times, one minute before jump time. When the green light comes on, kick them out of the door. Be sure they've all got their gear."

Wilson unfastened his harness buckle and made his way to the rear of the airplane.

All the men stood ready at the door. Wilson scurried around in the back of the cargo area as if he was searching for something.

Finally, the red light came on. Leo Sanders, who had been a paratrooper instructor, checked the men to be sure they were ready. He looked at Wilson and said to him, "Are you jumping too?"

"No…I mean, yeah…I found this chute in the back. I put it on just in case I fall out of the door." Leo studied him for a moment and arrived at the conclusion that the man had never jumped out of a plane in his life.

"Are you sure you want to do this, something doesn't look right about the way it's packed. I wouldn't jump with that if I were you."

"You ain't me."

"Okay, just thought you'd like to know."

Suddenly the red light blinked three times.

"One minute to go," Wilson said, his voice quivering. Leo Sanders announced, "We got green. *Go, go, go. Everyone out now.*" Leo waited until the last man was out of the door and turned to Wilson.

"You going too?"

In a panicked voice, he said, "Yeah, but I've nev—" Sanders grabbed hold of Wilson's belt and dragged him to the door; together, both men disappeared into the gray dawn.

Elmo waited another five minutes after he switched on the green light before he began his descent to the airfield. He could faintly see the compound and airstrip; though they were both nothing more than dots on the hilly terrain. The fog was not as dense as he had anticipated, but he knew that when he approached it laterally, his forward visibility would go to something less than zero.

He remembered what he had learned from the Padre. *Pick a spot for your descent point.* However, Captain Wilson was right. This was not only crazy—it was insane. Even the Padre had made practice runs and filled his notebook with volumes of information before he attempted landing in the fog at both Freeland and the headquarters.

Elmo had no choice; his friend was down there, and now his men were down there too. And even though they had fully understood the risk of this mission going in and freely accepted it, Elmo felt a responsibility to get them home alive.

He glanced at the left seat where only moments before Captain Wilson had sat—it was still empty. *I guess he doesn't like it up here*, Elmo mused.

Elmo looked at his hands; they were shaking. He adjusted his posture, clenched his jaw, and concentrated on what he needed to do. There, on the south end of the airport about a mile away from the threshold was an opening in the trees, a small clearing. *I'll line up with the center line and drop into the fog to about five hundred feet above the trees. When I cross that clearing, I'll start letting it down at three hundred feet a minute. That should put me on the runway immediately after I cross the threshold.*

Elmo made his last turn to final approach and leveled at five hundred feet. He could see directly below him but could not see a thing in front of him. He watched until he saw the clearing slide by below him and began a three-hundred-foot rate of descent. At that point, he unconsciously held his breath and didn't let it out until the wheels engaged the turf.

Leo Sanders let go of Captain Wilson as soon as they cleared the door, and the army pilot drifted away from him. He watched to see if his chute would deploy.

Wilson pulled the ripcord, and a trail of silk emerged from his half-opened parachute pack but did not catch air.

Looks like a zero going down in a trail of white smoke, Leo thought as he watched him. *Well, I better get him, or he'll be dead inside of two minutes. Looks like he passed out anyway, wouldn't even see it coming.*

Leo Sanders, still in free fall, maneuvered next to the limp pilot and unfastened his parachute pack. As the silk disappeared, he grabbed the unconscious pilot and clutched him against himself with one arm while deploying his own chute with the other. The ride down was considerably faster than normal due to the extra weight, but Leo had done this before as a master parachutist for the Army Air Corp. With over thirty thousand jumps to his credit, there wasn't much he had not experienced at one time or another.

Wilson woke up only a moment before they hit the ground. Clinging to Leo as if his life depended on it, giving Leo time to manipulate the guidelines and slow the descent before touchdown, miraculously, they landed directly in the middle of the runway. "Let's get this stuff off and get into the trees," Leo said quietly.

The rest of the men were already on the ground, and several rushed to help. Wilson was limping when he got up, and two of the men carried him to the trees. Whispering, Leo inquired, "Did anyone get to see the compound?" Several men nodded.

"Was there any activity? Could you see how many men were there?"

"I didn't see anybody," one of the men replied.

"Me neither," another answered.

A strange voice coming from the dark timber said to them, "You don't need to worry about anyone but me."

Everyone crouched and held their breath. Less than thirty feet away, a figure stepped out of the darkness and approached them.

"Who are you people?" the stranger said.

From low over the trees and two miles away, the sound of two 1,200 horsepower Pratt and Whitney radial engines broke the silence, growing louder the closer they came. Gradually the pilot increased power as the airplane slowed to 1.3 over stall speed as it descended down the final approach path.

Suddenly, out of the fog emerged the McDonald Douglas DC-3 with a huge Red Cross painted on the vertical stabilizer.

"We're with him," Leo Sanders said. "You must be Raylan Jaworski."

"That's me, boys. How did you know?"

"That guy," Leo said. "The one that just brought that airplane down in the fog."

As the aircraft rolled out, Elmo looked around to determine if there were any of his men that had found the airstrip or if they had missed the drop zone entirely. He wondered too if any of them had seen the fuel truck on the way down.

Suddenly he realized, *The flare…I forgot to wait for the flare.*

Elmo's heart jumped into his throat as he spun the tail around to face to the south and cut the engines. He had no more than unbuckled his harness when he heard voices and someone was climbing aboard. Elmo reached for his gun belt but was unable to retrieve his pistol before a figure burst through the door. To his great relief and delight, he found himself looking into the face of Raylan Jaworski.

"Elmo…buddy, you came back!"

"Of course I came back, why wouldn't I?"

"Well…I can think of about two hundred reasons."

"Oh, you mean your diamonds, I can get diamonds anywhere, but I haven't found very many friends that would have done what you did. How the hell did you live through that anyway?"

"Long story, Barker."

"Listen, I brought a dozen paratroopers with me. Do you think that will be enough to take over this place?

"There's no Mafia left here to worry about. I'll tell you all about it later. It's a long story. You can send a couple of men to get the truck if you want. There's no hurry. The key is in it, and it runs good. All they need to do is follow that road at the end of the airstrip. The compound is about three quarters of a mile northwest. When they get back, we can all climb on, and I'll show you to your quarters."

Elmo said to Leo, "Can you take a couple men and get that fuel truck?"

"Sure can, Mr. Barker."

Elmo was aghast; he knew that Raylan was capable of many things, but this? *How on earth did he...?* he wondered, but down inside, he already knew, and to tell the truth, he did not want to know anymore. Elmo knew too much about Raylan already, to the point that the man actually scared him.

"You amaze me, son, you are an incredible individual, and I just thank God that He put you on my side."

Raylan put his hand on his friend's shoulder and said to him, "I got a surprise for you, brother."

"What kind of a surprise, and how could it beat this one?" Elmo waved his hand toward the runway that was obviously void of the Russian Mafia.

Raylan answered, "You'll see, I'll tell you about it later."

"Yeah, I know, part of the long story, right? You sure got a lot of long stories. Are you ever going to find time to tell them all?"

"We got nothing but time, brother."

"So when did I become your brother?"

"The minute you came back, my friend...the minute you came back." Raylan patted Elmo on the back and gave him another hug.

Forty-five minutes later, Leo returned with the fuel truck.

THE FRUIT OF ATROCITY

"Some of you men give these guys a hand with this hose," Raylan ordered. Several of them came to help, and the refueling of the DC-3 began.

On the way back to the compound, Elmo rode with Raylan in the truck while the rest of the men found places to ride on the back.

"So what is this big surprise you got for me?"

Raylan looked at Elmo with a grin on his face and a sparkle in his eye. "I'm getting married, and you're going to be my best man."

"Married? Who the hell…I mean…who in tar-nation would marry you?" Raylan studied Elmo for a moment.

What did he do, quit swearing or something?

Elmo noticed that Raylan was staring at him.

"I've been around Ah-lam too much. She doesn't like me swearing in front of the orphans."

"I know how it is. I been doing the same thing, especially around Alyona."

"Around who?"

"Alyona, that's her name…my fiancée. She lives with her papa about four miles from here, and they put me up for the winter."

"I see, so you've already been—"

"No! I haven't."

"You haven't? You mean you've been living there all winter and haven't even…well good for you, Jaworski, I'm proud of you. Maybe a little of the Padre's religion has spilled onto both of us," Elmo said.

"Maybe, well, here we are. This is the compound, what do you think?"

"Wow, it certainly looks deserted. How did you manage… never mind. So what are your plans for the place?"

"It all belongs to me and you now, brother, that is if you want to be involved."

Elmo looked at Raylan not sure what he meant by that.

"Involved in what?"

353

"I am…I mean *we*… are taking over the smuggling operation the Russians were running out of here. I figure you and me and those paratroopers will be able to pick up where the Russians left off, and the outside operators will never know the difference." Elmo scratched his head.

"Are you talking about living here indefinitely?"

"That's right."

"Well, I'm all for taking over their operation, but I'm certainly not going to promise to live *here* forever."

"You'll be flying most of the time anyway. For all I care, you could have a family in every port of call you go to, just as long as you keep your side of the bargain—that is if you agree to the bargain in the first place."

"Well then, spell it out for me, what's the bargain consist of?"

"I run the show. You do the flying. You can even use your new copilot. We'll talk to these men you brought with you and see if they want in. They'll be richer than they ever dreamed. After expenses, you and I split everything down the middle."

"What all are we going to get involved in?"

"Gold, diamonds, airplanes, fuel, freight, munitions…you name it."

"Who will we sell the munitions to?"

"Whoever pays the most."

"Why don't you take the full share and just pay me for each individual job I do for you, and I get to choose what I do and reserve the right to refuse any job I don't want to be involved in."

"Elmo, if that's the way you want to do it, then that's okay with me. Except I'll make sure you still get your share. We're partners right down the middle. I won't settle for anything less."

"Let's get these men situated and brief them to see who's with us and who isn't."

"When did you say you were getting married?"

"This coming weekend. I'll take you to meet her tomorrow. But first I want to show you something."

THE FRUIT OF ATROCITY

Raylan showed Elmo and the thirteen other men around the compound and ended up at the barracks where the Mafia gangsters had once lived

Then he briefed the men on the opportunity he had for them. All seemed more than eager to be a part of the operation.

Next, Raylan took them to the three weapons bunkers strategically located around the encampment. Pointing to the one located in the center of the compound, he said, "This is where the larger weapons are stored, such as: grenade launchers, fifty-caliber machine guns, mortar launchers, and such. Your small arms are to be kept with you at all times. Well, that's it, gentlemen. Tomorrow we'll go into town, and you'll meet the Steward." Elmo was surprised and wondered who that might be.

"What's a Steward? And what does he have to do with anything?"

"Only a month ago, the Steward, was the big boss of the Russian Mafia. But now he works for me." Elmo looked puzzled.

"Why didn't he go to the same place the rest of them did?"

"*Aah*, the Steward is our connection to every underground organization from here to the middle east and beyond to the gold fields of Africa. He is the connection that connects the east to the west, sort of like a railroad track, and we are the train or the mules that pick up and deliver the goods.

"The good news, gentlemen, is that the war in Europe is over, and it won't be long before the war with the Japanese will end. In fact, they're already leaving China in droves. So for the next four or five years, the borders to every country from Europe and the Middle East and on to Canada and the United States will be wide open for just such a business as ours. You will all be richer than you ever imagined in your wildest dreams."

Raylan had them wrapped around his little finger before he even got to the part about the Steward.

"Raylan, aren't you going to need more airplanes and pilots?" Elmo asked.

"Yes, that will come in due time, but most of the goods will come and go by boat. All of you men will have to learn to conduct yourselves as businessmen, international tradesmen, with legitimate business buying and selling commercial goods. We'll have many meetings with the Steward. I'll have him come to the compound and train you all."

"Where's the mess hall?" Elmo asked.

"I figured you'd be the first one that would ask about that." Raylan chuckled as he turned to take them to the chow hall.

"It needs some attention. We'll have to hire a couple of cooks and kitchen labor. But there's still some food left from last month when the Mafia lived here. You all can help yourselves to whatever you can find." Elmo called Raylan aside for a moment while the men prowled through the cupboards.

"What about the Padre?" he asked.

"What about him?"

"Are you planning on helping me find him? I made a commitment to him and his family that I would find him and get him back home."

"That's fine, Elmo, you're going to be in China plenty of times, and you can look for him all you want, but if we make commitments to other organizations, there will be time restraints involved. We'll have to meet our obligations."

"Sounds to me like your priorities have changed since I last saw you."

Raylan thought for a minute and said to Elmo, "Okay, you can take all the time you want. Go find him and get him back home. I'll make out until you finish your obligation. Actually, Elmo, that's what I like about you, you're as faithful as a Saint Bernard, you always come back. So I'll wait for you one more time."

"There is one other thing," Elmo said.

"What's that?"

"I hired those men out of the unemployment lines in Anchorage, and I hired them to go with me and help me find the

The Fruit of Atrocity

Padre. They agreed to help me until that's accomplished, but now you got their heads all full of enormous wealth and riches to be had in the smuggling trade. What if now, they don't want to finish their obligation to me?"

"I'm sorry, Elmo, you're right. I got way out in front of you on this. Listen, we'll all go together. We'll find him and bring him home. Then we start our business, fair enough?"

"All right, that's good enough for me, thank you...*brother*," Elmo said, tentatively.

Raylan continued, "Now, I have one more thing to show you, remember?"

"I remember."

Raylan leaned close to Elmo's ear and whispered, "Follow me."

Elmo followed Raylan to the far side of the compound to a building that looked like it had once been used as the headquarters for the Russian Mafia's smuggling operation. It was the longest building in the compound and seemed to be the most secure.

Raylan opened the front door, and they entered into a family sized room with ranch-style décor complete with fireplace, pool tables, bar, and kitchenette. Just inside the door, Raylan made a right turn down a long hallway leading to additional rooms on each side of the hallway. Some appeared to be only guest rooms, others offices, and meeting rooms. It was designed similar to a hunting lodge and gave Elmo the feeling he was suddenly back in Alaska.

"This is where you'll stay when you're here. You can have any room you want."

"Pretty nice place. I'm surprised they gave it up so easy."

Raylan looked at his friend and, without smiling, said to him, "They didn't have any say in the matter, never even saw it coming."

Elmo realized that killing was not a humorous subject to Raylan.

"Here we are," Raylan said as he opened a metal door with four heavy sliding bolt locks mounted on the face. A stairway led down to a large underground room with two-foot-thick steel reinforced concrete walls. It was obvious that the room had been heavily secured or even guarded during the Russian Mafia occupation.

Raylan turned on a light, and they descended the stairs. Suddenly, Elmo gasped and inhaled for a long time before slowly exhaling.

"My god. How much is here?"

"Millions, brother, literally millions and millions. There's everything from cut and polished diamonds to gold and silver bars and script money from every economy in Europe and the USA, even paintings…you name it, it's here."

"What are you going to do with it all?"

"Good question, for now we'll bolt that door and keep it locked."

"Are you going to put guards at the door?"

"I don't think so. I believe it would create curiosity to the point that the men might want to know what's inside. One thing I do know, that Mafia bunch milked the village of Magadan for everything they had, for at least four years, while they were sitting on this pile of treasure. So I think we should use some of it to reinforce their economy and to make their lives easier."

"Like how? Do you mean just give it to them?"

"Not exactly, but we could use some of the script money to build streets and put in a city power plant and other utilities for them. It would put a lot of their people to work."

"Sounds like a good idea to me. I'm all for it. How do you want to go about it?"

"We can donate these art pieces, paintings, and artifacts to the town, and they can hold a international auction that would bring in all kinds of revenue for the town."

THE FRUIT OF ATROCITY

"What if some of the town fathers decide to line their own pockets with the proceeds?"

"I'll keep an eye on them. They've been under the Mafia thumb for so long they'll jump at any chance to make a real profit for a change. They now know the Mafia is no longer a threat to them, but they aren't sure exactly who's responsible for that. I want them to think it was a rival gang of cutthroats that did the exterminating."

Elmo walked among the piles of boxes full of coins, jewels, solid gold, and silver artifacts.

"Where do you suppose all of this come from?"

"I imagine a lot of it was stolen from the Third Reich, even the Jews, Germans, Russians, Polish, Yugoslavs…you name it. The rest of it was probably stolen from art galleries and personal collections by thieves who turned around and sold it to the underground."

"Yeah, you mean, tried to sell it to the underground, and then wound up dead."

"I expect you're right, that's just about the way it went down too."

"Well, we better get out of here before someone finds us."

The next morning, Raylan found Elmo in the kitchen scrounging for something to eat, along with several of the other men.

"Good morning, Elmo. As soon as you've finished, I want to take you to meet my fiancée and her papa."

"I can't wait, do you think she could fix me a decent breakfast?"

"Sure, no problem. But there's something we need to discuss."

"What's that?"

"We need to get these men squared away with a squad leader, so we'll have to pick one of them to take over command."

"Leo," Elmo mumbled between bites of a stale sweet potato he had found in the root cellar.

"Captain Wilson is the highest ranking man among them, how about him?"

"This ain't the army."

"Okay then, we'll need to have a meeting with Leo and fill him in on what we expect from him."

Elmo had put down the stale sweet potato and started on a stale beet.

"What's that exactly?"

"We need him to keep those men disciplined and in line. They'll need to work in shifts to guard this place around the clock as well as the airstrip. We never know when a plane will land here or a boat will dock, and on board will be some of the people the Mafia boys were doing business with."

"I see your point. What did you say her name is…Ally… something?"

"Alyona."

"Right. Alyona. Is she a good cook?"

"She's not going to come out here and cook for you every day, if that's what you're getting at."

"Well, we're sure going to need someone, and someone that can stay here full time too. It certainly isn't like you can't afford it."

"Hey, not so loud. Okay, we'll find someone from the village to do that. Did you hear what I said about the Mafia?"

"Yeah, something about the Mafia flying in…that's a good idea. We'll be sure and show them a real good time."

"Whatever, listen, now that this war in Europe has ended, there's going to be a huge surplus of airplanes. Everything from freighters to fighters. Do you hear me?"

Elmo stopped eating for a moment and looked at Raylan.

"You're right, there will be. We could pick up a few of them. Where do you suppose we can find them?"

"Well, if we get them legally, we would have to wait for the United States government to decommission them and sell them at auction, stateside, should go for about a nickel a piece."

"You're crazy, they'll be more than that, but I get your point. In other words, they'll go for cheap. I want to pick up a few for myself and start an aircraft salvage and restoration yard back in Anchorage, something a little more legal and less lethal."

"So you're not going to work with me?"

"I didn't say that, I just don't want to do this the rest of my life."

Raylan stroked his chin, his mind still forging the future of his new business.

"Anyway, I don't intend on waiting for all of that to happen. We'll need a few of them now, and I'll bet there will be some sitting in Shanghai or Rangoon or maybe Calcutta—all crated up and waiting to be put on a freighter. We might even be able to get them rerouted to Magadan under some other designation."

"Who are we going to get to put them together for us?"

"We'll worry about that later, for now we'll need to stockpile more fuel at Khabarovsk and make sure we have dependable fuel supplies at Yinchuan.

"Who will we work with there?"

"We'll have to work with whoever is willing to work with us."

Elmo thought for a minute and said to him, "It won't be long... maybe in six months or so. We won't have to fly so far north to stay away from the Japs. We'll be able to fly into Shanghai and Nanking and anywhere else along the South China Sea coast, and because it would be a direct route across the water, we should think about putting floats on a couple of C-47s and land right in the harbor."

Raylan's eyes grew wide with amazement.

"Elmo, you are a genius, brother. That's an excellent idea. If we did that, we wouldn't even need those other fuel rendezvous."

"Don't get ahead of yourself just yet. We'll still need them because there will be plenty of freighters that won't be equipped with floats, pontoons for a C-47 will be hard to find."

Raylan's optimism ignored Elmo's pessimism.

"We'll find them. Then, we'll have the only C-47s on floats in the world. Anyone who wants them will have to come to us."

"Not to burst your bubble, but I've already seen some in Alaska. Nonetheless, it'll be a great operational cover, and legitimate at that."

"Speaking of which, Elmo, I need to fill you in on one more small detail."

"What's that?"

"I still work for Army Intelligence."

Elmo choked on his food, sputtering beets all over the table.

"You what!"

"That's right, I still work for army intel. When Captain Prichard assigned me to Jay Baldwin, it was for the purpose of getting me into Russia and into this Russian Mafia compound. I was supposed to go in undercover and infiltrate the organization. Never in a million years did either of us expect that I would take over the whole compound. Now, this entire operation will be a front and will be the source of information into the network of hundreds of smuggling outfits just like this one all over the world. But we have to make it look real. It has to be a legitimate underworld organization. Legitimate from their point of view. Are you still with me?"

"Still with you? I actually feel a lot better about the whole thing, kind of like illegal yet still legal. Best of both worlds, above ground and underground, can't do better than that?"

"I'll have to get in touch with Captain Prichard before it actually becomes an official undercover operation, but when we do, then we'll be able to move around the whole world pretty much untouchable."

"Hey, maybe Prichard will have information about the Padre."

"Could be. Well, we got a lot of work to do and a short summer season to do it in. So as soon as this wedding is over, you should get going."

"Me? Aren't you going with me?"

"No, I'll be working from here."

"You mean taking a honeymoon."

The Fruit of Atrocity

"Of course, that too, you can take a few of those men with you, and I recommend that you go straight to Ledo and look up Prichard. He might have some men he could give us for this job, people with more…specialized training…if you know what I mean. We're going to need at least another dozen. However, I wouldn't tell him about…you know…what I showed you last night."

"Yeah, I get it. That's for the town."

"Well, some of it is anyway."

"Before you go, you might want to fill your teak chest up with some of that foreign currency, Chinese yen and US dollars, etc., even Russian rubles. Take some extra diamonds too. You may need them."

"I might need a bigger treasure chest."

"Take whatever you want, and whenever you're ready, I'm ready."

"Ready for what?" "To meet my fiancée."

"I've been ready for that since I gagged down that first sweet potato…mold and all."

"Lets go then. We'll take the jeep."

"What about the other guys. I thought they were going too?"

"We'll come back for them and then go on into town to meet the Steward."

"So this Steward, is he like a mayor or something?"

"I guess you could say that."

Raylan and Elmo climbed into the jeep and headed southeast down a dirt road for about two-miles before turning off into the woods due east. Soon the road disappeared, and the jeep was bouncing and lurching along over the forest floor. At one point they had to get out and manually lift it to get it over a downed tree.

"Wouldn't it have been easier to walk?" Elmo asked.

"I'm looking for the best way through here to my fiancée's home. When I find it, I intend to build a road through."

"She lives with her father, is that right?"

"Yeah, her mother died about a year and a half ago. They're tough people, though hardy as they come."

"What did she see in you?"

Raylan didn't answer at first. "What do you mean?"

"I mean what sparked the romance?"

"They think I've been sent by God to deliver them from the Mafia."

"Well, what's wrong with that? You did deliver them, didn't you?"

"Oh, yeah. I did do that."

"Then let her believe it. What's the problem, don't you feel worthy enough to be held in that high esteem?

"I suppose, but it seems to me that if God was going to send someone to deliver someone, that someone would be a righteous man like David or Joshua…or Pastor Jay Baldwin."

"How do you know they were righteous? You weren't there anymore than I was. They could have been men just like you and me, men who were doing what they believed was right at the time. Then later, some other *righteous man* wrote about it, happens all the time. You remember what the padre said, righteous is what God *calls* us, not what we actually are, and He calls us that because He gave us the righteousness of His own Son as a free gift. In other words, He can see it in us, but we can't see it in ourselves, which is the only way it works. Because the minute we see it in ourselves and start walking around with our nose in the air, it isn't there anymore."

"Hey, Elmo, that was pretty good. You should become a preacher."

"I'm a smuggler, remember?"

"A righteous smuggler?"

The Fruit of Atrocity

"Yeah, a righteous smuggler." Raylan and Elmo looked at each other and chuckled.

Soon the jeep emerged from the forest, and Raylan accelerated across an open field to a small farmhouse. They had made it barely halfway when the door flew open and a young girl with long flowing blond hair wearing a long blue work dress and white apron came running out to meet them.

Elmo also saw a man coming out of the barn door not far from the house. He was a large, muscular man, broad at the shoulders and slender at the waist, the type of man Elmo decided he would rather have as a friend as apposed to an enemy.

"Hey, Raylan, is that guy friendly?"

"I'll introduce you."

Raylan stopped the jeep as the girl came running to them.

"Raylan, where have you been?" she said in an exasperated tone.

"Been busy, my sweetness. I want you to meet someone."

"Is this Elmo Barker?"

"Yes, he—"

"Oh, I am so glad to meet you at last. Raylan has said many good things about you. There is my papa. Papa, this is Mr. Barker. Mr. Barker, this is my papa."

Elmo scratched his head again.

"Raylan, I didn't understand a word of that except my name. Are you going to translate or what?"

"Alyona, you'll need to speak English. Elmo doesn't speak Russian."

"I am too sorry, Mr. Barker. I am Alyona and this is my papa."

"How do you do, ma'am. How do you do, sir?"

"Anton, the name is Anton, so glad to acquaint with you. Please come to our home. We will have meal together. Alyona, go and make meal for our guests."

"You don't need to do that for us. I already ate anyway," Elmo said in an effort to appear less starved than he actually was.

Alyona looked at Elmo and said to him, "And just what did you eat, stale sweet potatoes or perhaps beets from that retched cellar? I will make for you a breakfast that will fill your belly the right way while you men talk of important business. Please, sit at our table."

Elmo looked at Raylan and said to him, "I want me one of them. Are there any more like her in this town?"

"Not like her, Elmo, she's one of a kind, and she's mine. But I'm sure you'll be able to find a wife. They're standing in line waiting for any kind of husband they can find that would marry them and take them to some lavish city, be it the United States or England or even Moscow, wherever they can live in the lap of luxury."

"Well, they don't need to wait any longer. I'm in town and I'm—"

Raylan kicked him in the shin from under the table thinking that he might say something about how he was *rich*.

"I mean…I'm…looking for a wife too."

Anton looked at Elmo with curiosity and said to him, "So you have flown your airplane all the way from United States?"

"No, Anchorage, Alaska."

"Will you come to the wedding of Raylan and me? It will be in the Russian Orthodox Church of Magadan. It will be this Saturday. There will be many people. Maybe you will find a wife there," Alyona said.

"I'd love to, Alyona, wouldn't miss it for the world."

The wedding ceremony lasted two hours, and the reception lasted two days. Elmo studied Raylan through it all and was amazed at the side of him he had never before seen—happy to the point of giddiness, completely stricken with his new bride.

Alyona was so beautiful Elmo began looking around for a single girl that he could marry that would be as beautiful as her but found none.

The second day of the reception proved even more rowdy than the first. Even the men Elmo had hired, who were supposed to be guarding the airstrip, came to join in on the fun and festivities. As the party began to wind down, Elmo was sitting alone at the end of a long table when he saw Raylan approaching him. Another man, whom Elmo had never met, accompanied him.

"Elmo, I'd like you to meet the Steward of our organization. This is Yuri Solomonovich."

Elmo stood and greeted the short, sturdy man wearing a wrinkled suit that looked like it had come from the Salvation Army.

"I'm Elmo Barker, how do you do, sir? Raylan has spoken of you."

"Really, Mr. Barker, and what did he tell you?"

"That you were the man who ran the Russian Mafia." Yuri looked at Raylan and chuckled.

"That is not precisely true, Mr. Barker. I am the man the Russian Mafia *worked for*, not *with*. They ran themselves and not too intelligently either."

"You'll have to explain that to me. I'm not sure I see the difference."

"I work with, not for, but with a large group of investors worldwide. Unfortunately, we must sometimes engage in business with very unscrupulous men, men such as the Russian Mafia. When Mr. Jaworski and I first met, it was at a time when my relationship with the Mafia had reached a point that neither they nor I or my fellow investors could continue to do business with them any longer. When I informed them of the fact, they took me captive and began to torture me in an attempt to extract information from me. Their intention was to cut me out of the loop.

It was at that time that my friend Raylan Jaworski and his beautiful fiancée, who is now his beautiful bride, came to my rescue.

Now, I and my fellow investors are most pleased to conduct our business with Mr. Jaworski and his newly formed organization."

"I get it..." Elmo said, "You're the head guy, and Raylan's the boss, is that right?"

"Not exactly, Mr. Barker. Your friend Raylan saved my life, and in doing so, he demonstrated his most excellent qualifications. Now, our relationship is much more than just business. He is more like a son to me, part of my family."

Raylan stepped closer behind Yuri and put his hand on his shoulder.

"Yuri is the head of the family, the 'godfather' if you get my meaning, kind of like Al Capone."

Elmo looked at Raylan not sure how far undercover he had actually descended. Then he turned to Yuri and said to him, "Who are some of these other investors you referred to?"

"Aha, Mr. Barker, you will never know who they are. But what you must know is that you have become part of a worldwide family that will take care of you and yours for the rest of your life. But you must also know this: to do business with us on any level greater than that of a mule, you must take an oath of secrecy, protected by pain of death to any who break this oath. So if you are not willing to take this oath and become part of the *family*, then you will work directly for Mr. Jaworski as only a mule, and you will know nothing of the family's inside structure or business.

"If that is all you wish to be, then that is all that will ever be expected of you. But understand, you will be subject to investigation, harassment, even arrest, from every law enforcement agency in every country in the world at any time and at their own discretion. However, if you are part of this family, you will travel the world at *your* own discretion and according to *your* own agenda. The gateway to every country in the world shall be wide opened to you without questions or harassment. And because you are Raylan's good friend, I will give you a week to decide before the invitation to become part of this family is withdrawn. But, Mr.

Barker, I must ask that you do not leave in your airplane before you have made this decision, do you agree?"

"That's okay, I ain't planning on leaving for a while anyway. I'll let you know before I do."

"It has been delightful to meet you, Mr. Barker, if there is anything you need or require, please let me know. And please visit my jewelry shop whenever you like. Mr. Jaworski will take you there. Maybe you will find a 'bride to be' here at this beautiful wedding, and you will want to purchase a ring for her. It would, of course, be my privilege to size it and set it for her. Good-bye for now, Mr. Barker."

Raylan and Yuri stepped away from Elmo and talked for a short while out of Elmo's hearing. Raylan soon returned and said to him, "Well, this is it, buddy, this is the end of the diving board. Are you going all in?"

"All into what? Al Capone gangland, only on a worldwide scale? Do I have stupid written across my forehead?"

"Just think about it for a while. Think about how it will help you find the Padre."

"How's it going to help me find the Padre?"

"These people have connections. They can find anyone. You know yourself that Charlie was planning to get into smuggling after the war that was why he wanted the lieutenant and his airplane. It could be that he's even connected to these people."

"You say, *these people* as if you are not one of them. Does that mean you haven't taken the oath yet? And what about army intelligence? How are you going to do both and stay alive at the same time? Or didn't you hear what he said about *pain of death*."

"Don't worry about me. I'm programmed for this kind of thing. The question is: do *you* want in? I'm going to need you with me on this to make it work. And I'll make sure Prichard takes you on as part of the team and gives you the same criminal investigation immunity that I have."

"What about 'pain of death' immunity?"

"Don't worry, when this whole thing goes down, as far as 'the family' is concerned, it will look like we've gone down with it. They'll never know the difference."

Elmo looked out at the people dancing on the church patio and saw a young woman who was alone, holding two drinks and smiling at him.

"I'll think about it. Right now I'm going to go ask that girl to marry me while the preacher is still on his feet."

A week passed, and Elmo had not seen hide nor hair of Raylan Jaworski. However, it was no surprise to him; one look at Alyona, and he knew that Raylan would be otherwise occupied for sometime.

The next day, a jeep arrived at the compound. Jaworski was driving, and Yuri was his passenger. Elmo knew exactly what Yuri wanted.

The mechanic had quartered up in a guest room directly across the hall from the underground vault. He had also done what Raylan had suggested and filled his teak chest with as much currency, diamonds, and gold and silver coin as he could stuff into it and still get the lid fastened. He had talked to the men that he planned to take with him and was ready to go except for one last detail—the *oath*.

Elmo opened the front door of the building and greeted the two men with a handshake.

"Good morning, Mr. Solomonovich."

"Good morning, Mr. Barker."

Then, with a facetious grin, he said to Raylan, "You look a little tired."

"Good morning," Raylan said, ignoring the comment.

Elmo saw that Raylan was carrying a basket that smelled of fresh-baked biscuits.

"What's in the basket?" he said.

THE FRUIT OF ATROCITY

"Alyona sent coffee and biscuits, have some. By the way, how'd you make out with that girl? Did she say yes or no?"

"What girl?"

"The one you said you were going to propose to."

"Oh, that girl. Well, her husband decided it would be a bad idea. So we're going to hold off on that for a while."

Yuri chuckled at their humor and said to them, "I see you have a fire burning. We'll sit by the fireplace. I am very glad to see that you two get along so well. It will make working with you a great pleasure. That is if you, Mr. Barker, have decided that you are going to work with us."

"I've decided. It wasn't a difficult decision. I'm in all the way."

"Good, Mr. Barker, very good. I am very pleased and looking forward to our association together."

"However, I have a condition," Elmo said.

Yuri frowned faintly and waited until he seated himself next to the fireplace before he replied.

"And what is this condition, Mr. Barker?"

"I have an obligation to fulfill to the family of a friend of mine, also a friend of Raylan's. We left him in China because we had no choice. It was either that or risk the lives of his family and the sixteen six-year-old orphans that were on the plane with us. I need to go back and find him and get him home to his family. Raylan even suggested that your organization might be able to help me with that."

"This man you are looking for, is he American?"

"Yes, he is a pastor, part of the Protestant League of Churches working with the Red Cross."

"Where did you last see him?"

"Last year, when we were on our way here, we stopped at Yinchuan for fuel. It was a previously arranged fuel rendezvous. However, we were about three weeks late in getting there. Well, when we landed, the Padre, that's what I call him, was taken captive, and before they could get to me, I slammed the power forward and got the...hell out of there."

"Mr. Barker, isn't it true that this man is not a pastor at all but a lieutenant in the Army Air Corp, and his real name is Lieutenant Jayson Bold?"

Elmo's mouth dropped open as he suddenly realized that he was most likely talking to the very man Clair Chennault had originally made the rendezvous arrangements with."

"Yesir, it is. That's the man, are you the one Chennault contacted?"

"If you are referring to General Claire Chennault, yes. Although I have never met the man, but I have met a Chinese gentleman by the name of...Charlie Nee. I am sure you are familiar with him, is that correct?"

This time, even Raylan looked astonished, and for the first time, they both felt a little behind the eight ball. And as they would soon discover, the eight ball was much farther ahead of them than they ever could have imagined.

Raylan looked at Yuri, suspiciously, "When is the last time you saw Charlie?"

"He was last here only two months before you came to me for the ring."

"What ring?" Elmo interjected.

Raylan looked at Elmo and replied, "When Alyona and I became engaged, I took one of my diamonds to Yuri to have it set as an engagement ring. That was when we first met."

Raylan turned to Yuri and said to him, "What did Charlie want?"

"He wanted to do business. He understands that the Japanese are losing ground in the war they started with the United States, and now they are losing in Burma and China as well. Mr. Nee has concluded, as also we have, that the markets for profiteering will be wide open for the next five years at least, especially for guns, ammunition, and surplus war materials. It is his intention to build up a supply of these materials as quickly as he can and

THE FRUIT OF ATROCITY

stockpile them for use against the communist. And of course he is interested in diamonds and gold as well."

"So will we actually be doing business with him…personally?" Elmo asked.

"Oh yes, I'm sure you will be, Mr. Barker. I am in the process of recruiting more pilots, and our organization already has in place the labor, including many dockworkers required for loading and unloading. These people are already stationed at every level of shipping and transportation to make certain that portions of the shipments of materials will be lost or misdirected in our direction. Then after the war has ended, when most of the surplus war materials are being sold at auction to the highest bidder, we will also steal from every staging area and skim from every transaction.

"Many of the aircraft of course will be flown back to the US. However, those that cannot fly for mechanical reasons, will of course disappear, and the government will never know what has become of them.

Charlie has the men and the capability of making things of that nature take place, but he does not yet have the pilots. That is why he would not let your Lieutenant Bold or, as you choose to refer to him, Pastor Baldwin leave his country. It was his intention that Mr. Baldwin would train pilots that Charlie would use to confiscate these materials, materials that we wish to purchase from him."

"I could fly them, and we could cut Charlie out of the loop and put more profit in our pockets."

"That is a very commendable offer, Mr. Barker, but this operation will be conducted on a much larger scale than only one man would be able to do alone. We will need many pilots and many people in many places, all working for the same organization, filtering and skimming from every shipment leaving from every port and harbor, every day and every night.

"You will find, Mr. Barker, that we have both ports and harbors of our own. We have stockpiles and warehouses and fuel caches that would amaze you if you were to see them for yourself."

"What else is your organization into?"

"If you are referring to the sex trade and the trafficking of woman and children, no we are not involved in things that are of such a despicable nature. We do have our pride and our scruples, Mr. Barker. However, you will meet people who are involved in such things. Unfortunately, it is part of the nature of the business, I regret to say."

Elmo was thoughtful. He stroked his chin and shifted in his chair while he considered how he would, or could, work for Yuri and still accomplish his obligation to his friend, Jay Baldwin.

"Do you know where my friend is right now?"

"No, Mr. Barker, I do not. And please believe me when I tell you that I understand completely your need to fulfill your obligation to his family, but seriously, from what I understand, the man unfortunately did not survive the winter in Yinchuan. I also understand that he had made agreements with Mr. Nee that he failed to honor, unlike you, Mr. Barker, whom I highly respect because you take your agreements very seriously."

Elmo felt anger rising in him; he said to Yuri, "It wasn't the Padre that didn't keep his word. It was Charlie. The Padre was more than glad to honor his commitment with Charlie until he kidnapped his family and hid them away in Chungking, then lied through his teeth about it. So if you are planning on doing business with Charlie Nee, you better get ready for the same thing. He's the biggest liar and manipulator you'll ever meet, even in this business. And furthermore, I don't believe for a minute that Jay Baldwin is dead."

"I am sorry, Mr. Barker, but I'm afraid that it is so, and I appreciate you informing me of that unfortunate quality of Mr. Nee's. However, we are not here to discuss the lesser qualities of our business associates but rather the future of the three of us as busi-

THE FRUIT OF ATROCITY

ness partners. I do hope that your experience with Mr. Nee will not influence your decision in regard to our business here.

"Now, if you are ready, I have prepared a document that we refer to as 'The Oath.' It is merely a contract that I will need you to sign. You may take time to read it if you wish. For that matter, I must insist that you do. When you are finished, Mr. Jaworski will give you your first assignment.

Raylan and Yuri excused themselves from the discussion. Elmo picked up the document. It read:

> The undersigned, Mr. Elmo Patrick Barker, hereby does agree to, and with, all partners of: TRADE INVESTMENTS INTERNATIONAL that from this date:_____1945 until _____1950. Mr. Elmo Barker's personal and physical life shall be on lease to the above named firm, which is to mean and imply that all personal resources, talents, skills, and abilities shall be the property of TRADE INVESTMENTS INTERNATIONAL.
>
> This agreement shall be bound by PAIN OF DEATH for any failure, sabotage, or refusal of any or all obligations deemed as obligations by the aforenamed institution: TRADE INVESTMENTS INTERNATIONAL.
>
> I, ELMO PATRICK BARKER, DO HEREBY TAKE THIS OATH TO HONOR, CONFORM, AND PERFORM ALL ASSIGNMENTS AND OBLIGATIONS PROVIDED ME BY TRADE INVESTMENTS INTERNATIONAL, INCLUSIVE WITH THE ABOVE DATES OF THIS CONTRACT. AND TO INTEND, PROVIDE AND PROMOTE THE PROFIT AND SECURITY OF THIS ORGANIZATION UNDER PAIN OF DEATH FOR ANY FAILURE, OR CONSPIRACY OF FAILURE, TO DO SO.
>
> Signed:_____ Elmo Patrick Barker.

Elmo finished reading the document and set it on the table. He considered carefully the ramifications of signing it, as well as those of not signing it. First, if he chose not to take the oath, he would most certainly be killed outright, or at the very least be sent away on a boat with no life raft that would most certainly sink. He already knew too much about Yuri, enough that he would be too great a liability to the firm, not so much because of what he knew but whom he knew.

As for Raylan, he wondered if he really was undercover or had actually turned and literally become one of them. Certainly, the kind of money involved in an operation of this magnitude would be enough to turn just about anyone.

It really boiled down to one issue: was Yuri really telling the truth about Jay Baldwin, was Jay really deceased? If so, Elmo would have to see for himself before he informed Jay's family of the fact. And for him to survive long enough to know for sure, he would need to take the oath.

Elmo picked up the pen and signed his name: *Elmo Patrick Barker*.

Chapter 14

Pastor Jayson Baldwin's eyelids fluttered as he squinted and turned his head away from the light. For the first time in over a week since his arrival, he was waking up. Sharp pains shot through his brain. He blinked repeatedly as his eyes slowly adjusted to the light—light he had not seen since his abduction. All recollection of what had happened to him in Yinchuan, and since, had for the time left him. Through blurry vision, he began to realize some of his surroundings. *Hospital, I must be in a hospital*, he reckoned.

Jayson lay on a bed in a large ward with at least twenty hospital beds lining each side of a long hallway, separated by only a few feet of space.

Jay had no idea where his hospital was located and wondered why he was receiving medical attention. He would have to wait until a nurse or doctor came by, and then, God willing, he would learn what had happened to him and his family.

Jay lifted the linen and looked at himself. His legs looked like mummies, bound in bandages, from his ankles to his thighs. His arms and hands too had been bandaged as if he had been burned.

He lifted one arm and pressed it against the side of his face and head. He could feel more bandages there as well. *What has happened to me?* he wondered. Soon he lapsed back into another deep sleep.

The next time he awoke, a young Chinese nurse was standing over him. In her hand she held a cup of water, in the other, a paper cup with a pill in it. Jay gulped the water down along with the pill, then spoke to her in her native tongue.

"Can you tell me where I am and what has happened to me?"

She looked at him, surprised, not only that he was awake but that he spoke such fluent Chinese.

"You are in the hospital in Nanking, China. You have been in an accident."

"Can you tell me what kind of accident?"

"No, I cannot, I only understand that you had an accident."

"Can you tell me how I come to be here?"

"The doctor will be along to see you in a while. You may ask him."

"What is your name?" he asked her.

"Lihua, I am the floor nurse for this ward."

"Lihua, you are about the same age as my wife who went to the university here in Nanking before the Japanese came. Maybe by chance you knew her? Ah-lam…Ah-lam Nee. Do you remember her?"

Lihua appeared bewildered. She quickly turned as if to go.

"The doctor will see you soon. I have work to do and cannot linger."

Lihua finished tucking the bedding and quickly moved to the next patient.

The huge room had windows, but they were high above his bed close to the ceiling. Jay expected that it would be some time before he would be able to climb up and see what there was to see through those windows.

He tried to move his legs but couldn't feel them. It was as if they were made of wood.

Accident, what kind of an accident? I don't remember an accident.

Jay tried to think back to the last thing he could remember, anything. *The dream, I remember the dream. I shared it with Elmo. What happened to Elmo? He was in the airplane. We were all in the airplane. We landed, I remember landing in Yinchuan. That was a short strip. Elmo wondered if we were going to make it out of there. What happened after that?*

THE FRUIT OF ATROCITY

The pain medication began to have its effect, and Jay's thoughts turned to dreams, as once again he drifted off to sleep.

Soon he awoke to the sound of voices. Jay opened his eyes to see an older Chinese gentleman bending over him.

"Aah, young man, I see you are waking up. I am Dr. Shoo. How are you feeling?"

Jay wasn't sure how to answer his question. For one thing, he couldn't feel anything.

"I can't feel my legs," he said.

"We are going to take you into one of the examining rooms and remove your bandages. Don't worry, you will soon begin to feel your legs. They are only asleep from the trauma."

"Dr....what...has happened to me, and do you know what has become of my family?"

The doctor looked puzzled.

"I am sorry, I do not know your name?"

"Jay Bol...I mean Baldwin. Pastor Jay Baldwin."

"I am so sorry, Mr. Baldwin, but I know nothing of your family. The man who brought you here only told us that you had been in an accident. He did not provide us with any details."

"Who was this man, and how long have I been here?"

"He gave his name as Mr. Yuan. That is all we know. He delivered you to us one week ago. But we can worry about all of that later. For now, we must concentrate on your recovery."

Two orderlies and the nurse, Lihua, transferred Jay from his bed to a gurney and took him to the examining room.

Jay was lying flat on his back and was unable to watch as Dr. Shoo and Lihua cut away the bandages. He could hear them mumbling in very low tones and felt the pressure of Dr. Shoo's fingers as he poked and prodded at the tissue of his extremities.

"Can you feel my finger poking you, Mr. Baldwin?"

"Yes, but I don't seem to have any sensation on the skin surface."

D.L. WATERHOUSE

"It will take time, but I believe it will return eventually. You almost lost your legs. I wasn't sure they would recover, but now I am much more optimistic."

Lihua brought Jay an extra pillow and propped him up where he could see. As they removed the bandages on his arms, Jay could now see the dark black and purple color of his skin. The doctor poked and squeezed at his arms.

"Mr. Baldwin, you are healing slowly, but you are healing. However, I am going to prescribe for you a routine of physical therapy that will include daily massage, combined with hydrotherapy—that is, alternated immersions into hot and cold water along with applications of hot and cold towel packs against the surfaces of the damaged tissue. This will help promote circulation, and circulation will bring about more rapid healing. Nurse Lihua, will you help Mr. Baldwin to sit up?"

Lihua and one of the orderlies took hold of Jay from each side and helped him to sit upright on the table.

"That will be all for now, nurse, I will call you when the patient is ready to return to his bed."

After the nurse and the orderlies left the room, Dr. Shoo pulled up a chair and sat directly in front of Jay.

"Mr. Baldwin, I have been a doctor at this hospital for the last fifteen years, and I have seen many patients with the kind of flesh trauma that you have experienced, especially since this terrible war began. I want you to know that I do not believe you have been in an accident. Your condition is completely consistent with having suffered a vicious beating. I have seen soldiers brought to me who have experienced the same horrible kind of beatings by the Japanese, and their injuries were perfectly consistent with yours. So if you can remember anything at all, I need to know exactly what happened to you."

"I'm not sure, Doc. I am starting to remember a few things, but I can tell you this: I don't remember any Japanese soldiers,

THE FRUIT OF ATROCITY

and I don't believe I was in an accident either. I remember landing my airplane. I just can't remember what happened after that."

"So you are a pilot? What sort of airplane was it?"

"It was a DC-3 Red Cross plane. I'm with the Protestant League of Churches in China and was flying one of the Red Cross planes.

"Well, I can tell you this, you were viciously beaten and left for dead, and if another day had elapsed without medical attention, you may have lost one, or both of your legs, or even perhaps have died. Where did you land this airplane?"

"In Yinchuan."

"Why were you landing in Yinchuan?" Jay thought for a moment. Until now he had not thought to ask himself that question.

"I'm not sure, but I remember my wife and child were on board the airplane along with my crew and sixteen orphans."

"Orphans?"

"Yes, they were of mixed race—Japanese and Chinese, refugees of the Rape of Nanking in 1937. We were trying to get them out of China." Jay suddenly received another spark of memory.

"That must be why we landed at Yinchuan, maybe we needed fuel. Anyway, I don't remember what happened after that until I woke up in this hospital.

"Very well, Mr. Baldwin. That is enough for now. I am here to help you in any way that I can. We will get you back to bed now so you can rest. Please remember, if there is anything I can do for you, just let the nurse, Lihua, know. She will contact me."

"Thank you, Doc, there is one other thing."

"Yes, Mr. Baldwin."

"Did you say the man's name was…Yuan?"

"You mean the gentlemen who brought you here? Yes, I believe he said his name was Mr. Yuan."

"As in Major Yuan?"

"It could be, however, to me, he only referred to himself as Mr. Yuan. Now, Mr. Baldwin, after you rest a few days, or whenever you feel up to it, there is someone on our staff that may be able to help you with your amnesia. Would you like for him to pay you a visit?"

"Sure, Doc. That would be great. I could use someone to talk to. What is he, a shrink?"

"His name is Watchmen Chow. He is a Christian minister." Jay's eyes lit up.

"I'd like that, Doctor Shoo, thank you."

Another week passed, and Jay began to look forward to the regularly scheduled three-a-day massages and hydrotherapy treatments. The Chinese massage therapist was a young man of about Jay's age, and they talked of better days when the war would someday end.

The nurse Lihua was a very beautiful girl who took great care to make her patients comfortable, and due to Jay's extensive injuries, Lihua seemed especially committed to his recovery. It was she who administered the hydrotherapy treatments.

Jay grew more intrigued with her each day. He would watch her as she moved around the hospital ward and noticed the extra care she gave to each of her patients. She reminded him of Ah-lam. His heart ached for Ah-lam and for his daughter Ching-Lan. He tried not to think about them because it hurt him so, but their memory was all he had left. His memories of before Yinchuan were full of both dread, that he would never get his family back, and the elation he had felt when he discovered them in Chungking. He recalled the last moments he had spent with Ah-lam, how precious and intimate they were. Tears began to stream from his eyes, and his breathing became labored.

Jay began to wonder what had become of Charlie. He could not remember when he saw him last. *Was he still alive? Had Charlie taken the airplane and his family? Maybe Ah-lam and Ching-Lan were back in Chungking. Maybe they are waiting for me to return, to rescue them again.*

All the events of that last flight were perfectly vivid in his mind, right up to the point when he landed the airplane. "Oh God," he cried out, "what happened to my family, are they alive, or are they all dead?"

Jay surmised that something terrible had taken place after he landed. *Maybe I did crash…maybe I was the only survivor. Then, again, what if I didn't crash at all? Maybe someone did beat me like Dr. Shoo said, and maybe it was Charlie. That could only mean one thing.* A terrifying thought occurred to Jay. *My God, did Charlie kill them all: Elmo, Raylan, the orphans, and even his own sister and niece? Would he actually do that?* Jay tried to tell himself, Charlie would not be capable of such a thing. But his arguments in Charlie's defense were so unconvincing he became completely overcome with grief. As the ensuing day's passed, Jay sank deeper and deeper into depression.

Every day Jay discreetly watched Lihua from the corner of his eye. He thought of how easy it would be to fall in love with her. He saw the way she looked at him and lingered about his bedside. He wondered too if she also felt something for him. Maybe it was love or maybe it was only pity. Jay rolled over on his side so he could not see her. He could never marry again. He could never take the chance to love again, not as long as there was the remotest chance his family or Charlie was still alive and certainly not as long as Jay was still in China. He closed his eyes and wept again—like the day before and the many days before that.

"Are you Mr. Baldwin?" Jay heard the voice, but it sounded so far away. He imagined it too was a dream. Slowly he rolled over to see if by chance it was real.

A Chinese man dressed in a blue wool suit stood at the foot of his bed with a newspaper tucked under his arm. He was much older than Jay but spry, and a wisdom beyond his years told in his eyes.

"Yes. Who are you?"

"My name is Watchman Chow. Dr. Shoo asked me to drop in to see you. Do you feel like talking?"

"Not really." Jay turned his head away and stared at the empty bed next to him.

"Well, if you don't mind, I'd like to sit and rest awhile. I have walked a rather long way." Jay turned back to face Mr. Chow and scooted around in the bed as he propped himself up with a pillow.

"I'm sorry, I didn't mean to be rude. I'm just not in the mood for a social call."

"I understand, Mr. Baldwin. Do you have a first name?

"Jayson, Jay Baldwin, is what I go by."

"Are you saying that is not your real name?"

"It is now…it's a long story."

"As you wish, Jay Baldwin. I haven't come here to investigate you or anything of that nature but to aid you in the healing of your mind. I understand you are suffering from a case of amnesia, is that correct?"

"I guess you could say that. I'm sitting here in this hospital all busted up and don't know how I got here."

"Dr. Shoo told me you have a family, is that correct?"

"I once did, I'm not sure what happened to them. I believe they might all be dead."

"Why do you think they are all dead?"

"Because of my brother-in-law."

"What would your brother-in-law have to do with your family being dead, do you think he may have killed them?"

"That or hired them killed."

"How many members of your family are we talking about?"

"My wife and child and all the members of my crew."

The Fruit of Atrocity

"I see, well it appears to me that there is a lot of history involved in your conclusion concerning your brother-in-law and your wife and child, maybe too much to go into at this time. So for the present, let us put that subject on the shelf for a later discussion. Would that be all right with you?"

"Sure, it only makes me depressed to think about it anyway."

"I certainly do understand. I'm sure it would make anyone depressed. If indeed that has happened to you, then you have every right to be depressed. Actually, I would like to begin visiting you on a frequent basis, if you don't mind. And don't worry, I have no other agenda than to become your friend. I am of the opinion that when someone has suffered something as traumatic as you have, it is important they have support, either from family, which you evidently have lost, or from friends. Therefore, I feel I could play a very important role in your psychological health, and maybe even recovery. Would you be open to that, Jay?"

"Sure, Mr. Chow, I already told the doc I wouldn't mind having someone to talk to."

"Excellent, and you can call me Watchman if you like." Jay didn't answer.

"Very well then, I will visit you again tomorrow, shall we say about this same time?"

"Fine with me, sir, I won't be going anywhere for a while."

"It was very nice meeting you, Jay Baldwin, is there anything I can bring you, books or magazines for instance?"

"I lost my Bible."

"Then I will bring you a Bible. You speak excellent Chinese, do you read it as well?"

"No, I only read English."

Watchman Chow studied Jay for a moment, then said to him, "It is most unusual that one would speak another language so fluently and not have learned the caricatures. Are you a deeply spiritual man? I have known of men to whom the Lord has given the special gift of tongues in a foreign land for the purpose of the special work he has called them to. Have you heard of this as well, Mr. Baldwin?"

Jay averted Watchmen's all-knowing eyes for a moment and acted as if he didn't understand.

"Can't say as I have."

"Very well, Jay, I will return tomorrow with an English translation Bible for you. But if you don't mind, I would like to pray with you before I leave, would that be all right?"

"I guess so," Jay answered, barely audibly.

Watchman knelt beside Jay's bed and placed his hand on his arm. The moment he began to pray, Jay felt the power of God come upon him.

Like a warm breeze in the middle of winter, it crept over him, and as it did, the feeling in his body returned. Shocked, Jay sat straight up in bed. He grabbed Watchman's arm and held him in a firm grip.

"I can feel again! I can feel again!" Suddenly, emotion came spilling out of him, and he began to sob uncontrollably as the Spirit of God came over him. Watchman held Jay tightly as the flood of depression, pain, and sadness drained out of him replaced, by faith, hope, and a life renewed by the spirit.

Jay threw off the bedsheet and looked at the skin on his legs and arms. The black and purple color had given way to a healthy pink hue.

"Young man, I believe the Lord has healed you," Watchman said.

Jay looked excited and rolled out of bed to kneel beside his new friend.

"My Lord and Savior..." he prayed. "I claim the life of Jesus Christ in substitution for my own wretched and faithless life. I claim the blood of Jesus Christ for the forgiveness of my sin and lack of faith, the greatest sin of all. I claim the resurrection of the Lord Jesus Christ as my right to heaven, and I claim the gift of the Spirit of God as the power in me to live a new and Holy life, a life full of faith and righteousness instead of unbelief and despair. Father, your ways are not our ways, and by thy Spirit, I will walk in the ways of God from this day forth. Thank you, my Father in heaven, for this man whom you have sent to me for my restoration. In the name of our Lord and Savior, Jesus Christ, I pray…amen."

Jay opened his eyes. He looked for Watchman, but he was gone. But there, standing at the foot of his bed, was Lihua. Her eyes were closed, her hands clasped together, and her lips moving in prayer. She opened them, and their eyes met. She moved to his side and knelt beside him. He reached out and drew her close to him; they embraced but said nothing.

"I will bring you some clothing," Lihua finally said.

Jay felt weak. He crawled back into his bed only to collapse exhausted against the pillow. A warm glow coursed through his body. He moved his arms and legs; he rubbed his feet. His body once again was a picture of its former health.

"Praise God, praise you, oh God," he whispered to himself.

"What would you have me do? Oh Lord. You have done this great thing for a purpose known only to you. Whatever you would have me do, I will do. I only ask of you this one thing, if it is thy will, show me what has become of my family."

Lihua continued to help Jay with the kind of physical therapy that would strengthen his muscles and endurance. When he became strong enough, he moved into a spare room in the home of Watchman Chow.

Every day, he and Lihua would walk together, first through the halls of the hospital and eventually, the path leading to the University of Nanking, the school where long ago Ah-lam had studied to become a doctor and from where she had saved not only the orphans but the lives of so many other women stranded in the war torn streets of Nanking.

Jay thought of his family less frequently now. They had become a painful memory to him, a memory he would rather not recall. The thought of losing her and especially his beautiful daughter brought great distress to his heart and soul.

Lihua was a wonderful girl and beautiful as well. Deep feelings for her continued to grow within him as the days and weeks passed. But Jay kept the feelings to himself. He still was not sure if his family was alive or, he could barely bring himself to think it, *dead*. Somehow, and soon, he had to face the prospect of discovering the truth.

Winter quickly passed, and as Jay grew stronger, each day he gradually became more of a help to Brother Watchman Chow in his ministry. However, several times a week Jay would go out of his way to make sure that his *helping* took him to visit the hospital where Lihua would eagerly run to him the moment he arrived.

Then, one day, his mentor Watchman Chow said to him, "Jay my friend, I have observed your growing feelings for Lihua. Have you settled in your heart that your family is truly deceased, or do you still have reservations in regard to it?"

Jay thought carefully.

"It is true that I am falling in love with her. Yet I must confess that I am still not certain of whatever become of my family, and it haunts me to this day."

"My friend, the Lord does not want you to be in anguish. He wants only your happiness and peace. You must settle this in your mind once and for all, before your feelings for Lihua continue to the level they cannot be reversed and something more becomes of it. Especially, it would not be fair to her."

"I know you are right. I suppose it would be best that I quit seeing her entirely. In fact, I should just leave."

"I am not suggesting that you go, only that you settle the matter in your mind. Where will you go?"

The Fruit of Atrocity

"Away somewhere, maybe Chungking to look for my family."

"But my friend, if they are all dead, you would be looking for a very long time, and your life would be of no purpose. I would like to suggest an alternative, because I see great potential in you as a fine minister for our Lord here in China. The gift God has given to you, of the Chinese language, would serve the Lord's ministry in a powerful way."

"What's the suggestion?"

"I suggest we make a trip to Yinchuan and find this Major Yuan, the man who brought you to Nanking. Maybe he can tell you what you need to know."

Jay's eyes lit up. He said to him, "I would like that, when can we go?"

"I have already checked the train schedule, and there will be a train leaving for Yinchuan next week on this same day."

"Wonderful, Brother Chow, will you go with me?"

"I would be delighted to go with you, my friend."

Jay sat at a desk in his room. He had not seen Lihua since his conversation with Watchman, and they would be leaving for Yinchuan the next day.

Jay took up a pen and paper and began writing Lihua a letter. It said:

> Dear Lihua, my feelings for you have reached a level that causes me great concern, especially for your own emotional well being. I can tell that you are experiencing the same feelings for me.
>
> You know I must discover the truth of what has become of my family before I could ever give you my whole heart. It would not be fair to you for me to do otherwise.
>
> Watchman and I are leaving on a train tomorrow for Yinchuan. God willing, the Lord will lead me to the answers that I seek.

May God be with you, and pray for me as I shall pray for you. Love in Christ, Jay.

Jay folded the letter and placed it in an envelope with Lihua's name on it. He then took it to the front desk of the hospital and left it at the nurse's station. He knew they would give it to her when her shift ended before she left for the day.

That evening while Jay was sharing a meal with Watchman and his family, there was a knock at the door. Jay opened it and there before him stood Lihua.

"May I speak with you?" she said. Jay excused himself from the family and stepped outside with Lihua. She looked at him with tears in her eyes and said to him, "I understand what you must do, but it is too late if you think the feelings in me as yet have not risen to the level you described. I love you, and I want you to know that my heart is ready for you, whenever your heart is ready for me. However long it takes, I will be waiting for you." Lihua threw herself against him, and he held her in his embrace. They said no more for a long while.

"Lihua…I will come back for you, but I must know. Please forgive me, I am so sorry."

"You don't need to be sorry. Just come back." She pulled herself away, wiped the tears from her eyes, and looked at him. He leaned down to meet her lips as hers rose to meet his. The kiss was gentle and soft; her lips were moist and full. Their mouths opened, and he could taste the hot wetness of her tongue. Then Lihua quietly slipped from his arms and vanished into the darkness.

Jay sat next to Watchman, staring out of the window as the train slowly clattered its way through the countryside. Out across those rolling hills and beautiful steep mountains of cliffs and jungle, there was nothing to indicate that a war raged over that beautiful land.

"You are very quiet, my friend," Watchman said.

"I have a great many thoughts to keep me quiet."

"I wish for you the will of God in this matter and that you will find peace, along with the answers that you seek."

"Thank you, Watchman. And thank you for coming with me on this journey."

"Do you know what you would prefer the facts to be?"

"What do you mean?"

"I mean would you rather to learn that your family is indeed perished, so you could go back to Lihua, or do you wish to learn that they are yet alive?" Jay became annoyed.

"That's a crazy question. Of course I want them to be alive."

"It is not so crazy a question if you find that Major Yuan has no knowledge of them whatsoever. Then you must decide what to believe without any evidence one way or the other. What then will you choose to believe, my friend? You must believe one or the other and believe it with your whole heart, or you will be a most miserable person for the rest of your life."

Jay pondered what Watchman had said. He realized he was right. It would have to be one way or the other. Then he realized which way he truly wanted it to be. He sat up in his seat and mentally prepared himself for the rest of his life. *Unless I find absolute proof of my family's demise, I will never cease waiting for them.*

It took two days for the train to reach Yinchuan. Jay and Watchman found a rooming house where they rested and recovered from their arduous trip. The streets of Yinchuan were of dirt, and the hard monsoon rains had left them muddy and eroded, yet vendors and patrons alike lined the streets, selling, buying, and trading their goods and provisions. Three-wheeled bicycles and wooden carts pushed by men and boys or pulled by water buffalo slipped and slid from side to side as they transported their oversized loads of commodities along the muddy, slippery road.

Jay said to his friend, "I'm not sure how we'll ever find him in all of this confusion."

"Aah, my friend, but it would not surprise me to find that Mr. Yuan is well known by a great many people."

"I'm sure he must come to town occasionally to buy food from these many vendors, unless he is totally self-sufficient. I see a fish market across the way. Let us ask the proprietor."

Jay approached a man sorting and adjusting an assortment of fish and a few other types of meat that Jay did not recognize as edible. He said to him, "Excuse me please, sir, my friend and I are looking for someone. Do you know him? His name is Mr. Yuan or perhaps Major Yuan."

"The elderly man only glanced at Jay, grunted something, and began shaking his head. "No, no, no, do not know, do not know, so sorry."

Watchmen said to Jay, "Let me try." Jay stepped away, and Watchman approached the man. He talked to him in a low voice and picked out a few fish to purchase from him. The old man began to smile and looked more enthusiastic. Watchman paid the man for the fish and returned to Jay.

"Follow me," he said.

They walked for a while through the hustle and bustle of the only road through town until they came to a building that actually had a front door. The sign on the window read Yuan's Laundry and Tailoring. Jay stepped aside and let Watchman enter before him.

"You go ahead, you seem to have a way with them that I don't."

"It is because you are a foreigner, and they don't trust you."

A bell jingled above the door as they entered, and instantly a man appeared from a curtain behind the counter. He was about the same age as Watchman and slightly taller than the average Chinese man. A startled look came across his face, and the man appeared a bit nervous. Jay had the impression the man may have recognized him. Watchman spoke first.

THE FRUIT OF ATROCITY

Addressing the man in his native tongue, he said to him, "Excuse us, sir, but we are looking for a man called Major Yuan."

The man first looked at Jay, then at Watchman, and somewhat hesitantly said to him, "I am Major Yuan, what is it you want with me?"

"We are wondering if you recognize this gentleman." Watchman made a gesture toward Jay.

Major Yuan quickly looked at Jay, then back at Watchman. He said, "Yes, he is the man I carried on the train to Nanking. It has been at least nine months since then. What is it you want with me? I am not responsible for his hospital cost. I was only helping."

"Don't worry, Mr. Yuan, we are not here about the hospital expenses. We are here to discover how this man became injured in the first place and what may have become of his family. Did you see any of his family?"

"No, I know nothing of his family. Unless…"

"Unless what, Mr. Yuan?"

"Nothing, it is no matter."

"Mr. Yuan, it seems that you may have information that would help my friend a great deal. You see he has a case of traumatic amnesia and cannot remember anything that happened to him after he landed his airplane. Do you remember the airplane?"

Major Yuan's nervousness seemed to relax when Watchman mentioned Jay's amnesia.

"Come, please. Come with me into my home. I will make some tea."

Watchman and Jay followed Major Yuan into his back room apartment where he obviously lived alone.

"Please, sit."

According to custom, they slipped off their shoes at the door and sat cross-legged on a carpet around a flat coffee table of sorts on which the major placed a pot of hot tea and cups. For the first time Yuan addressed Jay personally.

"Mr. Jaisonn, I seem to recall that you speak our language quite fluently, so I will speak to you directly. It appears that you have recovered very well from your wounds."

"Yes, I have, and I would like to thank you deeply for going to the trouble of carrying me to Nanking. I must insist that you let me reimburse your expenses. However, I would very much like to know how I received those wounds."

"Reimbursement will not be necessary, Mr. Jai-sonn. I was paid well for seeing to you. I only know that I found you in the street a short distance from here. I can show you if you wish."

"You found me in the street? Yes, I would like to see."

"Very well then, when we have finished with the tea, I will take you there."

"Who paid you to see to me? Did you see anyone around me when you saw me in the street or maybe someone running away?"

"No, Mr. Jai-sonn, I am so sorry, I did not."

"Mr. Yuan, neither my friend nor I have mentioned my name to you since we arrived, how is it that you know me by the name my brother-in-law called me? Do you know Mr. Charlie Nee? Is it he who paid you to take care of me?"

Major Yuan stopped sipping his tea for a moment and slowly sat his teacup on the board before them.

"Mr. Jai-sonn, I have not been entirely forthcoming with you. I am so sorry. The truth is, I did not find you by accident. The man you speak of, Charlie Nee, knocked at my door and informed me of a person who had been beaten and left naked to die on the road to the airport." Major Yuan waved his arm in a southerly direction toward the same airstrip where Jay had landed.

"The man asked me to attend to you and see to it that you received medical attention. He paid me money to take you on the train to Nanking."

"Did you know Charlie Nee prior to that time? And was there anyone else with him?" Jay demanded.

"No, Mr. Jaisonn, sir. I had never seen the man before that day. However, yes, there were also two Chinese soldiers who accompanied him."

Jay looked at Watchman. Watchman said to him, "Who is this Charlie Nee?"

A stern faraway look came over Jayson's face.

"My brother-in-law." Jay turned to Yuan. "Did this man say anything about the airplane or what happened to the people onboard?"

"I am so sorry, Mr. jai-sonn, I can say no more. It is all I know."

Jayson studied Mr. Yuan.

"How do you know Claire Chennault? He told me to find you when I arrived in Yinchuan, said you called him…Claire-sonn. Do you remember General Claire-sonn?"

Mr. Yuan appeared startled. Jay continued, "General Chennault told me you could make arrangements for refueling the airplane. Is that you? Aren't you the same Major Yuan that Chennault was referring to?"

Mr. Yuan was quiet for a long minute. Then he said, "General Chennault was my boss from 1937 to 1939 and prior to the Rape of Nanking. I was in charge of a squadron of flyers, training under Chennault. We became good friends. But Charlie—"

"So you did know Charlie, after all?"

"Yes, Mr. Jai-sonn, sir. I am so sorry. I have not been entirely truthful with you."

"You mean you are a bald, faced liar…isn't that right, Mr. Yuan?"

Major Yuan could no longer look Jay in the eye.

"Chennault is also a friend of mine." Jay interrupted. "He assured me that you would help us. Did Charlie Nee pay you to work for him?"

"Charlie Nee is very important man in China. Mr. Yuan is no longer in the Chinese Air Force. I now only do what Mr. Nee tell me."

"What all did he tell you to do? Did he tell you to help him kidnap me?" Mr. Yuan hung his head.

"Yes, I am afraid it is so. I am so sorry. I only did as Mr. Nee ordered me to do. I am so sorry."

"What happened after he finished beating me?"

"Out of my own kindness, I brought you to my home to care for you until the train arrived. Then I went to the airport to see for myself the airplane."

"Was it still there?"

"No, it had flown away, but this man, Mr. Nee, and the two other men with him, they dug many graves in the woods by the airport."

"Graves? What Graves?"

"Yes, twenty-one graves. He told us that the pilot had flown too high in the sky and the passengers had all died from lack of oxygen. He told us that you, Mr. Baldwin, were the only survivor."

Jay sat back and clasped his hands over his face. He struggled to keep control of his emotions; both grief and anger raged within him.

"That is another bald-faced lie. When I landed that plane, Elmo was still perfectly alive and awake. So was everyone else. We never went above fourteen or fifteen thousand feet and only long enough to cross that last mountain range before descending into Yinchuan. Charlie is lying through his teeth. If there were bodies, Charlie murdered them. They certainly didn't die in that airplane."

"Mr. Yuan, did you see for yourself the bodies they were burying?" Watchman asked.

Major Yuan thought for a moment before answering, "Yes, but they were already wrapped in tarpaulin. Mr. Nee told me there were seventeen children, a woman, and three men. One of which was a Chinese soldier who had deserted the army."

Jay was stunned.

"My God, Charlie murdered his own sister, my daughter, and all those orphans. That…how could he kill his own…?"

Watchman placed his hand on Jay's shoulder.

"My friend, you must rise above this grief and live the life that the Lord has spared for you."

Jay rocked back and forth, his head in his hand.

"Why do you think he did not kill you too?" Watchman asked Jay.

"He wanted his revenge. He wanted me to hurt for the rest of my life."

"What did you do that would make him hate you so?"

"He had the notion that he owned me because he rescued me when I crashed into the Himalayas two years ago. He thought that made me his property to buy or sell or use for as long as I lived."

"Then you must not give him the satisfaction of being overcome by this. Leave the vengeance to God, and rise above this terrible crime, or it will destroy you as it has your family. You must not give it that power."

Jay brought his emotions under control and said to Major Yuan, "Will you show me the graves?"

"Of course I will, Mr. Jai-sonn."

On the train ride back to Nanking, Jay was terribly distraught. He locked himself in his sleeping berth and wept nonstop the entire way. Watchman tried to console him, but it had no effect. When the train arrived in Nanking, Jay went directly to his quarters where he lived with Watchman and his family. There he shut himself away in his room and remained a recluse for the next several weeks.

One day, there was a knock at the door. Watchman came to Jay's room and said to him, "There is someone to see you, my friend."

"I don't want to see anyone." A familiar voice from behind Watchman spoke to him.

"Jay, it is Lihua. Would you please talk to me?"

Slowly Jay emerged from his depression. Each day Lihua would visit him until finally it was Jay who was initiating the visits.

Over the next year, Jay worked with Watchman Chow ministering to his several churches in Nanking and the surrounding villages.

The war had ended in Europe. On August 9, 1945, the United States dropped devastation from high in the sky over Hiroshima, Japan. Three days later, another atom bomb exploded upon the city of Nagasaki, and shortly thereafter, the Japanese surrendered the war against the United States, China, and the South Pacific.

The war in China had already diminished to only skirmishes around the perimeters of certain port cities that the Japanese held for the purpose of their own evacuation. Soon, however, it was the Chinese soldiers who were once again in charge of their borders and Ports of Entry.

By 1949, after decades of war, the rebuilding of China was well underway. The leader of the *Peoples Republic of China*, Chairman Mao Zedong, worked feverishly to accomplish a stabilized socialist economy through industrialization and farming. Though his efforts proved to be a failure, for a short time, it brought the masses of people together in farming communes where the message of the true God and His Son Jesus Christ was spread to the throngs of people through the ministry of Watchman Chow and his associate—Pastor Jay Baldwin.

Jay and Lihua were married in one of the churches pastored by Watchman. By the spring of 1949, they had two small boys— Erick, two and a half, and Phillip, who was only six months old.

It was a beautiful spring morning. Jayson and Lihua had their own home now, and Jay was caring for Erick and Phillip while Lihua worked her shift at the hospital.

Pastor Baldwin had taken up writing as a means of communicating the gospel in parables to the people who dwelt in the countryside. They were mostly simple, short, human interest stories the peasants could relate to stories that demonstrated the grace of God to all of humanity through His Son Jesus Christ. Lihua had taught Jay the Chinese caricatures, and though he still was learning, he could write well enough for the peasants to understand, and they loved them. Every month they would arrive by mail at no cost. Occasionally Jay and Watchman would travel to the many places where the articles had circulated, and large crowds of people would gather to hear the American Pastor speak of the love of God, love so great that He gave his one and only Son that all of mankind might have the option of everlasting life through believing, only.

Jay could well identify with the pain of losing a child, and when he spoke of the agony of God the Father and the agony of the Son of God in the garden of Gethsemane as the Father gave over His Son to the ignominy of death that all the world might have eternal life, it would break his own heart over and over again. But each time, hundreds of souls would come in faith to receive the promise of eternal life by grace through faith, and faith alone. As they came, the Holy Spirit of God would descend upon them, and the songs of rejoicing that come from their lips reverberated against the mountains surrounding the villages. Jay soon realized that God had a purpose for his life all along, a purpose far greater than anything he could have ever imagined. Hundreds of thousands had come to the Lord Jesus Christ through the former Army Air Corp pilot's ministry and testimony.

One morning as Jay sat writing at his desk, the telephone next to him rang. It was Lihua.

"Jay my darling, would you go to town with me? I would like to visit the fish markets and shops at the piers. I am off early today and must shop for food and cloth. My mother has generously offered to watch the children for us."

"That sounds like fun, Lihua, I'll meet you at your parents' home with the children."

"I love you, my husband, more than I can find words to say."

"I love you too, my dear, a great deal. I'll see you there."

Jay and Lihua walked together through the streets of Nanking to the wharfs overlooking the great Yangtze River. Lihua shopped for cloth for making pants and shirts for her family.

"We should go to the fish market. I will make a fish for your supper. Would you like that?"

"I would like that, Lihua, thank you."

The fish market with the best and freshest fish was down by the docks next to the harbor where the merchant ships, fishing boats, and ocean liners docked.

The huge ocean going liners dropped anchor well out into the deepest part of the Yangtze River. Smaller boarding vessels would ferry the passengers boarding and disembarking from the passenger liners.

The streets were crowded with people coming and going and buying and selling. Other, more unscrupulous types, also frequented the harbor areas, watching for anyone they might catch unaware that they might abscond with their purses or luggage. Jay kept his eye open for any such scoundrels.

Through the throngs of people, Jay noticed a man standing with his back to him. He was talking to several other men who fit the description of *unscrupulous*. Jay said to Lihua, "I'll be back in a moment, my dear, don't leave this market until I return, will you?"

THE FRUIT OF ATROCITY

"Where are you going?"

"I think I see someone I once knew. I'll be right back."

"Please do not be long," Lihua said.

Jay left Lihua and made his way through the crowd of people to the place where he had last seen the man whose back he had only briefly caught a glimpse of. There was something very familiar about the way the man had gestured and moved. Jay had not seen his face and was sure that it could not possibly be who he thought, but he had to make sure. Suddenly, there he was again, walking away from him toward the docks. Jay whistled—a sharp, shrill whistle, heard even above the noise of the crowds. The man stopped and turned to look at where the whistle had come from.

Jay stopped abruptly, his heart pounding within his chest. *No, it can't be. Surely it is only someone who looks like him.* Jay had to be sure; he yelled out his name.

"Elmo, Elmo Barker." The man looked again, glancing back and forth at the throngs of people.

Suddenly their eyes met. The man hollered, "Padre! Well, I'll be…my god, where the h…I mean, where have you been for the last four years? I've looked all over the world for you."

Jay felt weak in the knees. He ran to Elmo and clutched him in a huge bear hug. "My God in heaven, Elmo, you're alive."

"Of course I'm alive, why wouldn't I be?"

Jay clung to him to keep from collapsing to the ground. Elmo realized he was weak and shaking.

"Padre, are you all right?"

"Yes, Elmo, I just need to sit for a minute."

Then they both heard a voice saying, "Jay, my dear husband, are you all right? Who is this stranger that has caused you to become weak in the knees?"

Jay turned to see his wife coming toward him. She wrapped her arms around him to protect him from the large man standing over him.

"Who are you?" she demanded.

"My dear, he is an old friend. Mr. Barker, I would like you to meet my wife. This is Lihua."

Elmo stepped back; he was about to ask Jay what had happened back in Yinchuan after they landed five years before. But suddenly, he was too shocked to remember the question.

"*Your… wife?*"

Jay looked at him sternly and said to him, "Yes, we were married a little over a year after I lost my family. We live just out of town. Lihua works at the hospital, and I am an associate pastor. I work with the evangelist Watchman Chow, in case you have heard of him."

"Your wife died—?"

"Yes, Elmo, I lost both my wife and child. Why don't you come home with us? You can stay for supper, spend the night, and we can talk, catch up on old times."

Jay had put it together. Now he realized that he must keep Elmo from saying anymore in front of Lihua until he had had a chance to figure out how to deal with this realization.

"Of course, Padre, that would be great. I haven't had a home-cooked meal since…well, never mind about that. Lead the way."

In the shadows, behind the many stacks of crates and freight sitting on the loading docks, there was another man who had also heard Jay's whistle, stepping from behind a large shipping crate he watched carefully as Jay Baldwin, Elmo Barker, and Lihua made their way through the throng of people away from the crowded wharf. Inconspicuously, the tall, sinewy Chinese man followed from a distance.

Elmo and Jay talked of life in Nanking, China, as they walked with Lihua the five miles to their humble home. Lihua made a meal of fish and rice while Jay and Elmo continued to visit and talk of the new world politics taking place since the wars had ended. Jay made no mention of their previous relationship, nor did Elmo, who also had realized the predicament Jay now faced.

After Lihua took the children off to bed, Jay said to him, "Mr. Barker, would you like to take a walk with me?"

"Whatever you want, Padre."

Jay and Elmo walked along the country road that passed in front of his home. The moon was full, and it lighted their way. Neither of them remotely aware that they were not alone; a dark figure lingered in the shadows, an enemy from their past who silently listened to every word of their conversation.

"Well, Padre, is there anything you want to know about me, or would you rather I just disappear and leave everything the way it is?"

Jay thought for a moment before answering.

"Back there, at the market when you turned around, and I realized it was really you, *then* was when I wanted you to run. But now…heavens no, it's too late now. And besides, ignoring the fact will not change it." Jay's voice began to break.

"Tell me, Elmo, is she well? Are my wife and child well?" The pain that lay hidden in his breast once again bubbled to the surface. Jay struggled to control his emotions.

"They're all well, Padre. I took them to Alaska just like you told me."

Jay gripped Elmo's arm.

"Has she…remarried? Did she give up on me and marry again?"

"No, Padre, she has not given up on you. She is still waiting for her husband to come home and your child…well, she only knows what her mother has told her about you. Every day, the two of them stare out at the western sky thinking that any minute an airplane will appear, bringing you back to them. Yes, your daughter also waits for you."

"Please tell me about Ching-Lan."

"Oh, Padre, you'd be so proud of her. She just turned five you know and is pretty as a butterfly. Ah-lam has told her every story about her daddy there is, how he's the bravest man in the whole wide world."

Jay could not hold the emotion back. Tears flooded his eyes, and he shuddered uncontrollably as he wept. "I was told they were all dead, that you, the children, all of you were dead. I even saw the graves."

"Dead! How could we be dead? I hightailed it out of there as soon as I saw Charlie and those two Chinese guards dragging you into the woods. That's what you told me to do, and you were right because if I hadn't have gotten us out of there when I did, that's exactly where we might be—in those graves."

"There was just the three of them, couldn't you and Raylan have stopped them?"

"I'm sorry, Padre, but I had no way of knowing what was going on. I just did as you said. The minute it went sideways, I slammed the power forward, and as we were rolling down the runway, I saw a troop truck full of Chinese regulars already coming down the goat trail toward us. At the last second, I jerked that Douglas into the air and almost took their antennas off when I went over their heads. By the way, what happened after we landed, and you went to the back of the plane?"

"I don't remember what happened. All I remember is waking up in the hospital in Nanking, been here ever since. What happened with you?"

"We went on to Khabarovsk."

"How did you make it to Khabarovsk on only seven hours of fuel?"

"Well, you kept telling me to learn to pray, so I tried it, and he…that is, God, stretched our fuel out a little bit for us. So Padre, are you telling me you don't even know what happened to you after we left?"

"I've been told what happened, but to this day I remember very little."

"What were you told?"

"Remember the name General Chennault gave us, Major Yuan? Well, I went back to Yinchuan and looked him up."

"Why did you look *him* up?"

"The doctor at the hospital told me that a man named Yuan had brought me there. So I went to Yinchuan to find him. Major Yuan told me he found me on the side of the road: naked, beaten, and unconscious. Then he told me Charlie Nee had given him money to take me on the train to Nanking. I had been beaten severely, and according to Major Yuan, it was Charlie who beat me."

"He must have beaten you pretty bad for you to not remember it. It takes a lot of trauma for that to happen."

"Yes, he nearly beat me to death. Then Yuan told me that everyone on the airplane had died of something…he said it was hypoxia. But I didn't believe that. I was sure if everybody had died, it had to have been Charlie who killed them. At any rate, Major Yuan told me everyone was dead—my family, crew, all the orphans. Then he took me to the airstrip and showed me the graves."

"Graves?"

"Yes, twenty-one graves."

"You should have dug up those graves because there isn't a single thread of that story that's true. Charlie did that to get back at you. We should go back to Yinchuan and pay this Major Yuan a visit he'll never forget."

"No, Elmo, it's all been for the Lord's purpose. God has given me a ministry here in China that has brought many souls to the foot of the cross. I have no regrets."

"But, Padre, you have a family back in Alaska. What are you going to do about them?"

Jay looked wistfully at the moon. He turned to Elmo and said to him, "When is the last time you've seen them?"

"I make it back there about a half dozen times a year. Ah-lam bought a large house in Wasilla on the outskirts of town and started an orphanage, except she won't adopt out any of those kids. She also works for a clinic. She's done quite well for herself, but I'm telling you, she stares out the window a lot, and it wouldn't take a rocket scientist to figure out what's on her mind."

"When will you go there again?"

"I can go there whenever I want. When do you want to leave?"

"I'll let you know. How can I get in touch with you?"

"I'll be in Nanking for three more days. Then, I'll be heading back to Magadan, Russia."

"What's in Magadan?"

"That's where Raylan is. He lives there with his family."

"How did Raylan wind up living in Russia?"

"It's a long story, Padre. Believe me, you don't want to know the details. Suffice it to say, Raylan met his wife in Magadan when I left him there the first time on the way to Alaska with your...other family and the orphans."

"So Raylan married and settled down, that's good. I'd like to meet her."

"I have a family now too, wife and kid, and a little boy."

"Do they live in Magadan too?"

"No...Alaska, we got a place on Lake Hood, shoot moose right off the front porch."

"What keeps bringing you back to the orient?"

"Like I said, I've been looking for you for the last five years. Plus, Raylan and I are business partners along with—"

"You're right, I don't want to know," Jay interrupted.

"Just take me with you when you're ready to leave. I'll go with you to Alaska."

"What about your family?"

"I'll talk to Lihua, and see if she will go with me. What are you flying? Would there be room for my family too?"

"I'm flying an Antonov AN-2, got it brand new in '47. It's sitting in the harbor on a set of floats. You can't miss it. It's the only one there."

"I see, what about fuel. What's the fuel range on the AN-2?"

THE FRUIT OF ATROCITY

"Around eight hundred miles, but we have…I mean, I have places set up where we can get fuel along the way. Stockpiles, you know?"

"You must go back and forth frequently. What ever happened to the DC-3?"

"I started a salvage business in Anchorage, and the old hospital plane is setting in the back lot. I still fly it occasionally, mostly for stockpiling fuel caches along my route of flight. Other than that, I keep it as a kind of memento. Nostalgia thing, you know? Hey, when we get there, we'll have Loretta take a picture of the two of us beside the Douglas for old time sake.

"Sounds great, who is Loretta?"

"That's your sister in-law, Arthur's wife."

Jay looked surprised. "Do you know them?"

"Yeah, remember way back when I told you I once worked for Arthur, well, I spent the winter with him and his wife before I came back in '45. Your brother has a place there in Wasilla. I landed that Douglas right on his private runway. Arthur and Loretta put all those kids up in his hangar for the winter until Ah-lam got them into that house."

"How is Arthur?"

"He's doing great, got a good flying business going, flies everything for everybody, from one end of Alaska to the other, owns three airplanes now."

"That's awesome, I'm glad for him. It will be good to see him again and meet his family. I remember he was sweet on a girl back in Sikeston named Loretta Ponder. I wonder if—"

"That's her, Padre. He went back there, married her, and took her to Alaska."

"That's exciting, I can't wait to see them…okay then, I'll spend the next three days trying to help my wife come to grips with this whole thing, and we'll meet you at the docks. Are you sure you want to do this for me?"

"Absolutely, my friend, you bet your biscuit."

"It's a long way back to town, and that road is dark at night. You're welcome to spend the night here. We have an extra room."

"Naw, I got to get going. Besides, there's a full moon, and I carry a .38 caliber Colt revolver in my pocket. Tell your, lovely wife…I said thank you for a wonderful meal and for her gracious hospitality. And you know, Padre, these oriental women don't make such a big deal out of a man having more than one wife… like us Westerners do."

"I know, Elmo, it's me that is trying to deal with this. She has known all along that nobody knew for sure what happened. We were blinded by love at first sight and still are for that matter. Now, I couldn't think of living without either one of my families, even now that I know what actually happened."

"Seeya, Boss." Elmo turned and waved as he disappeared into the dark night.

From behind a tree that hovered over Jay's home, a shadowy figure stepped into the moonlight to watch Jay Baldwin as he entered his home to retire for the evening. Then, like a ghost, he too melted into the darkness silently following Mr. Elmo Barker down the dark and deserted road to town.

Chapter 15

The door shut quietly behind him as Jay carefully slipped back into his home having just said good night to his old friend, Elmo Barker. Light from several candles danced against the walls as he made his way to his desk. A few feet away, the remnants of a fire burned in a cook stove. He opened the cast iron door and fed more wood onto the dying embers. Suddenly, Lihua appeared from behind the curtain to their bedroom.

"Do you plan on coming to bed soon, my husband?" Lihua said in a low tone so as not to wake the children.

Jay looked at her beautiful form standing in the flickering light of the fire. Tears welled in his eyes. What words could he possibly find that would make her understand or condone his decision?

"Come to me, my love," he said, extending his hand toward her. "Sit here." He patted the cushion next to him.

"I have something to tell you."

Jay began at the beginning when he encountered the Japanese Zero. He told Lihua of Charlie, who had rescued him from the crashed C-47 and of his men, who had carried him for many days through the jungle to safety. Then, he told her of Ziyou-di, of Ah-lam and how they had fallen so rapidly into love, and, finally, of their marriage. He told her of his first child Ching-Lan, how his heart ached for her and longed to watch her grow into a beautiful young woman like her mother.

Jay told her of his evil brother-in-law Charlie, who had kidnapped his wife and child, and of his own struggle to get his family and the sixteen orphans out of China. Finally, he told her what had actually happened in Yinchuan, that the death of his family had all been staged, and how they were even now yet alive and waiting for him in Alaska.

Lihua listened quietly, her head bowed, her hands folded across her lap. Suddenly, she buried her face in her palms, her body shuddered as she sobbed…until there were no more tears to shed. Lifting her head, she said to him, "My husband, I feel so deeply the pain you have carried all these years. It is terrible what that man has done to you. You must go to her. You must find your wife and daughter. They need you, and it is not fair that I should have you, and they should not. Go to them, and I will give you the marriage annulment for their sake and for yours."

Jay reached for her, but she withdrew from him. "No, no, Lihua, I cannot live without either of you. You must come with me. We will all go together. We will all be one family together." Jay rushed to her and clasped her in his arms. She did not resist but clung to him, frightened that he might take her advice.

"What if your first wife does not want me in her house? What if she hates me and our two sons?"

"Nonsense, Ah-lam would never hate you, Lihua. You will see, it is not in her to hate. She is gentle and kind and gracious, and very wise. She will understand that it was her evil brother who made this happen. You will see."

"If you are sure, my husband, if it is what you want. If you will continue to love me and love our sons, then I will go with you, and if she will have me as her sister, then I too will make her *my* sister."

"She will have you, my beauty, do not fret, she will have you for a sister, and you will always be my wife, as will she."

"When must we leave?"

"Three days, my love, we must leave in three days."

"Will we take any of our belongings with us?"

"We can pack our things and keep them in a store room at the university. I can come back for them. I will have a bigger airplane to carry them, and if your parents would like to come with us, there will be room for them as well."

"But what would my father do to make a living in this place called Alaska? He is too old to be a soldier anymore."

"Do not worry. I will take care of your parents for the rest of their lives."

Early in the morning on the third day, Lihua, Erick, and Phillip climbed into the back of Watchman's car. Jay shut the car door after them and pulled Watchman to the side.

"My brother," he said, "I don't know what else to do in this matter. I must confess, I am no longer sure what is right and what is wrong anymore. I am like the man who must jump into the fire to escape the frying pan. If God condemns me, then I will bear it, but I will bear it knowing that I cared for my two wives and the children I have brought into this world."

Pastor Watchman Chow looked empathetically at Jay and said to him, "My dear brother in Christ, have you forgotten the grace and mercy of God that you yourself have preached to the thousands of country folk. Have you forgotten that grace applies also to you? Do you not believe that the life of our Savior stands in substitution for you, just as surely as it does for all the thousands of souls you brought to the Lord and to the foot of His cross?"

"Of course I do, but what about—"

"Wherefore then, do you doubt the love of God? Think of what he has done to save your family and the hundreds of other souls that have heard of his sacrifice and salvation through your own preaching and testimony. I only have this to say to you my friend: Have faith in God. Always, and forever, have faith in God, that he will give you an expected end. Do you know what that means?"

"I don't know if I know anything anymore."

"It means that whatever your *expectation* is that God will do for you that is your expected end. When *you* can say the great *I AM* is *my* life, the great *I AM* is *my* provision, and *my* salvation, and the great *I AM* is *my* righteousness and salvation. When *that* is the final judgment *you* expect from God, then God will give you *your* expected end. It is all about *your* faith, my friend. *Have faith in God.*

"Remember this also, we are all made from the dust of this earth and operate out of our mortal existence. We calculate on the basis of today and tomorrow and the evidence of what we can see and touch and what, with our feeble understanding, we believe is right or wrong. But *God* is *Divine.* And Divinity operates on the basis of *eternity*: not today but *forever*, not tomorrow but *forever*, and not by the things that can be touched and felt or the things that can be seen but by the evidence of the word of God. In that word, he says to you: *I AM* your eternity. *I AM* your family's eternity. Take no thought for what seems so right or what seems so wrong to you at the moment. Man looketh on the outward appearance, the Lord looketh on the heart. Our ways are not His ways, and His ways are not our ways. Trust the Lord in all things and in all places and at all times. That is what I have to say to you, my friend. Now, go in peace, and care for all those that God has given to you and put into your trust." Jay's eyes were wet as he hugged his mentor.

"I will, my brother, thank you. We will meet again. If not in this life, then the next, but we will meet again."

On the way to the harbor, Jay and his family sang songs of praise to God, and Erick, with wide-open eyes asked questions of what it would be like in Alaska—the strange faraway place where they were going to live.

Jay spotted the Antonov AN-2 tied to the floating dock at the bottom of a hinged ramp leading down to the water. He looked around for Elmo but did not see him.

Jay said to Watchman, "We'll wait for him on the dock. You won't need to wait with us. I'm sure he'll be along soon."

"Are you sure, I don't mind waiting."

"It's okay, we'll be fine, and thank you again. I am forever in your debt, my friend."

"Nonsense, Jay Baldwin, you will never be in my debt. You have blessed me beyond what you will ever know. God bless you and your...all of your family." Watchman Chow smiled facetiously, waved, and drove away.

Jay climbed the ladder attached to the huge pontoons to see into the cabin of the Antonov AN-2. For a single engine airplane, it was monstrous in size and looked extremely heavy. Jay wondered how much of a payload it could carry.

He said to Lihua, "I hope he has a lot of fuel caches along the way. This beast looks too big to be very fast."

Lihua replied, "Are you sure this is Mr. Barker's airplane?"

"I'm sure. I don't see another one like it in the harbor."

"Can we get in and wait for him inside?"

"No, we should wait out here. I'm sure he'll be along soon."

Suddenly Jay heard Elmo call to him, "Hey, Padre, glad you could make it." Jay looked up to see Elmo descending the ramp with a canvas duffle slung over his shoulder.

"Yes, Elmo, we're ready to go. When will we be leaving?"

"I'm ready whenever you are, Boss. I'll open that side door so your family can get onboard." Elmo reached in his pocket for a key to unlock the passenger door located on the portside of the empennage, aft of the wing.

"Hmm, that's strange. I could have sworn I locked that door," Elmo said bewildered.

Inside were four seats located near the rear, while the area before the seats and aft of the cockpit was occupied by five fifty-five-gallon drums.

Jay didn't ask what the drums contained but assumed they were filled with 91 octane aviation fuel. He directed Lihua and the boys to their seats and showed them how to fasten the seat harnesses that keep passengers from being lurched about and possibly injured in the case of rough air.

Jay took their sacks of food for the trip and along with their bags of clothing and stowed them in the rear in front of the bulkhead. As he did, he noticed two things: a mattress lying on the floor in front of the bulkhead and the wooden bulkhead itself that appeared to be loose. He checked and saw that the screws holding it had been left unfastened, yet the bulkhead remained in place.

He said to Lihua, "Sweetheart, whenever you or the boys get tired, there's a mat back there you can lie on."

"Thank you, my husband, I am sure we will use it often."

Elmo called to Jay, "You can ride shotgun with me, Padre, if you want."

"Be right there," Jay called back. "By the way, if you have a screwdriver, you may want to tighten the screws on that bulkhead. They're loose."

"I'll have a look," Elmo said.

"Lihua, I'll be up front a lot but will come back to check on you often. If you need anything or any of you show signs of getting sick, let me know. I love you, my love."

"I love you too, my husband. I am so happy you will get to see your wife and child. I am just so—" Lihua choked back the tears as she cast herself against her husband.

"Don't think about it right now, my precious, we'll make it work, you'll see. Take care of our sons for me and make them comfortable while I help Elmo get us to our new home."

On his way to the cockpit, Jay passed Elmo as he headed back to tighten the screws on the bulkhead. A minute later, he returned.

"Must have vibrated loose or something…probably didn't get tightened enough during the last inspection.

"Padre, will you climb out onto those pontoons and untie them from the dock. You can use one of the oars strapped to the driver's side pontoon to push us away."

"You bet, Elmo."

"When you push off, step out on that crossbar between the floats and pull that prop through fifteen or twenty times. This engine has been sitting a few days and needs to be purged."

"I'm on it, Elmo. Just don't kick it over till I'm back inside and be sure the master switch is off before I pull it through."

Jay did as Elmo asked. Already he was growing less and less impressed with seaplanes. Finally, he returned to his copilot's seat.

"You can fire it up any time, Captain," Jay said.

Elmo started flipping switches. Finally he clicked the master on and fired the huge four-bladed radial engine. It coughed and sputtered, then backfired. Smoke and oil belched from the circular exhaust system as the one thousand horsepower R-1800 cyclone exploded to life.

"Good grief, this thing sure makes a fuss about going to work," Jay said.

"It's a beast that's for sure, but it lands and takes off slower than anything you've ever seen. That's one of the reasons it's called the *ANT*, along with the name. You can land this thing at 30 mph. And take off at full gross weight at less than 40."

"What's its stall speed at gross weight?" Jay asked.

"Doesn't have one, just reduce the power, pull the yoke back against your chest, and let it sink. You can't get it to break stall, add a little power just before touchdown, and it will be stopped in four hundred feet—fully loaded."

"Wow, must come in handy for the kind of work you're doing these days." Jay looked at Elmo with a concerned expression on his face.

"It does work well for what I do. Not so much for long distance though, like now, sure would be nice to have that Douglas… you know?"

"Yeah, I know."

"So, Padre, you want to learn to fly this trap?"

"Maybe later, I'd rather watch for a while."

"You'll have plenty of stick time by the time we get to Anchorage. It's a real truck, hard as h…I mean really hard to fly—wear you plum out."

"How much will it carry?"

"About five thousand pounds if you round it off, 4,486 according to the book, almost as much as the Douglas."

"Looks like the cruise speed might be a bit slow. I'm guessing not much over a hundred knots?"

"Good guess, Padre, 105 actually, a little over 120 mph of airspeed in calm air."

"So which way we headed, and where's our first fuel stop?"

"Seoul, South Korea. We'll water taxi out of this congested area so we don't run into anyone's sloop, and open it up when we get out on the river. Then we'll turn northeast to a heading of 048 dg magnetic for about two and a quarter hours, then make it 053 dg for the remainder. With a few other adjustments for wind corrections along the way, we should make Seoul in about four hours."

"Does that mean we're not going direct?"

"I have one other stop in Dalian, Manchuria, won't be long."

"What's there?"

"A port. Someone dropped off a crate for me that come from Africa, and I need to pick it up, shouldn't take long, maybe a half hour."

"Are we going to fuel at Dalian?" Jay asked.

"No, just pick up the crate. We'll fuel in Seoul."

"Where do we get fuel in Seoul?"

"We won't be going into Seoul proper. We'll land on the water in an inlet. I got some fuel stashed at a dock there."

"Aren't you afraid it might be gone when you get there?"

"I work for a pretty big outfit, most people, if they don't respect us, at least, are afraid of us, so don't worry about that. It'll be there."

"What are you hauling in those drums?"

THE FRUIT OF ATROCITY

"Fuel."

"Is it for a stockpile somewhere?"

"No, it's for us. After Seoul, South Korea, our next stop will be Vladivostok, Russia, and then Khabarovsk. The next leg from Khabarovsk to Magadan, where Raylan lives, is the longest leg. We'll land in an inlet at the north end of the strait of Tartary between the mainland and the island of Sakhalinskaya. There isn't any fuel there, so we'll set up the hose and pump from those barrels in the back."

"How about the rest of the way, it's almost two thousand miles to Anchorage, Alaska, what kind of range do you get with this thing, seven or eight hundred miles?"

"That's right, 800 nautical miles, about 920 statue miles, enough to make it almost halfway to Anchorage, depending on the wind. I have fuel caches every six hundred miles, and we'll carry whatever extra fuel we need to get us the rest of the way."

"Sounds like you've done this before."

"Oh yeah, plenty of times, at least a half dozen since I got this biwing two years ago, and that doesn't even count the seven or eight times back and forth in the Douglas."

"This...*business* you and Raylan are into, is it dangerous?"

"Shucks, Padre, everything has risks associated with it, look at you. I never came so close to dying so many times in a row over such a short span of time in my whole life since I met you. You want to know if my job is dangerous? I'll tell you. Since Raylan took over running this outfit—"

"Raylan is running the outfit? What kind of an outfit is it, a smuggling outfit?"

"Some would call it that, we call it business. Since the war in Europe ended and especially since the Japs went home, there have been enormous business opportunities for the especially skilled entrepreneurs, who happen to own an airplane or two. Just wait till you see what we got going, Padre. We got our own airstrip, our own town, even a shipping harbor with docks for merchant ships. And we got it all sowed up so that everything moving from the far west to the far east and back has to go through us. It's big money, Jay, more money than I've ever seen. So I'm grabbing my share while it's there, you know what I mean?"

Elmo talked on and on, for hours, telling Jay the whole story of how Raylan took over the Russian Mafia in Magadan, Russia. Jay listened politely, but his mind was not on Raylan or smuggling or all the money they were making. His thoughts were on the hours and minutes that slowly ticked away until he would once again be reunited with Ah-lam and Ching-Lan.

The stop in Dalian was uneventful except Elmo had one of the dock boys take a picture of the two men standing next to the Antonov AN-2.

Soon they were again on their way. At Dalian, there was no opportunity for Lihua or the boys to deplane, and Jay knew they were going to soon need to stretch their legs.

He said to Elmo, "I'll be back, I'm going to check on my family." Jay retreated to the back of the airplane.

"How are you all doing?" Jay said to his wife as he brushed her hair from her face. He bent over to kiss his two sons who were still asleep.

"We're doing fine. Will we be landing soon? We would like to take a walk. I am getting the jumpy legs," Lihua said.

"I'm sure we will. I'll check with Elmo."

Jay returned to the cockpit in time to watch Elmo set the monster seaplane down onto the glassy surface of the inlet and taxi to a pier jutting out from a wooded shoreline encased in brush.

"Doesn't look like this dock gets used much," Jay said. "Lihua and the boys are getting a little saddle sore, will they have time to go for a walk?"

"Sure, it'll take us about an hour to refuel this thing. You'll find some fuel drums in a little shed at the other end of the dock.

THE FRUIT OF ATROCITY

There should be a hand truck in there you can use to bring the drums out on the dock. I'll get the hose hooked up."

"Okay, I'll tell Lihua to get the boys ready."

Jay went to the back and opened the passenger door. Lihua lingered, waiting for the boys to wake up.

Jay headed to the little shed and found the hand truck in the shed where he counted twenty-one barrels full of fuel and six empty fifty-five-gallon drums. He moved four of the full drums to the end of the dock. Jay said to Elmo, "Do you want me to load the empties on the airplane?"

"We'll just leave them for now. I'll refill them on the dock so I don't have to unload or load full barrels anywhere. How many full barrels are there left in the shed?"

"Sixteen."

"Good that will do for a while till I get back from dropping you off in Anchorage."

Jay suddenly remembered something.

"Speaking of which…what ever happened to my passport and money?"

"Hey, glad you reminded me, I got your passport in my teak chest. It's under a false bottom in the floor of this ANT. Remind me when we get to Wasilla I'll get it for you. You won't need it before then anyway. In fact, you won't even need it there because we won't be going through any international check point."

"I could have used it back in Nanking when I woke up in that hospital trying to figure out who I was."

"He beat you pretty bad, didn't he, Padre?"

"I guess it was him, bad enough that I almost lost both legs."

"Well, my friend, if I ever run into the scoundrel, I'll—"

Elmo stopped in midsentence and gasped. Jay heard a whimper coming from the passenger door of the seaplane and then a familiar but dreaded voice.

"Jai-sonn, my brother-in-law, what is it the fat man is telling you he will do to me?"

D.L. WATERHOUSE

Jay's heart froze in his chest. Standing in the door of the Antonov AN-2 was none other but his old nemesis, Charlie Nee, his left arm held Lihua around her middle while the other, held a fish-gutting knife against her throat,

Elmo was standing on the wing holding the refueling hose. Jay was on the dock, aft of the wing holding the hand truck less than twenty feet from the door.

One terrifying thought after another raced through Jay's mind. *My wife, he's going to kill my wife—the boy's, what has he done to my boy's?*

Charlie held Lihua so tightly her feet hardly touched the floor of the floatplane as it rocked up and down with the motion of the sea. One slip or the slightest move from her even the pontoons bumping against the dock could cause her throat to be slashed.

Jay quickly looked around for something he could use to distract Charlie. There was nothing. Then he saw the oar he had used to push the seaplane away from the dock. *Have to get to that oar*, he thought. Then, a picture reminiscent of the past flashed through Jay's mind, a picture of Charlie standing over him with a big stick. He was tied up in the corner of a cage, and Charlie was beating him mercilessly. He could see his legs, and he could see Charlie striking them again and again. Suddenly it all came back to his mind. The cold metal of the gun Charlie had pressed behind his head before he knocked him out; the beating and the man, the man who stood behind Charlie watching it all. Suddenly he could see the face of Major Yuan. Jay became furious.

Elmo hollered, "Jay, stay back." Jay glanced at Elmo still standing on the wing of the aircraft. He was now pointing his .38 caliber revolver at Charlie and Lihua.

"No! Don't shoot. You might hit my wife or blow us all up!" Elmo remembered the gas fumes and lowered his gun.

Slowly Jay turned to face Charlie.

"How did *you* get here?" he asked, panic struggled to turn itself into a plan. Jay studied Charlie's eyes.

THE FRUIT OF ATROCITY

"Jai-sonn, you have never learned that Charlie is everywhere. Jai-sonn no can run from Charlie. There is not place in the world Jai-sonn can go to hide from Charlie. Charlie has come for Jai-sonn. Did you think I had forgotten that you still belong to me? Have you forgotten that if Charlie had not found you and saved your life you would not have lived to even marry my sister? And now, it is I who has saved your life again. It is I who paid Major Yuan to take you to the hospital."

"Why didn't you just kill me in Yinchuan?" Jay asked as he took a few steps closer to him.

"Because that fat mechanic flew away with my airplane. Charlie let Jai-sonn live so that someday Jai-sonn will lead Charlie to sister and her stupid orphans. Charlie follow Jai-sonn home. Charlie overhear all Jai-sonn say to the fat mechanic as you talked under the big tree. Charlie listen outside window and see Jai-sonn with this whore."

"So now you plan on killing your own sister?"

"Yes of course. Sister traitor, Charlie kill sister and her stupid orphans. Make Jai-sonn watch. Then, Jai-sonn will know the penalty of betraying Charlie."

Jay began inching his way toward the pontoon where the oar was lying.

"Charlie, please forgive me, I will do whatever you want, just don't hurt my wife."

Charlie took Lihua by the hair. "Do you mean this stupid whore?" Then, in one terrible instant, he shoved Lihua head first out of the door. As if in slow motion, Jay watched Lihua fall the twelve feet to the wooden dock below where she landed motionless in a heap.

For a moment, Jay hesitated. He wanted to run to Lihua's side to see if she was still alive. Suddenly he heard a gunshot and knew it had come from Elmo's .38 caliber revolver. His hesitation ceased, and in that instant, he lunged for the oar.

Charlie stepped out of the doorway where he had ducked away from the bullet. This time he was holding the dagger to the throat of Jay's oldest son, using the boy as a human shield between himself and another bullet from Elmo's gun. Charlie began to descend the ladder.

Jay had lost all regard for his own safety; he desperately wanted to help Lihua, but the first priority was to rid their world of its immediate threat—the devil in the form of Charlie Nee.

Jay knew already that this day would eventually come, and now that it was here, he felt completely unprepared with no idea how it would end. He breathed a prayer to the only one he knew he could trust.

"Strengthen me, Oh Lord, that I might bring this to an end, right here and right now. Amen."

He unlashed the oar from the pontoon and held it over his shoulder like a spear.

Charlie kept the boy's body between him and Elmo, who still held his pistol trained on him from on top of the wing. Jay watched intently, waiting for Charlie to make only one small mistake.

Then, as Charlie attempted to step from the bottom of the pontoon ladder to the dock, he glanced for one brief second to the ground to see where to place his foot.

In that instant, Jay made his move. Silently, he sent up a prayer to God that the wooden oar would find its mark and no harm would come to his son. With every fiber of the strength that was in him, he launched the heavy oar, aimed directly at Charlie's head.

The oar arrived at the same moment Charlie looked up, only glancing off the side of Charlie's head. But it was enough. Charlie dropped both the child and the knife.

In one second, Jay was there, snatching Erick away from Charlie. Charlie lashed out at Jay striking a glancing kung fu blow to the side of Jay's head.

THE FRUIT OF ATROCITY

Jay turned and tossed his son to the floatplane dock and hurled himself against Charlie, sending both men airborne into the salt water below.

Jay felt Charlie move like a cat around to his back and hook his arm around Jay's throat and neck. Jay took one last deep breath, knowing he had only seconds to fight his way free from Charlie's death grip.

As they squirmed and wrestled against each other, the two men sank to the bottom of the inlet. Jay's energy was draining. Charlie's choke hold around his throat would soon crush his windpipe. Jay reached out with his leg and felt one of the pilings with his foot. Using it as leverage, he flip the two men backward in a somersault, face down in the sand.

Jay knew his only chance was to find the dagger that Charlie had dropped when the oar hit him. Frantically he searched through the mud and silt of the ocean bottom. Suddenly he felt it. In an instant, the dagger was in his hand. Jay's lungs were screaming for air, and he knew it would only be moments before he would black out from Charlie's choke hold around his throat. Turning the knife blade toward Charlie's face still pressed against his right ear, with all his might, Jay thrust the sharp blade into Charlie's face.

Jay felt the hardened steel penetrate through Charlie's cheek. His hand slid part way up the blade from the impact against Charlie's cheek bone, gashing open the flesh on the palm of Jay's hand. Charlie's grasp around his throat relaxed, and Jay wriggled loose in time to plunge the blade once again, this time into Charlie's throat. The blade slid easily through the front of his throat and spine until it protruded out the back of his neck. Charlie's whole body went limp, and Jay, holding Charlie's body with one hand, desperately struggled to the surface.

Jay gasped for air as he emerged out of the water. Pulling Charlie's body to the surface, he pinned him against the corner piling that supported the dock. Jay looked into Charlie's eyes.

With his last breath of life, he tried to speak, but all that would come from his mouth was his last breath of air mixed with red bubbles of blood. Jay said to him, "I'm sorry, Charlie, you gave me no choice."

Charlie's hand came out of the water and took hold of Jay's shoulder. A slight grin appeared across his mouth as the final bit of life left his body. Jay knew what that grin meant, and he would forever be haunted by it. *You are really no different than me after all, aren't you?*

As Jay reappeared, Elmo stood above him at the end of the dock holding the revolver.

"My god, Padre, is he dead?"

"You never know, maybe. Help me get him out of here, will you?" Jay sputtered as he panted for air.

Jay tossed the dagger onto the dock and tried to push Charlie's lifeless body high enough for Elmo to get hold of him.

"I can't do it, Elmo. I'm too tired."

"Why don't we just tie him to the peer for now until we're ready to go? I'll throw a tarpaulin over him.

"All right then."

"Here, I got him," Elmo said. "There's a wooden ladder on the side of the platform. You can climb up over there."

Jay climbed onto the dock as Elmo tied Charlie's body to the piling. He looked toward the place where Lihua had landed on the dock, afraid of what he might find. His son Erick sat beside his mother, cradling her blood-soaked head in his lap.

Slowly Jay crawled on his hands and knees toward Lihua and sat beside his wife's crumpled body. Elmo followed him and knelt beside them.

"Is she alive?" Jay whispered.

"I think she'll be all right," Elmo said. "I checked on her a minute ago and couldn't find anything broken."

Gingerly Jay lifted her limp body into his arms.

THE FRUIT OF ATROCITY

Lihua groaned and opened her eyes.

"Lihua, my dear, can you hear me?"

Lihua sat up and began to look about.

Jay watched her carefully for any signs of a concussion.

"Do you remember what happened?" he asked.

She looked at him and reached up and touched the wound on her head but said nothing.

Jay asked his wife, "How do you feel? Do you think you can stand up?"

Lihua pulled Erick toward her with one hand and began running her fingers through his hair.

"You are such a sweet little man. What is your name?" she said.

Jay looked at Elmo, and Elmo looked down at the wooden deck. Shaking his head, he said, "Maybe there's a doctor in Magadan that can check her out, Padre. I think she's just got a concussion. I'm sure she'll be all right."

Jay reached out and touched his wife's arm.

"Lihua, look at me. Do you know me?"

Lihua looked into his eyes but did not seem to understand.

"All right, we'll go on to Magadan and wait for her to rest up a bit."

Jay made Lihua and the boys comfortable in the front of the airplane, forward of the fuel drums where he could keep a close eye on his family. In the back, wrapped in a canvas tarpaulin, was the body of Charlie Nee.

Jay and his family spent two weeks in Magadan, Russia, visiting Raylan, Alyona, and their three boys while Lihua recovered from her fall.

Jay took Lihua to a family doctor who examined her and confirmed Jay's suspicions—the trauma to her head from landing headfirst on the dock had left her mentally diminished.

Jay dug a grave for Charlie and buried him in Magadan. No one attended his funeral accept Jay, Elmo, and Raylan—Jay wept.

✪✪✪

A week later from far away against the gray horizon, Jay Baldwin began to see the misty outline of the Aleutian Chain. To its left was Kvichak Bay and beyond…the village of Naknek.

"Do you want to stop or keep going?" Elmo asked.

"How much farther past Naknek?"

"About three hundred miles, two and three quarter hours, and we'll be on final approach into Lake Hood."

"How will we get over to Arthur's place?"

"We can take the Douglas. There's a hard surface runway next to the lake. By the way, Jay, are you going to tell Ah-lam you killed her brother?"

"No! Nobody needs to know what happened at the bottom of that inlet."

"Are you going to tell her Charlie beat you near to death?"

"Yes, she'll have to know all about that. I'll just tell her the truth about everything, except the last part."

"Before we go to your brother's, I want you to meet my wife and kid."

"I'm looking forward to meeting them. Did you say you have a son?"

"Sure do, his name is Raylan, we call him Ray, and by the way I changed my name, as far as everyone in Alaska is concerned, it's Sumner—Elias Sumner. I even got new ID."

Jay looked at Elmo.

"You named your son after Raylan Jaworski?"

"Yeah, except now I wish I'd named him after you."

"Just make sure he doesn't grow up like Raylan."

"Why do you think I keep my family in Alaska?"

"Good thinking."

Elmo looked intently at his pilot for a long moment.

"Something on your mind? Jay asked.

"I just have a question that's all."

"What is it?"

THE FRUIT OF ATROCITY

"Well, I guess I don't understand something. Remember when we were waiting in the underground bunker at Charlie's headquarters and you prayed that prayer?"

"Yes."

"You prayed that God would deliver us from every unexpected *rough spot*. Not only that, you told us all along that God would provide in every circumstance and difficulty."

"Yes, so what's your point?"

"Why did everything have to go so sideways for us?"

"Do you mean why did I wind up staying in China for an extra five years while you and my family escaped? Or why was I deceived into believing my family was dead and ended up marrying again? Or why am I coming home with another family to live happily ever after with two wives and children from two mothers?"

"That's it, brother, and one more thing. How come God put you into circumstances that required you to do things you wouldn't have otherwise ever done?"

"You mean like killing another human being?"

"Exactly!"

Jay was quiet for a long minute.

"Well, Elmo, I've given all of your questions considerable thought over the years since I first went down in that meadow.

I remember the night we all spent in that cave on our way to retrieve the Douglas. You inside the cave, all alone, and me outside in the brush with a dead man's M-1 Carbine to keep me warm, do you remember that?"

"I sure do! I didn't even have a sidearm."

"I think that was when I first realized that when it comes to war, it's more than just one nation against another. It's really right versus wrong, righteousness versus unrighteousness, good versus evil. It's the same struggle that goes on in the life of a Christian, the carnal man, the flesh at war against the spiritual man—that is, the indwelling Holy Spirit of God. It is the great controversy between God and Satan, regardless of whether the battle is spiritual or physical. Either way, God is on one side and the devil is on the other."

"How are you to know which side God's on?"

"That's the easy part. God is on the side that recognizes his Son Jesus Christ as Lord and Savior of the human family."

"But why do you suppose God wanted you to fall prey to Charlie's schemes and wind up beat half to death, with two families out of the deal?"

"Looking back, I can see clearly that I let my faith falter on a number of occasions. For instance, when Chennault first offered me the deal to take the children straight from Anshun to Alaska, it was the Lord offering the deal. If I had placed unadulterated faith in God at that moment, that He would provide for my family and ultimately reunite us together, I would never have experienced those difficulties that ultimately came as a result of my lack of faith.

"Secondly, when Charlie kidnapped my family and Madam Chiang promised me she would care for my family and the children, I was not willing to settle for that either. Thirdly, when Major Yuan told me my family and the children were all dead, I had another opportunity to either believe my human senses, which included my grief and the graves he showed me, or believe God and what *He* had promised."

"But, Padre, how were you to know the truth?"

"Because long ago when the Lord first gave me the gift of tongues and I emerged from our family prayer room, speaking fluent Chinese, God had given me the vision that *all* would be saved."

Elmo scratched his chin and replied, "Did you think he meant, *all* the children or *all* as in all of us too?"

"At the time I thought it meant all of the children. But now, I can see clearly, it included my family and the crew as well. All of the ensuing tragedy happened because of my own lack of faith,

THE FRUIT OF ATROCITY

my own failure to believe God's promise no matter what. I felt like I needed to take the bull by the horns and do it my way."

"Padre, I think you're being a little hard on yourself, aren't you?"

"Not at all, I am actually seeing the truth for the first time. Stop and think about the story of Moses when he struck the rock instead of speaking to it as the Lord had instructed him to do. And Cain, the brother of Abel, who brought a garden variety sacrifice, the fruit of his own hand, instead of the blood sacrifice the Lord instructed him to bring. Or Abraham when the Lord had promised him a son, and he grew impatient with the Lord and, following his wife's human reasoning, took for himself another wife. Just think about all the ramifications and curses that have plagued the entire human race as a result of just those incidents alone. Not to mention the hundreds and thousands of identical cases where man has followed his own reasoning instead of God's revealed will."

"I think I'm starting to see what you mean, Padre."

"There is one more thing that you need to know, Elmo."

"What's that?"

"It has to do with why the whole thing came down to either me or Charlie."

"Do you mean, why you had to kill him? That's no mystery, he was trying to kill you and your family, and if you had let him live, *again*, he would have followed you home and eventually done just that."

"I know that, Elmo, I mean, why from a spiritual standpoint."

"I don't get it."

"When Charlie kidnapped my family, he was saying that he didn't trust me, thought I would not keep my word and return like I said I would. That really offended me. I have always taken a great deal of pride in keeping my word with people. Then, here was this…this liar of liars calling *me* a liar. It not only infuriated me but brought out of me a hatred for him that I never imagined existed in myself."

D.L. WATERHOUSE

"Anyone else would have felt the same way, Padre, again, you're being too hard on yourself."

"That's just the point, anyone else would have. But not anyone else would have felt so self-righteous about it. I believe it was because of my pride and self-righteousness that the Lord required that I experience the ultimate fruit of my hatred, taking the life of the very one I hated."

"Most people would pray for that privilege," Elmo replied.

"I prayed that it wouldn't happen, yet the pride and self-righteousness in me dictated that inevitably it would of necessity happen. In other words, I created it."

"Now you're talking like the Buddhists and Hindus."

"Well, there's a lot of truth in what they teach in the realm of cause and effect."

"So do you know what you're going to do now, Padre?"

"I'm not sure, get reacquainted with my...family. After that, I suppose I'll raise up a church and begin preaching the gospel. What are your plans, Mr. Sumner?"

"I'm going to spend some time at home and then head back to Magadan. There's still more money to make."

"Why don't you stay at home with your family and work for Arthur?"

"I might do that too, for a while at least. Can I ask you another question?"

"Sure."

"What's going to happen with Lihua now that she's...you know? Will you put her in a home somewhere?"

"No, she can live with us. I'll get her whatever medical help she needs and take care of her the rest of her life, like I promised to do in my wedding vows."

"How do you think Ah-lam will take all of this?"

Jay was quiet as he stared out of the window.

"Sorry, Padre..."

"That's okay, Elmo…I'm not sure, but I believe she'll be as gracious about it as she is about everything else. If there is anyone in this whole world that has taught me anything by example, it has been Ah-lam."

"Are you getting anxious to see her?"

Jay looked at Elmo and grinned. "My stomach is in knots and quivering like a bow string that just launched its arrow."

Elmo smiled. "Hang in there, Padre, we're almost home."

Two days later, Jay and Elias Sumner climbed into the Douglas DC-3. Lihua stared blankly at the inside of the airplane as the two boys sat beside her.

Jay looked around inside. Nostalgically he imagined the many flights he had made in the airplane. He thought back to the day he encountered the Japanese Zero and how he plummeted over eight thousand feet into the long canyon that terminated at the miracle meadow. He thought of the paratroopers and chuckled at their bumbling efforts to jump out of the plane. He thought of Wonlukee and wondered what ever happened to him.

"Elmo…I mean, Elias, whatever happened to Wonlukee?"

"You'll see him shortly. He's Ah-lam's house boy, helps her with the kids and their schooling, and everything from shopping to gardening."

"Really, that's great. I was just remembering how he survived that jump…that was the darndest thing I've ever seen. I can still see his face when he…" Jay stopped. He saw something familiar hanging on the wall. It was his army issue Colt .45 still in its holster.

"You saved my Colt .45!"

"Sure did, Boss, it's all yours if you want it."

"Naw, you can have it. Thanks anyway. You'd need it before I would."

"Are you about ready to do this? You've been waiting a long time."

Jay thought a moment. A note of sadness clouded his face. "I'm ready. It's just that…"

"That…what, Padre?"

"It's just that, it isn't like I thought it would be. I feel like I am a stranger invading her life. What is she going to think of me after all these years, returning with an extra wife and two more children?"

"Well, Padre, if I know Ah-lam, and I think I know her pretty well, she'll be so excited to see you she won't even care. If they're yours, as far as she'll be concerned, they'll be hers too, so fire up this Douglas and go to her before you get so old and wrinkled she won't want you for sure."

Jay turned to Elmo and embraced him. "Elmo, you've been the best friend a man could ever have. I love you, brother."

"Just keeping a promise, Padre…a man has to keep his promises."

The end.

Epilogue

"Forty-three years prior to the time I landed my little Cessna on the gumbo-covered airstrip at Alfred Creek and during Arthur Bold's long flying career in Alaska, the local news media reported that a Russian pilot, thought to have smuggled diamonds into the US, had apparently gone down somewhere north of Nome. The date was given as October 1953.

"No one would have even known there was such an airplane or if it was loaded with diamonds or chicken feed for that matter, except for an old-timer and his dogs that were out for a walk one evening near the little town of Port Clarence on the west coast of Alaska, fifty miles northwest of Nome.

"The Russian designed Antonov AN-2 came out of the north-northwest, flying low under a solid overcast in less than two miles visibility due to fog and light snow less than fifty feet above the old-timer's head. As it passed over the little village of Singigyak, the huge floatplane turned due east toward the Feather River airstrip, which, at that time of the year, would most likely have been covered with a layer of ice and snow. After circling the field at Feather River several times—possibly calculating if there was enough room to land and take off—the AN-2 turned east up the Glacial Lake drainage toward Salmon Lake.

"The next morning, the old man notified the coast guard, but no one ever saw the aircraft again. Some say it flew all the way to the Yukon without even landing in Alaska at all. Others speculated that it crashed in the Kiglua mountains from fuel exhaustion. Arthur Bold was sure he knew exactly where. There was a note from Arthur attached to one of the maps. It read."

To Lou Worley:

I always said, if I ever got the time, I would go look for the Russian smuggler. I never did, but I sure hope you will. I want you to have everything I compiled over the years. All the information you need is in this envelope. Take my word for it, that old Russian airplane is right where I believe it is.

I don't know exactly where the Russian plane took off from, but if he was indeed a smuggler, he probably had a load of diamonds coming from India, or Russia, in which case he had flown all the way across Siberia to the Alaska territory on his way to either a fuel cache or a rendezvous. One thing is sure, he would have had some fuel quantity issues by the time he reached the northwest coastline. It is my guess that due to the weather conditions at the time he had burned too much fuel trying to figure out where he was in relation to where he wanted to go. I don't think he got very far after the old man last saw him. If I were you, I would start where I have made an X on the map about twenty five miles due east of Singigyak. You may find him at the bottom of Glacial Lake, and I'll tell you why I think that.

Judging from the description of the airplane provided by the eyewitness, the Russian was flying a 1947 Antonov AN-2, a Russian-designed and Polish-built biwing with an eight hundred nm (nautical mile) fuel range under ideal conditions. The weather that night was anything but ideal, and the pilot may have already been running on fumes as he crossed the Bering Strait and the coastline at Port Clarence.

It occurred to me that he may have had extra fuel on board in the form of four or five fifty-gallon drums, giving him an extra two hundred or more gallons, enough to get him to his next rendezvous—that is, if he could find a frozen lake where he could land the big floatplane and refuel. I believe that is why he paused to circle the airstrip at Feather River.

THE FRUIT OF ATROCITY

At that time of year, it would have been unlikely the pilot would find a lake frozen with a sufficient amount of ice to support the weight of the AN-2, even it were loaded lightly. However, most of the lakes would have had more than enough ice to support several inches of snow, which could deceive a tired pilot in poor visibility conditions. He would have been looking for a lake remote enough that he could refuel and wait out the deteriorated weather without detection. Glacial Lake would have met every criterion, and with the freshly fallen snow on the thin layer of ice in reduced visibility and out of fuel, attempting a landing on Glacial Lake was probably the only option he had left. I believe that as the big floatplane transitioned its weight onto the thin layer of ice. It broke through and flipped the airplane upside down, which immediately sunk to the bottom of the lake. I'm sure that by the time anyone investigated that area for the wreckage of a downed aircraft, the lake had again frozen over, leaving no trace of what had happened. I know it's speculation, but I'm sure you can see why I believe that Glacial Lake is precisely where that smuggler ended up.

(Excerpts from *The Sequel to Alfred Creek* by D. L. Waterhouse)

The first time Pastor Jay Baldwin ever landed an airplane in Alaska was the day he set his McDonald Douglas DC-3 Red Cross plane on the ground at his brother's private airstrip in Wasilla. Before he could extricate himself from his pilot seat, a swarm of ten-year-old (soon to be eleven) kids, his wife, and their five-year-old daughter converged upon him. Jay's long lost wife, Ah-lam, welcomed the additional family members he had brought with him, as beautiful extensions to her family.

Jay and Ah-lam sought professional help for Lihua's special needs, but her mental handicaps caused by her fall never improved, and for the rest of her life, she could only function on the level of a ten-year-old. Lihua no longer comprehended who she was or even who Jay or her children were. Jay and Ah-lam

435

cared for her and their children along with the orphans for the rest of their lives.

After his return, Jay moved them all to Juneau, Alaska, and built a church where he began a ministry that he left as a legacy to others who would come behind him carrying the torch of the gospel of grace through faith in the Son of God who gave his own life as a propitiation for the sins of the whole world. Neither Jay nor any of his family ever mentioned the three additional family members that had returned with him from China almost five years after Jay had gone missing.

It remained a family secret for many decades until the day— at the request of Genneta Williams (Arthur's daughter)—Lou Worley began the investigation into the facts surrounding the lost Russian smuggler.

Over the next four years since rescuing his friend Jay Baldwin and his additional family from China, Elmo continued to make occasional trips to Magadan, Russia. No one ever knew for sure what he did when he was away on those trips. In July of 1953, he departed Lake Hood for the last time and was never seen or heard from again by any of his friends or family. Elias Sumner continued to operate his Used Aircraft Salvage, Sales, and Service business until the day he disappeared. His wife LeAnn and her son Ray Sumner took over the business, and it was from him that Lou Worley bought his first Cessna 180 many years later.

In the Fall of 2012, Lou Worley sent Genneta Williams a copy of the investigation report concerning the uncle she never knew she had. Having only learned of his existence from the pictures found in the ancient teakwood chest that Worley had found in the decayed remains of the Antonov AN-2, at the bottom of Glacial Lake. The identity of the young man in the picture had finally been revealed as her father's (Arthur's) younger brother, Jayson Bold.

The investigation had begun with interviews of Jay Baldwin's own children. Other interviews came from many of the orphans

THE FRUIT OF ATROCITY

themselves, rescued as a result of Lieutenant Jayson Bold's courage and tenacity.

Investigators also traced the children of Raylan Jaworski. Raylan had died in Magadan, Russia, in late 1972. The information he provided the Central Intelligence Agency proved invaluable in the apprehension and convictions of thousands of Russian Mafia along with many other smuggling organizations operating on a worldwide scale. Raylan Jaworski was posthumously awarded the Medal of Merit within the intelligence agency.

Jay Baldwin raised his daughter and two sons to understand the history of their family and the incomprehensible grace of God in his dealings with mankind.

One year after arriving in Alaska, Jay and Elmo made one last trip to China in the Douglas. They returned with Lihua's parents. They too became a fundamental extension of Ah-lam's family.

As missionaries, Jay's sons spent their adult lives in China preaching the Gospel of Jesus Christ and His unmerited favor extended to all men through His sacrifice on the cross of Calvary in substitution for mankind for the wages of sin conferred upon the human race through the fall of the first Adam in the Garden of Eden.

Ching-Lan remained with her mother throughout her mother's life and provided the investigators the majority of information in regard to her parents' background.

Genneta Williams sat in her office at the William Shearer Center for Learning in Bettles, Alaska. She finished reading the report she had received from Lou Worley and set it on the desk in front of her. She pressed a napkin against her eyes, saturated from the never-ending stream of tears she had shed. *My God*, she thought. *It is just as Mr. Worley said, my uncle really was a hero.*